WHO KILLED THE EARL OF MORAN?

THE CASEBOOK OF BARNABY ADAIR

BOOK THIRTEEN

STEPHANIE LAURENS

ABOUT WHO KILLED THE EARL OF MORAN?

THE THIRTEENTH VOLUME IN THE CASEBOOK OF BARNABY ADAIR NOVELS

#1 NYT-*bestselling author Stephanie Laurens is back with a challenging case in which, from the first, the Adairs and Inspector Stokes are under significant pressure to identify the murderer of a powerful nobleman. When the Earl of Moran is found bludgeoned to death in his study, the finger is pointed at his mother's companion, Mary Alder, who the earl had dismissed and who was found standing over his body. Mary is the mother of Julian, one of Barnaby Adair's Lads Network's brightest stars, and in desperation, Julian and his employer, Curtis, appeal to the Adairs and Stokes for help in saving Mary from the hangman. While the investigators quickly establish that Mary couldn't have been the murderer, pressure builds to quickly declare the murderer's identity, yet who actually accomplished the deed is difficult to imagine, let alone prove.*

After being dismissed—for no apparent reason—from her position as companion to the Dowager Countess of Moran, Mary Alder believes she is fulfilling her last duty to the earl before leaving his employ the following morning, only to discover, on entering his study, that the earl has been struck down and is very dead. Then she's discovered standing, horror-struck, over the body, and is accused of committing the crime.

On learning of his mother's predicament, Julian seeks help from his employer, Curtis, who immediately enlists the assistance of the Adairs and Stokes on Mary and Julian's behalf. As the investigators have already been directed to solve the politically and socially sensitive case without delay, they are swiftly on the scene—only to find that all their prime suspects were in the drawing room at the time of the murder, under each other's eyes.

Indeed, despite a plethora of potential suspects, there's a dearth of evidence that places any of them anywhere near the earl's study at the fateful time.

In solving this case, the investigators are forced to look past the obvious and confront their own prejudices before—fact by fact and motive by motive—they finally answer the question of who killed the Earl of Moran.

A historical novel of 78,000 words interweaving mystery, crime, and a touch of romance.

PRAISE FOR THE WORKS OF STEPHANIE LAURENS

"Stephanie Laurens' heroines are marvelous tributes to Georgette Heyer: feisty and strong." *Cathy Kelly*

"Stephanie Laurens never fails to entertain and charm her readers with vibrant plots, snappy dialogue, and unforgettable characters." *Historical Romance Reviews*

"Stephanie Laurens plays into readers' fantasies like a master and claims their hearts time and again." *Romantic Times Magazine*

Praise for The Curse of the Ill-Gotten Gains

"An improbable murder. An excess of suspects. A confluence of unintended consequences. The Adairs and their allies face their most challenging case yet. *Who Killed the Earl of Moran?* interweaves an intriguing, unpredictable mystery with a thoughtful exploration of the meaning, responsibilities, and rewards of family."
Irene S., Proofreader, Red Adept Editing

"In Mayfair, a family dinner party turns deadly after the host, the Earl of Moran, is discovered with his skull bashed in, and for this investigation, the question seems to be not 'Who wanted him dead?' but 'Who didn't want him dead?' As if that weren't mystery enough, the earl's butler dies by poisoning the very next morning. With suspects and motives aplenty, this Regency tale proves that readers can never be sure what's going on behind those elegant, stately walls."
Angela M., Copy Editor, Red Adept Editing

"Regency-era high-society sleuths Penelope and Barnaby Adair are back on the job to figure out who killed the Earl of Moran. Because the earl was disliked for his political views and his miserliness, there's no shortage of suspects; the list includes his entire family and many of his business associates. Even with the Adairs handling the financial and social aspects and Scotland Yard's Inspector Stokes acting as the long arm of the law, the complex case proves especially challenging."

Kim H., Proofreader, Red Adept Editing

OTHER TITLES BY STEPHANIE LAURENS

Cynster Novels

Devil's Bride

A Rake's Vow

Scandal's Bride

A Rogue's Proposal

A Secret Love

All About Love

All About Passion

On A Wild Night

On A Wicked Dawn

The Perfect Lover

The Ideal Bride

The Truth About Love

What Price Love?

The Taste of Innocence

Temptation and Surrender

Cynster Sisters Trilogy

Viscount Breckenridge to the Rescue

In Pursuit of Eliza Cynster

The Capture of the Earl of Glencrae

Cynster Sisters Duo

And Then She Fell

The Taming of Ryder Cavanaugh

Cynster Specials

The Promise in a Kiss

By Winter's Light

Cynster Next Generation Novels

The Tempting of Thomas Carrick

A Match for Marcus Cynster

The Lady By His Side

An Irresistible Alliance

The Greatest Challenge of Them All

A Conquest Impossible to Resist

The Inevitable Fall of Christopher Cynster

The Games Lovers Play

The Secrets of Lord Grayson Child

Foes, Friends and Lovers

The Time for Love

The Barbarian and Miss Flibbertigibbet

Miss Prim and the Duke of Wilde

A Family Of His Own

Lady Osbaldestone's Christmas Chronicles

Lady Osbaldestone's Christmas Goose

Lady Osbaldestone and the Missing Christmas Carols

Lady Osbaldestone's Plum Puddings

Lady Osbaldestone's Christmas Intrigue

The Meaning of Love

The Casebook of Barnaby Adair Novels

Where the Heart Leads

The Peculiar Case of Lord Finsbury's Diamonds

The Masterful Mr. Montague

The Curious Case of Lady Latimer's Shoes

Loving Rose: The Redemption of Malcolm Sinclair

The Confounding Case of the Carisbrook Emeralds

The Murder at Mandeville Hall

The Meriwell Legacy

Dead Beside the Thames

Marriage and Murder

The Murder of Thomas Cardwell

The Curse of Ill-gotten Gains

Who Killed the Earl of Moran?

Bastion Club Novels

Captain Jack's Woman (Prequel)

The Lady Chosen

A Gentleman's Honor

A Lady of His Own

A Fine Passion

To Distraction

Beyond Seduction

The Edge of Desire

Mastered by Love

Black Cobra Quartet

The Untamed Bride

The Elusive Bride

The Brazen Bride

The Reckless Bride

The Adventurers Quartet

The Lady's Command

A Buccaneer at Heart

The Daredevil Snared

Lord of the Privateers

The Cavanaughs

The Designs of Lord Randolph Cavanaugh

The Pursuits of Lord Kit Cavanaugh

The Beguilement of Lady Eustacia Cavanaugh

The Obsessions of Lord Godfrey Cavanaugh

Other Novels

The Lady Risks All

The Legend of Nimway Hall – 1750: Jacqueline

Medieval (As M.S.Laurens)

Desire's Prize

Novellas

Melting Ice – from the anthologies *Rough Around the Edges* and *Scandalous Brides*

Rose in Bloom – from the anthology *Scottish Brides*

Scandalous Lord Dere – from the anthology *Secrets of a Perfect Night*

Lost and Found – from the anthology *Hero, Come Back*

The Fall of Rogue Gerrard – from the anthology *It Happened One Night*

The Seduction of Sebastian Trantor – from the anthology *It Happened One Season*

Short Stories

The Wedding Planner – from the anthology *Royal Weddings*

A Return Engagement – from the anthology *Royal Bridesmaids*

UK-Style Regency Romances

Tangled Reins

Four in Hand

Impetuous Innocent

Fair Juno

The Reasons for Marriage

A Lady of Expectations An Unwilling Conquest

A Comfortable Wife

WHO KILLED THE EARL OF MORAN?

This is a work of fiction. Names, characters, places, and incidents are either products of the writer's imagination or are used fictitiously and are not to be construed as real. Any resemblance to actual events, locales, organizations, or persons, living or dead, is entirely coincidental.

WHO KILLED THE EARL OF MORAN?

ISBN: 978-1-925559-80-4

Cover design by Savdek Management Pty. Ltd.

First print publication: March, 2026

Savdek Management Proprietary Limited, Melbourne, Australia.

www.stephanielaurens.com

Email: admin@stephanielaurens.com

❀ Created with Vellum

CHAPTER 1

APRIL 11, 1842. MORAN HOUSE, PARK LANE, MAYFAIR.

After placing the last of her neatly folded dresses into the suitcase lying open on her bed, Mary Alder straightened and glanced once more around the room that had been hers for less than a year. It was of a decent size and functional, and being in the attics, it was reasonably warm, but now, denuded of all that had made it comfortable and welcoming to her, the space seemed cold and impersonal. Although presently curtained against the night, the small dormer window gave an uninspiring view over the roofs of neighboring houses, but if one squinted to the left, across the busy street, the trees in Hyde Park offered the promise of pleasanter vistas.

Ten years ago, three weeks after she'd been informed of her husband's death at sea, she'd accepted the position of companion to the Dowager Countess of Moran and had considered herself blessed. There hadn't been many places to be found where having a three-year-old toddler in tow was accepted without a blink. At that time, the dowager had lived in a house in Regent's Square, and for nearly ten years, Mary and her son, Julian, had called the town house home. Then, in the middle of the previous year, the earl had decided to move the dowager into the huge mansion on Park Lane that, for generations, had been the London home of the Earls of Moran.

From Mary and Julian's perspective, the move had been neither here nor there; through shared summers at the earl's country estate, the staff of Moran House had already known Mary and Julian well and had accepted them and the dowager's other staff into the larger household without fuss. They'd settled in and become a part of the Moran House staff.

Then, three days ago, the earl had called Mary into his study and informed her that he was terminating her employment. He'd given no reason, leaving Mary to surmise that the dismissal was more by way of restructuring the staff than any reflection on her performance, which she knew to be exemplary. However, along with the rest of the staff, the dowager had been shocked by the news.

But the dowager was ageing and growing frailer; soon, she would be better served by a nurse rather than a companion. Mary was genuinely fond of the old lady and truly wished only the best for her, and if that meant Mary and Julian leaving the household, so be it. The dowager had helped them when they'd needed it; it was only fair that they return the favor.

Initially, Mary had felt stunned by the abrupt change that had come without warning, but literally within a day, some until-then-unrecognized inner voice had started suggesting that moving on might not be a bad thing. She'd joined the dowager's staff as a way to gain time to find her feet after her husband's death. Now, ten years on, she was a different woman from the anxious gentry-born mother with a small child in her arms, desperate to find a safe place to lay their heads.

She'd saved diligently, adding to the sum her husband's employer had paid in compensation for his death, and over recent years, Julian had found what work he could and had insisted that virtually all he earned was tipped into their communal pot. Recently, he'd found full-time employment with the Curtis Inquiry Agency, under the wing of Mr. Curtis himself, who, according to Julian, could do no wrong.

Mary smiled at the thought of Julian's enthusiasm for his new position, and she couldn't deny that having met and assessed Curtis for herself, she was relieved that her son had settled on Curtis as his mentor. Although reserved, the man exuded steady, dependable common sense.

In part due to Julian's wages from his work with Curtis, Mary and Julian's nest egg was now sufficient to allow them to find lodgings in a decent area of the city and live quietly while they decided what to do with their lives.

Like the trees in Hyde Park, the possibility of a different and potentially better life beckoned.

Only one more night, and then we'll be off on the next stage of our lives.

Smiling at the thought, she glanced around again, searching for items she'd yet to pack. Her gaze fell on the small clock on her shelf, which showed the time as five minutes to ten o'clock. She widened her eyes. "I'd better go." She shook out her skirts and turned to the small mirror that hung above the washstand.

Large hazel eyes fringed by long brown lashes stared back at her. A swift scan of her heart-shaped face confirmed that her pale English-rose complexion bore no errant smudges, although several silky mid-brown tresses had escaped her otherwise neat bun to bounce about her ears and throat. Deciding that taming them would take longer than she could afford, she ignored the curls and picked up the list she'd earlier prepared. "Wouldn't want to be tardy in performing my last duty."

When the dowager had returned to Moran House, the earl had decreed that Mary was to deliver a list of the dowager's appointments for the following day to his study desk every evening at ten o'clock. Although the earl had never explained his need of the information, the staff had speculated that knowing the dowager's movements allowed him to make greater use of the footmen and coachman and carriage on which the dowager had first call.

The walls between the attic rooms were paper thin, and Mary could hear that in the room next door, Julian was moving about; he, too, was packing.

She walked into the narrow corridor and paused in the open doorway of Julian's room.

He was bending over the narrow bed, placing a jacket into his small case. Hearing her step, he glanced her way. His gaze found her, and his face lit.

As she smiled at him, Mary's heart turned over. His features were a blend of hers and his father's; his hazel eyes he had from her, while his golden-brown hair he'd inherited from Jonathon. Although Julian was nearly fifteen years old, his countenance remained wide-eyed and youthful, yet he was growing quickly—*so* quickly—and already there were discernible hints of the handsome man he would become.

He straightened; he was of average height but adding inches by the month, his frame still coltish, his build slight but filling out.

Mary waved the list. "I'm heading down to the study." She arched her brows. "My last duty, as it were."

Julian smiled encouragingly. "And then you—we—will be done with Moran House."

She nodded and glanced at his case, then surveyed the room. "You're nearly finished, it seems. I'll be back to tuck you in as soon as I've delivered this."

"Muu-*um*." Julian rolled his eyes. "I'm nearly fifteen!"

She laughed. "Indeed, you are, but you're still my little boy."

The frequent exchange was something of a joke between them, yet the affection that underlaid it was valued by them both. With a chuckle and a wave, Mary continued along the corridor, passing the doors of the rooms of other members of the staff.

She reached the head of the dark staircase the servants used, glanced down, then moved back as Polly, the parlor maid, came trudging up.

Polly stepped into the passage and blew out a breath. "Right. I'm done for the night. Everyone's in the drawing room again, the dining room's cleared, and Winslow and the boys"—by "boys," she meant the footmen—"are hovering in case they're needed."

The door one back from the stairs opened, and Orla, dresser to Lady Victoria, the current countess, looked out. Her gaze landed on Mary. "I thought it might be you. Don't you and Julian dare leave tomorrow without saying goodbye."

"Indeed, you'd better not!" Polly looked outraged. "Bad enough you're going at all."

Many of the staff were still up in arms on Mary and Julian's behalf.

Hoping to defuse the situation, Mary laughed. "I promise we won't slip away without saying goodbye to you all." She waved the list. "But I'm off to leave this on the earl's desk, so I'd better hurry."

All the staff knew about the earl's insistence on being informed of the dowager's movements. Orla and Polly nodded, and Mary stepped past Polly and onto the stairs and hurried down.

On reaching the small foyer at the stairs' foot, Mary turned away from the short corridor to the servants' hall and walked briskly along the passages that served the front of the sprawling mansion. Eventually, she reached the corridor that led to the earl's study and fetched up outside the study door.

As usual, the door was closed.

Mary smoothed her skirts, then, as the clocks throughout the house chimed for ten o'clock, she rapped on the door and waited to hear if the earl was inside.

She listened but heard nothing. The earl had instructed that if he was not in the study, she was to enter and leave the list on his desk. Mary knew the entire Fitzhugh family had been summoned to dinner that evening—she'd been the one who'd penned the invitations—and Polly had just said that everyone was in the drawing room. Assuming that meant the earl was there, too, Mary opened the door and walked into the study. She halted over the threshold, leaving the door ajar.

The room was well-appointed, with a solid mahogany desk placed squarely across one side wall, before a low sideboard topped by and surrounded by shelves. On the other side of the room, the wall opposite the desk hosted a central fireplace, flanked by more bookshelves, with two leather-covered armchairs angled toward the hearth. A fire burned brightly in the grate, usual for that time of the evening, and together with the twin lamps on either end of the desk shed warm light over the room. The wall facing the door was largely filled by two sets of French doors, the long windows currently concealed behind drawn curtains, while book-filled shelves covered the wall shared with the corridor.

At first glance, nothing appeared amiss, yet Mary's instincts prickled.

As she'd expected, the admiral's chair behind the desk was empty, but curiously, the lamps were not only lit but turned high. Family gathering or not, she wouldn't have been surprised to find the earl at his desk, working on his papers. Perhaps he had been but had stepped out for a moment.

She walked toward the desk. An odd metallic scent reached her and sent premonition flaring, then she noted the chair was swiveled sideways and papers were fanned over the desk as if swept to one side.

She halted before the desk with her hand, holding the list, hovering over the polished surface, then she saw a cloth-clad shoulder, tucked down between the chair and the desk.

Stifling a gasp, she leaned over the desk and saw a body slumped on the floor.

The earl had collapsed.

She dropped the list and rushed around the desk, then pulled up in horror at the sight that met her eyes.

The earl lay crumpled on the carpet, his skull misshapen, the back dented so deeply that bone showed white and brain matter was oozing free. A widening pool of blood was seeping into the thick carpet, forming a dark halo around his head.

Rooted to the spot, she stared in shock at her very dead employer.

The door opened.

Mary jerked her gaze from the awful sight to see the butler, Winslow, walk in, carrying a decanter of amber liquid.

Staring at Winslow, she opened her mouth and tried to find words, but her mind had seized.

Winslow frowned at her, then looked at the desk, at the empty chair behind it.

Pacing forward, the butler frowned even more.

Unable not to, Mary looked at the earl.

Tall and thin, Winslow followed her gaze.

She heard the hitch in his breathing when he saw…

The decanter clunked on the desk. Winslow, his face pale, his expression incredulous, leaned over the desk.

Winslow stared at the earl's lifeless body, then lifted his horrified gaze to Mary's face. "Mrs. Alder! What have you done?"

Curtis sat before the fire in his parlor, his gaze on the page of the book he was endeavoring to read, but the spitting of a log in the grate had jerked his mind out of the story, and the silence of the house had, as it sometimes did, wrapped about him and impinged in a way he'd never imagined silence—the simple absence of sound—could.

He'd bought the town house in Red Lion Square primarily because he'd thought he should. He'd seen that the place was for sale, and when he'd been shown around the property, it had, somehow, felt right to him. As if the house had been built for him, with a man like him in mind. He hadn't needed to be told that such a property was a wise investment for someone at his stage of life. With a well-established and growing business and having moved beyond the age of forty, a house such as this was almost an expected purchase, as if the mere owning of it declared to the world that he had succeeded in life.

But had he?

Success came in many forms and on multiple planes. The silence…

The oppressive quiet seemed to mock him and, inevitably, prodded him into contemplating the true reality of his life. Into considering what his life was and what he would prefer it to be.

Into focusing on what was lacking—on what *he* was lacking.

His professional life and his business were thriving, but his private life was more by way of a blank page he hadn't yet got around to filling in.

The truth was, he wasn't at all sure what, exactly, he wanted within his personal sphere, other than that he wanted something to fill the empty space—both the space inside him and in the house around him.

He wanted something that would engage him, that would give a personal purpose to his life and leave him, at the end of every day, satisfied and supported. Happy and content.

He dwelled on the amorphous sense of what he needed for several minutes, then he grunted, shook his head at himself, and refocused on the open page.

Knock! Knock! Knock!

The battering of the knocker on the front door had him setting aside the book, pushing to his feet, and striding rapidly into the front hall. Mrs. McGinnis, his cook-housekeeper, would be tucked into her bed in the dormer room and snoring by now.

The knocking recommenced.

"I'm coming!" he called. As he strode to the door, he mentally reviewed his current cases; all had seemed relatively benign. He couldn't imagine which of the men he had out and about, gathering information on those cases, might need help, yet the tenor of the knocking screamed of a need for urgent assistance.

He reached the door, threw open the locks, and hauled the panel wide.

His gaze fell on his protégé, Julian Alder.

Curtis felt his eyes widen in surprise.

Shadowed eyes met his gaze. Julian's young face was pale and drawn as he seized Curtis's sleeve. "Oh, thank God you're home! Mr. Curtis, sir, you've got to help. We have to save my mum!"

Looking past Julian into the dark night, Curtis saw a hackney, with a familiar jarvey on the box, waiting by the curb. Curtis nodded at Wallace, who nodded back and tipped his head toward Julian.

Curtis looked down at Julian, who he sensed was trembling. "Take it easy, lad, and tell me what's happened. What's this about your mum?"

His jaw setting stubbornly, Julian shook his head. "We don't have time for a full report. They'll take her away!"

Curtis's attention sharpened. He'd met Mrs. Alder on two occasions. Two memorable occasions, at least for him. "They who? And to where?"

His tone had sharpened and hardened.

Julian dragged in a breath, held it for a second, then blurted, "The police! They'll take her to jail because that dunderhead Winslow said she murdered the earl!"

"The Earl of Moran?" Curtis knew Mrs. Alder had until very recently been employed as companion to the dowager countess and that Mrs. Alder and Julian lived at Moran House, on Park Lane.

Frantically, Julian nodded. "She went to deliver a list to his study, just as she does every evening at ten o'clock. Tonight, she went in to leave the list and, instead, found the earl dead. I was upstairs, packing—we're to leave in the morning like I told you—and Thomas, one of the footmen, came racing up to tell me that old Winslow, the butler, had found Mama standing staring at the earl's body, and Winslow decided she'd killed the earl, and he sent for the police!"

The act of reciting what he knew was helping Julian to calm and focus his mind. "I don't know any more details," he added. "I went downstairs, and everyone was shocked, but they confirmed what Thomas had said—that Winslow accused Mama of killing the earl and the police had been sent for."

Beseechingly, Julian raised his gaze to Curtis's face. "I didn't know what to do, so I ran out and found Wallace"—he gestured at the hackney—"and came here."

Curtis squeezed Julian's shoulder. "You did the right thing."

Julian searched his face. "You'll help?"

"Of course." Curtis moved back and reached for his hat and coat. He settled the first on his head, shrugged into the coat, then, steering Julian ahead of him, stepped onto the narrow porch and closed the door. "The first thing we need to do"—he urged Julian down the steps to the pavement—"is to call on some very able folk you and I both know."

Approaching Wallace's hackney, Curtis added, "If anyone can deal with this bramble patch quickly and without getting scratched, it'll be them."

~

Seated beside her husband, Barnaby, Penelope Adair sighed contentedly as their carriage rocked to a halt outside the door of their home in Albemarle Street. They'd spent a very pleasant evening at the opera. She glanced at Barnaby and, smiling through the enveloping shadows, admitted, "Although *La Bohème* will never be my favorite opera, you were right in predicting that Madame De Livra's performance would be a delight."

Amused, he smiled back. "Sometimes, it's necessary to wade through dross to experience a jewel."

"Indeed." She turned to the door as Connor, her groom-cum-guard, appeared and swung open the portal.

Barnaby rose and moved past her to descend to the pavement, then reached back and helped her down the steps.

On gaining the flagstones, she shook out her silk skirts and resettled her velvet cloak, then linked her arm with Barnaby's, and they started for the steps leading to their front door.

"Hoi!"

They halted and looked along the pavement. At that hour, in that neighborhood, there weren't many people about.

Recognizing the figure striding their way, his greatcoat billowing about his long legs and a grimly serious expression on his dark-featured face, Penelope exclaimed, "It's Stokes."

"And someone's dead," Barnaby murmured.

"So it seems," Penelope replied. "I wonder who?"

She didn't have to wait long to hear the answer. The instant Stokes halted before them, he bluntly stated, "The Earl of Moran has been murdered."

"Moran?" Barnaby's incredulous tone echoed Penelope's astonishment.

Her wits whirled with the implications, and her eyes widened. "Good Lord!"

"Indeed." Stokes had glanced around and confirmed that only their coachman, Phelps, and Connor were near enough to overhear, and he trusted both men. Returning his gaze to Barnaby and Penelope, Stokes added, "The Commissioner himself came to fetch me from home."

In addition to being a high-ranking noble, Moran was a large and significantly wealthy landowner and, even more pertinently, was a major player in the government ranks in the House of Lords.

"Needless to say," Stokes continued, "the pressure is already well and truly on to solve the case as soon as possible, and the pair of you are hereby conscripted."

"Of course," Barnaby murmured.

"Naturally," Penelope concurred.

"Where was he killed?" Barnaby asked.

"In his study at his London house," Stokes replied.

"Moran House is in Park Lane," Penelope informed them absentmindedly. "Not far at all." Frowning, she went on, "Now I think of it, I didn't see any of the Fitzhugh family at the opera, which is rather strange. Lady

Cleome—one of the earl's sisters—is a regular patron, yet I'm sure she wasn't there tonight."

"There was some sort of family gathering at Moran House earlier in the evening," Stokes said, "but the earl had left the company and gone to his study."

Barnaby glanced up at Phelps and Connor, waiting patiently—and rather interestedly—atop the carriage. "It appears we'll need you both shortly. Give us ten minutes or so."

Both coachman and groom dipped their heads, plainly very ready to embark on a new investigation.

Amused and inwardly shaking his head, Barnaby waved Stokes and Penelope to their front door. "Let's go inside, and you can tell us what you know." He led Penelope forward.

Stokes grunted and followed them up the steps. "Sadly, as yet, I know precious little. I've dispatched O'Donnell, Morgan, and Walsh straight to Moran House, and Findlay's been sent for. I doubt he'll arrive for some time—he has to come from Islington—but we should make haste to get to Park Lane sooner rather than later."

"Indeed," Penelope concurred as Mostyn, their majordomo, opened the door at their approach. She bent a frown on Barnaby as he ushered her into the foyer. "We can go—"

"After you change your gown." He grinned at her. "Not even you can charge into a murder scene dressed as you are."

As Mostyn shut the door behind Stokes and Barnaby lifted the dark-blue velvet opera cloak from her shoulders, Penelope glanced down at her gown. Created from midnight-blue silk shot through with iridescent silver, it was eye-catching and, for most observers, distinctly distracting, especially when combined with the impact of the magnificent sapphire-and-diamond necklace that graced her throat and dripped tantalizingly down her décolletage.

And then there were the blue and silver feathers in her dark hair.

Catching sight of her reflection in the hall mirror, she grimaced. "Unfortunately, that's true."

She was about to say that changing her gown would take only a few minutes, but Mostyn, relieving Barnaby of her cloak, earnestly said to Stokes, "I'm very glad you're here, Inspector."

Mostyn collected the top hat Barnaby doffed, but both Barnaby and Stokes elected to retain their coats. In explanation, Mostyn continued, "Mr. Curtis and young Julian are waiting in the drawing room. It seems the Earl of Moran has been bludgeoned to death, and the butler has, entirely falsely, accused Julian's mama of the crime. Julian went to Curtis and appealed for his help, and in turn, Curtis brought the boy here, no doubt hoping to elicit your assistance in saving poor Mrs. Alder from the gallows."

Along with Barnaby and Stokes, Penelope stared at Mostyn for a few frozen seconds while she absorbed that information, then she swung on her heel and made for the open drawing room door.

On crossing the threshold, she beheld Julian, sitting tentatively on the edge of one of the twin sofas and anxiously twisting his cap in his hands.

He saw her and leapt to his feet, blushing furiously.

Penelope smiled, she hoped reassuringly, but in truth, she was beyond curious.

Curtis, who'd been sitting alongside Julian, lumbered more slowly upright. To her surprise, Penelope sensed an unexpected tension in Curtis, as if this case meant more to him than she'd imagined it might. She knew he was fond of Julian and approved of the lad and saw a great deal of promise in him, but this seemed something more.

More focused. More committed. More determined.

Before either unexpected visitor could speak, she informed them, "We've just heard that Moran has been murdered." With a swish of her silk skirts, she sat opposite Curtis, on the twin of the sofa he and Julian had been occupying, and waved at the pair to resume their seats. Briskly, she asked, "What can you tell us?"

Curtis and Julian paused to exchange polite nods with Barnaby and Stokes. All had met before, while working on a previous case. Barnaby sank onto the sofa beside Penelope, and Stokes claimed one of the armchairs.

Stokes nodded at Julian and, in a reassuring tone, stated, "Don't worry. We'll sort this out."

With an inward smirk, Penelope noted that Stokes had already taken the position that Julian's mama could not be the guilty party.

His gaze on Julian's face, Barnaby leaned forward, elbows on his thighs. "We need to get to Moran House as soon as we can, but first, tell us what you know."

Curtis glanced at Julian, then rumbled, "Young Julian here came to fetch me about half an hour ago." Julian glanced at Curtis, and Curtis nodded encouragingly at the boy. "Go on, lad. Tell them what you told me in the hackney on our way here."

Pale-faced, Julian swallowed, then, returning his gaze to Barnaby, said, "All I actually *know* is that, last Friday, the earl told Mama that her services were no longer required so she and I had to leave the house, and we were to go tomorrow morning." Julian paused, then added, "Just like that. But Mama was to continue with her duties to the dowager—she's the dowager's companion—until tomorrow morning, so, as usual, Mama went to the study to give the earl a list of the dowager's appointments and meetings for tomorrow. Mama does that every night at ten o'clock. That's what the earl ordered."

Julian paused to draw breath, then went on, "So tonight, we were upstairs in our rooms, packing for tomorrow morning, and just before ten o'clock, Mama stopped at my door to tell me that she was going down to the study with her list. And so she went." Julian's chest rose and fell. "The next thing I knew was that one of the footmen—Thomas—came rushing up to tell me that old Winslow, the butler, had found Mama standing over the earl's dead body, and Winslow was saying that Mama had killed the earl."

Julian's fingers tightened and twisted, mangling his cap even more. "I went straight down to the servants' hall. They wouldn't let me go to the study where Mama still was, and all the staff were in a flat panic, but everyone was saying the same thing and that the police had been sent for." His breath came faster. "I didn't know what to do, so I dashed out and found a hackney—most of the drivers around Mayfair know me—and Bill Wallace took me to Curtis's house." Julian paused, then carefully—as one trained to report accurately—added, "I don't actually *know* more than that."

Penelope exchanged a look with Barnaby and Stokes, then nodded. "Right, then." She rose, waving at the men to remain seated. "Give me five minutes to change my gown, and we can go."

Stokes growled, "Five minutes. I can't dally any longer."

Haughtily, Penelope looked down her nose at him as she swept past.

~

Six minutes later, Barnaby handed Penelope, now gowned in sober gray, into their carriage and followed her inside.

Stokes, Julian, and Curtis climbed in as well and crammed themselves onto the opposite bench seat.

Connor shut the door, and a second later, Phelps set the horses trotting.

"Julian," Penelope said, studying the boy, "can you tell us a little of your mother's background? Was she born in London?"

Julian shook his head. "Her family lives in Shropshire. It's quite large, the family—I have three uncles and two aunties who live out there. But when Mama married m'father—he was a captain of a merchantman—she came to live in London with him."

Barnaby knew that Julian's father had perished when his ship went down in a storm in the Bay of Biscay. Gently, Barnaby asked, "When was your mother widowed?"

Matter-of-factly, Julian replied, "Back when I was just three."

"So," Penelope said, "about eleven years ago?"

Julian nodded. "Mama thought of going home to Shropshire, but by then, London had become her home, and she had a payment from the shipping company to tide her over, so she looked for a position and was offered the post of the dowager's companion." Julian shrugged. "We've lived with the dowager ever since. Mama made it a part of her employment that I lived with her, and the dowager said that was all right."

"So you have a room in the servants' quarters?" Stokes asked.

"Yes. My room is next to hers." Julian paused, then added, "At Moran House, all the staff have rooms in the attics. The house is huge, so the attics are roomy as well."

The carriage turned onto Park Lane, then slowed and turned through a pair of gates, onto the crescent of a gravel drive before the looming bulk of a rather gloomy-looking house.

The carriage halted. The dark of the night was only slightly alleviated by the carriage lamps and the beam of a distant streetlamp. It was a cloudy night, so the moon and stars delivered only fitful illumination.

Connor opened the door, and Barnaby alighted first. He glanced briefly at the massive house shrouded in shadows, then gave Penelope his hand and helped her out of the carriage.

They stepped to the side to allow Curtis, Julian, and Stokes to alight. Once they had, the trio joined Barnaby and Penelope in examining the dark edifice before them.

Moran House was one of the older mansions gracing Park Lane. Julian had described it as huge, but that didn't do the sprawling bulk justice. Built of old dark-red bricks, with what appeared to be a central section flanked by substantial wings to either side, the three-storied house squatted heavily in the center of its plot, squarely facing the thoroughfare and the dark expanse of Hyde Park beyond.

Penelope murmured, "It reminds me of a crouching beast."

"Indeed," Barnaby concurred. "A dark, brooding, and potentially malevolent one."

Stokes softly huffed and turned to Julian. "I've been thinking. If you and your mother are already packed, almost completely, it might be best if you slip inside via the servants' entrance and finish packing for both of you, then bring down your and your mother's things, and tell the butler or housekeeper that you've got another place to stay and you're leaving as per the earl's orders."

Through the gloom, Curtis studied Julian's face. "Are they likely to make a fuss about you leaving now, before morning?"

Julian thought, then shook his head. "We get on well, like a big family. They know I was upstairs when it happened—Gwen, one of the maids, saw me up there, and Thomas, the footman who told me about Mama, found me there." Julian shot a look at Curtis. "If I tell them I'm going to stay with my employer…"

Curtis nodded. "Yes, you tell them that." He glanced at Stokes, Barnaby, and Penelope. "I'll wait outside the back door and help Julian with the suitcases and take him and them home."

Stokes glanced at Barnaby and arched a brow.

"Actually," Barnaby said, having understood Stokes's unvoiced question, "I've a better idea, but by all means, Curtis, wait for Julian by the rear door and help him take the luggage to the carriage." Barnaby tipped his head at the carriage behind them, on which Phelps and Connor were perched, listening. "Wait in the carriage, and let's see what we learn inside."

"And what we can manage regarding your mama," Penelope said to Julian.

Stokes, who'd been staring at the dark door of Moran House, softly added, "Unless the evidence against your mama is uncontestable, and I see little likelihood of that, then we'll arrange to send her out to join you."

Julian's relief was palpable, and Curtis's nod indicated that he approved, too.

Barnaby lifted a hand to Julian's slight shoulder and lightly gripped. "As Stokes said, we'll sort this out." Gently, he pushed Julian toward the side of the house. "Go and get your bags."

Julian drew in a breath, nodded, and went.

Curtis gave them a look and followed silently at his protégé's heels.

With Stokes and Penelope, Barnaby waited for the pair to fade into the shadows, then Penelope headed for the steps leading to the porch. "So," she declared, "let's see what there is to see."

They paused before the door, and Stokes pulled the bell chain.

A full minute passed, then the door was swung wide by a transparently distracted butler.

He was tall, thin, and garbed in the ton butler's traditional black suit. His white hair formed a corona about his head, rendering his pallid complexion even more wan. His faded-blue eyes were wide, and his gaze held incipient panic as he gulped and inquired, "Yes?"

Stokes calmly stated, "I'm Inspector Stokes of Scotland Yard. Mr. and Mrs. Adair"—he indicated Barnaby and Penelope—"are consultants who will be assisting with this case."

Relief replaced panic in the butler's pinched features. "Oh, thank God!" Then he pulled himself up and, more formally, bowed and stepped back. "Please come in."

Penelope led the way inside, and Stokes and Barnaby followed.

As the butler—presumably the Winslow Julian had mentioned—shut the front door, a door to the right of the foyer opened, and O'Donnell slipped out of the room beyond, then quietly closed the door behind him.

Approaching them, O'Donnell nodded to Barnaby and Penelope, then halted before Stokes. "I hoped it was you, sir." The experienced sergeant tipped his head toward the room he'd left. "The whole family, root and branch, were here for a dinner, it seems. They're all still here and were in the drawing room when the body was found. So far, they're shocked enough to stay put, although I gather two of the gentlemen—the brothers of the deceased—went to look at the body, but they'd already returned to the drawing room when we got here."

Stokes asked, "Morgan and Walsh?"

"Walsh is in the study, keeping an eye on the body, and Morgan's in the servants' quarters with Mrs. Alder, the lady who found the body."

Stokes nodded approvingly. "Good." He cocked a brow at O'Donnell. "Findlay?"

"Not here yet, but he should turn up soon."

Stokes inclined his head and turned to the butler. "Winslow, isn't it?"

Surprised that Stokes knew his name, the butler nodded. "Yes, Inspector."

Stokes continued, "The body was found in the study?"

"Yes. And no one's touched or moved anything." Reluctantly, Winslow added, "As the sergeant said, Mr. Frederick and Mr. Christopher did go in to look at the body, but they didn't touch anything and came straight back out again."

"Excellent." Stokes gathered Barnaby and Penelope with a glance. "We'll start in there. When the medical examiner arrives—name of Findlay—show him straight to the study."

"Yes, Inspector." Winslow gestured to a corridor leading away from the rear left corner of the foyer. "If you'll come this way?"

With Penelope and Stokes, Barnaby followed the butler down a poorly lit corridor that led ever deeper into one of the massive house's wings.

"Winslow," Penelope said, "the sergeant mentioned that *all* of the family were here for a dinner. Did that include the younger members?"

"Yes, ma'am." Winslow threw her a glance. "All the way down to the youngest, Miss Lydia and Miss Ella."

Penelope arched her brows. "Is that usual? That the children attend?"

Winslow waggled his head. "Yes and no. When the dowager calls a family dinner, as she did for this evening, then everyone in the family, including the children, generally attends."

"I see." Penelope said no more, but clearly, like Barnaby, she remained curious as to why the children had been present. At this time of year, with the Season in full swing, children of the ton tended to be relegated to their schoolrooms. The Season was all about adult society rather than family in the wider sense.

"Had any of the family left before the body was found?" Stokes asked.

"No, Inspector. They were all still in the drawing room."

Barnaby glanced at Penelope and, from her frown, deduced that she also found that strange. The Season was at its height, and there were so many events held every night that, normally, attendees at a dinner would move on to a ball, a soirée—or the opera. And as Penelope had mentioned, Lady Cleome, who was presumably sitting in the drawing room, was an avid patron who rarely missed a performance.

Winslow halted before a door. Reaching for the doorknob, he declared, "His lordship's study," then he opened the door and pushed it wide.

Penelope swept through, and Barnaby and Stokes followed. All three halted just over the threshold and paused to take in the scene.

Walsh was there, standing at ease before the wall directly opposite the door.

The room was rectangular, but not that large. The long wall behind Walsh was broken by two tall windows, both presently screened by heavy amber-velvet curtains. To Barnaby's right, the wall played host to a good-sized fireplace, the fire in the grate now little more than glowing coals. Two armchairs were angled before the hearth, with small side tables beside each. Glancing around, Barnaby located a tantalus positioned against the inner wall, half concealed by the open door.

The left half of the room was dominated by a massive, highly polished mahogany desk. It sat square within the room, facing the fireplace and positioned a good yard in front of a sideboard and the ceiling-high bookshelves lining the side wall. An imposing leather-covered admiral's chair was stationed behind the desk and was presently swiveled as if the last occupant had stood and walked toward the nearer curtained window.

After nodding respectfully to Stokes, Barnaby, and Penelope, Walsh tipped his head toward the area behind the desk. "Doesn't look like anyone's disturbed the body."

Stokes walked toward the desk, and Barnaby and Penelope followed.

On rounding the desk, they halted and looked down at the body of a large man, well dressed, heavily built, lying on his left shoulder, his face toward the desk, and his right hand extended but limp. His left arm was trapped beneath him, and his legs were bent at hips and knees. Most notable was the vicious dent in the man's skull, so deep that the ivory of bone showed in several places. Blood matted his sable-brown hair and had congealed in a pool of darkening red beneath his head.

Stokes eased his way farther behind the desk, and Penelope shifted and leaned forward until she could peer over the man's raised shoulder at his half-hidden face.

After a second, she sighed and straightened. "Definitely Moran."

Barnaby nodded at the head wound. "That was quite a blow."

Stokes pointed to a small marble bust lying on the carpet closer to the sideboard, near where he was now standing. "The murder weapon, perhaps."

Stokes raised his gaze to Winslow, who had shut the door and, with his hands nervously clasped, was waiting before it. "Who found the body?"

Winslow looked uncomfortable. "It was Mrs. Alder, sir. The dowager's companion. Well, ex-companion, I suppose. I came in and found her standing over there"—he pointed to the space at the far end of the desk, closer to the window—"looking down at the master."

Barnaby shifted and fixed his gaze on Winslow. "I understand there's been some speculation that Mrs. Alder killed the earl."

Winslow colored, dull pink flushing his thin cheeks. "I did…er, leap to that conclusion, although on calmer reflection, I suspect I was overhasty."

"What made you think it was her?" Penelope asked.

Winslow hesitated, then offered, "Well, ma'am, it's common knowledge among the staff that the master had dismissed Mrs. Alder and given her and her son, Julian, who also lives here although he's not a member of the staff, their marching orders. They were to leave the house tomorrow morning. And then there was the timing. The master had called me in and ordered the whiskey decanter refilled."

Winslow pointed at the decanter that, now full, sat somewhat incongruously on the corner of the desk closest to the door rather than on the tantalus with the other decanters and glasses.

"So, you see," Winslow continued, "I knew the master was alive and well when I took the decanter and left the study. By the time I went down to the cellar and refilled the decanter and returned here, only about fifteen or twenty minutes had passed. Then I walked in and found the master sprawled on the ground dead and Mrs. Alder standing there, looking down at him."

From his expression, Winslow was vividly recalling the scene, then he winced. "Mrs. Alder looked so horrified. In that moment, I thought she was horrified by what she'd done, but now I realize she might simply have been horrified by what she saw." Winslow swallowed and confessed, "I know I was."

"I see," Stokes said, very clearly nonjudgmentally. "So you're no longer convinced that Mrs. Alder struck down the earl."

Winslow straightened and raised his head. "Yes, Inspector. That's correct." He paused, then added, "Mrs. Alder has been a part of the dowager's household for over ten years. We, the staff here, all know her as a decent, hardworking lady, come down in the world, perhaps, but she's never been one to give herself airs or complain. Her being let go was a shock—to everyone. But she didn't rail or carry on. Very dignified about it, she was. To think she did this…" He tipped his head toward the earl's body. "That doesn't fit at all with what we know of her. I was very wrong to even suggest it, regardless of how shocked I was."

Stokes inclined his head. "Thank you. That's very clear. Where is Mrs. Alder now?"

"She's with Mrs. Pratchett, the housekeeper, in the housekeeper's room."

Penelope asked, "Where was this bust—which appears to be the murder weapon—kept?"

Winslow pointed to the first shelf above the sideboard behind the desk. "Just there. You can see the spot—that bust has stood in the same place for years."

Penelope, Stokes, and Barnaby all turned and looked, and sure enough, a lighter area on the polished surface seemed to match the base of the bust.

Penelope swung back and considered the position of the body, then asked Winslow, "When you left to fill the decanter, was the earl busy with his correspondence?" She shifted her gaze to the papers strewn over the desk. "Was he sitting in his chair, reading those papers?"

"Yes, ma'am. If he was at home, he usually worked through the evening. He was a night owl, as they say. He rarely went upstairs before one o'clock."

Barnaby asked, "Was there a reason Mrs. Alder came to the study? Did the earl send for her?"

Winslow conceded, "It was more by way of a regular appointment. The master insisted on being kept informed of the dowager's planned outings for the next day, and as the dowager's companion, it was Mrs. Alder's duty to deliver a list of the dowager's plans to the study at ten o'clock every evening."

Puzzled, Penelope asked, "Why did the earl need to know of his mother's plans?"

"It was to do with the carriage and the two extra footmen, ma'am. The dowager isn't strong, and as she uses a Bath chair, she needs two footmen to get about, and she has to have the larger carriage. The earl liked to know when he would need to use the smaller town carriage and also to avoid any clash with the countess, as well."

"Ah. I see." Penelope assumed that her tone would convey to Barnaby and Stokes that, in truth, she didn't see at all.

The distant sound of the front doorbell reached them.

Instantly, Winslow turned to go. "If you'll excuse me?"

Stokes nodded. "That'll likely be Findlay, the medical examiner. Please show him straight here."

Winslow bowed and left.

Barnaby looked questioningly at Penelope. "The family?"

Rapidly organizing her thoughts, she supplied, "The dowager, a widow of many years, is Lady Imelda Fitzhugh. As you heard, she's elderly and frail, but still manages to go about socially, although most likely keeping to a narrow circle of acquaintances. The earl"—she tipped her head toward the body—"is her eldest child, Gordon. He's presently married to Victoria, who was a Carrington. She's his second wife—the first died of a fever decades ago—so Victoria is some years younger than Gordon, although nothing too unusual in ton terms."

Stokes had pulled out his notebook and was jotting. "How old was he?"

Barnaby replied, "About fifty-five, I think. Mid-fifties, at any rate."

Penelope continued, "The dowager's second child is Frederick—the Honorable Frederick Fitzhugh. He married Imogen Farrer. They have six children and live in a house in Hertford Street. Next comes Cleome—Lady Cleome, who married Damien, Lord Mitchelmore. They have four children—two boys, two girls. The older girl, Lizbet, married Lord Brompton last Season. The Mitchelmores spend most of the year in Somerset, but during the Season, they live in Mitchelmore House on Charles Street."

The door opened, and Winslow stood back to allow a rumpled-looking Findlay to enter.

Findlay grunted a greeting at Barnaby, Stokes, and Penelope, then irascibly waved them aside. "Let me get at our body, and we'll see what I can see."

Barnaby, Penelope, and Stokes quickly filed out from behind the desk, and Findlay dove in to crouch beside the body.

Stokes looked at Winslow, who was hovering by the open door. "You may go. We'll ring if we need you."

Winslow bowed, backed out of the room, and shut the door.

Stokes settled on his feet, raised his notebook and pencil, and returned his gaze to Penelope. "Go on. Who else?"

Penelope duly continued, "In order of age, after Cleome comes Constance, who married Viscount Southerly. They have three children and live in Southerly House in Mount Street. The youngest of the dowager's brood is Christopher. He's mid-forties, now, and a dyed-in-the-wool bachelor and general man-about-town." Penelope glanced at Barnaby. "I believe Christopher still lives under this roof."

Barnaby confirmed, "He does."

Stokes frowned at his jottings. "How old are the children? Meaning the dowager's grandchildren?"

"All but two," Penelope replied, "the younger girls Winslow mentioned, would, I judge, be capable of committing this crime." She paused, plainly consulting her capacious memory, then added, "Frederick's two sons and Cleome's pair are out on the town, while Constance's two sons would still be at Eton, but the Lent term ended a week ago, so they're probably here, in the drawing room, as well."

Stokes raised his gaze from his notes and regarded Penelope and Barnaby. "How well do you know these people?"

Penelope wrinkled her nose. "Not that well. We cross paths at balls and parties, so we know them well enough to chat to, and of course, I know all that's generally known of them, but we're not what one would term 'friends.'" She sighed and admitted, "I don't know the family's secrets. That said, I know who to ask."

Barnaby smiled and added, "I know the men well enough to pass the time with, but no more than that. However, with the earl's standing in politics, the Fitzhughs are a family of note."

Stokes grunted and returned his attention to his notebook. "So I gathered. I've never seen the Commissioner in such a flap."

From behind the desk, Findlay's voice drifted up. "Well, I'd say that's conclusive enough."

With Penelope and Stokes, Barnaby shifted to peer over the desk.

"What's conclusive?" Stokes asked.

"That he was struck on the head, hard, with this bust." Without looking up, Findlay angled the bust so they could see that its shape mirrored the damage to the earl's skull. "One decisive blow by someone who's right-handed, which doesn't help all that much." He held up the bust. "But this is your murder weapon, and judging by the extent of the damage, he would have died more or less instantly."

"Time?" Stokes asked.

Findlay pulled a face. "Between one and three hours ago. I can't say more than that."

Stokes offered, "He was seen alive and well at about nine-forty and found dead at ten o'clock."

Findlay happily nodded. "That fits, then."

Barnaby had been studying the body's position. "The chair's a swiveling one. Was he working at his papers when he was struck?"

Findlay raised his head to look at the papers strewn across the desk, then returned his gaze to the body. "Looks like he was. He was struck, all unsuspecting, and then slid sideways as the chair rotated a little due to the force of the blow. Then, with him insensible and slumping, his weight dragged him out of the chair and onto the floor."

Stokes glanced at Barnaby and Penelope. "That means..."

Barnaby obligingly completed the thought, "That whoever murdered him was someone he viewed as absolutely no threat."

Stokes looked at the nearby window and the thick curtains that screened it. "Or he had no idea they were there, creeping up behind him."

"Regardless," Penelope stated, "that means that the murderer was definitely not Mrs. Alder. She came in through the door. If she'd tried to circle around behind the earl, he would have turned and watched her."

Stokes looked at Findlay. "Could a woman have struck the blow?"

"In this case," Findlay replied, looking back at the body, "definitely. Even a delicate young lady might have managed that." He hefted the bust in one hand. "This has lots of weight in a small package, and this marble is very hard. It was an excellent choice as a weapon with which to accomplish the deed."

Stokes sighed. "So everyone's a suspect."

Findlay grunted and clambered to his feet. "One thing. There's a draft down there. Is there a window open?"

Stokes, Barnaby, and Penelope regarded the long curtains, then Stokes went to check the window closer to the desk, while Penelope walked to the other window, with Barnaby close behind.

Nearing the window, Penelope said, "These curtains aren't sitting quite straight." She pushed the two long curtains apart and looked out. "And yes, the window—well, it's actually a French door—is ajar."

She spread the curtains wider and gently pushed open the glassed door. "There's a courtyard out here."

She stepped through the doorway, and Barnaby followed.

They found themselves on a gravel pathway that ran around a pretty courtyard. There was a plinth in the center supporting a fountain, and beds of flowers bordered the rectangular space.

Stokes joined them and looked around.

"Those are different wings of the house." Barnaby pointed to the left and right, where the walls of the courtyard were punctuated by windows and two more French doors. "But that wall"—he nodded at the high stone wall directly opposite the study—"might well have a lane on the other side."

Penelope added, "One of those narrow little alleys that lead to the mews behind these old houses."

Stokes surveyed the wall. "Even from here, I can tell that's a very old wall. Lots of little pockets between the stones. Easy enough to climb over."

Staring at the wall, Barnaby observed, "Moran was widely known for his politics, which weren't appreciated by all."

"Perhaps," Penelope said, "someone slipped in from this courtyard, hid behind the curtains closer to the desk, then after Moran had sat and grown absorbed with his papers, stepped out and took him by surprise."

Barnaby arched his brows. "That's possible, I suppose."

Stokes grunted and turned back to the study. "We'll need to check if anyone was seen in the vicinity around ten o'clock."

He led the way inside, and Barnaby and Penelope followed.

Findlay was standing beside the desk, repacking his black bag. "I've finished here. I'll have my men remove the body to the morgue."

Stokes nodded in agreement, then the study door opened, and O'Donnell looked in.

Focusing on Stokes, O'Donnell reported, "The natives are growing restless."

Stokes sighed, then looked at Barnaby and Penelope. "Looks like it's time to face the family and see what they can tell us."

CHAPTER 2

It was now past midnight, so it was hardly surprising that the assembled family were growing fractious.

Penelope led the way into the drawing room, with Barnaby and Stokes close behind.

She was immediately aware that hers and Barnaby's appearances caused, if not consternation, then at least rapid reassessment. In such situations, their reputations very much preceded them.

She paused inside the door, looking down the long room toward the massive ornate fireplace at the far end. Barnaby halted on her right, while Stokes took position to her left, and O'Donnell, having followed them in, quietly shut the door.

Penelope scanned the room, taking rapid note of the faces she'd expected to see. The dowager sat in a Bath chair angled beside the hearth. With her gray hair pulled high into a bun, accentuating the fineness of her features but also the lines that were, now, deeply etched in her cheeks, she'd immediately fixed her pale-blue eyes on Penelope, her gaze shrewd and almost challenging, even as her crabbed fingers idly picked at the fringe of the shawl that was draped over her lap.

On either side of the dowager's chair stood one of her grandsons, much as if the pair were sentinels. Like all the Fitzhugh men, save, curiously, the late earl, who had been heavier and more robust, the duo sported dark hair, tall, athletic frames, and handsome features.

Dismissing the grandsons for the moment, Penelope found Imogen,

Frederick's wife, sitting in the corner of the chaise nearest the dowager. Imogen was a buxom, comfortable, and comforting sort of person, with brown hair and hazel eyes and a round face that, despite her forty-plus years, still held elements of sweetness. Penelope had always found Imogen to be straightforward and sensible and very awake to the ins and outs of ton life.

Her husband, Frederick, stood behind the chaise, one hand resting on the chaise's back behind Imogen's shoulder. He cut a tall, upright figure, his straight dark hair shared with his male relatives, along, in large part, with the austere planes of his face and the ineluctable traces of his aristocratic forebears.

Both Frederick and Imogen appeared openly concerned, although in light of the glances they cast the dowager, their worry was for her rather than any indication of a guilty conscience.

In an armchair on the other side of the fireplace sat Victoria, the current Countess of Moran. Younger than the earl by a good decade, she was an elegant pattern card with a good figure and glossy blond hair artfully arranged about her heart-shaped face. She had large dark-brown eyes and an excellent complexion. The slight primming of her lips combined with a faint frown suggested she was still grappling with shocked surprise at finding herself a widow.

Behind Victoria stood Christopher Fitzhugh, the youngest of the dowager's children, now in his mid-forties. Like Frederick and the dowager's grandsons, Christopher was tall, lean of build, and sported dark-brown hair and blue eyes. He looked more puzzled and surprised than anything else.

At the nearer end of the chaise sat Lady Cleome, a handsome matron of rather haughty mien whose expression gave little away. In the chair alongside Cleome sat her husband, Damien, Lord Mitchelmore, an elegant gentleman with black hair and mid-blue eyes. He looked faintly shocked and, like his wife, appeared to be awaiting further news.

Penelope shifted her gaze to Lady Constance and her husband, Viscount Southerly, who were seated on the second of the twin chaises, then glanced over the rest of those assembled—the numerous children gathered around, the girls on straight-backed chairs and the males standing in small groups behind them.

There was not one tear, not a single sign of sorrow to be found. No hint of anything resembling grief.

Instead, like Mitchelmore and the Southerlys, the wider family looked faintly shocked, rather surprised, and keen to hear more regarding the murder of the head of their house.

Penelope wasn't sure what to make of that.

The entire company had fixed their gazes on them and were waiting for their next move. She glanced at Barnaby, then at Stokes, on her other side.

Barnaby opened proceedings with "Many of you are acquainted with myself and Mrs. Adair, and no doubt, you will have heard that, in cases involving serious crimes within the ton, we assist Scotland Yard"—he tipped his head toward Stokes—"represented by Inspector Stokes. In this particular case, the involvement of Mrs. Adair and myself has been requested by the Commissioner of Police and the Governors of Scotland Yard in order to ensure the murderer is apprehended in as expeditious a manner as possible and with the least disruption to your lives."

Penelope saw faint frowns and thinned lips among many of the older Fitzhughs, eloquent signs of resigned acceptance. In contrast, the expressions of the grandchildren—all of them—displayed interest and, indeed, burgeoning curiosity.

And still, she could not detect the slightest hint of grief.

"We understand," Stokes said, his tone grave, "that you've been informed that the earl was killed—murdered—this evening in his study."

The dowager raised her chin. "Indeed. And it's utterly preposterous to imagine Mrs. Alder is guilty of the crime." The dowager's tone rang with defiance. "Just because Winslow found her in the study, hovering over the body. And now I've discovered that Mary was ordered to deliver an accounting of my prospective social engagements to the study every night at ten o'clock, so it's hardly any wonder that she was there at that time, and her finding Gordon's body was sheer bad luck."

Penelope was struck by the trenchant belligerence in the old lady's gaze.

Calmly, Stokes inclined his head. "Given the hour, we'll keep this as brief as we can. Do you"—he met the dowager's challenging stare, then swept the company—"or anyone else have any idea who might have killed the earl?"

"I've no idea," the dowager stated with marked finality. "Gordon had his fingers in many pies, and not everyone agreed with his opinions. I wouldn't be the least bit surprised if he was killed by someone linked to his political enemies, and of those, he had more than his fair share."

Frederick shifted, drawing the investigators' gazes. "It does seem that might be it." He hurried to add, "Although, clearly, we're not pointing our fingers at any group in particular." He shrugged. "Well, we can't, because we don't know which of those groups might have thought to put an end to him, do we?"

The rest of the family stared at Frederick for half a minute, then all gazes returned to the investigators as if to see what they would make of that.

Penelope decided it was time to get to the facts. "If we could confirm —you were all here tonight for a family dinner?"

In unison, the dowager and Lady Cleome replied, "That's correct."

"When did you last see the earl?" Penelope asked.

The dowager looked peeved. "After dinner, in here. He took himself off the instant he'd downed his tea, leaving the rest of us to our own devices."

As if in exculpation, Frederick offered, as much to the dowager as Penelope, "Well, he did usually work in the evenings. Really, after any event. And I daresay he had official matters to see to."

The dowager haughtily turned her head away, clearly dismissing the excuse.

"You say you all remained here, in this room," Barnaby said. "Did anyone leave before the body was found?"

The family's gazes swung back to the dowager, and she grudgingly stated, "I always retire at nine-thirty. At my age, I need my rest." She gestured to her chair, with its big wheels and handles at the back. "I summoned my footmen, bid the company good night, and had the footmen carry me upstairs to my chamber."

Barnaby glanced at the rest of the company. "And no one else left this room prior to the body being found?"

Imogen spoke up. "No. We"—she included Cleome and Constance with a wave—"Cleome, Constance, and I, were discussing various arrangements to do with our daughters' come-outs. The rest were chatting, waiting for us. We'd just reached agreement and were about to get ready to leave when Winslow came in and told us the shocking news."

Frederick added, "Christopher and I went to the study—really, we couldn't quite believe what we'd heard. Not without seeing…" He blanched at the memory of what he'd seen, swallowed, and concluded, "But we didn't touch anything and came back in here straightaway." He glanced around. "Other than that, none of us have left this room since Gordon went to the study."

There were nods all around, and Christopher, a touch defiantly, affirmed, "We went to the study and returned all but immediately, and other than that, no one left."

Victoria put in, "We were all simply too stunned. That a murderer could actually come into this house and kill Gordon in the study, while all of us were sitting here talking, only yards away." Artfully, she shuddered. "It's truly too shocking to contemplate."

Barnaby looked at Stokes, then at Penelope. They needed to speak with this group individually, but the clocks had struck midnight long ago. Seeing the realization that time was not on their side in Penelope's and Stokes's eyes, Barnaby turned to the group and stated, "We realize that this has been an immense shock, and at this hour, you'll all wish to return to your homes and your beds. However, we do need to speak with each of you individually—purely routine, but a necessary and expected step in the investigative process. Those interviews can be put off until later today. If you would confirm your addresses, specifically where you can be found this afternoon, you may then leave."

Stokes drew his trusty notebook from his pocket and stepped forward, pencil poised. After the dowager responded in haughty tones that she would be there, at Moran House, Stokes progressed from adult to adult around the room.

Barnaby seized the moment to study the younger members of the company. They ranged in age from early teens to about their mid-twenties, and all exhibited signs of being intrigued by the investigators' process. None projected any degree of concern or anxiety, much less showed any hint of a guilty conscience or, indeed, grief.

Stokes completed his circuit of the company and respectfully nodded to the group. "Thank you. We won't detain you any longer."

The ladies promptly rose, gathered their families, and ushered them toward the door.

With Penelope and Stokes, Barnaby stood back and allowed the family groups to file past them, into the mansion's foyer.

The dowager, in her chair, pushed by one of her grandsons, brought up the rear. Imogen had called for Winslow and dispatched the butler to summon the dowager's footmen; the burly pair were now hovering just outside the drawing room.

As the dowager drew level with Barnaby, Penelope, and Stokes, she raised a hand, and her grandson obligingly halted the chair. The dowager's sharp if faded blue gaze scrutinized their faces, then she asked, "Mrs. Alder and Julian?"

There was a demand for reassurance couched in the words.

Stokes stated, "We'll be speaking with Mrs. Alder in a moment, and Julian is currently in the care of his employer."

The dowager considered that, then nodded. "Good." She looked at Stokes. "I want them taken care of. I have no idea what bee got into Gordon's bonnet that led him to dismiss Mary, but"—her lips tightened—"he wouldn't be swayed. I wish you to know that I have nothing but admiration and affection for Mrs. Alder and for Julian as well. He's a bright and caring lad."

"We think so, too," Penelope said. "As does his employer."

"In the circumstances," Stokes stated, "we'll be removing Mrs. Alder from Moran House, but at this point, we have no grounds on which to believe she killed the earl."

The dowager snorted dismissively. "Of course you don't. Because she didn't." She waved toward the open door. "Now, if you'll excuse me, these fellows are here to escort me upstairs."

Stokes half bowed. "Of course."

Her grandson propelled the dowager's chair through the doorway and on to where the footmen now waited at the foot of the stairs.

After halting the chair and farewelling his grandmother, bending to place a kiss on her paper-thin cheek, her grandson turned and left, presumably to join the rest of his family in quitting the house.

With Stokes and Penelope, Barnaby watched as the footmen bent and, between them, hoisted the Bath chair with the dowager in it and started up the stairs.

Barnaby followed Stokes and Penelope into the foyer, where they found Winslow waiting.

Stokes nodded to the butler. "We'll speak with Mrs. Alder now."

~

Penelope followed Winslow through the green-baize-covered door at the rear of the foyer and into the bowels of the huge mansion.

The butler led them to the servants' hall and on into an adjoining corridor to where Morgan was standing, apparently on guard, outside a plain wooden door.

On seeing them approaching, Morgan straightened. As they halted before the door, he tipped his head toward it. "Mrs. Pratchett, the housekeeper, is inside with the lady." To Stokes, he added, "There's no other way out, so I left them to talk."

Stokes nodded his approval.

Penelope noted Morgan's designation of Mrs. Alder as a lady. The fresh-faced constable was too experienced to make a mistake.

Morgan reached for the doorknob and opened the door, and more than passingly curious to meet Julian's mother, Penelope led the way inside.

The housekeeper's room was rather small and contained a neat desk with two chairs. The one behind the desk was occupied by a worried-looking older woman, an upright figure with iron-gray curls half concealed by a housekeeper's mobcap, while the second chair, angled before the desk, had been claimed by a younger woman, presumably Mrs. Alder.

And yes, Morgan was correct. Mrs. Alder was definitely gentry-born.

She sat upright, her hands clasped in the lap of her neat blue day gown. Her glossy brown hair was restrained in a no-nonsense bun at her nape, and her hazel eyes—quite fine hazel eyes—reflected concern and anxiety in equal measure.

The set of her eyes reminded Penelope of Julian, but Mrs. Alder's tapered chin and delicately molded lips were distinctly feminine. She possessed a well-rounded figure and an English-rose complexion, but there was something about her that hinted at strength and resilience beneath the apparent delicateness.

At Penelope's entrance, Mrs. Alder's eyes widened, then as Barnaby and Stokes filed in, her gaze flitted to them. With her fingers spasming tightly together, along with the housekeeper, somewhat uncertainly, Mrs. Alder came to her feet. In a clear, even tone, she stated, "I didn't kill the earl."

Stokes inclined his head. "Having seen the body, we don't believe you did." His gaze shifted to the housekeeper. "Mrs. Pratchett?"

Stiffly, the housekeeper nodded, then defiantly said, "One thing I think you should know. One of our maids—Polly—and the countess's dresser, Orla, both spoke with Mrs. Alder in the attics when she was on her way to the study to leave the list. She was up there then, where she should have been, just two minutes before the clocks struck ten, and it takes that long to get down the stairs and around to the study. No way did she have time to kill the earl and then be found by Winslow at a minute after ten o'clock."

Stokes had pulled out his notebook and took down the names. "Thank you." He nodded to the housekeeper. "Every extra fact helps."

Mrs. Pratchett, pink rising to her cheeks, looked mollified.

Barnaby smiled at her. "I assure you that Mrs. Alder will be safe with us, but we do need to speak with her alone."

Penelope added an encouraging smile.

Glancing at Mrs. Alder, reluctantly, Mrs. Pratchett came out from behind the desk. "I'll be just outside, dear, if you need me."

Mrs. Alder smiled gratefully. "Thank you, Mrs. Pratchett."

As the housekeeper made for the door, and Morgan, remaining outside, closed it behind her, Mrs. Alder regarded Penelope, Barnaby, and Stokes with the air of one who didn't quite know what to make of them.

Penelope grinned and went to claim Mrs. Pratchett's vacant chair and waved Mrs. Alder to resume her seat. "Please sit."

Sinking into the housekeeper's chair, Penelope watched as Barnaby moved to lean against the wall behind her, while Stokes remained before the door. Space was limited, and both men were on the large side.

"Now." Placing her hands flat on the desk, Penelope met Mrs. Alder's gaze. "The first thing we need to tell you is that, immediately Julian heard that you had been accused of the earl's murder, he rushed off and found his employer—Curtis—and appealed for Curtis's help. Subsequently, Curtis brought Julian—whom all three of us here have met before, when he helped us solve another murder—to our house, to our attention, which in part is why we are here. Julian is safe and well and is currently finishing packing his and your things, after which he'll join Curtis outside to wait in our carriage." Penelope paused, taking in Mrs. Alder's stunned expression, then concluded, "So you don't need to worry about Julian."

"Oh, thank God!" The relief that flowed through Mrs. Alder was obvious to any observer. She glanced at Barnaby and Stokes. "Thank you. Thank you all."

"Well, then, with that explained," Penelope continued, "as Julian might have mentioned, I am Mrs. Penelope Adair, and my husband, Barnaby"—she waved over her shoulder at Barnaby—"and I often assist Inspector Stokes"—she indicated Stokes—"in solving crimes involving members of the ton. Officially, that's why we're here."

Mary Alder nodded. "Julian has told me of your association with Scotland Yard." She glanced at Barnaby. "I understand that it's through your offices, sir, that Julian found his way into the information-collecting business and, through that, secured his position with Curtis."

Barnaby smiled. "Julian's a bright lad, and we all believe he'll go far."

Penelope saw that Mary Alder was now a great deal more relaxed, at least in terms of trusting them. "Getting back to the here and now," Penelope said, "we've seen the body and we—and, indeed, Winslow, now he's calmed down—do not believe it was you who killed the earl. We've spoken with the family, and the dowager said she'd just learned that a part of your duties was to give the earl an accounting of her planned engagements for the next day."

Mary nodded. "Yes." She looked at Barnaby, then at Stokes. "That's why I went to the study—to deliver the list."

"Do you have the list?" Stokes asked.

Mary blinked, then said, "I had it in my hand…and I dropped it on the desk when I realized there was a body on the floor and went around to see…"

Barnaby glanced at Stokes. "So it'll be there, on the desk."

Stokes nodded. "We'll check before we leave."

"We need to look over the papers on the desk, regardless," Penelope pointed out.

"We should have a gander at what he was working on," Barnaby agreed.

Penelope returned her attention to Mary. "If you would, could you take us through what you did from, say, nine-thirty, when the dowager retired and left the drawing room?"

"I was waiting for her at the base of the stairs with the footmen—the pair who carry her chair when needed, Edward and Thomas." Mary drew in a breath and continued, "They picked up the chair, and I followed them up the stairs and around to the dowager's room." She smiled faintly, fondly. "Despite what she allows people to think, the dowager doesn't normally get into her bed until later. I think she uses her infirmity as an excuse to escape the noise of the family, even on those occasions, like tonight's, when she was the one who organized the gathering."

"She arranged for the dinner?" Penelope asked.

"Yes, but that wasn't unusual. She insisted on having family dinners every three or so months. The last was in February, just as the Season started, and all her children came up to town."

"So," Stokes said, "you followed the dowager to her room, and then?"

"Sometimes, I read to her, but this time, she was in one of her testy moods and said she wouldn't need me further that night. I confirmed her appointments for tomorrow—well, today, now—and then I left her with Hilda, her dresser and maid."

"So that was, what?" Barnaby asked. "Nine-forty?"

Mary nodded. "It must have been about then."

"What did you do next?" Penelope asked.

"I went upstairs, checked over the list—I'd written it based on the dowager's diary earlier in the day—then I packed more of my things until just before ten o'clock." Mary met Penelope's gaze. "The earl was a stickler for time, and he insisted that I give him the list or, if he wasn't in the study, leave it on the desk on the dot of ten o'clock. He got irritated if I didn't do exactly that." She shrugged. "So I did."

"So you spoke with"—Stokes consulted his notes—"Polly and Orla, then went downstairs to the study." He looked at Mary. "Did you knock?"

"Yes, of course. But he didn't answer, so I assumed he was in the drawing room with the rest of the family, and I opened the door and went in."

"And?" Penelope asked.

"I couldn't see him and thought the room was empty, so I walked toward the desk. But then I noticed the lamps were turned high, and his papers were strewn all over… That wasn't like him. He was usually very tidy and precise. I kept walking toward the desk, puzzling, and started to put the list on the corner where I normally leave it when the fact the chair was swiveled to one side struck me, and I looked over the desk and saw…"

Her gaze distant, Mary swallowed. "At first, I thought he must have collapsed—his heart or something like that. So I dropped the list and rushed around the desk." She paled and put her hands to her face. "It was awful."

After a moment of reliving the horror, she drew in a steadying breath and lowered her hands. "I was horrified. I froze. And I was still standing there, staring down at the earl, when Winslow walked in and saw me."

Penelope exchanged a quick glance with Stokes, then asked, "Did you see or hear anyone else, inside or outside the study? In the corridor or even in the courtyard?"

Mary blinked and looked puzzled. "The courtyard?" When Penelope merely arched her brows, Mary shook her head. "No. I saw no one while making my way to the study—which was not surprising given I came from the servants' stair—and I didn't see or hear anyone outside, either."

"Tell us about Winslow," Barnaby said. "When he walked in, how did he appear?"

"Just as normal, until he saw me standing there and walked to the desk to see what I was staring at."

"Was he carrying a decanter?" Penelope asked.

Mary nodded. "Yes. I remember that, when he saw the earl, he started shaking and almost dropped it on the desk. The last I saw of it, it was still there."

Stokes nodded. "It is. Now, we understand that the earl had decided to let you go. Do you know why he made that decision?"

Mary faintly colored. "No. He gave no reason, which left me mystified. Frankly, all the staff, and the dowager, too, were equally at sea." Mary paused, then, patently uncomfortable, revealed, "Higgs, his lordship's valet, mentioned to me that over recent months, the earl had been grumbling about missing small amounts of cash and had wondered if Julian was to blame, but Higgs had told him, and all the staff know this as fact, that Julian never goes through the green-baize-covered door. He never ventures out of the servants' side of the house. He never has."

Mary's lips tightened. "Regardless, the earl never mentioned the matter of the missing money to me. Or the dowager. As I said, he gave no reason for my dismissal at all. Not to anyone."

Penelope frowned. "But that would leave the dowager with…whom?"

"Just her maid-cum-dresser, Hilda. And her two footmen, Edward and Thomas, who are more or less at her beck and call." Mary hesitated, then added, "I did wonder if, perhaps, the earl was preparing to replace me with a full-time nurse, as, of course, the dowager has aged significantly over the time I've been with her."

"Hmm." Penelope didn't point out that, in such circumstances, the common practice would be for the dowager to be left with all the staff she'd grown accustomed to having around her, and a nurse would be added to the group.

"Did you have much interaction with the earl?" Barnaby asked.

Mary shook her head. "None of the staff did, not really. He held himself aloof from the lower orders. Winslow and Higgs would have spent the most time in his orbit, but he said very little to any of the staff, even them."

"Who runs the household?" Penelope inquired. Given there were two countesses in residence, that was a valid question.

Mary's lips quirked upward. "Outwardly, Lady Victoria, but in reality, ever since the dowager returned to this house last year, the reins have, bit by bit, slid back into her hands."

"Is there tension between the two?" Penelope couldn't see how that would impinge on the earl, but if Lady Victoria was violently unhappy…

Mary grimaced lightly. "To a degree, but no more than you would expect given that this was the dowager's home and household for decades before Lady Victoria married the earl."

Penelope had run out of immediate questions, and a quick glance at Barnaby suggested he'd reached the same point. She looked at Stokes and arched her brows.

Stokes duly addressed Mary Alder. "At this point, we have no more questions for you. However, given the circumstances, namely of an earl being violently murdered in his own study, coupled with Winslow's earlier speculation, even though he's retracted that, and also given that you and Julian were expecting to quit Moran House"—he glanced at the small clock on a cupboard against the wall—"this morning, we believe it would be best all around if you and Julian were to come with us, at least for the immediate future."

"To that end," Barnaby said, "Julian should, by now, have taken your cases outside, to where Curtis was waiting."

"I would like to send you in the care of Constable Morgan"—Stokes tipped his head toward the door, behind which Morgan would presumably be standing—"to join Julian and Curtis in the Adairs' carriage and have the carriage convey you all to the Adairs' residence in Albemarle Street."

"Although the night has already been a long one," Barnaby explained, "we need to interview Winslow and Mrs. Pratchett and take another look at the study. After that"—he glanced at Penelope and Stokes—"we'll reconvene at Albemarle Street and decide on our next steps."

"And part of that," Penelope declared, rising to her feet, "is to keep you and Julian far away from the press."

"Oh, I see." Mary's expression cleared. She studied their faces, then nodded. "If you think it best, Julian and I will fall in with your wishes."

"Excellent." Stokes stepped away from the door, opened it, and called Morgan inside, then firmly shut the door on all interested ears. In a low voice, Stokes gave Morgan orders to take Mrs. Alder out by the rear door to join Julian and Curtis in the waiting carriage.

Barnaby said, "Tell Phelps to take you to Albemarle Street. It's so close, he can take you lot there and return for us in good time. We still have several things to do here before we can leave."

"Just don't tell anyone where you're going," Penelope warned. "Behave as if you're escorting Mrs. Alder to Scotland Yard."

Morgan's face cleared. "Ah. I see. So I'll take the lady, and we'll all go and wait for you at the Adairs'."

Barnaby and Stokes both stated, "That's right."

Morgan smiled at Mrs. Alder, bobbed his head, then reached for her elbow. "If you'll allow it, ma'am, that's what I'd normally do if I were escorting a lady to the clink."

Morgan's cheeriness was difficult to resist. Mrs. Alder strove to straighten her lips and inclined her head. "Of course, Constable. Lead the way."

Morgan's expression leached into one of stern authority, and Mary adopted a bland, blank expression as he opened the door and, with gentle care, steered her out and along the corridor.

~

Barnaby followed Penelope out of the housekeeper's room. Stokes, having been closer to the door, had led the way, and they followed him into the servants' hall.

There, they found Winslow and Mrs. Pratchett. Beyond them, the servants' hall was empty.

Winslow noticed Barnaby looking and quickly explained, "It being so late, sir, and what with the shock of the master's murder, Mrs. Pratchett and I sent the rest of the staff to their beds. Everyone is so discombobulated, and tomorrow is already here."

"Understandable," Stokes allowed. "That said, we have a few questions we need to put to you, but we'll try to keep it brief."

Both Winslow and Mrs. Pratchett looked unhappy but resigned, and both complied with Stokes's gesture to seat themselves at the long deal table in the center of the room.

Barnaby sat on the bench on the table's opposite side, beside Penelope, who was on Stokes's left.

Stokes began by stating, "We understand that the earl had terminated Mrs. Alder's employment, the dismissal to take effect this morning. Do either of you have any idea why he took that step?"

Mrs. Pratchett looked at Winslow, who briefly met her gaze. When Winslow looked back at his clasped hands and volunteered nothing, Mrs. Pratchett raised her head and replied, "Honestly, none of us have any notion of what was in the master's mind, but we did wonder if it had something to do with a wild idea the master had taken that young Julian, Mrs. Alder's son, was responsible for the thefts of small amounts of cash that the earl says have been happening, but truly, that's just daft. Aside from Julian never going into the front of the house, which is where the cash went missing from, there's not a bad bone in that boy's body, and I'll take an oath on that."

His tone lugubrious, Winslow added, "All of us would. A very good lad all around, is young Julian. We're all very sorry to see him and Mrs. Alder go."

Stokes eyed the pair. "Do you have any idea who might have been responsible for those small thefts?"

Again, Mrs. Pratchett and Winslow shared a glance, then Winslow offered, "It seemed to us—all the staff who work in the front of the house—that the thefts the earl was complaining about always occurred, or at least were always noticed, after Lady Constance's boys had been around."

"Mr. Vincent and Mr. Theodore," Mrs. Pratchett supplied. "Rascals, the pair of them, and very good at slipping unseen all over the house."

Barnaby wondered what connection, if any, a series of small thefts might have to the earl's murder.

After a moment, Penelope asked the butler and housekeeper, "How did Mrs. Alder react to being dismissed?"

Mrs. Pratchett's expression lightened, and a degree of approval invested her features. "Gracious about it, she was. Truth to tell, many in the servants' hall were a bit up in arms about it on her behalf, but she said as it was well within the master's rights as he was her employer, and that after being with the dowager for over ten years, perhaps it was time for her to move on."

Winslow shifted on the bench. "She did mention that with the dowager growing so old and frail, perhaps the master was thinking of replacing her—Mrs. Alder, that is—with a nurse."

Mrs. Pratchett angled her head. "And indeed, that might be a good thing and what was intended, but regardless, we're all sorry to see Mary and Julian go."

"Most of us here," Winslow said, "have known Julian since he was a little tyke, because whenever the dowager visited here—she used to live in Regent's Square—Mary and Julian came as well and would spend their time back here with us, so in a way, to us, Mary and Julian are a bit like family."

Stokes had pulled out his notebook and was scribbling. "All right." He looked across the table at the pair. "To last night. We've heard that Mrs. Alder had been ordered to deliver a list of the dowager's appointments for the following day to the earl's study every night at ten o'clock." He focused on Winslow. "I take it you were both aware of that."

Winslow and Mrs. Pratchett nodded, and the latter added, "Every night, regular at ten. That's what the master wanted."

"Mrs. Alder kept the dowager's diary," Winslow explained. "And after writing the list, which she usually did every afternoon, she would tell the dowager's footmen, Thomas and Edward, and also the coachman, Hollis, so they would know when they would be needed the next day."

Mrs. Pratchett added, "Quite aside from letting the master know where his mama and some of her staff would be, it helped that the staff knew what to prepare for come the next day. Helped things run more smoothly, knowing when we'd have extra footmen about and also if the big carriage would be here or not."

"I see." Stokes focused on Winslow. "At what time did you first go to the study?"

The butler glanced at the housekeeper. "We think it must have been about nine-forty when the master rang the study bell, and I went to see what he wanted." Mrs. Pratchett nodded her agreement, and Winslow returned his gaze to Stokes. "It seemed the whiskey decanter was empty, and the master wanted it refilled, of course, so I took it with me and came back here." He tipped his head toward the corridor, which led to Mrs. Pratchett's room and, it seemed, also the butler's pantry. "I had to fetch the key from my room, then I went down to the cellar, filled the decanter from the stock there, and brought the decanter up again. I stopped to return the key to my pantry before I headed back to the study."

Mrs. Pratchett put in, "The clocks struck the hour—for ten o'clock—while Winslow was putting the key back."

Jotting that down, Stokes nodded. "Thank you."

"When you first went to the study," Barnaby said, "was there anyone else with the earl?"

Winslow shook his head. "No. He was quite alone, as usual."

"Did you see anyone in the corridors after you left here with the refilled decanter?" Stokes asked.

Winslow frowned and, clearly, replayed his memories, but eventually, he shook his head. "No. There was no one about that I saw." He refocused on Stokes. "As far as I know, at that time, the rest of the family were all still in the drawing room, even the younger ones. I'd fetched away the tea trolley about ten minutes before the master rang, and I saw them all there then."

Mrs. Pratchett volunteered, "When Thomas and Edward went to fetch the dowager—and that was at nine-thirty, as usual—they crossed paths with Winslow, bringing the tea trolley down."

Stokes nodded. "We'll check with Thomas and Edward tomorrow, to confirm they didn't see anyone leave the drawing room." He studied his notes, then looked at Winslow. "The first time you entered the study, did you notice if the French door to the courtyard was open?"

Winslow frowned. "Was it open?"

"It's open now," Barnaby said. "We believe it might have been open when the earl was killed."

"Heavens!" Mrs. Pratchett looked taken aback. She glanced at Winslow.

Deep puzzlement was evident in the butler's frown as, slowly, he said, "I'm sure that door was shut earlier. The master would have noticed if it wasn't. Very sensitive to cold drafts, he was."

Penelope said, "The wall at the far end of the courtyard, opposite the study. What lies on the other side?"

"A lane," Winslow replied. "A very narrow one. It runs between Park Lane and the mews behind the houses."

Stokes stated, "We'll check with the rest of the staff tomorrow, but were either of you aware of any person the earl might have been expecting last night?"

"No." Winslow's reply was definite. "And the master never had meetings he didn't tell me about."

In a scandalized tone, Mrs. Pratchett added, "Much less meetings with the sort of people who might come over the wall from the lane."

Barnaby clarified, "Regardless of their route of approach, is it correct to state that neither of you were aware of anyone expected to come to the house and meet with the earl yesterday evening?"

Both Winslow and Mrs. Pratchett nodded emphatically.

Winslow insisted, "There was no one expected."

"And why would there be?" Mrs. Pratchett asked. "It was a big family dinner, one the dowager had called. When she calls, they all come, and they know better than to expect to do any other business while they dance attendance here."

Barnaby saw Penelope tip her head consideringly, no doubt assimilating what that statement said of the family and the dowager's place in it.

Stokes looked over his notes, then shut his notebook and inclined his head to the pair across the table. "Thank you both." To Winslow, he said, "We'll be back later today, but for now, you can lock up."

With obvious relief, the butler and housekeeper rose, as did Barnaby, Penelope, and Stokes.

"Before we leave, we need to check the study," Penelope reminded Barnaby and Stokes, and they headed for the foyer.

They made straight for the study. During their absence, the body had been removed and, presumably, transported to the morgue at Scotland Yard.

On halting before the desk, they surveyed the papers strewn upon it.

Penelope picked up a sheet of notepaper that had been lying on the front edge of the desk. "Here's Mrs. Alder's list." She scanned it. "Just what one would expect of an ageing dowager countess at the height of the Season."

Barnaby rounded the desk and, without disturbing the papers, bent to read them. After a moment, he reported, "These appear to be submissions to a parliamentary committee on workers' rights." He straightened. "Nothing overtly threatening or revealing in them."

Stokes grunted. "I suppose it's too much to hope that the murderer might have left anything to point his way."

Penelope sighed. "Apparently so." She handed Mary Alder's note to Stokes, then looked around the room again. "I can't imagine we're likely to learn anything more here." She returned her gaze to Barnaby and Stokes. "Phelps should have returned with the carriage by now. Let's leave poor Winslow to lock up and continue discussing our next steps at home."

Stokes nodded and waved her toward the door.

After one last glance at the disarranged papers, Barnaby left the desk and followed his coinvestigators as Penelope led them to the front door.

CHAPTER 3

Curtis sat perched on a sofa in the Adairs' drawing room, feeling even more awkward than he usually did in the refined ambiance of the Mayfair home. He was, however, determined to triumph over his uncertainties—which, after all, were a form of shyness and thus a weakness to be overcome—because the lady seated beside him needed his support.

Mary Alder's gaze was fixed on Julian, who was standing before one long window and peering between the curtains, keeping watch for the Adair carriage that would deliver Barnaby, Penelope, and Stokes to the house. Then they would all learn what was what and decide what to do next, but in the meantime, while gazing at Julian, Mary Alder was worrying something fierce.

If Curtis possessed one talent, it lay in reading people, and from the set of her lips and chin and the faint frown tangling her delicately arched brown eyebrows, Mary Alder was imagining all sorts of unlikely outcomes.

Feeling compelled, even in the teeth of his shyness, to try to alleviate her worry, he ventured, "You can put your faith in the Adairs. They may be top-of-the-trees, yet they're good people. Ones you can rely on." He thought, then grunted and added, "Stokes, too, even if he is an inspector of police."

His comment had, at least, drawn her attention and distracted her. Plainly curious, she asked, "Have you known them long?"

"A few years now." He paused, then, seeing that she was still watching him, as if eager to hear more, he went on, "I was working for a client—another nob by the name of the Honorable Mr. Richard Percival. I was helping him find his missing niece and nephew, who he'd thought had fled with his stepniece, who was older but still a youngish lady. He—Percival—wasn't sure why the trio had done a bunk in the dead of night from the ancestral home, but it turned out, they were in fear of their lives, and to top it all, they thought it was Percival—Richard Percival, my client—who they were fleeing from. A right mess, it was, but it was all the work of another Percival, a cousin who was trying to kill the nephew—who was a viscount having inherited the title from his father—and make it seem that it was Richard Percival who'd done the deed. That way, the cousin's path to claiming the title and the estate would be free and clear. It was through untangling all that and getting it sorted out that we—Percival and I—crossed paths with Stokes and the Adairs. Once we'd got all squared away and realized who the real villain was, we worked together, and in the end, the villain was caught."

Curtis felt he could drown in Mary's hazel eyes. Lamely, he added, "That was how I came to know the Adairs and Stokes, and since then, I've worked with them on a few other cases." He forced himself to look across the room at Julian. "As you no doubt know from young Julian, my business deals in information, and these days, if we stumble on anything untoward, I pass it on to Stokes."

Mary followed his gaze to her son. "I see." After a tiny pause, she went on, "I have to say, your story makes me even happier about Julian working for your firm."

Quietly, so the boy wouldn't hear and get a swollen head, Curtis responded, "Not half as happy as we are to have him. He's got a good head on him." Curtis tipped his own head toward Julian. "As he's shown in this case."

He met Mary's eyes. "He didn't panic when he learned the earl had been murdered and you stood accused of the crime. Instead, he did the wise and sensible thing and came straight to me for help."

Mary searched his eyes, then nodded. Looking back at her son, she murmured, "He's growing up so fast. Sometimes, I think he's much older than he should be for his years, yet at the same time, he's content and happy with what he's doing, and I tell myself that that's enough."

"It's more than enough," Curtis gruffly said. "It's far more than most his age can claim."

Mary sighed and glanced at the open doorway. "Maybe so, but for how long? At this moment, I feel that we—Julian and I—are in limbo, but we're also at some sort of crossroads. The sort where there are multiple ways we could go, but which we choose will be vital for our future." She shook her head. "It all happened so quickly, I can barely take in the whole of it."

At the window, Julian straightened. "I think I see the carriage." A second later, he shut the curtains and, with his young face full of hope, turned to Mary and Curtis. "They're here!"

Instantly, Curtis was aware of the tension that gripped the lady beside him. He glanced at her profile as she stared at the doorway. "Trust me," he murmured. "It'll all come out right."

Penelope led the way into their drawing room to find Curtis standing unexpectedly close to Mrs. Alder. Both were on their feet before the sofa, and Julian—who had apparently been keeping watch on the street—was on his way to join his mother.

Smiling reassuringly, Penelope waved at Mary Alder and Curtis to resume their seats. "Finally, we're here."

She claimed the position on the sofa opposite the pair, and Barnaby came to sit beside her while Stokes claimed his usual armchair, angling it so he could view the occupants of both sofas.

Although Curtis wore his usual imperturbably stoic mask, Penelope noted the faintly concerned look he directed at Mary. For her part, Mary was looking with incipient trepidation at Stokes.

Noting that, Stokes mildly stated, "We've asked all the questions we reasonably can to this point, and what we know is this." He raised his hands and, with one index finger, ticked off his points on the fingers of his other hand. "First, yesterday evening, the Earl of Moran was seated behind his desk in his study, reading some documents." He moved on to his next finger. "At about nine-forty, he summoned his butler, Winslow, and ordered him to refill the empty whiskey decanter."

Shifting his attention to his third finger, Stokes continued, "At some moment between Winslow leaving the study at nine-forty and Mrs. Alder entering it at ten o'clock, someone struck the earl on the head with a small marble bust that was kept on the shelf behind the desk. The blow was sufficiently hard to cave in the earl's skull and kill him, most likely instantly."

Tapping his fourth finger, Stokes tipped his head Mary's way. "Mrs. Alder entered the study because she'd been ordered by the earl to leave a list of the dowager's plans for the next day on his study desk every night at ten o'clock. Consequently, she was the one who discovered the body and was, soon after, found in the study by Winslow, returning with the refilled decanter."

Stokes told Mary, "Winslow has recanted his assertion that you had anything to do with killing the earl. In addition, it's well-nigh impossible to imagine that the earl would have allowed you to walk behind him in such a way that you might have struck the blow that killed him. Further, there are several staff members who can testify to your presence upstairs, in the attics, until you left to go to the study just before ten o'clock. You could not have been hidden in the study prior to Winslow seeing the earl alive, and you could not have gone to the study earlier than you did, so you could not have committed the crime."

Tiredly, Stokes smiled at Mary. "All of that means that, as far as Scotland Yard is concerned, you are not a suspect."

"Thank God!" Mary breathed, her hand at her throat.

Stokes sighed. "However, to continue with our findings, no one was seen going into the study or lurking elsewhere inside the house during the critical period, namely, between nine-forty and ten o'clock. All the other members of the earl's family were in the drawing room, save only the dowager, who had been carried upstairs to her room at nine-thirty. Our one potential lead is that the French door to the courtyard was open—unlocked and left ajar—and the courtyard is bounded by a narrow alley that runs between Park Lane and the mews behind the houses along there."

A pause ensued while they all digested that summary.

Then Barnaby said, "One point. We gathered that the dowager hadn't previously known of the list of her engagements that you supplied to the earl every evening."

Mary colored. "She knew I always checked with her every evening regarding her engagements—I also kept her diary, but I would check, nonetheless. I…didn't know if the earl had told her of his order or not, and I didn't feel it was my place to mention it if he hadn't." She faintly grimaced. "Truth to tell, it seemed rather intrusive and a touch callous in that his only interest appeared to be where her staff—the footmen and coachman—and also the carriage were at any time. It wasn't any interest in his mother's life that lay behind the order."

Penelope studied Mary's expressive face. "We also heard that the dowager and the staff and, it seems, everyone else are mystified as to why the earl dismissed you. They know of no reason for his action, yet Winslow and Mrs. Pratchett said you'd accepted the dismissal with notable grace." Penelope cocked her head. "Why was that? Normally, if a member of staff of your long service and seniority was given short shrift, I would expect you to make some protest, even if that was merely to grumble to the housekeeper."

Mary sighed. "I didn't because of the dowager." She paused, then went on, "When I was newly widowed and seeking a position, the dowager behaved as something of a white knight for me and Julian. Few would have so readily accepted a maid-companion with a young child into their households, but she did without a blink, and she was always encouraging and supportive when it came to Julian." Mary frowned slightly. "And then there was the situation with the earl—whatever was behind that." She met Penelope's eyes and explained, "Over recent years, there's been a steadily building tension between the earl and the dowager—driven by the earl, I hasten to add. I've heard them arguing, but I've never been sure about what. I know she doesn't agree with his approach to...something to do with the family or possibly the estate, but I never heard details enough to be sure of what the actual issue was."

"How did she react to the news of your dismissal?" Penelope asked.

"She was furious but...I would say controlled, for she knew that it was within the earl's purview to dismiss me. He was the one paying my wages and supporting our board, not her." Mary hesitated, then admitted, "If I'd protested the dismissal, even to Pratchett, the dowager would have heard of it, and she would have argued even more than she did, and despite her iron will, she's no longer as strong as she once was."

Mary met Penelope's eyes, then glanced at Barnaby and Stokes. "All in all, I knew Julian and I could survive well enough—we've saved well over the years, and there will be other positions for me, and"—she smiled at Julian, then glanced at Curtis—"Julian now has steady employment as well." She looked back at Penelope. "So I decided I didn't want us to be the cause of a serious—more serious—rupture between the earl and the dowager. I didn't want that on my conscience, not after she's been so kind to us over the past ten years."

Impressed and, indeed, reassured by the sentiment, Penelope nodded in understanding.

Stokes had been studying Mary. His gaze flicked to Curtis, who was watching her closely, then Stokes stated, "I want to be abundantly clear. After viewing the scene of the crime and interviewing the staff and the family, we see no reason to think that you, Mrs. Alder, were in any way involved with the murder of the earl."

"Indeed," Penelope put in. "You were merely the one who was unlucky enough to first come upon the body."

"And the reason you did," Barnaby added, "was because of a pre-arranged meeting decreed by the deceased."

"Exactly." Stokes took back the reins. "However, all that said, there will be considerable—*considerable*—pressure brought to bear to apprehend the earl's killer with all speed. While we will certainly do our level best to oblige, for the next several days at least, it would be in everyone's best interests if you officially 'remain in police custody.'"

Mary's eyes widened, and Curtis tensed, but it was Julian who, aghast, exclaimed, "You're going to put Mama in jail?"

"Good gracious, no!" Penelope smiled reassuringly at Julian and at Curtis and Mary, too. "Not at all." She glanced at Stokes, who nodded for her to continue. Looking back at the three on the sofa opposite, she explained, "We discussed our options on the way back here, and we think it would be best if you—Mary and Julian—remain here, in this house. At present, no one knows where you are, and it might well be preferable to keep your whereabouts from the press, at least until we're further down the road with this investigation."

"If you will agree, Mrs. Alder," Stokes rumbled, "to remain within the house, then I believe that, in the circumstances, that solution will be acceptable to the Commissioner."

"To put matters bluntly," Barnaby said, "the powers that be and the press will be howling for a quick arrest, and you don't need to be the one arrested for something you didn't do."

Mary stared at them, then glanced at Curtis.

He felt her gaze, met it, and nodded. "I think they're right, and it's a good idea. You'll be safe from any bounders of the press in here."

"Julian, of course," Barnaby said, "would be free to come and go." He looked at Curtis. "And I expect you'll have work for him."

"Too right," Curtis averred. He leant forward and, across Mary, caught Julian's still-wide-eyed gaze. "I'm thinking I'll be putting men on to watch the earl's house, just to see who comes and goes. Who takes an interest."

Barnaby inclined his head. "That could prove helpful."

Curtis looked at Stokes. "With your permission, I'll also send some of my crew around to see if they can turn up any sightings of someone in that lane or in the mews at the time of the murder." Curtis switched his gaze to Julian. "You can help with that. Enough of those 'round about the area will know you and speak to you more freely than they will to anyone else."

Stokes nodded eagerly. "That would be a great help."

Barnaby caught Stokes's eye. "Later today, we'll need to follow up with individual interviews with all the family members who were at Moran House last night. They might have been in the drawing room throughout the murder itself, but it's possible they'll have insights into the earl's activities and who might have been motivated to strike the fatal blow."

Penelope nodded. "At present, given the family seem to have all been in the drawing room, it seems most likely that someone came in from outside the property. They might even have already been in the study when the earl entered." She frowned, then pulled a face. "Short of Curtis and Julian learning of someone lurking outside at the right time, that's going to be difficult to prove."

"Obviously," Stokes said, pushing out of the armchair and getting to his feet, "we need more information. Lots, lots more information."

Barnaby rose, too, bringing Curtis and Julian to their feet as well. Barnaby smiled tiredly. "And if we're to make sense of what we learn, we all need to get some sleep."

Penelope stood and, beckoning, took Mary and Julian in charge. To Mary, Penelope said, "Come and I'll introduce you to Mostyn. Julian and he are already acquainted, but Mostyn will arrange everything we need—he always does."

Inexorably, she steered Mary and Julian ahead of her and out of the room.

Standing with Stokes and Curtis, Barnaby watched the trio depart, then turned to Stokes. "I'll go and speak with my father later this morning, in case the Commissioner needs any assistance in keeping the howling hordes at bay."

Curtis nodded at Stokes. “As early as I can, I’ll get my people on the job. I’ll let you know if we find anything useful.”

Barnaby asked Curtis, “You’ll take Julian with you?”

Curtis nodded. “Never fear. I’ll keep him busy and keep an eye on him as well. The truth is, if there was any cove lurking around Moran House last night, young Julian’ll be the one to find his trail.”

CHAPTER 4

Later that day, Barnaby was sitting at the table in the dining room, with an array of dishes representing breakfast and lunch combined spread before him. He'd just finished reading the black-bordered front-page article in *The Times*, announcing the murder of the Earl of Moran in respectful yet somehow lurid terms, and Penelope, seated opposite, had finished her slice of toast slathered with marmalade and picked up her teacup to take a sip when the front doorbell pealed.

And pealed again.

Then the knocker was plied.

Startled, across the table, Barnaby locked gazes with Penelope.

They heard Mostyn's hurried footsteps cross the front hall, and a second later, Stokes's rumbling tones reached them.

Then Stokes came striding rapidly toward the dining room.

From the way Penelope's eyes widened, she, like Barnaby, recognized that this was not Stokes arriving to join them in continuing their interviews.

Penelope broke eye contact and swung to face the doorway as Stokes loomed, filling the space.

He hadn't even stopped to remove his greatcoat.

"Who's dead?" Penelope demanded.

That was the only viable explanation for the intensely grim look on Stokes's face.

"Winslow, the earl's butler, was found dead this morning."

"A heart attack?" Barnaby asked.

"No such luck," Stokes ground out. "Judging from the scant details I have thus far, he was poisoned. Findlay's already on his way there." Stokes tipped his head toward the front hall. "Coming?"

Penelope was already out of her chair and making for the door.

"Silly question." Barnaby rose and followed.

~

They were forced to descend from the carriage in Park Lane because the wrought-iron gates to the Moran House drive were closed, with a bevy of constables pacing before them, ostensibly to deter a horde of hovering reporters from making a run at the front or side doors.

Barnaby took Penelope's arm, and with Stokes on her other side, they put their heads down and strode rapidly toward the gates.

Unfortunately, several of the newshounds recognized Stokes and rushed toward them, yelling their questions—mostly "Who's the murderer, Inspector?"—as they came.

Two constables raced forward and intercepted the reporters before they reached Stokes, and the three investigators managed to slip between the gates, manned by another constable, before being accosted.

As they walked up the drive, Stokes glanced behind them and muttered, "The Commissioner wants to keep the press as far away as possible, far enough that they don't hear about this latest development immediately."

Barnaby nodded, and they went up the steps, and Stokes rapped on the door.

Seconds later, they were admitted to the house by a tall, pale, and rather frightened footman.

As soon as the footman had shut the door behind them, Stokes demanded, "Where's the body?"

The footman swallowed. "Upstairs, sir—Inspector. In the attics. I'll… er, show you the way."

They followed the footman deeper into a warren of corridors to what was plainly the servants' stair. The footman waved them up, and they swiftly climbed to the attics on the third floor.

On the uppermost landing, they encountered a teary-eyed Mrs. Pratchett. The previously unflappable woman was wringing her hands. The instant she saw Penelope, Mrs. Pratchett all but wailed, "Lord save us, ma'am! What's to become of us?"

Deciding to take the question literally, as she stepped off the stairs, Penelope briskly asked, "Who of the family have been told of Winslow's death?"

"That's just it, ma'am." Mrs. Pratchett's fingers tightened even more. "They're all still abed. Mr. Christopher, Lady Victoria, and the dowager."

Penelope cast a swift look at Barnaby and Stokes, then instructed Mrs. Pratchett, "Go downstairs and rally the staff so they can cope with their duties over the rest of the day. Much will go on as usual. If any of the family wake and ring for their attendants, their maids or their valet will need to tell them Winslow has died."

Mrs. Pratchett, her gaze locked on Penelope's stern face, drew in a deep breath, then nodded and bobbed a curtsy. "Yes, ma'am. I'll see to it."

Before she could step past them and start down the stairs, Stokes asked, "Who found Winslow?"

Mrs. Pratchett's face fell. "I did, Inspector. We'd left him until late—well, he's not young, and we all thought, what with the drama of last evening and him being last up to bed after locking up, that he was due a little sleep-in, so as the family weren't up and about and needing him, we let him be and got on with our usual chores. But then it was getting on for eight-thirty, and he still hadn't come down, so I came up…" She teared up and, on a half sob, waved along the corridor. "And I found him…like that. Horrible, it was."

"Did you touch anything in the room?" Stokes asked.

Mrs. Pratchett shook her head. "I didn't need to." Again, she waved farther down the corridor to where the door to a room stood open. "You'll see. As soon as I saw him, I knew he was gone." She sniffed, then raised her head and added, "I closed the door and went straight downstairs and sent Jeffrey—the footman who would've opened the door to you—to send one of the constables outside to Scotland Yard."

Stokes inclined his head. "Thank you. That was precisely the right thing to do."

Mollified, Mrs. Pratchett sniffed again, then offered, "Your man—the medical one—arrived a few minutes ago, and I brought him up. He's in there now. No one else has been up here since I found Winslow and went downstairs."

Penelope nodded reassuringly. "You did just right." She gently pushed the housekeeper toward the stairs. "Go down, now. The staff will need your direction."

Mrs. Pratchett dipped in a curtsy, straightened, and started down the stairs, her footfalls heavy on the wooden treads.

Penelope turned and, with Barnaby and Stokes at her back, hurried down the narrow corridor to the open door.

The room was the last along the corridor, tucked under the eaves and, given Winslow's rank, no doubt slightly larger than the other servants' rooms.

As she halted in the open doorway, Penelope saw what Mrs. Pratchett had meant. There was no need to go any closer to see that Winslow was definitely dead.

He was a pathetic sight, his features fixed in a rictus suggesting horrendous pain, the bedclothes soiled and massively disarranged. He'd clearly thrashed about in extremis.

Findlay, who'd been standing by the head of the bed, glanced their way. "Poison, obviously. And I would wager it was strychnine."

From behind Penelope's left shoulder, Stokes heaved a heavy sigh.

Glancing back, she saw him draw out his notebook.

"The poison virtually every household has tucked away somewhere." Stokes shook his head.

She grimaced. "Especially with the rat infestation being what it currently is."

Barnaby leaned against the doorjamb to her right. "Any hint as to when he ingested it?"

"Or how?" she added.

Findlay sucked his teeth in thought, then offered, "Assuming it is strychnine, then given the way it acts, I'd say he must have consumed the dose close to the time he got to bed. Say, in the hour before." Findlay looked at Stokes, then at Barnaby and Penelope. "But I assume you three were here later than I was last night."

Stokes nodded. "Into the small hours. We left at what?" He looked at Penelope and Barnaby. "Two o'clock?"

"About that," Barnaby said. "And after seeing us out of the front door, Winslow would have completed his rounds and locked up before he came up here."

Findlay waggled his head. "That fits well enough. He ate or drank something before he came upstairs."

He sighed and waved them back, out of the room and into the narrow corridor. "I'll have the men from the morgue take the body out. I've already sent for them."

Stokes pulled a face. "There are reporters by the dozen in Park Lane. See if you can go out via the mews. The fewer people who learn of this second death in Moran House, the better for all concerned."

Findlay grunted. "The morgue men and I are all for avoiding the press. We'll do our best."

Penelope turned and led the way down the servants' stairs. Halfway down, she glanced over her shoulder at Barnaby and Stokes, who were following her. "Why kill the butler?"

From behind Stokes, Findlay said, "It might have been an accident."

"Faint hope, my friend," Stokes muttered.

They reached the small foyer at the bottom of the stairs and parted from Findlay, who headed for the back door and the mews beyond.

As they tacked through the corridors, making for the front of the house, Barnaby said, "Accident or murder? Was poisoning Winslow a deliberate act? If so, by whom?"

"Or," Penelope replied, her tone grim, "was the poisoning a deliberate act but Winslow wasn't the intended victim? If so, who was?"

From behind them, Stokes growled, "Indeed."

Penelope emerged from the maze of corridors into the rear of the mansion's foyer. The lower flight of the mansion's grand staircase rose beside them, and with Barnaby and Stokes at her back, she made for the front door, but as they cleared the side of the staircase, they found Christopher Fitzhugh distractedly pacing.

He swung to face them, and from the way his features eased on sighting them, it was them he was waiting to waylay.

Gone was his debonair defiance of the small hours. Christopher looked ashen and shaken, his movements less assured, his overall appearance one of nervous uncertainty. "Thank God you're still here!"

When Penelope, who, with Barnaby and Stokes, had halted beside the newel post, arched her brows in question, Christopher approached and explained, "My man told me about Winslow dying. Of poison, of all things!" The last word ended on a near-hysterical note. Christopher dragged in a breath and, clasping his hands before him, rushed on, "I was so shocked, I came down and decided I needed a drink to steady my nerves, so I went into the study—the decanter there is always kept full of the better stuff."

Turning toward the corridor leading to the study, he beckoned. "Come and see. It'll be easier to show you."

Mystified, Penelope exchanged a quick glance with Barnaby and Stokes, then they followed in Christopher's wake.

He led them into the late earl's study, then stopped just over the threshold and stood aside to allow them to enter the room. The instant they had, dramatically, he pointed at the tantalus that stood against the corridor wall. "I came in and saw that and realized something was wrong."

Following the direction of his accusing finger, Penelope saw the decanter—the same one they'd seen the previous evening—mostly full of amber fluid with a glass, presumably used, sitting upright beside it. Other glasses were arrayed, upside down, on the tantalus's lower shelf.

Stokes rumbled, "When we left the room last night, the decanter was full and was standing on the corner of the desk."

Christopher nodded. "It was there when Frederick and I came in to look at Gordon's body." He glanced at their faces and added, "It was the used glass that struck me as odd. As wrong. Winslow is the last one in here every night, when he locks up, and he would never normally leave a used glass sitting with the decanter."

"Except," Penelope said, "last night—or more accurately, early this morning—wasn't the least bit normal, and Winslow was, no doubt, in something of a state."

"Exactly." Christopher went on, "I wondered if he'd felt the need for something to steady his nerves, to help him sleep, and he helped himself to a tot, and then, with Gordon dead, just left the glass, thinking to clear it away later today."

It was a plausible scenario.

Stokes and Barnaby were frowning.

Barnaby crossed to the tantalus and crouched to examine the glass without touching it. "This has definitely been used. There's a film of dried whiskey in the base."

He straightened, and they heard footsteps, several pairs, coming slowly and heavily down the main stairs.

Stokes had raised his head, listening. "That'll be Findlay and his men, removing the body."

Stokes looked at the decanter, then pulled a handkerchief from his jacket pocket, shook it out, and using it, picked up the decanter, along with the glass, and carried both out, into the corridor and on to the foyer.

Penelope followed, with Barnaby at her heels and Christopher trailing behind.

They reached the foyer just as Findlay, who'd been following the men from the morgue as they carried Winslow's sheet-draped body down on a stretcher, joined Stokes on the black-and-white tiles. "We had to come down this way because the servants' stairs are too narrow for the stretcher." Findlay directed the morgue attendants to the green-baize-covered door. "On and out through the servants' hall and the back door. You won't want to run into any of those pesky reporters carrying that."

The men's expressions stated they were in total agreement. They maneuvered the stretcher around and continued toward the rear of the house.

Findlay returned his attention to the investigators. Curious, he nodded at the decanter. "What do you have there?"

Stokes proffered the decanter and glass. "You saw these in the study last night. Mr. Fitzhugh went in there this morning and noticed that the decanter had been moved and one glass used, apparently for the whiskey."

"You think the butler had a tipple?" Findlay set his big black bag on the tiles and bent to open it.

"That seems the most likely explanation," Barnaby said. "Regardless, you'll need to test what's in the decanter."

Findlay drew out a paper bag, opened it, and held it out. "Drop the glass in here."

Stokes obliged, and Findlay wrapped up the glass and set it in his black bag. Then he pulled out a bigger piece of paper and wrapped it about the base of the decanter, dislodging Stokes's handkerchief. "Don't use that without washing it first."

Tucking the cloth into an inner pocket, Stokes grimaced. "I won't."

"Now, hold this." Findlay had Stokes support the decanter while Findlay used twine to tie down the stopper.

Eventually satisfied, Findlay finished wrapping the decanter and wedged it upright in his black bag.

Rising, he carefully picked up the bag, then nodded to Christopher. "We'll return the glassware to you eventually."

Christopher looked faintly appalled. "If that's where the poison came from, I'm not sure we'll want it back."

Findlay shrugged, nodded to them all, and followed the morgue attendants into the rear of the mansion.

Stokes turned to Christopher. "If you could instruct the staff to leave the study undisturbed for the moment?"

Christopher blinked. "Yes, of course." He hesitated, then said, "If you'll excuse me, I…er, need to return upstairs."

With the barest of inclinations of his head to Barnaby and Penelope, Christopher moved past them and started up the stairs.

With Barnaby and Penelope, Stokes watched Christopher go, then murmured, "We need to find somewhere private to talk."

Penelope thought, then suggested, "Winslow's office—his butler's pantry—might be the perfect place."

~

They followed the same route Findlay had taken into the bowels of the house. On reaching the servants' hall, they found Mrs. Pratchett endeavoring to do as Penelope had suggested and keep the rest of the staff focused on their daily chores.

Shock and sorrow showed on many faces, and most were working with gazes downcast, occasionally pausing to wipe their eyes.

Stokes, who'd led the way, caught Mrs. Pratchett's eye and quietly said, "We were hoping to find somewhere private to discuss our findings and thought Winslow's office might suit."

Penelope put in, "There, we would be out of your way." She glanced at the staff at various stations around the room. "And out of sight, as well."

Holding herself staunchly upright, her expression fixed, sternly suppressing all emotion, Mrs. Pratchett stiffly inclined her head. "Yes, of course. I'll show you where it is."

She led them into the short corridor that gave access to her housekeeper's room but turned in the other direction. Winslow's pantry was two doors along. As Penelope had supposed, while the room hosted three large sideboards accommodating the Moran silverware and plate, the space was set up as a working office with a good-sized desk and three chairs, one behind the desk and two set in front.

"Thank you," Barnaby said. "This will do admirably."

Her gaze on the floor, Mrs. Pratchett bobbed and left them.

Stokes closed the door, then made for the chair behind the desk.

Barnaby held one of the chairs before the desk for Penelope, then subsided onto its mate.

Stokes had opened his notebook on the desktop. "First, given the poison seems likely to have been in the whiskey in the earl's study, does that mean the earl was the intended victim?"

Stokes looked up, and meeting his gaze, Barnaby admitted, "It certainly seems that way. Given that, by his own testimony, it was Winslow himself who filled the decanter, it clearly wasn't he who introduced the poison."

"Yes, but"—Penelope was frowning—"why bludgeon the earl to death as well as try to poison him?" She met Barnaby's gaze, then Stokes's. "Are we dealing with a single murderer who set out to poison the earl, but before the poison plot could work, something changed, and the murderer felt they had to act immediately, and so they bashed the earl on the head?"

"That's one possibility," Stokes allowed. "Or we could be dealing with two completely separate attempts on the earl's life."

"Either is possible," Barnaby conceded. "One killer pushed into immediate action, or two separate attempts, with the caveat that if we have two independent attempts, then those behind each attempt did not know the other attempt was going forward."

Penelope inclined her head. "And if we are dealing with the latter scenario, then ipso facto, more than one person or group of people wanted the earl dead."

Stokes flicked back through the pages in his notebook, then paused on one, his eyes scanning. "Considering the poison, is Mrs. Alder's motive—that of resentment at being dismissed without cause from a position she'd held to everyone's satisfaction for more than ten years—sufficient to move a woman of her ilk to murder?"

Penelope considered the point, then shook her head. "I can't see it."

"Nor I," Barnaby stated. "Especially as, at least by her accounting, the move wouldn't have cast her and Julian penniless onto the streets."

With one finger, Stokes tapped the page. "In light of the open terrace door, we have to allow for the possibility that someone came in from outside—perhaps an enemy the earl had made in public life—and hid behind the curtains and killed the earl at his desk. However, it's difficult to imagine that same unknown outsider sneaking in and slipping poison into the decanter."

Barnaby tipped his head in agreement. "It's theoretically possible but seems highly unlikely. An outsider couldn't have been sure the earl would drink a glass of whiskey before someone else did."

"As, indeed, happened." Penelope sighed. "Poor Winslow. He didn't deserve to die like that."

"No, he didn't." Barnaby looked at Stokes. "While the earl's actual murderer might well have come from outside the house, the attempted poisoning, which has now ended in unintended murder, is most likely the work of someone much closer to the Moran household."

"I imagine," Penelope said, "that a man like Moran, absorbed with his politics and his business endeavors, would have spent much of his time in his study. Consequently, surreptitiously introducing the poison into that decanter wouldn't have been easy. Indeed, it had to have been carefully planned to avoid both Moran and the staff."

"The poison has to be the work of someone with ready access to the study," Stokes said.

Penelope nodded. "Someone who, if found there, wouldn't raise any meaningful surprise, much less alarm."

Silence fell as they dwelled on the implications of that.

Eventually, Stokes shut his notebook and tucked it away. "Because of the earl's rank, we need to make sure we do everything expected of us. That means interviewing everyone who was in the house at the time of the murder, so all the family members. In addition to that, in light of the poisoning, we need to conduct a thorough search of the premises for any possible source of the poison as soon as possible."

Barnaby said, "Findlay seemed sure it was strychnine, for which rat poison is a common source."

"And," Penelope said, "virtually every house will have some of that tucked away somewhere."

Barnaby frowned. "That said, I seriously doubt rat poison was used in this instance." He met Stokes's eyes. "It comes in pellets, and introducing them into a glass decanter and hoping they would dissolve completely and no cloudiness would remain to tip off Moran sounds…unlikely. I can't see a conscientious butler like Winslow not noticing something like that."

"More to the point," Penelope put in, "the decanter had been emptied, remember? Winslow filled it himself, presumably from a bottle in the cellar."

Stokes frowned. "Not a cask?"

"Highly unlikely for the likes of Moran," Barnaby said. "Christopher told us the whiskey in the study was 'the good stuff,' implying it was the best in the house that Moran kept for himself, and that would certainly come in bottles, not casks."

"Indeed." Penelope went on, "So Winslow would have opened a bottle, filled the decanter, then taken it back to the study. Obviously, Winslow himself didn't poison the whiskey, and someone introducing poison into an unopened bottle in a way that a butler of Winslow's experience wouldn't notice is very hard to imagine, which means—"

"That the poison was already in the emptied decanter." Stokes frowned. "How was that done?"

"Someone emptied the decanter or found it empty and introduced a solution of strychnine, then swirled it around and restoppered the decanter," Penelope said. "I believe the coating would be virtually invisible."

Stokes had reopened his notebook and was scribbling again. "How do you make a solution of strychnine?"

"Just water, I believe," Penelope said. "And in this case, most likely, the poisoner used the powdered form. It's readily available through apothecaries and used on estates and in the country in general for making baits."

Stokes shot her a glance. "Your knowledge has few bounds."

She grinned, then sobered. "The use of the powder, however, means that your men will need to search the whole house, not just the kitchens."

Stokes grimaced. "I've enough men here to mount a thorough search. I'll put O'Donnell and Morgan onto it. However"—he looked at Barnaby—"regarding who among the family might have cause to do away with the earl, we'll need to look into their finances and, specifically, the details of the inheritance."

"In this case," Barnaby said, "the inheritance will be straightforward. The title and entailed estate, which, I might add, is substantial, will go to Frederick, the earl's oldest surviving brother and next in line. But regarding the finances of the various family members, you're right. We need Montague, and Thomas as well, running their eyes over the various family members' accounts. The earl's brothers, brothers-in-law, and nephews."

"I'll ask my usual sources as well," Penelope said. "They're sure to have some valuable insights."

Stokes nodded. "An excellent idea, and in this case, the ladies are likely to be even more helpful than usual. However, for now, our immediate task is to do what we were unable to accomplish earlier this morning, namely interview all the family members who were under this roof yesterday evening."

Barnaby, Penelope, and Stokes looked at each other, waiting for any further insight. When none came, Stokes rose and sent a footman to fetch O'Donnell and Morgan from the front of the house.

Meanwhile, Barnaby sorted through Winslow's desk to find paper, pen, and ink, then he sat behind the desk and composed missives to Montague and Thomas Glendower, outlining the case and requesting what help they and their offices could provide.

When O'Donnell and Morgan arrived, Stokes gave orders for a search to be conducted. "However," Stokes said, "we'll need to get permission from at least one of the family."

O'Donnell nodded. "So we'll organize and wait for the word."

Penelope looked up from mentally composing a list of all the Fitzhugh family members they needed to interview to say, "If you find any suspicious powder, don't forget to use gloves or paper or something to stop you getting any on your hands."

O'Donnell and Morgan grinned, and both tipped her a salute. "We will, ma'am," O'Donnell averred.

Satisfied, Penelope returned to her task of defining the optimal order in which to interview the members of the House of Moran.

CHAPTER 5

As they knew Christopher was in the house and out of bed and dressed, he seemed the ideal Fitzhugh with whom to commence their interviews. On leaving Winslow's erstwhile domain, they headed for the drawing room and, on discovering the lanky footman, who was apparently standing in as butler, hovering in the foyer, after ascertaining that the man's name was Jeffrey, Penelope dispatched him with a request that Christopher meet with them downstairs.

They went into the drawing room, and Penelope and Barnaby chose to sit on the long sofa, while Stokes claimed the armchair opposite, leaving the other chair facing the sofa for Christopher.

Three minutes later, the door opened, and Christopher walked in. He had to have been awaiting their summons, knowing it would come. He bestowed a vague nod of greeting, and when Penelope waved him to the vacant armchair, he came forward and claimed it.

To her eyes, as Christopher sank into the chair, behind his outward assurance, he appeared wary and a trifle anxious. Doubtless, he'd realized that all of the family residing at Moran House would be suspected of the attempted poisoning.

Stokes opened proceedings with all due deference. "Thank you for your time, Mr. Fitzhugh. As you will have guessed, we are now investigating two murders—that of your brother, the late earl, and that of his butler, Winslow. We have yet to establish whether the killings are connected and would welcome any insights you can offer us."

Christopher faintly frowned. "I'm not sure there's much I can tell you, Inspector. I was here, in this drawing room, from the time my brother left for his study until he was found murdered."

"Nevertheless," Stokes said, "we wished to ask if you know of anything at all that might be pertinent to the earl's murder or to the poisoning of Winslow."

His frown deepening, Christopher replied, "If you mean, did I see anyone around who might have committed either act, then no. I didn't."

Barnaby shifted, drawing Christopher's attention. "Do you know of anyone who had threatened the earl?"

Christopher hesitated, then more carefully replied, "No one I can point to specifically, but given Gordon's championing of numerous reactionary policies, I wouldn't be the least surprised if someone in the labor movement had wished him dead."

Penelope saw the suggestion as an obvious deflection. Hoping to jar Christopher into revealing what was making him so wary, she abruptly stated, "We understand that your brother Frederick will succeed to the title."

Christopher's jaw firmed, and with somewhat petulant bitterness, he confirmed, "Yes, Frederick is now the earl and will, no doubt, move his family into this house with all speed. I know Mama will be delighted by that."

Tilting her head, Penelope regarded him curiously. "Why do you say that?"

"That Mama will be over the moon?" When she nodded, Christopher stated, "Frederick was always her favorite, and she gets on like a house afire with Imogen and, indeed, all their brood."

Christopher's lids lowered to half mast, and nonchalantly, he added, "Besides, I'm sure Frederick will seize the chance to reduce his expenses forthwith."

"Oh?" Innocently, Penelope inquired, "Are Frederick's finances a trifle strained?"

Christopher plainly toyed with the notion of playing up Frederick's state of financial need—thus increasing Frederick's motive to murder Gordon—but ultimately, Christopher metaphorically balked at that fence. "Well," he temporized, "I suppose any gentleman with four daughters to marry off, what with all the associated costs of puffing each chit off, would feel a pinch or two."

Penelope inclined her head. "Indeed. That would hardly be surprising."

Christopher shifted in the chair, then in a more challenging tone, asked Stokes, "What I want to know is what the police are doing to protect the family from the likes of whoever poisoned Winslow."

Mildly, Stokes replied, "You'll find that we have a sizeable number of constables in and around the house, and with the poisoning deemed the more immediate threat to the residents, our first step must be to search the premises for any sign of the source of the poison."

Christopher's frown returned.

Imperturbably, Stokes continued, "It's important to establish how the poison got into the whiskey. We need to determine if there's any possibility that it happened by accident or, alternatively, if the introduction of the poison into the earl's whiskey was a deliberate act."

Puzzled, Christopher asked, "Could it have been an accident?"

"Strange to say," Stokes replied, "such things have been known to happen, especially with strychnine, which is the poison the medical examiner believes was used."

Before Christopher could say anything more, in a formal tone, Stokes asked, "As you are the oldest Fitzhugh male currently residing in this house, do we have your permission to search for any remnants of or evidence relating to the source of the poison?"

Christopher blinked, then after a few seconds, slowly inclined his head. He moistened his lips and stated, "Yes, of course. If there's any lying about somewhere, it needs to be found and taken away."

"Indeed." Stokes inclined his head. "Thank you."

He glanced at Barnaby and Penelope, and both shook their heads.

Returning his gaze to Christopher, Stokes stated, "That's all the questions we have for you at this juncture."

Stokes rose, and Barnaby and Penelope followed suit, bringing Christopher to his feet. His expression suggested he was surprised that there weren't more questions—more harrowing and difficult questions—but then, many thought a police interview would be more like an inquisition.

Stokes nodded deferentially to Christopher. "We'll be commencing the search momentarily. We will, of course, avoid any private rooms currently in use by family members—the dowager, the countess, and yourself. Beyond that, however, our search will be comprehensive. If you could convey that to the staff, along with the fact that we have your permission to go forward?"

"Er, yes, of course. I'll tell..." Christopher caught his breath and, for an instant, looked stricken, then he amended, "I'll tell Jeffrey." With that, he turned and strode for the door.

~

After Christopher opened the drawing room door and walked into the foyer, the investigators heard him give Jeffrey the gist of Stokes's statements, then Christopher continued up the stairs, and a second later, Jeffrey peered rather warily around the drawing room door.

Penelope smiled reassuringly. "We would like to speak with Lady Victoria next. Would you please ask her if she's willing to indulge us for a few moments, to address some questions regarding her husband's death?"

Frowning slightly, Jeffrey repeated Penelope's words beneath his breath, then bowed and departed, and through the open doorway, they heard him hurry up the stairs.

Penelope shook her head and sank onto the sofa. "Frederick will need to hire a new butler. Poor Jeffrey won't make the grade, not for an establishment of Moran House's social status."

Stokes seized the moment to speak with O'Donnell, who was waiting in the foyer. After confirming that the search could commence, Stokes returned, and they waited.

Two minutes later, the lanky footman-cum-butler was back to inform them that Lady Victoria would see them in her private sitting room. Jeffrey bowed and gestured to the foyer. "If you'll come this way, I'll show you up."

They rose and followed him up the stairs, through the rather gloomy gallery, and on along a corridor leading deeper into the mansion's central wing. Jeffrey stopped outside a door, tapped on the panel, and on hearing a command to enter, he opened the door and announced, "Mr. and Mrs. Adair and Inspector Stokes to speak with you, my lady."

From the depths of the shadowy room came "Thank you, Jeffrey. Please show them in."

Jeffrey stepped aside and bowed them over the threshold.

Penelope led the way into a largish chamber that immediately struck her as cold in the sense of being impersonal. That seemed strange for a private sitting room. As Barnaby and Stokes entered behind her, she glanced around curiously.

A fireplace with a mantel graced only by an ormolu clock filled one side wall, while the wall opposite hosted a delicate-legged escritoire with a matching chair, placed beneath a painting of a rather drab landscape in a heavy, ornate frame. Covering two long windows, heavy damask curtains were drawn almost shut, leaving twin beams of daylight to penetrate the resulting gloom, providing just enough light to navigate the space.

Not that there was all that much furniture to avoid, but as she walked forward to where Lady Victoria was seated in an armchair in a grouping comprising a chaise and two chairs set between the long windows, Penelope found herself wondering if the deliberate lack of illumination was intended to conceal the extent of the occupant's grief or the dearth of personalized comfort in the room.

Victoria was garbed in a fashionable day gown of pale-gray cambric, beautifully tailored to her figure, with the collar and sleeves trimmed with a narrow band of fine white lace. As a temporary substitute for the mourning attire she would need to have made, the gray gown was an inspired choice.

Glancing past Penelope, Victoria, her lips tight, nodded to the footman. "Thank you, Jeffrey. That will be all."

Jeffrey, who'd dithered uncertainly in the doorway, bowed, backed out of the room, and closed the door.

With a polite nod for Victoria, who returned the greeting with an inclination of her head, Penelope sat on the chaise facing the long windows. After exchanging nods with Victoria, Barnaby came to sit beside her, while Stokes claimed the chair to Penelope's right.

Something about the room niggled at Penelope's brain, but she focused her attention on Victoria, who, whether by accident or design, had her back to one of the beams of daylight. Her face, therefore, was not well lit.

While Stokes began by thanking Victoria for agreeing to speak with them, Penelope took stock of what she could, despite the shadows, discern in Victoria's features. Moran's widow seemed strangely composed, and no matter how hard Penelope looked, she could see no sign the now-dowager countess had shed any tears; her eyes and her complexion appeared unmarred and undimmed by the impact of grief.

However, when Penelope lowered her gaze to Victoria's hands, clasped in her lap, she saw that Victoria's interlaced fingers were tight, her grip tense. Swiftly, Penelope confirmed that Victoria's shoulders—indeed, her whole body—seemed braced. For whatever reason, the newly made dowager was on edge and doing her best to hide it.

With her vision adjusting to the dim light, Penelope studied Victoria's dark-brown eyes. Eyes of that hue were often difficult to read, but in this instance, Penelope felt confident in judging that Victoria was troubled. Anxious and concerned.

Over what?

Possibly over unexpectedly being made a widow.

Deciding that she didn't know Victoria well enough to make any deductions, Penelope realized that Victoria had noticed her scrutiny. Hard on Stokes's calming words about needing to ask a few standard questions, with her gaze on Penelope, Victoria hurried to state, "I heard about the poisoning." She waved toward the door through which Jeffrey had left. "Obviously. But on top of Gordon's brutal murder!" Her gaze shifted to Stokes. "What's next? First Gordon, then Winslow. Who will be the next to be struck down?"

Penelope resisted the urge to tip her head and openly scrutinize Victoria even more closely. Although there'd been a hint of the hysterical in Victoria's tone, she appeared more anxious and uneasy than overcome by nerves and unbridled imagination.

Calmly, Stokes reassured Victoria, "We have no reason to believe anyone else is a target of whoever is behind these deaths. In addition, there are a significant number of police both in and around the house." He paused, then added, "I should mention that, as is police procedure in such cases, we are presently conducting a thorough search of the premises to establish whether the source of the poison lies within the house. Mr. Fitzhugh gave permission for the search. Although the search will be extensive, it will not include any private room currently used by the family. You will not be inconvenienced."

Victoria blinked. The information did not noticeably reduce her tenseness.

"Now." Stokes drew out and opened his notebook. "We've already asked similar questions of Mr. Fitzhugh and need to ensure you have nothing to add." Stokes raised his steely gaze to Victoria's face. "Do you know of any threats made against your husband?"

"No," Victoria stated.

Stokes persisted. "Do you have any idea of anyone who might have wanted him dead?"

"None at all." Sensing some explanation was called for, Victoria offered, "Gordon wasn't one who shared details of his life. I suspect you'll get the same answers from all the members of the family. There might, indeed, have been some threat made, but I doubt any of us would have heard of it."

Penelope asked, "Were you involved with the earl's political life? For instance, did you host political dinners for him on occasion?"

That would have been the normal way of things, but Victoria shook her head. "No. I had no interest in Gordon's political views and his subsequent machinations, and he never encouraged me to develop any interest in his affairs, either. Indeed, he actively discouraged me—and everyone else in the family, for that matter—from taking any such interest." Victoria paused, then added, "That might have been because, by the time we married, he was already set in his ways. He was a very private man and preferred to keep all his doings to himself."

"And as earl," Penelope musingly said, "I suppose he was able to do that."

Victoria inclined her head. "Indeed." She glanced at Barnaby and Stokes, then went on, "Before you ask, Gordon spent most of his waking hours deeply immersed in his own pursuits—in the maneuverings of his political life and in his investments and all to do with those. He occasionally visited his clubs—White's and Brooks—but otherwise, not much in ton life, or even in life more broadly, impinged on him."

Shifting her gaze to Penelope, almost bitterly, Victoria stated, "Gordon saw little point in socializing in general. He would only attend those events that might, in one way or another, further his political aims or his investment projects. Those were the two arenas that were important to him, and he was a very focused man."

"I see." The reason why Penelope couldn't recall meeting the late earl all that much in ton circles was growing clearer. "How have you found the rest of the family? I'm aware they are more socially active."

Victoria lifted her shoulders in a slight shrug. "They are, and generally speaking, we've rubbed along well enough, but my sisters-in-law—Imogen, Cleome, and Constance—are, all too often, absorbed with one or other of their distracting broods, and that makes them rather dull and uninteresting company for me."

Beneath the disparaging words, Penelope detected a note of bitter longing. It seemed Victoria's childless state wasn't by her choice. And, Penelope recalled, the late earl hadn't fathered any offspring with his first wife, either.

Leaving that issue aside, Penelope engaged Victoria in a discussion of upcoming family events. "Sadly, it seems," Penelope observed, "the three girls' come-outs will be disrupted."

Victoria's eyes widened. "I hadn't thought that far, but I suppose you're right." She thought, then sighed. "That will no doubt lead to more drama and histrionics the next time the family gather."

With a few further queries, Penelope established that Victoria tolerated the rest of the Fitzhugh family and was tolerated in return, but beneath that superficial level, there was little real connection and certainly no love lost between Victoria and the rest of the Fitzhughs.

Finally, Penelope baldly stated, "It seems you have no real interest in the late earl's nephews and nieces."

"That's correct." Victoria met Penelope's gaze and, with an almost-amused glint in her dark eyes, added, "And I can assure you that the late earl—Gordon—didn't, either. He barely saw them even when they were planted in front of him, and he paid zero attention to them and their existence." She arched her fine brows. "Why would he? None of them could help him with his political maneuverings or his investment projects. They were, therefore, of no interest to him, and he treated them accordingly."

Barnaby stated, "Frederick was Gordon's heir apparent, and Frederick's oldest son, William, will eventually become earl. In such circumstances, society—the ton—would have expected the late earl to take an interest not only in Frederick's circumstances but also William's."

Victoria tipped her head, conceding the point. "Indeed, and when I, being rather more attuned to society's expectations than Gordon ever wished to be, raised that very point, he stared at me as if I was a numbskull, then told me that he saw no purpose in cultivating any interest in either Frederick or William, as they wouldn't become earl until he was dead. And if he was dead, then he wouldn't have to deal with them." Victoria's lips almost twitched. "If I recall correctly, at that point, he went back to eating his ham and eggs as if his reasoning was so obvious that no one could ever question it."

Sensing that continued probing wouldn't get them much further, Penelope looked at Stokes and arched her brows.

He saw and turned to Victoria. "It appears that Winslow died after ingesting poison dissolved in the earl's whiskey. We understand Winslow had only recently refilled the decanter from a bottle in the cellar. Can you confirm who has keys to the cellar?"

Victoria blinked, twice, then waved the question aside. "You will need to ask Mrs. Pratchett. Or the dowager. The household arrangements currently followed were in place long before I came to the house."

"I see." Stokes made a note, then looked back at Victoria. "As it happens, we'll be seeking to speak with the dowager next. However, we will also need to interview the staff, possibly at some length, and would like your permission to do so."

Victoria frowned, then, lips pursing slightly, reluctantly said, "You have my permission to speak with the staff, but I strongly advise that you also seek the dowager's permission." She raised her brows. "In fact, I insist that you gain her agreement as well."

Penelope frowned.

Seeing that, Victoria added, "In large part, the dowager still rules this house."

Unable to help herself, Penelope asked, "Really?"

Victoria had been the Countess of Moran for close to eighteen years.

Her lips twisting, Victoria nodded. "Yes, really. Ever since she returned to this house…well, it was hers for decades before I married Gordon, and old habits die hard and all that." Lightly, she shrugged. "The truth, my dear Mrs. Adair, was that it was simply easier to let the reins slide from my hands to hers. Much less effort required."

Watching Victoria closely, for just a second, Penelope felt she saw beyond the mask Victoria presented to the world. Victoria genuinely didn't care all that much that the dowager had, it seemed, usurped her role.

Penelope concluded that while such an arrangement wouldn't suit her, it did, indeed, suit Victoria.

"Thank you for your help." Stokes rose and bowed to Victoria. "My men will endeavor not to disturb you with their searching."

Graciously, Victoria inclined her head. "Inspector. I wish you luck in pursuing Winslow's murderer, and Gordon's, too, of course."

Along with Barnaby, Penelope rose. After exchanging nods with Victoria, she and Barnaby followed Stokes across the room. Again, this time idly, Penelope's gaze passed over the furnishings.

And her earlier niggle flared and grew clear.

Everything in here is old. Good quality but very dated...possibly to the time when Victoria first came to the house as a new bride. That was nearly eighteen years ago!

Penelope paused before stepping through the door Stokes was holding open and swiftly scanned the room one last time. Then facing forward, she walked through the door and into the corridor.

How many ladies of countess or equal rank went eighteen years without refurbishing their private domain?

Puzzling over that, she led the way to the stairs.

CHAPTER 6

They didn't reach the stairs. Instead, they were intercepted by a nervous Jeffrey, who was waiting in the gallery to inform them that the Dowager Countess of Moran requested their attendance in her private sitting room.

Amused by the dowager's summons—as distinct from her acceding to a request of theirs—Penelope readily followed Jeffrey down yet another corridor. The house was truly a warren, with wing begetting wing until it was difficult to be sure which way one was heading.

The room to which Jeffrey led them exuded a very different ambiance to Victoria's cold chamber. This room looked out over a pretty rear garden and, with its pale-colored curtains fully open, felt airy and light. The well-padded older-style armchairs, upholstered in chintz, held the promise of comfort, and there were framed prints on the mantelpiece, while from its prime position above the fireplace, a large portrait, possibly of the previous earl, the dowager's husband, looked down in benign complacency.

All in all, this was a room that held numerous clues as to the personality of its owner, and inwardly, Penelope approved.

The dowager, already garbed in full mourning, sat waiting to greet them in her Bath chair, angled before the largest window. Her steel-gray hair, partially covered by a fine black-lace veil, was, again, pulled ruthlessly into a bun high on her head—a fashion of decades past—and her lips and chin were firmly set as she watched Penelope, Barnaby, and Stokes approach.

In contrast to Victoria, the dowager didn't shy from facing the situation head-on, and the light from the window, falling across her features, did not dim the shrewdness in her faded-blue eyes or soften the determination that kept her sitting rigidly upright in her chair.

As they neared, with much the same graciousness as a queen granting an audience, the dowager regally inclined her head. "Mr. and Mrs. Adair. Inspector Stokes." She waved at the three armchairs that had been arranged in a semicircle, facing her. "Please sit."

They dutifully returned her nod and settled.

Now they were closer, Barnaby briefly studied the old lady. Since they'd last seen her in the small hours, she appeared to have aged even more. Doubtless, the impact of her eldest son's murder was weighing on her, compounded, it seemed, by Winslow's unexpected demise.

Despite that and the present circumstances, Barnaby wasn't entirely surprised when the first words the dowager uttered were "Mary is clearly innocent, not only of murdering my son, but obviously, she can have had no hand in poisoning Winslow."

Uncertain how to react, Stokes shot an imploring look at Penelope.

She responded to the unvoiced plea by capturing the dowager's gaze and calmly stating, "Indeed. Like you, we do not believe Mrs. Alder is complicit in any way in either death. However, we also believe that, with the House of Moran so highly respected and well-regarded, the most certain path to ensure that Mrs. Alder is cleared of all blame, both legally and socially, is to identify the person or persons who actually committed the crimes."

Taking in the dowager's arrested expression, Barnaby sternly suppressed a grin. Trust Penelope to light on the approach most likely to get the old lady on their side. She was plainly very concerned over Mary being blamed.

After a moment of studied blankness, slowly, the dowager inclined her head. "You're right, I suppose…" She stared into space for several heartbeats, then her lips and chin firmed, and refocusing on them, the dowager dipped her head more decisively. "I agree. Identifying those responsible is the sensible way forward."

With that, she fixed her gaze on Penelope. "I have heard that you are intelligent and clever." Shifting her attention to Stokes, she demanded, "So what do you need to know?"

Stokes, who, to Barnaby, was being careful and feeling his way, said, "In terms of Winslow's death, we believe he ingested poison dissolved in the earl's whiskey."

The dowager blinked. "*Gordon's* whiskey?"

Stokes nodded. "We're currently seeking to determine how the poison came to be in the decanter, which Winslow apparently refilled from a bottle in the cellar. Can you confirm who has keys to the cellar?"

"Only Winslow," the dowager replied. "We never saw the need for anyone else to have access." She met Stokes's gaze. "All three of my sons grew up in this house, Inspector. It seemed wisest to limit the number of keys to the cellar to the one in Winslow's possession. Although my sons are long grown, that arrangement never changed."

"So only Winslow could have filled the decanter," Stokes concluded.

"Indeed," the dowager confirmed. "He's the only one who had access to the bottles in the cellar."

Rather more confidently, Stokes continued, "Moving on to the death of the earl, do you have any idea of anyone who might have wanted him dead?"

"None whatsoever," the dowager stated. "Gordon wasn't the easiest man with whom to get along, and as I understand matters, he certainly had his political opponents. However, I am not aware of anyone in whom he inspired a murderous rage."

Somewhat gently, Barnaby pointed out, "Given the poison appears to have been in the earl's decanter, from which Winslow imbibed a small amount, suggesting his death was entirely inadvertent, then in addition to whoever actually killed the earl, it appears he was also the target of a plot to poison him." He held the old lady's gaze. "Your son definitely had enemies, enemies sufficiently motivated to act."

The dowager looked distinctly peeved. "That may be so—indeed, must logically be so, as you say. However, I can assure you that neither I nor any of the family are acquainted with any such person. We cannot point a finger in any direction whatsoever."

"Are you acquainted with any of the earl's close associates?" Penelope inquired.

"No," the dowager replied. "Not at all." She paused, then went on, "In fact, now I think of it, I really have very little idea as to whom Gordon consorted with when out of this house. I know of several social acquaintances, but they are the obvious ones anyone would expect—his varsity friends and some from his days at Eton." She looked at Penelope. "I'm sure you could name them all. However"—she transferred her imperious gaze to Stokes—"as to those elsewhere with whom Gordon interacted while pursuing his political and business interests, they are entirely beyond my ken."

Glancing again at Penelope, the dowager added, "Over the past decade and more, ever since Gordon married Victoria and I moved out of this house, I've kept to my own circle, and because of that, I know very little of my late son's affairs."

Barnaby glanced at Penelope, and when she met his gaze, her brows faintly raised, he deduced she couldn't think of anything more to ask at that point. Neither could he. He looked at Stokes.

Stokes duly focused on the dowager. "Thank you, ma'am, for bearing with our questions."

He rose, and Barnaby and Penelope did the same.

To the dowager, Stokes continued, "I assure you, ma'am, that we will diligently pursue our investigations into your son's and Winslow's deaths. As part of those investigations, we need to interview the staff. We mentioned the matter to Lady Victoria, and she advised us to seek your approval."

The dowager raised her brows, but after a moment, she nodded. "Very well, Inspector. You and your consultants"—she glanced at Barnaby and Penelope—"may put your questions to the staff." She pointed to the door. "If you would summon Jeffrey—and I'm quite sure the nervy boy is waiting in the corridor—I will inform him that the staff should answer your questions freely."

"Thank you, ma'am." Stokes half bowed and made for the door.

Barnaby and Penelope exchanged formal farewells with the dowager, then followed in Stokes's wake.

~

On quitting the dowager's sitting room, they waited in the corridor while Jeffrey received the dowager's instructions, then followed him toward the main stairs.

In the gallery, they came upon a group of constables, searching rooms under O'Donnell's watchful eye.

O'Donnell nodded respectfully, and when Jeffrey had passed by and, expectantly, Penelope, Barnaby, and Stokes slowed, O'Donnell murmured, "Lots of unused rooms up here. Bit of a warren, too."

"Nothing yet?" Stokes asked without much hope.

"Nothing," O'Donnell confirmed. "But we've only just started up here."

Stokes nodded. "Carry on. We're off to speak with the staff."

Penelope and Barnaby lengthened their strides to catch up with Jeffrey, who'd noticed them dallying and obligingly paused.

With them once more in tow, Jeffrey walked on.

When they reached the head of the stairs and started down, Stokes informed the footman-cum-butler, "We've permission to speak with the staff."

"The dowager said." A trifle wide-eyed, Jeffrey glanced over his shoulder. "The servants' hall, then? Or the drawing room?"

"The servants' hall," Penelope firmly declared. They all knew how awkward staff became when interviewed in rooms in which they considered it was not their place to be.

"Oh. All right." More confidently, Jeffrey faced forward and, after gaining the foyer, led them into the staff's quarters.

They reached the servants' hall to find most of the staff rather desultorily going about their customary tasks—the cook and her assistants preparing luncheon, the maids wiping plates and glassware ready to serve the meal, the footmen and coachman waiting to answer any call—all under the eagle eye of Mrs. Pratchett, who stood on the far side of the deal table that ran down the middle of the long room, much like a general marshaling her troops.

Inwardly pleased—with the house quiet and solemn in the wake of the two deaths, now was clearly a good time to interview the staff—Penelope halted on the other side of the deal table, and while Stokes and Barnaby took up positions to either side of her, she inclined her head to Mrs. Pratchett, acknowledging the housekeeper's curtsy.

Their entrance had caused all conversations and activities to cease. As wide-eyed and expectant as Jeffrey, many of the staff drifted closer to Mrs. Pratchett as if she was their anchor, the solid center they all relied on to hold them together.

Only the outdoor staff held aloof. Penelope noted four individuals, who, judging by their apparel and age, she took to be a coachman, a stableman, a groom, and a stableboy, all of whom elected to cluster around a grizzled veteran of a gardener, who'd been sitting at one end of the table, but now rose to his feet.

"Mrs. Pratchett," Stokes began in a formal but reassuring tone, "we've permission from the dowager and also from Lady Victoria to question the staff regarding the deaths of the earl and Winslow."

Stoutly, Mrs. Pratchett clasped her hands at her waist. "Ask away, Inspector, and we'll see what we can tell you."

"First," Stokes said, "regarding the murder of the earl, did any of you see anyone in the house or lurking around it who shouldn't have been there?" He swept the gathering with his gaze. "The time period we're interested in is between nine-thirty and fifteen minutes past ten yesterday evening."

Stokes paused with his gaze on the outdoor staff, but along with everyone else, they, too, shook their heads.

Mrs. Pratchett looked around her troops, then stated, "Doesn't appear we know anything about any strangers lurking, inside or out."

Stokes nodded in acceptance and consulted his notebook. "The French door in the study, leading to the courtyard, was open that evening. Open and left ajar." He raised his head and looked at the housekeeper and the footmen ranged behind her. "Was that normal? Something the earl might have done? Gone for a stroll about the courtyard and forgotten to latch the door on his return?"

All the staff looked at each other, then, again, all shook their heads.

Mrs. Pratchett offered, "Far as I've ever known, the earl didn't appreciate drafts, and he wasn't one to seek out fresh air, either, and especially on a chilly night, as last night was."

Barnaby noted that Jeffrey shuffled uncertainly, then glanced at Mrs. Pratchett.

She didn't notice, so Barnaby asked, "Do any of you know why the French door to the courtyard was unlocked?"

Jeffrey looked up, went to speak, then caught himself and glanced at Mrs. Pratchett.

This time, she caught his questioning look, all but glared, and gestured for him to speak.

Jeffrey swallowed and focused on Barnaby. "I remember it was about a year ago. I heard Winslow muttering that the earl had ordered him to unlock that French door every morning and lock it again on his rounds at night. Winslow was grumbling that it was just another door he'd have to check every night, and the Lord only knew why the earl wanted it unlocked, as he wasn't given to wandering the courtyard."

Barnaby found that as strange as, transparently, the staff did. After a moment, he said, "We are correct in thinking that there is no gate between the courtyard and the lane?"

"Aye," the gardener said. "That wall there's solid all the way along. Only way past it is over the top."

Stokes nodded to the man. "Thank you."

Penelope ventured, "Regarding the earl's use of the study, was he often to be found there?"

All the front-of-house staff nodded emphatically.

"If he was in the house," Mrs. Pratchett declared, "and not in his bed or the dining room, he'd most likely be there, in the study. Forever working on his papers, he was."

Stokes looked around the faces, then said, "Turning to Winslow's death, we believe the earl was the poisoner's intended target, but sadly, Winslow took a small tot of the whiskey in the study decanter before retiring in the early hours of this morning."

That information caused something of a stir; clearly, many of the staff had not heard the details of Winslow's demise.

"In the circumstances," Barnaby said, "I think we can all agree that it was perfectly understandable for Winslow to help himself to a small whiskey. However, in this instance, that action led to a tragic outcome."

"At present," Stokes said, "we're trying to discover how the poison got into the decanter. Winslow himself told us that he'd refilled it last night, and when he returned to the study with the filled decanter, that was when he found Mrs. Alder there for her ten o'clock appointment, but by then, the earl had been murdered." He looked around at the faces, all of which wore serious and somber expressions. "Can any of you confirm that, at about nine-forty-five yesterday evening, Winslow went down to the cellar and refilled the decanter?"

Several heads nodded, and Mrs. Pratchett stated, "We were mostly all here, still clearing up after the family dinner, when he came past. He was grouching about the decanter being empty." The housekeeper looked at the footmen around her, and they readily nodded.

Jeffrey volunteered, "He was saying that he'd only filled it the day before and carrying on about how it was empty again."

Mrs. Pratchett pulled a face, then looked at Stokes. "Winslow blamed it on the younger gentlemen—Mr. Frederick's sons, and Lady Cleome's and Lady Constance's, and even Mr. Christopher. He claimed they'd filled their flasks, the ones they all seem to carry these days." She paused, then added, "Not that Winslow ever caught any of them at it—not that he said, and he would have if he had. But that was what he thought."

"I see." Stokes had learned not to write notes while interviewing staff; it made many people nervous. Now, he looked at Barnaby and Penelope, then returned his attention to the staff. "You'll have heard that my men are searching the house for the source of the poison that killed Winslow. I believe they're still going through the unused rooms upstairs, but they will, eventually, need to search through here and also through your rooms as well."

Mrs. Pratchett tipped up her chin. "There's a box of rat poison in the pantry, on the top shelf."

Gruffly, the grizzled gardener volunteered, "We have some in the garden shed, too."

"And we've a box in the stable." The stableman shrugged. "These days, you have to, don't you?"

Stokes nodded. "Thank you all for that, but in this instance, we don't believe rat pellets were used." He glanced at the gardener and stableman. "I assume that's the form of rat poison you have?"

Mrs. Pratchett, the gardener, and the stableman all nodded.

"We believe it was a purer form that was used," Barnaby revealed. "A powder."

"Oh!" From their expressions, both the gardener and the stableman understood what that was.

The gardener said, "You mean the stuff they use in the country for larger baits?"

"Yes," Barnaby said. "That."

The staff exchanged glances, then the gardener volunteered, "I don't think we've ever had call to use that stuff here—in this house."

Mrs. Pratchett and the stableman nodded.

Penelope was frowning; Barnaby had noticed that she hadn't been paying much attention to the discussion of the poison but, instead, had appeared sunk in thought. Now, she said, "To return to the incident of the decanter being empty—empty to the point of needing to be refilled. Had that ever happened before? That it was found to be unexpectedly empty?"

Mrs. Pratchett looked uncertain and looked to the footmen.

All three footmen met her gaze and shrugged.

Mrs. Pratchett turned back to Penelope. "Not that we know of, ma'am."

Penelope inclined her head. "Thank you."

Stokes, who'd been quietly studying his notebook, said, "One last point. Can you confirm that, early this morning, when he completed his rounds and locked up the house, Winslow was the last member of staff downstairs? That he was the last to seek his bed?"

Everyone nodded.

"He always was the last up, every night," Mrs. Pratchett said, and a hint of sorrow crept into her voice.

Stokes nodded and tucked away his notebook. "That will be all for the moment. Thank you. All of you."

The staff nodded respectfully back, then started to disperse.

After a final nod to Mrs. Pratchett, with Penelope and Stokes, Barnaby turned and walked into the corridor that led to the front of the house, only to see O'Donnell, his expression eager, coming toward them.

Stokes waved his sergeant to a halt, and O'Donnell stopped and waited until they reached him.

"What have we got?" Stokes asked, his voice low.

O'Donnell held out his gloved hand. On his leather-covered palm lay a small brown-paper packet with one corner torn off and a label stuck to the front. Also speaking quietly, O'Donnell reported, "We found this tucked away in a drawer in one of those tall chests in a room upstairs. But it looks like the room's not been used for an age. No clothes hanging in the wardrobe or in the drawers, and decades' worth of dust in those places maids don't think to clean when they're just going through the motions."

Barnaby frowned. "So the room's been tended, but not as if anyone's sleeping there?"

O'Donnell nodded. "Aye. That's it."

They all leaned closer and peered at the packet. The label carried a warning in solid red letters: "Poison." Higher on the label, closer to the top of the packet, were the letters "Strychn—." The word was cut off where the packet was torn open.

"Can you turn it over?" Barnaby asked.

O'Donnell obliged, and they saw printing in tiny letters on the brown back of the packet.

Stokes squinted. "What does that say?"

Penelope huffed, opened her reticule, and hauled out her trusty magnifying glass. "Hold it still," she ordered O'Donnell and bent close to study the letters.

Then, slowly, she straightened. "Chifley's Chemist Shop. And there's a date, or part of one, in the corner. The seventh of April, but there isn't a year. That bit's been torn off." She looked at Barnaby and Stokes. "But assuming it was this year, then the packet was bought only last week."

They considered what that meant, then Stokes turned to O'Donnell. "Get that—with all due care—to Findlay."

"Get a sheet of paper from the study and wrap it inside," Barnaby suggested.

"And keep your gloves on regardless," Penelope instructed.

"Yes, sir. Ma'am," O'Donnell replied.

Stokes had glanced back at the servants' hall. "But before you go… Wait here."

Stokes returned to the servants' hall and asked Mrs. Pratchett to accompany him along the corridor to where Barnaby, Penelope, and O'Donnell waited.

When, with Stokes, the housekeeper joined them, Stokes nodded to O'Donnell. "Tell Mrs. Pratchett which room we're looking at." To Mrs. Pratchett, he said, "It would be helpful if you could tell us who last used the room in question."

O'Donnell promptly described the room in terms of which corridor it lay along and how many doors from the gallery it was.

Mrs. Pratchett, who obviously knew the mansion like the back of her hand, followed the trail in her head, and when O'Donnell reached the door at the trail's end, the housekeeper immediately supplied, "Why, that's Mr. Frederick's old room." She met Stokes's eyes. "But he—Mr. Frederick—hasn't used it in an age. Not since he married and left to live in Hertford Street." She paused, plainly consulting her memory, then added, "Indeed, I don't believe he's even been inside that room, not for more than two decades. Long before the old earl, the one before, meaning his father, died."

Barnaby met Stokes's eyes, then looked at Penelope.

Penelope smiled at Mrs. Pratchett. "Thank you. That's exactly what we needed to know."

"You've been most helpful," Barnaby assured her. "We're leaving now, so we'll be out of your hair."

Stokes added his farewell, then they turned and, ushering O'Donnell before them, headed for the foyer and the front door.

CHAPTER 7

After a brief conference on the pavement in Park Lane, Stokes dispatched O'Donnell to take the poison packet to Findlay and sent the constables from the search party back to their normal posts, leaving Morgan with a small group to maintain a cordon around the house.

A bevy of reporters were currently cooling their heels in a loose gathering under the trees on the other side of the street, kept at that distance by two watchful constables. Several of the press had perked up at the sight of the investigative team, but were being actively discouraged from calling out questions, which, regardless, Stokes, Barnaby, and Penelope ignored.

After seeing O'Donnell rumble off in a police wagon with the returning constables, Stokes joined Barnaby and Penelope in their carriage.

Barnaby had already directed Phelps to take them to Chifley's Chemist Shop. No further information was needed, and mere minutes after rolling away from Moran House, the carriage drew up in Piccadilly, just before the corner of Old Down Street.

Connor dropped to the pavement and opened the carriage door. Barnaby descended first, before the wide front window of Chifley's Chemist Shop. The place was a fixture in Mayfair, well known to most residents and their households.

Barnaby gave Penelope his hand and assisted her down the carriage steps, then Stokes climbed out, and the three of them paused to take in the colorful window display and the well-lit shelves and counters beyond. A shrewd and canny businessman, Chifley worked to make his shop welcoming and reaped the commensurate rewards.

For Stokes's edification, Penelope stated, "Everyone in Mayfair uses Chifley's to supply their medicines and tonics."

Stokes glanced at her, then looked at Barnaby. "So you're customers?"

Barnaby nodded. "Especially now we have the boys. Cough tonics are one of Chifley's specialties."

"And they work," Penelope said and started for the door. "Come on. Let's see what Chifley can tell us about the packet of strychnine bought on April seventh."

Penelope swept into the shop, and a bell tinkled melodiously, drawing the attention of the middle-aged man—neatly dressed in a suit and with a well-groomed head of brown curls—who was standing behind the main counter that ran the length of one side of the shop.

As Penelope approached, Barnaby and Stokes at her back, Chifley beamed. "Mrs. Adair! And Mr. Adair as well. How delightful to see you. And how are your two mites?"

"The boys are thriving, thank you." Penelope halted before the counter. "And how are you and Mrs. Chifley?"

"We're both very well, and I'll tell her you asked." Chifley's eyes shone with good humor.

Halting beside Penelope, Barnaby nodded cordially to Chifley. "Good afternoon, Chifley. As it happens, we"—Barnaby gestured to Stokes, who'd come up on Penelope's other side—"and Inspector Stokes of Scotland Yard are here on a matter in no way connected with our household."

"Oh?" Chifley was openly curious. "And what might that matter be?"

Penelope knew that the best way to engage Chifley's ever-inquisitive heart was to enlist him as a helper, so she hurried to explain, "We're trying to trace the source of some poison—strychnine powder, as a matter of fact—that was found in a nearby house, and we believe the poison was purchased at Chifley's."

"The packet we found bears your shop's name and also a date," Stokes stated. "The seventh of April, which was last Thursday."

Chifley's expression turned grave. "I must state that we've been very much against allowing the populace such easy access to the powdered form. There's a much higher danger of accidental poisoning, and strychnine is not a poison that affords much leeway, so to speak." He stepped back, his gaze lowering to the area beneath the counter. "Because of that, we've instituted a system that we always follow when selling the more dangerous powders." He reached down and drew out a scarlet-cloth-covered ledger. "We keep a register of all purchases of the more dangerous substances."

Stokes came alert. "A register?"

"Indeed." Chifley set the scarlet ledger on the counter and opened it. "Substance, amount, name of purchaser, date of purchase, and a signature." He started flicking over pages. "Now, let me see. Strychnine, strychnine—here we are." He ran a finger down one column. "April seventh, you said?"

Penelope held her breath and was sure Stokes and Barnaby were holding theirs, too.

Chifley flicked over another page, then his finger halted on one entry. "Ah. Yes." He straightened and read, "A quarter ounce of strychnine powder, sold on April seventh to Mr. F. Fitzhugh."

Chifley swung the ledger around so they could see the entry for themselves. He tapped the last column. "As I mentioned, we insist the purchaser signs."

Together with Barnaby and Stokes, Penelope stared at the neat figures of the entry—plainly made in one hand, presumably that of the vendor—and the signature at the end, which was in a very different script.

Barnaby straightened and nodded to Chifley. "Thank you, Mr. Chifley. That's a great help."

"Indeed," Stokes said. "This idea of yours of a dangerous-substance register is an excellent one." He nodded approvingly to Chifley. "I'll be mentioning it to the Commissioner."

Chifley beamed. "I'm delighted to have been of help."

But... Penelope studied Chifley, then asked, "I'm sure you must be acquainted with Mr. Fitzhugh—Mr. Frederick Fitzhugh?"

Chifley nodded. "I know the gentleman by sight, but it's more often his wife who comes in to make purchases for their household."

"Do you recall serving Mr. Frederick Fitzhugh last Thursday?" Barnaby asked.

Chifley's face fell. "I have to confess it wasn't I who served him." He tapped the ledger entry. "Judging by the writing, it was Joseph, my assistant, who handled the sale."

"May we speak with Joseph?" Penelope promptly asked.

"Of course." Chifley looked toward the rear of the shop, where a high counter cut off a section of the shop's space. Beyond the counter, several white-jacketed staff could be seen, filling packets with pills and bottles with prepared tonics. Among them was Joseph, whom Penelope had dealt with before.

Chifley caught Joseph's eye and beckoned him to join them.

After shrugging off his white jacket, the younger man hurried out from the rear through a side door and continued behind the long counter toward them. "Yes, Mr. Chifley?"

In avuncular fashion, Chifley placed a hand on Joseph's shoulder. "Joseph, you know Mr. and Mrs. Adair. This other gentleman is Inspector Stokes of Scotland Yard, and he and the Adairs are trying to trace a packet of strychnine powder, which seems to be one you sold last week."

Alarm flared in Joseph's eyes, and Barnaby quickly assured him, "There's no suggestion of any wrongdoing on your part."

Penelope smiled encouragingly. "Mr. Chifley has shown us this quite excellent register"—she laid her hand on the open ledger and tapped her finger on the pertinent entry—"and we wanted to ask if you could describe the gentleman, Mr. F. Fitzhugh, who bought this packet of strychnine last Thursday."

Joseph glanced at his employer. When Chifley nodded his approval, Joseph returned his gaze to Penelope's face. "Mr. Fitzhugh was a well-dressed man, definitely a gentleman."

When Joseph seemed to think that was description enough, Penelope prompted, "How tall was he?"

"Tallish—over six feet, I would say," Joseph replied and added, "Not heavily built, though. More on the lean side."

Penelope nodded. "Hair color?"

"Dark hair. Very dark brown," Joseph said and obligingly went on, "He had a pale complexion—notably pale—and black eyebrows and blue eyes."

Penelope paused. Joseph's description fitted Frederick and Christopher and, indeed, all four of the older Fitzhugh nephews. She glanced at Barnaby and Stokes and, from their expressions, deduced they'd come to the same conclusion.

As if sensing their conundrum, Joseph glanced at Mr. Chifley and said, "I did speak with the gentleman for several minutes. If I saw him again, I'm sure I could with certainty say that it was him."

Along with Stokes and Barnaby, Penelope beamed.

Stokes tapped the counter. "Excellent!" He nodded to Joseph. "It may not be necessary, but it's possible that, at some point, we might need to call on you to do that. But for now"—he inclined his head to Chifley—"thank you both. That's all we need to this point."

To Chifley, Barnaby said, "Please keep this register safe. It might be needed as evidence."

Chifley bowed and assured them that he, and Joseph, too, were more than happy to assist in whatever way they could.

Leaving both Chifley and Joseph patently chuffed at being involved in an investigation, with Barnaby and Stokes, Penelope quit the counter and made for the door, which Joseph hurried across to open for them.

With a gracious nod for the young assistant, Penelope walked out onto the pavement and paused, raising her face to the afternoon sunshine.

When Barnaby and Stokes joined her, she observed, "Chifley's is not at all far from Frederick's home in Hertford Street." She tipped her head and went on, "That said, Piccadilly is not far from any of the houses of those involved in this case."

"True," Stokes said. "And given we were planning to interview the families this afternoon, I suggest we go to Hertford Street and see what Frederick Fitzhugh is willing to tell us."

~

Penelope stood beside Barnaby on the doorstep of the Fitzhugh house in Hertford Street and watched as Stokes plied the knocker with authority.

Less than a minute later, the door was opened by a sober, quietly assured butler, who, on hearing their names, stepped back and bowed them into the house. "The master and mistress mentioned you might drop by."

Walking into the front hall, Penelope noted the black armband adorning the butler's coat sleeve, a very proper observance in response to the earl's death.

Even more striking was the contrast between the severely austere Moran House foyer and the space in which she now stood. The Fitzhugh front hall projected an image of relaxed tonnish life more commonly found in country houses, where strict adherence to the ton's expectations of appearance and exactitude was often allowed to slide. A clutter of assorted reticules and shawls was piled around the base of the large ornate vase that stood on the round hall table, and cloaks and greatcoats were tossed haphazardly on the coatrack, with hats balanced atop the mounds.

With unimpaired calm, the butler ushered them into the drawing room. "I will inform the master and mistress that you have called. As you might expect, given the events of last evening, the family have only just risen for the day."

Glancing at the mantelpiece clock, Penelope confirmed that it was just after one o'clock. She turned to the butler. "Have any of the family left the house this morning?"

"No, ma'am." The butler paused as if consulting his memory, then added, "Having only recently broken their fast, all the members of the family are presently still under this roof."

Penelope smiled. "Good, because we need to speak with all those who attended the dinner at Moran House yesterday evening. Please inform Mr. and Mrs. Fitzhugh of that, and please ask Mr. Fitzhugh if he would spare us a few minutes of his time."

The butler bowed. "Indeed, ma'am." He turned and went to fetch his master.

Penelope looked around. The room exuded much the same ambiance as the hall. The chintz-covered sofa and large armchairs were irregularly grouped around a low table, as if the seating had been shoved around by recent occupants and left wherever it ended up. Wide windows flooded the room with light, and the same chintz had been used in the curtains that hung to either side of the panes. A large fireplace filled quite half the wall opposite the door, while a profusion of flowers spilled from a vase on a sideboard against one wall.

Penelope moved to the sofa and sat—and promptly sank into the thick cushions.

Subsiding beside her, Barnaby grinned. "Much more comfortable than the usual ton effort."

After assessing the available seating, Stokes claimed an armchair beyond the end of the sofa on which Penelope sat. He, too, sank into the cushions. "Comfortable seems to be the watchword here."

"From what little I know of Imogen Fitzhugh, she has always been more focused on her family and their well-being than on meeting society's expectations." Penelope paused, then went on, "She and Frederick have six children. The eldest two, both young men now, are on the town, although I believe they still live at this address. The oldest girl is in the throes of being presented to the ton this Season, and I've heard that the

Fitzhughs are working with the Mitchelmores and the Southerlys to share expenses, with all three families having young ladies to puff off this year. And after the Fitzhughs establish their eldest girl, they have three more to follow, so Imogen will have her hands full in the years to come."

"Not that I know all that much about the costs associated with young ladies being presented," Stokes said, "but it sounds as if Christopher's assertion that Frederick's finances are a mite stretched could be well founded."

Barnaby nodded. "Almost certainly. The costs of bringing up children within the ton and meeting the expected standards along the way—for instance, Eton and Oxford for the boys—and then supporting them as they venture onto the town, let alone the expense involved in presenting and marrying off young ladies, are, indeed, considerable."

"And largely unavoidable," Penelope added. "That said, given that Gordon—the late earl—had no children of his own, most in the ton would have expected him to take an interest in Frederick's children. Certainly, most would assume that Gordon would have assisted Frederick with the costs associated with educating the eldest son—William—who, after all, will at some point accede to the title."

Approaching footsteps put an end to their discussion, and a moment later, the door opened, and Frederick Fitzhugh, now the Earl of Moran, paused on the threshold. He regarded them for a moment, then stepped over the threshold, closed the door, and walked to join them as they rose to their feet.

In the harsher, brighter light of day, Frederick's resemblance to Christopher, to Frederick's own sons, and his older nephews was even more pronounced. All possessed straight dark hair, and the shape of their heads, the set of their blue eyes, and their long, lean frames were notably similar.

Now, however, Frederick's features were drawn and tinged with what appeared to be genuine sorrow. That, however, seemed to be the extent of his grief.

Barnaby introduced them again, and Frederick half bowed to Penelope and shook Barnaby's and Stokes's hands, then waved them to resume their seats while he drew another armchair to face the sofa and sank into it with a small sigh. "I apologize in advance if I seem somewhat distracted. While I'm still in shock over Gordon's death—and the manner of it—I've discovered that the demands of the Moran estate wait for no man." Tiredly, he smiled at Penelope and Barnaby. "I have the steward in my study, wanting me to make decisions on issues advanced by the agents, the bankers, and several others. And then there's the polite note from the government whip in the Lords." Looking decidedly frazzled, he ran his fingers through his hair, then ruefully shook his head. "Of course, our father—the previous earl—made sure that, as second in line, I was taught the basics of managing the estate, but with Gordon as earl, I never imagined that I would have to remember those lessons."

"It must, indeed, be quite a shock," Penelope soothed, "coming on top of the shock of the murder."

"Exactly." Frederick looked at Barnaby and Stokes. "So I fear you'll have to excuse any mental disarray on my part."

Barnaby inclined his head. "That's understandable, and we'll endeavor to keep this interview as brief as possible. Our first question is whether, after having had a chance to think of the matter, you've remembered anyone with whom your brother had a falling-out. Or anyone he mentioned as being a threat."

Frederick frowned and shook his head. "No. Gordon never mentioned anyone he feared. That said, we rarely spoke of his activities, so there might have been something…" After a few seconds of silence, during which Frederick stared at the low table, he sighed and met Barnaby's gaze. "The truth is that Gordon and I weren't close. Not ever, really. We are—were—very different people. Gordon was always focused on being the earl and shaping his life as he thought it should be. He liked the prestige and the power the position afforded him, and while he was careful with money, he was also very set on keeping up appearances."

Regarding Frederick, Penelope tilted her head. "And you?"

Faintly, Frederick smiled. "I'm much more concerned with taking care of the people around me—my family, of course, but also the staff who serve us and, were it in my power, the people on our estates and farms."

Unstated was the fact that, with his older brother now dead, he was free to pursue those goals.

Barnaby shifted, drawing Frederick's attention. "You said Gordon was careful with money. By that, did you mean he was tightfisted?"

Frederick considered the point, then admitted, "When Imogen and I married, Gordon made it very clear that, as far as he was concerned, my allowance from the Moran estate would not be increased. As you can no doubt imagine, that's led to a degree of financial strain. Gordon even refused to give William an allowance, even though, eventually, William will be the earl. If we hadn't had Imogen's portion and the help of her family, I honestly don't know where we would be."

Barnaby caught a pointed look from Stokes and took a moment to find the right words. "I take it Gordon's attitude created a rift between you?"

Frederick's brows rose, but he answered apparently openly, "Yes and no. After all, I had to respect the fact that, beyond the allowances stipulated in our father's will, the estate's funds were Gordon's to do with as he wished. And as I said, we weren't close to begin with, and after I married, it's true to say that we grew even further apart. I daresay that, if we had been in the habit of exchanging views, we wouldn't have seen eye to eye on many, so perhaps the distance between us wasn't such a bad thing. Having Gordon and me at daggers drawn would only have caused Mama more angst."

Penelope's instincts quivered. "More? Was the dowager at odds with Gordon?"

Frederick frowned. After several moments, he offered, "I am aware that, over recent months, Mama seems to have felt a growing…frustration, I suppose one would call it, with Gordon."

"Did that in any way stem from his marriage to Lady Victoria?" Penelope probed.

"Oh, I don't think so." Frederick readily met her gaze. "This is more recent, and aside from all else, Gordon married Victoria to placate Mama and our aunts. They were adamant that, socially, he needed a countess at his side, and although he argued that, courtesy of my sons, the succession was secure, they kept pushing and prodding until he agreed. As Victoria was their chosen candidate, I don't think the issue between Mama and Gordon had anything to do with him marrying Victoria."

Penelope glanced at Stokes, a question in her eyes. When he fractionally nodded, she returned her gaze to Frederick and said, "I suspect you haven't yet heard the news, but Winslow, the Moran House butler, was found dead this morning."

Frederick's eyes flew wide. "Good Lord!" His expression sobered, and he went on, "That'll be a huge shock for the household and a major loss. Winslow was the family butler for decades."

Evenly, Stokes said, "He was poisoned."

"What?" Frederick stared at Stokes, then blustered, "When you said dead, I thought you meant his heart had given out with the shock..." His

voice trailed away, then after a moment, he refocused on Stokes. "Are you sure?"

Imperturbably, Stokes replied, "We believe that, early this morning, after the events of the night and before he went to his bed, Winslow helped himself to a small tot of whiskey from the decanter in the earl's study. It seems the whiskey had been laced with poison. Strychnine, to be precise."

Frederick stared, then blinked. Then he frowned. "Wait. Are you saying that Gordon was the real target? That the poisoner intended Gordon to die, but because Gordon had already been killed, old Winslow died instead?"

Faintly, Barnaby raised his brows. "You could put it that way."

Frederick was transparently flabbergasted. Looking at Stokes, he asked, "What on earth is going on in Park Lane?"

Stokes inclined his head. "That, indeed, is what our investigation is seeking to learn. However, given the most recent events, we have to ask if, at any time yesterday, you went into the earl's study."

Frederick shook his head. "No. Well, yes, I did, but only after we were told Gordon was dead. None of us could really believe it, you see. He'd been there, in the drawing room, drinking tea, less than an hour before, so Christopher and I went to check. We were in the study for perhaps three minutes. Just long enough to see, gawk, then catch our breaths and leave." He met Stokes's gaze. "That was it. Otherwise, I haven't been in the study for weeks."

Stokes glanced at his notebook, then asked, "Did you visit the house the day before—on Sunday?"

Frederick shook his head. "No."

Stokes continued, "When did you get to the house on Monday?"

Frederick paused to draw a leveling breath, then stated, "I arrived for the dinner at six o'clock sharp, with the rest of my family. Mama had called for a family dinner and had asked that the children attend, which she always prefers, so we usually gather at six in the drawing room and are home by about half past ten."

"So you arrived in the drawing room," Penelope said, "and you didn't leave the company at any time thereafter until the earl was found dead. Is that correct?"

Frederick nodded. "Indeed."

"And the rest of your family?" Stokes had his notebook on his knee and was making an entry.

Frederick opened his mouth, then paused. Then he paled.

Seeing that, Barnaby asked, "Which of your family left the gathering over that time?"

Frederick looked at Barnaby measuringly, but eventually answered, "George. He went elsewhere for...perhaps ten minutes. I assume he went to use the facilities."

"When was that?" Stokes's tone remained matter-of-fact.

"After dinner," Frederick said, "when the company left the dining room, and we were on our way back to the drawing room. George peeled off then."

Frederick looked at Barnaby. "William will likely be able to tell you where George went. At the time, they were walking together at the rear of the group."

Equably, Barnaby nodded. "We'll ask William, but likely it was simply as you assumed."

"Incidentally," Stokes said, his gaze on Frederick's face, "when Moran House was searched for any likely source of the poison introduced into the earl's whiskey, an open packet of strychnine was found in a drawer in the room that used to be yours when you lived under that roof."

"Really?" Frederick's expression reflected nothing more than surprise and curiosity. "Why on earth would such a thing be kept up there?"

Stokes studied Frederick's face, then nodded. "Indeed."

Stokes looked at Barnaby and Penelope, but both shook their heads.

Stokes returned his gaze to Frederick. "At the moment, that's all the questions we have for you."

Penelope held up a hand. "One last thing." When Frederick looked her way, with an understanding smile, she said, "If you would indulge us, it would be helpful if I could see a letter you've written but not yet sent or even a draft that you've discarded. Something with your signature and a few lines of text. I won't need to take it away or even actually read what's written. I just need to look and get some sense of your script. I'm something of a writing expert, and during our investigations, it's proved useful to be able to distinguish the writing of the various people involved. In this case, knowing your writing style will be helpful should we need to tell your writing apart from the earl's or even Christopher's."

Frederick blinked. "Oh. Yes, I see." He glanced at Stokes and Barnaby. "If you have, indeed, finished with me, I'll take a look in my study and see what I can find."

Penelope smiled. "Thank you. We would appreciate that."

Barnaby and Stokes rose with Frederick.

Stokes stated, "We would like to speak with your wife next, and after that, we will need to speak, albeit briefly, with each of your children in turn."

Barnaby added, "We will be interviewing every person who attended the dinner at Moran House."

Anticipating resistance regarding the younger children, Penelope added, "In the past, we've found that children, not being so involved in the conversations, are often more observant than their elders."

Frederick appeared to have no issue with them questioning his offspring; he readily inclined his head. "Imogen will summon the children for you. I'll send her in, then look for a letter for you."

After thanking Frederick for his assistance, Barnaby walked him to the door.

He and Frederick found Imogen loitering in the front hall.

Frederick smiled at her. "You're next."

"Of course." After pressing her husband's arm, Imogen came to the drawing room doorway, and when Barnaby stepped back, she exchanged a polite nod with him, then walked determinedly past and on toward the chairs.

On reaching the chair Frederick had occupied, Imogen nodded confidently to Penelope. "Mrs. Adair."

Having risen to greet her, Penelope nodded back. "Thank you for speaking with us, Mrs. Fitzhugh."

Imogen inclined her head to Stokes, who had also come to his feet, then, after Barnaby had returned to the sofa, Imogen and Penelope sat, allowing the men to do the same.

Penelope had always found Imogen refreshing in that she frequently displayed greater practicality than was customary among ton matrons. Today, Imogen was gowned in a midnight-blue day gown, perfectly presentable but not in the latest style, combined with a black fichu to denote her mourning state. With her rounder face and comfortable figure, she exuded a no-nonsense, direct, and unrufflable air that was reassuring, and it was clear she wore her motherhood as a badge of honor.

Penelope reflected that, as Imogen was the mother of six grown children, few would argue her right to the status.

Predictably, Imogen took the bull by the horns. "I was waiting in the hall. You said you would wish to speak with me."

Penelope said, "As we explained to Frederick, we need to interview all those present at last night's dinner."

Imogen nodded. "Indeed. While Frederick was with you, a footman from Moran House arrived with the news of Winslow's death. Apparently by poison!" She looked at Stokes. "What is the world coming to?"

Stokes made no reply, and Imogen turned her attention to Barnaby. "Is it thought that the poison was intended for Gordon?"

Cautiously, Barnaby inclined his head. "It does seem that way."

Imogen shook her head in sorrowful disparagement. "To have multiple people willing to murder you. I always thought Gordon would one day push someone too hard. Everything always had to be done his way." Imogen brought her hazel eyes to meet Penelope's gaze. "He was an abrasive character and could be quite aggressive, especially toward those he considered his inferiors. I saw that trait displayed often enough, but he was always one to show a smooth exterior to those whose goodwill he courted."

"I see." Penelope asked, "Do you know of anyone who wished Gordon ill?"

Frowning, Imogen admitted, "No, I don't. Not specifically. But I have to say that I'm not surprised that someone did."

"We understand," Barnaby said, "that financially speaking, Gordon didn't make life easy for Frederick and your family."

"He didn't." Imogen patently had no qualms about admitting that. "However, courtesy of my portion and my family, we manage well enough." She gestured about them, then went on, "Very soon after we married, I saw how things would be with Gordon, and since that time, I've been at pains to make clear to Frederick and, more recently, the children that we are not dependent on the Moran estate and Gordon's goodwill. In the wider scheme of things, we want for nothing that matters and have everything we actually need to go forward as we should."

That firmly independent attitude resonated with what Penelope knew of and had previously sensed in Imogen. Penelope arched her brows. "You weren't surprised when Gordon refused to help support William, even though he will eventually be earl?"

"Well," Imogen conceded, "I was surprised at the time, but truly, it's all of a piece with Gordon's attitude to money. Even Victoria grumbles about it. His direction to her has always been that she must keep up appearances, yet still, he was difficult over her expenses."

"And the dowager?" Penelope asked.

"Imelda doesn't grumble as such," Imogen replied, "and of course, while she lived in Regent's Square and had less to do with Moran House, she wasn't constantly reminded of Gordon's ways, but ever since she returned to live in Park Lane, she's grown increasingly annoyed at Gordon, although over what, I have to admit I'm not entirely sure." Imogen faintly frowned, apparently over not being able to pinpoint the reason for the dowager's reaction.

Penelope hesitated, then, as Imogen was being so forthcoming, ventured to ask, "What about the earl's sisters?"

"Luckily, both married well, but even they scoff at Gordon's secretly tightfisted ways."

Curious, Barnaby inquired, "Secretly?"

Imogen glanced at him and faintly grimaced. "It's difficult to explain, but Gordon was miserly only in ways that wouldn't be obvious to any observer outside the household or family." She raised her head. "For instance, the entire family believes he sold the house in Regent's Square that the dowager used to live in and moved her back to Moran House purely to swell the estate's coffers, which, of course, are almost certainly already overflowing!" Imogen raised her hands. "None of us could imagine any reason for doing that other than his never-ending pursuit of funds. And then there's his insistence on knowing what events the dowager plans to attend each day. That, I assure you, is not due to any concern for her but so that he knows where her footmen and the coachman are." Lips primming, Imogen revealed, "I understand that he ensures the footmen, who are specifically employed to assist the dowager up and down stairs and into and out of the carriage, are fully engaged in running errands and the like for him during the hours they're not out with her. Likewise with the coachman."

Shifting her focus to Penelope, faintly incensed, Imogen continued, "And then he dismissed the dowager's companion for no reason that anyone knows." She shook her head. "With Gordon, it was all about minimizing expenses, and he'd been doing that for decades."

Imagining such a scenario, Penelope murmured, "And no one can criticize, at least not openly, because he can simply say he's managing his resources to best effect."

Imogen threw up her hands. "Exactly! The whole family, even the children, know he does it." She paused, then, in a calmer tone, added, "That said, I honestly can't imagine that, for any of us, the impact of Gordon's miserliness has ever reached the point of moving anyone to murder." She sighed and returned her gaze to Penelope, then glanced at Barnaby and Stokes. "But what I do wonder is, if he was like that with family, who else did he 'manage' in the same way? Others might have been more seriously affected and…"

Barnaby inclined his head. "And maybe there's a motive for murder there." He met Imogen's gaze. "Thank you for being so frank."

Imogen's lips twisted, and she shrugged. "Well, he's dead. And as much as I might have disapproved of his ways, he was family, and the murder of an earl cannot be condoned."

"No, indeed," Stokes grimly replied. He consulted his notes, then looked at Imogen. "When you were at Moran House yesterday evening, did you see anyone unexpected—anyone not of the family or the staff?"

"No. No one."

Barnaby said, "We understand that you and your family arrived at six o'clock, and of course, you were there until after the murder. Do you know if any of the family left the gathering at any point?"

Imogen blinked. "Well, Gordon did—he went to the study at about nine-thirty."

"Before that?" Penelope prompted.

Imogen frowned as she thought back, then her lips firmed. "George. He slipped away while the company was progressing from the dining room to the drawing room, and he returned as Winslow wheeled in the tea trolley, so George was apart for only a matter of minutes." She met Penelope's gaze openly. "I assume he went to use the facilities." She paused, then went on, "The only others who spent time away from the group were Vincent and Theodore, Constance and Southerly's sons. They—Constance, Southerly, and Lydia, too—were already in the drawing room when we arrived, but Vincent and Theodore were absent. They came in about fifteen minutes later."

Envisioning the scene, Penelope asked, "When did Gordon join the gathering in the drawing room?"

"He came in a minute or so after we arrived," Imogen replied.

"So," Barnaby clarified, "Vincent and Theodore joined the company in the drawing room sometime after Gordon."

Imogen nodded. "As I said. A good fifteen minutes after Gordon."

"Thank you," Stokes said. "That's very clear." He looked up as the door opened, and Frederick returned, carrying a somewhat crumpled paper.

He smiled at them all and waved the sheet. As he approached, to

Imogen, he explained, "Mrs. Adair requested a sample of my writing so she can tell it from Gordon's and Christopher's."

Imogen looked surprised but merely nodded as Frederick halted before Penelope and offered her his find. "Best I could do. A letter I wrote to a friend who I thought was in the country still, but I ran into him two days ago, here in town, so this is now redundant, and I'd intended to throw it away." Apologetically, he added, "It's mostly about dogs—that's an interest we share."

Smiling, Penelope accepted the sheet and swiftly studied it. "This is perfect. Thank you for showing it to me." Still smiling, she looked up and handed the letter back. "That's really all I needed to see—enough to distinguish your writing from others."

And to get a firm idea of your usual signature.

"Good-oh." Frederick took back the letter.

Stokes glanced at Penelope and said, "If you would, sir, please keep that letter. Just in case we need it later."

Folding the letter, Frederick shrugged. "As you wish."

Stokes shifted his gaze to Imogen and inclined his head. "You've been most helpful, Mrs. Fitzhugh. Now, if we could have a word with your eldest son?"

Imogen rose and laid a hand on Frederick's arm. "We'll send William in."

Frederick offered, "He's waiting in the hall so that he and George can go out once you've finished with them."

Stokes, Barnaby, and Penelope rose, and with polite nods all around, the new earl and countess left the room.

Immediately—verifying Frederick's information—William Fitzhugh entered, giving Penelope no chance to convey the conclusion she'd reached after viewing Frederick's letter. Instead, she turned her attention to William.

In his early twenties, tall, lean, with the sable-brown hair, aristocratic features, and mid-blue eyes he'd inherited from his father, the young man was passably handsome and otherwise unremarkable. William's sole concession to mourning was a black armband fastened over his sleeve. While his neat dark suit, white shirt, oyster-silk stock, and subdued waistcoat were much the current fashion for his age, he carried himself well, and his attitude as he crossed the room and politely returned their greetings exuded quiet confidence.

Penelope could see William, in time, as a perfectly acceptable Earl of

Moran. Her appreciation of Imogen's mothering skills rose several notches.

Barnaby waved William to the chair his mother had vacated, and Barnaby, Stokes, and Penelope resumed their seats.

After settling comfortably, William, his expression turning serious and somber, said, "I say, this is rough news about old Winslow." William met Barnaby's gaze with clear-eyed directness. "He was a good egg. A bit stiff if you didn't know him, but he was a decent sort." William's features firmed. "And now he's dead because of Uncle Gordon." William shook his head in what appeared to be mild disgust.

From his manner and tone, Penelope felt it was safe to deduce that William felt more genuine grief over the loss of his uncle's butler than his uncle.

Stokes took William through the same questions they'd asked of his parents, and although William answered freely, with an easy, accommodating air, he offered much the same answers and no further insights.

Then, without warning, Stokes asked, "When the company was moving from the dining room to the drawing room, and your brother, George, parted from the group, where did George go?"

William blinked. He stared at Stokes blankly, then replied, "I assume he went to use the facilities."

"Did George say so?" Barnaby asked.

His expression much less relaxed, William admitted, "No. But…" He shrugged. "Where else would he go?"

"So George went off." Penelope caught William's gaze. "In which direction?"

William hesitated—plainly thinking furiously—then said, "We were in the foyer, and he went toward the corridor at the rear of the hall."

"The one that leads to the study?" Barnaby asked.

William's until-then-loosely-clasped hands tightened. "Yes."

Penelope arched her brows. "A strange place for a water closet. Is there one along there?"

William sat back and looked at her, then at Barnaby and Stokes. "I… don't know."

Not only was it plain that William was fabricating in an attempt to protect his brother, but also, he could see that he wasn't convincing them.

"Look," he said, adopting a conciliatory tone, "I don't know where George went, but he wasn't away for long. I don't know why you think it's important, but…there it is." He sat back, the set of his lips turning mulish. "That's all I can tell you."

After studying him for a moment, Stokes inclined his head. "In that case, thank you for your time."

"Right, then." Barnaby stood and waved an uncertain yet relieved William to his feet. "We'll speak with George next. You can take me to him."

Somewhat stiffly, William nodded in polite farewell to Penelope and Stokes, then made for the door, with Barnaby close behind him.

Penelope exchanged a faintly amused but long-suffering look over the predictability of certain witnesses' behavior with Stokes, then Barnaby was back, ushering in George Fitzhugh, Frederick and Imogen's second son.

Smiling easily, Barnaby informed them, "As it happened, George was waiting in the hall just outside."

Although in all respects similar in appearance to his older brother, George did not exude the same level of confidence, and he returned their greetings in a subdued tone. As he sat as directed in the armchair, he glanced somewhat nervously at Stokes, but when Stokes commenced by confirming that George had heard of Winslow's death, George responded readily, demonstrating that he, too, felt greater sorrow over Winslow's death than his uncle's.

Stokes followed with their now-standard questions regarding the time the family arrived at Moran House and who else had been in the drawing room at the time, and George replied with increasing steadiness and decreasing resistance.

Then Stokes baldly stated, "When the company was moving from the dining room to the drawing room, you were walking at the rear of the group, and in the front hall, you slipped away." Stokes met George's startled gaze. "You were absent from the group for over ten minutes. Where did you go?"

George stared at Stokes, then bit his lip and looked at Barnaby. Eventually, George glanced at Penelope and glumly stated, "I suppose I'd better tell you, or else you'll think I did something even worse."

Penelope nodded encouragingly. "That's the right decision."

George hauled in a breath, then shifted his gaze to Stokes. "I went into Uncle Gordon's study and checked to see if he'd left any money lying about. He sometimes did—just a few quid he'd taken from his pockets, that sort of thing. Small change for him, but it helped me and

William. Especially as Uncle Gordon refused to give William even a tiny allowance, even though, in most families, that would be the natural thing to do."

Barnaby confirmed, "So you were in the habit of removing small amounts of money from the earl's study."

Lowering his gaze to his clasped hands, George nodded.

"It might interest you to know," Barnaby continued, a thread of steely condemnation in his voice, "that your uncle blamed the thefts on the fourteen-year-old son of the dowager's companion."

George's head snapped up. Eyes wide, he asked, "Julian? He blamed Julian?"

Penelope nodded. "Yes, Julian." She studied George. "Do you know him?"

"Yes. All of us—the younger ones—do. He's been there—well, in Grandmama's household—forever. But for Uncle Gordon to think it was him…that's absurd!" George shook his head in disgusted disbelief. "Julian never came into the front of the house. You couldn't get him to cross the threshold out of the servants' side for love nor money. And trust me, over the years, several of us have tried." As if in explanation, George met Penelope's gaze and added, "He's a bright one, is Julian. He's really good at inventing games, and we all appreciated that."

Stokes stated, "The staff of Moran House have already confirmed what you've said about Julian, so we knew he wasn't to blame for the thefts. Now, we know it was you who took the cash."

George protested, "It wasn't just me! Sometimes William, and we know Byron, Hugh, Vincent, and Theodore all did the same. We've caught them at it, on occasion." George grimaced. "And they've caught us, so…" He paused, then, chin firming, said, "But truly, Uncle Gordon had it coming, given the way he treated all of us as if we were invisible. As if we didn't even exist."

Curious, Penelope asked, "You all stole only from him?"

Emphatically, George nodded. "We only took things that were his. All of us agreed to that, and really, that was why we did it in the first place. To at least *inconvenience* him. And after all, we're family, so"—George shrugged—"if one of us had been caught, I seriously doubt even Uncle Gordon would have wanted us prosecuted for theft."

Barnaby dipped his head, then met Stokes's gaze. "A valid point." He returned his gaze to George. "And strange as it might seem, we're grateful to you for being truthful. Now, we won't go searching for whoever was behind the thefts, just in case your uncle surprised a thief in action and that, somehow, led to his murder."

Stokes asked, "Can you recall if all the younger Fitzhughs, your cousins, remained in the drawing room after the earl left and went to his study?"

George readily replied, "Yes. After Uncle Gordon left, no one else did. We just sat and talked, and then Winslow came to tell us that Uncle Gordon was dead."

Frowning, Penelope asked, "When you slipped into the study, did you happen to notice if the whiskey decanter was empty?"

George was surprised to be asked but nodded. "As a matter of fact, it was." Then he blushed and glanced at Barnaby. "Sometimes, we fill our flasks from it, but this time, it was already empty."

Barnaby glanced at Stokes, who paused in his scribbling to shake his head, then Barnaby rose and waved a relieved George to his feet. "Come on. You can introduce me to your oldest sister."

When, two minutes later, Barnaby ushered a willowy young lady into the room, Penelope rose and smiled invitingly. "Good afternoon, Mathilda." She'd been introduced to the girl, better known as Tilly, at a ball only a few weeks before. Tilly was a taller, slimmer version of her mother, with the same glossy brown hair combined with wide hazel eyes. From the few phrases Penelope had exchanged with Tilly, she suspected the girl also shared her mother's practical bent.

A reassuring smile in place, Penelope waved the slightly hesitant girl to the vacant armchair opposite. "Please join us. We have a few questions for you regarding the gathering at Moran House last evening."

Very much on her dignity and cautious with it, Tilly glided forward, nodded politely to Penelope and, rather more wide-eyed, at Stokes, then, as Penelope, Barnaby, and Stokes all sat, Tilly gracefully subsided to perch on the edge of the chair's seat.

By way of an opening, Penelope ventured, "We've gathered that you and your cousins, Geraldine and Diana, are being presented this year, more or less as a shared endeavor."

Tilly nodded. "Yes." When Penelope waited, Tilly added, "It was easier that way—for the three of us, because we'd have each other for support, and also for our parents, what with the organizing being shared."

Penelope decided the query might bear fruit so evenly asked, "What was your opinion of your uncle Gordon?"

Tilly's eyes widened. "Uncle Gordon?" She blinked, twice, then offered, "Well, he was the head of our house, being the earl." She met Penelope's gaze, then shrugged. "Other than that, I really didn't know him. Our paths didn't cross, as they say." She paused, then stated, "I've haven't really thought much about Uncle Gordon, but I know Grandmama and the others—our parents, aunts, and uncles—always seemed irritated with him."

Other than confirming the absence of Vincent and Theodore from the drawing room when Tilly and her family had arrived, there was little more she could tell them.

Tilly's view of the earl was echoed, one after another, by her three sisters. Their knowledge of their uncle Gordon was next to nonexistent, and while all had sensed the tension between the earl and the other adults in the family, none had worried their heads about the reasons for it.

Ella, the youngest at twelve years old, simply said, "Uncle Gordon was snippy with everyone. I don't think anyone in the family liked him much, not even Aunt Victoria, which is rather sad, but then, he never seemed to like any of us, either."

Penelope escorted Ella out to the hall, then returned to Barnaby and Stokes, who had remained standing by the chairs. "It seems," Penelope said, "that the youngest in the family gave a fair summation of the family's attitude to the erstwhile head of their house."

Barnaby smiled, and Stokes grunted.

"Incidentally," Penelope continued, "I do not believe Frederick's was the hand that signed Chifley's register." She tilted her head. "However, I also think it would be unwise to show Frederick the register with his faked signature."

Stokes arched his brows. "Because he might recognize the writing?"

She nodded. "I think, in this instance, playing safe might be wise."

"I agree." Barnaby looked at Stokes.

Stokes grimaced. "Given the pressure that's already mounting over solving this case, we need to act expeditiously but, I concede, also without making mistakes."

Barnaby glanced at Penelope. "So should we ask Frederick to come with us to Chifley's and allow Joseph to take a good look at him?"

Penelope frowned, then stated, "The sooner we can establish that it wasn't Frederick who bought the strychnine, the better for all concerned."

"And, with any luck, the clearer our path forward will be," Stokes said.

"Indeed." Penelope marched to the fireplace and the bellpull that hung beside it. She tugged peremptorily, and when the butler appeared, asked him to convey their compliments to his master and mistress and request a further moment of their time.

After the butler bowed and withdrew, she returned to Barnaby and Stokes and answered the question she saw in their eyes. "We need Imogen because she's the more practical and also the more likely to see the implication and seize the chance to clear her husband of all suspicion."

No more than a minute later, Frederick and Imogen came in.

Penelope, Barnaby, and Stokes walked to join the pair nearer the door.

Halting before the new earl and countess, Barnaby swiftly outlined their findings at Chifley's and explained that the assistant who sold the poison was sure he would know the man who purchased the strychnine if he saw him again.

"Consequently," Stokes said, "we would like to ask you, sir"—he dipped his head to Frederick—"if you would consent to accompany us to the shop and allow the assistant to confirm that it wasn't you who purchased the poison."

As Penelope had predicted, it was Imogen who tipped the scales.

She looked at Frederick's face—at his slight frown as he considered the request—then she gripped his arm and lightly shook it.

When Frederick glanced at her, she pointedly said, "Go. It's the quickest way to ensure our investigators here don't have to consider you and this family any further and can focus their energies on finding the guilty party."

Penelope promptly confirmed, "That's the situation in a nutshell."

Frederick had shifted his gaze to Penelope's face. Now, he glanced again at Imogen, who nodded encouragingly, then looked at Stokes. "Very well, Inspector. I'm game."

"Excellent." Barnaby waved toward the front hall. "Best we get this issue cleared up so that we can move on."

~

Barnaby was delegated to wait with Frederick on the pavement outside Chifley's shop while Stokes and Penelope went inside and explained the situation to Chifley and arranged to have Joseph at the counter.

Frederick stood with his back to the window, ostensibly gazing across the street at the leafy expanse of Green Park. Barnaby glanced through the window and saw Chifley nod agreeably to Penelope and Stokes. Raising his hand, Chifley beckoned to someone in the rear, and in less than a minute, Joseph arrived, and Penelope turned and, seeing Barnaby watching, beckoned.

Barnaby tapped Frederick's arm. "Come on. All you need to do is to follow me to the counter and allow the assistant to study your face."

His jaw tightening, Frederick nodded, and Barnaby crossed to the shop door, opened it, and led the way inside.

He walked directly to the counter, and obediently, Frederick trailed him.

Approaching the counter, Barnaby smiled encouragingly at Joseph, who appeared distinctly nervous. Standing beside the younger man, Chifley waited with his hands clasped behind his back and his expression radiating intrigued curiosity.

Barnaby nodded to Chifley, then stepped to the side to stand beside Penelope, leaving Frederick to halt before the counter, directly in front of Joseph.

Stokes, standing by the counter on Frederick's other side, asked Joseph, "Is this gentleman the man who bought a half ounce of strychnine from you last Thursday?"

The pair stared at each other, and very seriously, Joseph ran his gaze over Frederick's figure, then focused on his face. It took only a second before Joseph's expression eased and, turning to Stokes, Joseph confidently declared, "This gentleman is definitely not that man."

A second of silence ensued, then Frederick turned to Stokes. "Is that it?"

Hiding a smile, Stokes nodded. "Yes. Thank you for obliging us. This will allow us to get on faster."

Joseph had been following the exchange, a curious look on his face.

Seeing that, Penelope asked him, "Are you quite sure?"

Joseph smiled and said, "Oh, indeed. I'm doubly sure now that I've heard the gentleman speak. His voice is different." He glanced at Stokes and continued, "While the other man is very like this one in appearance, with even the same accent and manner of speech, the tone of voice is quite distinct. The other man—the one who bought the poison—had a more forceful way of speaking, and his voice was not as deep."

Barnaby smiled. "Thank you, Joseph."

"Indeed," Frederick said. "Thank you, young man, for being so observant. *I* know it wasn't me who came in here and bought poison, but it's helpful to have you confirm that."

A general round of mutual thanks ensued, and several minutes later, Barnaby and Penelope steered Frederick out of the shop. Behind them, Joseph and Chifley were beaming at each other, delighted to have played a part in a real murder investigation.

Stokes hung back. As Barnaby held the door for Penelope and Frederick, he heard Stokes tell Joseph that they might have need of him later to confirm the identity of the gentleman who had, in fact, bought the poison.

Emerging from the shop, on the pavement, Barnaby and Penelope parted from Frederick, who happily settled his hat on his head and strode off toward Hertford Street with his mind, apparently, already full of the decisions that, as the new head of the House of Moran, it fell to him to make.

Stokes came out of the shop in time to catch a glimpse of Frederick before he turned the corner and disappeared into the streets of Mayfair. "Do you think he realized?"

"I don't believe so," Penelope said. "He seemed to have missed the implications of Joseph's observations entirely. Frederick was simply relieved to have been so easily cleared of all suspicion."

Given the blanket of noise cast by passing carriages, it seemed safe enough to take a moment to confer.

"I think," Penelope said, "the fact that the man who bought the poison pretended to be Frederick strongly suggests that the purchase wasn't for any innocent purpose."

"Indeed," Stokes agreed. "And given the stashing of the poison packet in Frederick's old room—presumably to focus our suspicions even more firmly on Frederick—then, clearly, Christopher Fitzhugh moves to the top of our list of suspects responsible for the poisoning. None of the other Fitzhughs looks quite so like Frederick, and Christopher's voice is, indeed, more tenor than baritone."

Barnaby shifted. "Yes, but why the poison? What was Christopher hoping to achieve? What was his motive and why? As long as we have no idea of the answer to those questions, any case you bring against Christopher based solely on Joseph's testimony will end up being a matter of Christopher's word against Joseph's, and we know how that will play out."

Stokes grunted dispiritedly.

"And," Penelope said, frowning, "demonstrating that it was Christopher who bought the poison doesn't get us any closer to identifying who actually killed the earl. If Christopher was behind the plot to poison his older brother, why not just let it play out? As it would have, if, after Christopher had, we presume, put the poison in the empty decanter, someone else hadn't killed the earl, leaving Winslow so shaken that he took a sip of the whiskey." She grimaced. "And no one could have predicted that."

Barnaby stated, "I have no difficulty imagining Christopher as the one behind the poisoning, driven by some motive we've yet to sight, but I can't see him somehow managing to circle behind Gordon and smash in his skull with that bust. For Christopher to be the earl's murderer, he would've had to have been hiding behind the curtains in the study when Gordon entered it, but instead, we have any number of the family swearing Christopher was in the drawing room with them the entire time."

Stokes pulled a face. "Christopher isn't the earl's murderer. But he was planning to murder the earl and, instead, killed Winslow."

After a moment, Stokes met Barnaby's and Penelope's gazes. "We need to get on with our interviews. Who knows? With any luck, Christopher's motive might become clearer."

Barnaby tilted his head. "Christopher's motive or even the motive of whoever did, in fact, kill the earl."

CHAPTER 8

Penelope stood before the glossy black door of Mitchelmore House, a fashionable town house in Charles Street that was the London home of Damien, Lord Mitchelmore, and his wife, Lady Cleome.

Beside her, Stokes tugged the bell chain, and mere seconds later, a youngish yet starchy butler opened the door, attempted to look down his nose at Stokes—rather difficult as Stokes was several inches taller—then the butler noticed Penelope, and at her back, Barnaby, and his expression underwent an almost comical change.

Stokes calmly stated, "Inspector Stokes of Scotland Yard and Mr. and Mrs. Adair."

"Oh. Yes, sir." The butler, looking faintly startled, bowed and stood back. "I was told to expect you."

Clearly, he hadn't quite believed his ears, which were now a trifle flushed.

After closing the door behind them, the butler hurried around to indicate the open door to their left. "If you would wait in the drawing room, I'll fetch her ladyship."

With polite nods, they consented to amble into the drawing room, and the butler went quickly up the stairs.

Penelope looked about her with some interest, then commented, "In contrast to the austerity of Moran House and the relaxed ambiance in Hertford Street, here we have a degree of style executed with a nod to comfort." She indicated the fashionable damask-covered sofa and chairs and the handsome gate-legged Pembroke table set between the long windows. As she sank onto one end of the sofa, she mused, "Now I think of it, most of Moran House was rather lacking in modern comforts."

Barnaby and Stokes looked at her. Neither ventured any opinion.

Footsteps on the tiles presaged the appearance of Lady Cleome. She swept in, a polite smile on her face, then paused as, at her commanding over-the-shoulder wave, the butler closed the door behind her.

Penelope rose. Like most of the Fitzhughs, Lady Cleome had dark-brown hair, which she wore gathered in a bun in the latest style, and blue eyes, in her case fringed by long lashes. She possessed a matronly figure, and having an excellent upright posture, she carried it well. Penelope knew that, normally, Lady Cleome favored gowns in shades of blue, but today, she was garbed in somber black.

However, beyond that adherence to society's expectations of mourning, there seemed little evidence of deep grief. Indeed, of any grief at all.

As she came forward to greet them, Lady Cleome's blue eyes were clear, as was her complexion, and her expression held no hint of sorrow.

"Good afternoon, Inspector. Mr. and Mrs. Adair." Lady Cleome exchanged nods with each of them, then waved to the chairs. "Please sit." She sank into an armchair facing the sofa, leaving its mate for Stokes. "We heard about Winslow dying." She shook her head. "Such a shocking thing." Fixing her rather sharp gaze on Barnaby, she asked, "Was Winslow's death in any way connected with Gordon's?"

Calmly, Barnaby replied, "It's possible there's a link."

"Exactly in what way," Penelope stated, "we cannot yet be certain, but we're here to ask if you are aware of anyone who wished your brother ill."

Lady Cleome took a moment to think, then widened her eyes. "I have to confess that I was not close to Gordon—not at all—and I have really no idea if he had any enemies or any cause for alarm." Cleome met Penelope's gaze squarely. "Gordon wasn't one to encourage others to take an interest in his affairs."

Penelope inclined her head. "We've heard as much from several people."

Responding to a subtle encouraging nod from Stokes, she proceeded to lead Lady Cleome through the events of the previous evening, from the time she arrived with her family at a touch after six o'clock and found everyone else already there to the moment when, seated in the drawing room with the rest of the family, she heard of her brother's murder.

Nothing Cleome said altered the picture they'd built from the testimonies they'd already heard, and disappointingly, she added little by way of extra corroborating detail. Her account suggested her attention had remained very much centered on her own family.

Finally, hoping for something—anything—more, Penelope bluntly asked, "Were you surprised that your brother was murdered?"

Cleome blinked once, twice, then admitted, "No." She looked faintly aghast and shot a nervous look at Penelope. "Isn't that a simply dreadful thing to say?" When Penelope looked interested rather than condemnatory, Cleome went on, "Gordon was always self-centered and hard with it, and over the years, he'd grown increasingly focused on his own consequence. That in pursuing his self-aggrandizing schemes, he might have crossed someone in a way that prompted them to murder him? No." She shook her head. "I can't say that surprises me."

After glancing at Barnaby and Stokes and receiving signs that they had no further questions for Lady Cleome, Penelope rose, bringing Cleome and the men to their feet. "Thank you for speaking with us. We would like to speak with his lordship as well."

With her customary brisk efficiency, Cleome said, "I'll send him in." With gracious nods to them all, she departed and closed the door behind her.

They resumed their seats, and Stokes observed, "That added little to our knowledge."

"Perhaps," Penelope returned. "But I find it telling that a lady so blinkered—so ruthlessly focused on her own family's affairs—had actually noticed that her brother had 'self-aggrandizing schemes.' That suggests that his pursuit of them impacted the entire family."

Barnaby arched his brows. "Because if that wasn't so, Cleome wouldn't have noticed?"

"Precisely."

The door opened, and Damien, Lord Mitchelmore, walked in. His gaze found Barnaby, Penelope, and Stokes as they rose to their feet, and he nodded amiably, then closed the door and walked to where they waited.

"Good afternoon." Mitchelmore was a dapper gentleman in his mid-fifties. With still-black hair and steely-blue eyes, he had pleasant features and a firm jaw, and his tall, upright figure belied his age, while his movements displayed more youthful vigor than customary among his peers.

All in all, he was a personable gentleman, and his manners were excellent. He half bowed over Penelope's fingers and shook hands with Barnaby and Stokes, then gestured that they should resume their seats while he claimed the armchair his wife had vacated.

As soon as they'd settled, Barnaby opened proceedings by asking, "Do you know of anyone who might have wished your brother-in-law ill?"

Mitchelmore frowned slightly. "Gordon and I weren't in any way close, and indeed, I spend much of the year on my estate in Somerset."

His gaze on Mitchelmore's face, Barnaby tilted his head. "Many would have thought that, as a fellow large landholder, you and the earl might have had interests in common."

Readily, Mitchelmore replied, "So one might think, but in this case, that wasn't the reality." He paused, then went on, "The truth was that Gordon and I barely crossed paths other than during family gatherings and, very occasionally, at our clubs. Quite frankly, I was and remain rather surprised by how little we had in common. As you say, that's contrary to what anyone would suppose."

Watching Mitchelmore closely, Barnaby asked, "What was your opinion of the earl?"

His gaze steady on Barnaby's face, Mitchelmore hesitated, plainly considering his reply, then offered, "He was very one-eyed about how things should be, and that was especially so with money." Mitchelmore frowned. "You could almost say he was obsessed with..." Faintly, he grimaced. "I can't say 'hoarding it,' but there was a sense of that, nonetheless."

"Tightfisted?" Barnaby suggested.

"Oh yes." Mitchelmore nodded. "But he was that way with everyone. It seemed to be his nature rather than an adopted policy."

Penelope ventured, "Would it surprise you to learn that your sons—both of them—along with all their male cousins have been pilfering small amounts of cash from the earl's study for months if not longer?"

"Have they?" His brows rising, Mitchelmore's lips twitched. "How very enterprising of them." He met Penelope's gaze. "But as for surprising me, no, I can't say it does. Gordon was just as tightfisted toward them as to everyone else, even toward William, who, as matters stand, will eventually accede to the title. William might not be the heir apparent at this time, but he will be, and yet Gordon showed no interest in him or his education. Not at any time. As for the others, as far as Gordon was concerned, they might as well not have existed."

An instant's silence fell, which Barnaby broke. "Thank you for your frankness. You won't be surprised to hear that your view of the late earl tallies with the opinions of others, but every fresh perspective adds to our image of the man and increases our understanding of him and, thus, informs our view of those he might have inspired to murder him."

Pushing to his feet, Mitchelmore snorted. "You won't find any shortage of potential suspects. The little I've heard of Gordon's political activities—not from him but from others—suggests he was not much liked, even by those of the same political persuasion, and he was positively detested by those in the organizations at which he took particular aim."

"Like the workers' associations?" Along with Barnaby and Penelope, Stokes had risen to his feet.

Michelmore nodded. "Yes." He paused, thought, then conceded, "While it's comforting to imagine some rough character was responsible for killing Gordon, the fact that Winslow was poisoned by accident, which, I assume, means the true target was Gordon, suggests a very different murderer."

Reflecting that there was nothing wrong with Mitchelmore's powers of deduction, Barnaby dipped his head. "Indeed. Thank you for your time." He waved Mitchelmore to the door and fell into step beside him. "We need to speak with your children—purely routine—simply to check their recollections of the gathering yesterday evening."

Mitchelmore halted and, glancing back at Penelope and Stokes, explained, "The only one of our children still living under this roof is our younger daughter, Geraldine. Lizbet is now Lady Brompton and can be found, no doubt, at Brompton House, and Byron and Hugh have lodgings in Duke Street."

Penelope exchanged a glance with Stokes, then said, "It might not be necessary to speak with your older children. Geraldine might well be able to tell us all we need to know."

Michelmore dipped his head to Penelope and Stokes. "I'll send Geraldine in now."

After exchanging a nod with Barnaby, Mitchelmore opened the door and left.

No more than two minutes later, a light rap on the open door had them rising to greet Geraldine Mitchelmore.

A pleasant-faced young lady, with her father's black hair and blue eyes more like his than her mother's, Geraldine was unfashionably tall and a touch mannish in build. She was also widely held to be bookish, and her mother, Cleome, was known for dressing Geraldine in a particular shade of petunia in an attempt to catch gentlemen's eyes.

Of course, today, Geraldine was gowned in somber black, and given her very pale skin and glossy black hair, the contrast was quite striking.

Penelope smiled encouragingly and gestured to the girl to join them. She suspected that Geraldine would prove to be an observer of other people, a hope bolstered by the way the girl readily glided forward, studying them as she came.

"Good afternoon." Penelope directed Geraldine to the armchair opposite, and after exchanging polite nods with Barnaby and Stokes, Geraldine sank onto the cushions.

Resettling on the sofa, Penelope observed, "It seems quite unfair that your uncle's death will put an end to your come-outs. Yours, Diana's, and Tilly's."

Geraldine lightly grimaced and nodded, then, with a faint smile, met Penelope's eyes. "To be perfectly candid, Mrs. Adair, while our mamas are no doubt dismayed at the disruption and delay, I'm not at all perturbed by the enforced hiatus, and I daresay neither are Tilly or Diana."

Curious, for it was patently clear Geraldine was, indeed, speaking truthfully, Penelope cocked her head. "Why so?"

"We are, one might say, half out," Geraldine said, "and given what we've seen thus far of the ton and the Marriage Mart, we really would prefer to have another year to look over the field, as it were, without the pressure of being officially out and, therefore, searching for a husband."

"Ah." Penelope smiled. "I hadn't thought of that, but I take your point." She did, and her assessment of Geraldine's intelligence rose several notches.

Before Penelope could pose any questions, Geraldine's expression clouded and, her attitude respectful and sincere, she offered, "I was deeply sorry to hear of Winslow's passing."

Penelope waited, but Geraldine made no comment regarding her uncle's demise.

Consequently, Penelope grasped the opportunity to elicit Geraldine's view of the earl, which, unsurprisingly, mirrored that of all the others in the family with whom they'd spoken.

"He was aloof and distant," Geraldine stated. "Always. I can't ever remember him freely interacting with us—the younger lot—or even with our parents. At family gatherings, he was there, much like a column might be. Not something anyone made an impression on nor something that contributed to the party."

She paused, then met Penelope's gaze. "I know Grandmama—the dowager—felt it, Uncle Gordon's distance from the rest of us, quite keenly. You could see it in the way her lips pinched whenever he said something dismissive about one of us. And he did that regularly."

"I see." Penelope was intrigued by the insight. "Now, one thing we need to check is the movement of your siblings during the evening. As they're no longer living here, we were hoping you could help us establish their movements." She met Geraldine's blue gaze. "Let's start with your sister, Lizbet."

Geraldine readily supplied, "Lizbet came here earlier in the evening and went with Mama, Papa, and me in our carriage to Moran House. Brompton was otherwise engaged."

Penelope questioned, and Geraldine confirmed that Lizbet did not leave the company at any point and that she departed Moran House with Geraldine and their parents and returned to Charles Street in the Mitchelmore carriage.

"As for Byron and Hugh," Geraldine volunteered, "they were already in the drawing room when I walked in with Mama, Papa, and Lizbet." Geraldine frowned slightly, plainly trawling through her memories, then her chin firmed, and she nodded. "And I'm sure neither Byron nor Hugh left the company at any point." She confided to Penelope, "They're both very fond of Grandmama, and they tend to hover beside her to help with anything she needs. I can't *absolutely* swear that neither slipped out for perhaps a minute, but I honestly don't think either did. Every time I glanced toward Grandmama, they were beside her, as usual. I would have noticed if they weren't."

Penelope could think of nothing else to ask. She glanced at Barnaby and Stokes, and when both shook their heads slightly, she returned her gaze to Geraldine, smiled, and rose. "Thank you. We have no further questions, and in light of your recollections, I doubt we'll have to hunt down your brothers and sister."

Geraldine smiled and curtsied, and Penelope waved her to the door, then fell in beside her.

Barnaby and Stokes followed.

They emerged into the front hall to find Lady Cleome waiting, and after confirming that there was no one else they needed to speak with at Mitchelmore House, Penelope assured her ladyship that it was unlikely they would need to speak with the family again, and they took their leave.

On the pavement, Stokes halted and fixed Barnaby with a questioning look. "I know what we just told her ladyship, but should we confirm Byron's and Hugh's movements with the lads themselves?"

Penelope frowned. "I vote no." She met Stokes's and Barnaby's gazes. "I trust Geraldine's insights, and we have others to speak with who are more likely to have observed something relevant."

Barnaby huffed. "Byron and Hugh sound like typical young gentlemen who spent the evening playing doting grandsons for their grandmother's benefit." He smiled ruefully at Stokes. "I seriously doubt either one paid any attention to anyone else. I would be very surprised if they had anything useful to tell us."

Stokes nodded. "You've convinced me." He looked at Penelope. "So who's next?"

"The household of Viscount Southerly," she replied. "And Southerly House is in Mount Street."

She waved at their waiting carriage and led the way.

~

As they climbed the steps of Southerly House, Penelope assumed that they would find a household much like the others they'd visited that day—fashionable, in some degree of respectable mourning, yet not really touched by the murder of the Earl of Moran.

Barnaby tugged the bell chain, and they waited.

And waited.

Frowning, Barnaby was reaching for the chain to tug it again when the door was flung wide, and without even looking at them, a panicked butler declared, "The family is not receiving!"

He started to shut the door, but Stokes stepped forward and leaned his shoulder against the panel, holding the door open.

The butler blinked at Stokes, who informed him, "I am Inspector Stokes of Scotland Yard, and these"—he tipped his head toward Penelope and Barnaby, and finally, the butler followed his gaze—"are Mr. and Mrs. Adair, who are assisting in the investigation into the murder of the Earl of Moran. Whatever's going on, I'm certain that the family is definitely at home to us."

For an instant, the butler stared at Penelope and Barnaby, then he blinked and, stiffly, stood aside. "Yes, of course. The master mentioned…" Still looking decidedly harassed, he cleared his throat and bowed them in.

Immensely curious, Penelope followed Stokes over the threshold.

His gaze downcast, the butler closed the door behind Barnaby, then waved them to the open drawing room doorway. "If you would take a seat, I'll inform the master…although I really don't know if he or the mistress will consent to come downstairs just now."

"Good Lord, man!" Barnaby rapped out in a tone that had the butler drawing himself up. "What is going on?"

In a more normal voice, the butler replied, "It's Master Theo, sir. He's fallen quite dreadfully ill, and the doctor has just arrived…" The butler looked hopeful. "Are you sure you wouldn't rather call back at a later time?"

"Quite sure," Penelope replied. "Please tell your master and mistress that we are here and wish to speak with them as soon as they are able to see us."

"The doctor, too," Stokes ordered. "He's not to leave the house before speaking with us."

Although transparently uncertain over the likely outcome, the butler nodded and hurried up the stairs, leaving them to find their own way into the drawing room.

Shaking her head, Penelope led the way. "How very odd." She dropped onto the sofa and looked at Stokes. "How old is Theodore?"

Stokes pulled out his notebook and consulted the pages. "Fourteen. He's the younger of Southerly's sons. The older one, Vincent, is fifteen."

Considering that, Penelope tipped her head. "I suppose it's possible that it was just a piece of bad meat."

"Except," Barnaby said, sitting elegantly beside her, "that it seems no one else in the family has fallen ill."

"Also of note," Stokes said, reading from his jottings, "is that Imogen Fitzhugh told us that when she and her family first arrived in the Moran House drawing room, Vincent and Theodore were absent. The rest of the Southerly family were in the room, but Vincent and Theodore didn't come in until about fifteen minutes later, sometime after the earl had joined the company."

"And don't forget," Barnaby said, "that George Fitzhugh told us that Vincent and Theodore were also involved in the cousins' occasional pilfering from the earl."

Penelope was frowning. "Theodore can't have poisoned himself with the whiskey, not if the poison was only mixed with the liquor when Winslow filled the empty decanter."

"More to the point," Barnaby said, "if he had, he would most likely have died before leaving Moran House." He met Stokes's gaze. "Judging by the time the poison took to affect Winslow, it's difficult to see how Theodore falling ill could be linked to the strychnine."

Stokes grimaced and nodded.

After a moment, he sat, and with eyes trained on the open doorway, they waited impatiently for someone to come.

Eventually, they heard brisk footsteps come down the stairs, and an instant later, an exasperated-looking gentleman, clad in a dark suit and carrying a medical man's black bag, walked into the room.

The man's sharp gaze focused on them, and as Stokes rose, the man raised his thick, bushy eyebrows. "Inspector Stokes?"

Stokes nodded and introduced Barnaby and Penelope, who had also got to their feet.

Politely, the man bowed, then stated, "I'm Dr. Gilroy, the Southerlys' family physician. I was called in to treat young Theodore."

"In your opinion," Barnaby said, "what is the cause of Theodore's sudden illness?"

Gilroy primmed his lips, then replied, "He's denying any link, but I've been told there was a case of strychnine poisoning at a house the family visited for dinner last evening." Gilroy eyed Barnaby shrewdly. "I know nothing of the circumstances and cannot account for the time difference—the lag in the time since Theodore was there and the onset of his symptoms, which apparently came on midmorning today—but to my mind and, I would think, in the opinion of any experienced medical man who examined Theodore, he is suffering from a mercifully slight exposure to the same poison. Indeed, in my view, he's deuced lucky to be alive."

"So," Barnaby said, "somehow, Theodore ingested strychnine."

Gilroy nodded. "So it seems." He looked at Stokes, who was busily jotting. "These days, my colleagues and I see enough cases of accidental strychnine poisoning through people mishandling rat poison or bait powder that we can be quite sure about the signs."

Stokes inclined his head and continued writing.

"Will Theodore recover?" Penelope asked.

"Oh yes. As I said, the exposure was mercifully slight. He's going to feel very sorry for himself for quite a few days, but I imagine the resilience of youth will kick in, and by next week, he'll be feeling much more the thing."

"Thank you, Doctor." Stokes looked at Gilroy. "Is there anything more you can tell us?"

Gilroy thought, then said, "I don't believe so. However, the viscount asked me to tell you that he would be down momentarily."

Barnaby and Penelope added their thanks to Stokes's, and Gilroy departed.

The front door had only just closed behind the doctor when they heard measured footsteps descending the stairs, then Viscount Southerly appeared.

A minor nobleman who could accurately be described as neat and conservative, and not just in his dress, Southerly was of average height, with an oval face and somewhat severe features. His brown hair was cut short, and while his hazel eyes appeared tired, his gaze remained sharp.

Barnaby had heard Southerly described as a careful man of sterling character. His manner was agreeable, quietly congenial, and he was not in any way in need of funds.

At present, Southerly's features were set in lines that denoted deep concern.

"Mr. and Mrs. Adair." Southerly half bowed to Penelope, then nodded to Barnaby and Stokes. "Inspector Stokes." He gestured at them to resume their seats, and he moved to claim an armchair facing the sofa, angled to the one Stokes occupied. Southerly leaned back with a small, half-suppressed sigh. "I take it Gilroy filled you in on Theo's sudden illness?"

Barnaby responded, "Gilroy believes it to be a survivable case of strychnine poisoning. Given Winslow's recent death from the same poison, it's difficult not to imagine a link."

"Indeed." Gravely, Southerly inclined his head. "However, to this point, Theo is maintaining that he only ate and drank what everyone else did while at Moran House." Southerly paused, then went on, "Other than that Winslow died in the early hours from a dose of strychnine, we have heard no further details." Southerly glanced at Stokes. "Do you know how he came to be poisoned?"

"We believe," Barnaby replied, "that the poison was in the whiskey decanter in the earl's study. It appears that Winslow helped himself to a small tot just before retiring. However, prior to the earl being found murdered, the decanter had been emptied, and Winslow was in the cellar, refilling the decanter, when the earl was killed."

"We've yet to ascertain exactly how the poison was introduced into the decanter and by whom," Stokes added. "Nevertheless, it appears that the decanter was the source of the poison that killed Winslow."

"I think," Barnaby said, "that we must assume that the poison was placed into the emptied decanter at some point during the day."

"Consequently, earlier in the evening," Penelope extrapolated, "the decanter would most likely have appeared to be empty."

Openly perplexed, Southerly shook his head. "I can't imagine how Theo came into contact with the stuff." He met Barnaby's eyes. "I'm aware that he and Vincent vanished from our sight for several minutes when we first arrived at Moran House. They say they went to the back of the house to see if they could find that lad—Julian, Mrs. Alder's son. They know him quite well, but they say they didn't find him and returned to the drawing room. After that, they remained with the company throughout the rest of the evening."

Southerly raised his hands, palms up. "How Theo managed to dose himself with the poison, and the doctor says that happened today, not last night, I simply cannot fathom."

Barnaby looked at Stokes, then at Penelope, but none of them had any viable suggestion.

After exchanging a glance with Stokes, Penelope ventured, "Setting aside the matter of Theodore's poisoning and turning to the murder of the earl, were you aware of anyone who wished him ill?"

"No," Southerly replied. "But Moran was a very private man and kept himself quite apart from the family. He had his own interests, both political and in business investments, and did not share any of that with anyone." He paused, then added, "I'm not sure he even had any close friends to whom I might direct you."

Penelope said, "We've spoken with others of the family, and without exception, everyone has commented on the late earl's…well, frugality." She met Southerly's gaze. "Do you have a similar view?"

Southerly's features hardened. "Yes, although I would label Gordon's attitude as simple stinginess. He was positively miserly toward everyone except himself. Even Victoria, who, in large part, he saw as an extension of himself, he kept on a ridiculously tight budget. Frankly, I didn't approve." He met Barnaby's gaze. "As far as I'm aware, there was no financial reason for Gordon's peculiar habits. More, as the years have rolled on, those habits only became more deeply entrenched and ingrained."

His gaze sharpening, Barnaby asked, "Do you have any insights at all into Moran's business dealings?"

Southerly waggled his head. "Only in the most general sense. I know he dabbled—increasingly, I suspect—in highly questionable schemes. Extremely risky endeavors, at the very least. I quickly grew wary of his continuing involvement in such ventures, and as I so strongly disapproved of his uncaring attitude to family members' financial situations, I long ago determined to exercise due prudence and keep my family as separate as possible from what went on at Moran House."

He paused, then amended, "Naturally, that distance didn't apply to the dowager. I've always found her to be clear-headed and sensible about all matters to do with her social position and her family."

Stokes had been scribbling in his notebook. He glanced at Southerly. "So, generally speaking, you avoided the earl but were happy to interact with the dowager."

Southerly inclined his head.

The patter of heels on the hall tiles heralded Constance. Gowned in black, with her features drawn and tendrils of brown hair escaping to form a corona around her head, she hurried in, looking flustered and harried.

She waved at the men to remain seated and claimed the empty armchair beside her spouse. "You will have to excuse my state. Such a panic we've had! But it does seem that Theo is on the mend." She caught an inquiring look from Southerly and, lips setting, shook her head. "That said, Theo is still being closemouthed. There's obviously something he's refusing to tell us that would account for him being poisoned, but I simply can't imagine what it might be." She laid a hand on Southerly's arm and met his gaze, then looked at Penelope. "I left Vincent with Theo in the hope that Vincent, who is a year older and a touch more mature, might convince Theo to make a clean breast of whatever it is."

Penelope nodded approvingly. "Let's give Vincent a few minutes to see if he can accomplish that task. Meanwhile, if you would answer a few questions?"

"Yes, of course." Constance sat straighter. "Ask away."

Penelope realized that the moment was propitious; because of her distraction with her sick son, Constance's normally astute social screens were well and truly scattered. "To begin with, can you outline what you saw when you first walked into the Moran House drawing room yesterday evening?"

Constance readily replied, and when Penelope led her through the subsequent events to the time of the earl's murder, Constance's answers matched those of all the other adults.

On reaching the end of her recitation, without further prompting, Constance raised her chin and declared, "I have never approved of Gordon's ways and am thoroughly grateful not to have to live beneath his roof." She paused, then amended, "Or what used to be his roof. He was always a parsimonious soul, but with the years, he's grown decidedly worse. I know Mama had words with him on the subject, but he was never one to listen to anyone else, let alone a female, even his own mother."

Penelope felt her brows rise.

Has anyone else mentioned that?

After glancing at Barnaby, she returned her gaze to Constance. "Do you have any notion of who might have killed your brother, either in the way it was actually done or via the attempt we assume was directed toward him by poisoning his whiskey?"

Baldly, Constance replied, "I have absolutely no idea who wished him dead. And I certainly have no inkling about how the poison got into his whiskey." She sighed, and her face fell. "I'm really quite broken up over old Winslow dying, especially if it was by accident and the intended victim was Gordon. That seems doubly cruel, coming on top of Gordon's death. Poor Mama will feel Winslow's loss keenly—beneath the starch and his prissy exterior, he was a kindly soul."

For a moment, Constance remained sunk in gloom, then appeared to shake off her megrim. "But returning to Gordon's death, while I might have no idea who killed him, I can't say I'm surprised that someone did—that Gordon incited someone to the point of murder."

Penelope noticed that Southerly was nodding.

Constance continued, "He was stubborn and could be quite aggressive and stone-cold hard when he felt like it." She paused, then, eying Barnaby and Penelope, went on, "Gordon maintained a polished exterior, one commensurate with being the Earl of Moran, and he was always careful to keep up appearances, as they say. But inside, he cared for nothing and no one but himself, or so it seemed."

Constance cocked her head as if reviewing her last statement, then amended, "Himself or whatever it was he was always working on." Frowning, she said, "There seemed to be some sort of private project he was intent on pursuing, but I've no idea what it was."

"Private project?" Barnaby said. "You're the first to mention that. What led you to think he was working on some project?"

Constance lightly shrugged. "That's just my interpretation of a few remarks I overheard him making to Victoria and Mama. Gordon seemed to have some purpose to which he was devoting himself—all of himself—but I never heard him or anyone else mention exactly what that was. I don't believe it was political in nature—it seemed more personal than that."

All in the group paused to ponder the point.

Eventually, Penelope said, "In the interests of all our schedules, can you tell us where your daughters were during the visit to Moran House?"

Blithely, Constance replied, "Diana, Geraldine, and Tilly had their heads together the whole time, and Ella and Lydia—they're the same age—also spent the hours talking nonstop to each other, as they usually do. Josephine and Martha, Imogen's other two, were talking mostly to themselves and also to Vincent and Theo, who are much of an age. As far as we know"—Constance glanced at Southerly—"the children remained with the company throughout."

Southerly nodded. "After Vincent and Theo joined the company in the drawing room, as I mentioned earlier."

Constance's lips tightened. "If Theo was poisoned by strychnine, perhaps the same poison that, sadly, did for old Winslow, I can't imagine how Theo came into contact with it."

A tap on the door frame had them all turning to see Vincent, looking distinctly green about the gills, gingerly holding something wrapped in a sheet of rough paper.

Southerly beckoned his elder son and heir to join them. "Vincent—come in. I daresay"—Southerly threw a questioning glance at Stokes—"that the investigators would like to speak with you as well."

Stokes nodded. "We would."

Her gaze fixed on the package Vincent was holding so cautiously, Penelope asked, "What do you have there?"

Reluctance all but poured from Vincent; he came forward as if having to force himself to take each step. On reaching the grouping of chairs, he looked around the faces, then focused on his mother and said, "I—we—think this is how Theo was poisoned."

Vincent held out the package and released the top of the paper. It unfolded, revealing two fat cigars, one pristine, the other slightly burnt at one end.

The adults all stared.

Vincent swallowed and stated, "We took them from the box in Uncle Gordon's study yesterday. Before we joined everyone else in the drawing room."

"What?" Southerly looked shocked and pained.

Eyes round, Constance confirmed, "This was when we first arrived and you two vanished?" Her color rising, Constance accused, "You said you went to look for Julian."

Vincent hung his head and mumbled, "Yes. Then." He tilted his head. "Or close to then." Tentatively, he raised his gaze and, avoiding looking at his parents, focused on Barnaby. "We thought Uncle Gordon would either come out of his study or come down the stairs and go to join everyone in the drawing room, and he did. He came down the stairs and went straight to the drawing room. He didn't see us watching from the other corridor."

Sternly, his expression severe, Southerly said, "So you slipped into the study and stole those?"

Vincent swallowed again and admitted, "We knew it was wrong, but…well, they're just two cigars out of a whole box. The chances were that Uncle Gordon wouldn't even notice they'd been taken."

"From talking to your male cousins," Barnaby said, "we've learned that all six of you have been filching small things—a bit of cash left lying about, this and that—from your uncle for years."

Vigorously, Vincent nodded. "Yes. Exactly." He glanced sideways at his father. "It wasn't just me and Theo. It was all of us."

Plainly mystified, Southerly asked, "Why?"

Vincent met his father's gaze, then shrugged. "It was because he was always so stiff with us—so stingy. And I don't mean just with money. He barely acknowledged we were alive. And in the same fashion, he never seemed to notice the little things we took. Or if he did, he didn't really care. He just liked being mean and tight and nasty to all of us. At least, that's how we all saw it."

Vincent glanced down at the two cigars resting on the paper supported by his palms. "So anyway, yesterday evening, there wasn't anything else about to take, so Theo and I each took a cigar and hid them in our pockets."

Gently, Penelope asked, "When you were in the study, did you notice if the whiskey decanter was empty?"

Vincent frowned and nodded. "Yes. It was." He looked even more uncomfortable, but bravely admitted, "We sometimes took a sip, but last evening, it was empty. Completely empty. I remember thinking that Winslow had fallen down on the job, and Uncle Gordon wouldn't like that."

Breaking the ensuing silence, Stokes asked, "Why do you think those cigars are the source of the poison affecting your brother?"

Vincent straightened. "Because this morning, Theo decided to light his, but he took one puff and choked. I took it off him and stubbed it out, and he said it tasted horrible—ghastly. And then he said he was feeling woozy, and I could see he was struggling to breathe, and then he just collapsed!"

It was obvious that witnessing that moment and the subsequent trauma had deeply frightened and shaken Vincent.

Barnaby rose and crossed to carefully take the cigars from Vincent. After wrapping them safely within the sheet of paper, Barnaby caught Vincent's eyes. "Thank you for having the courage to come down, tell us the whole, and hand these over. We'll have them tested, but I suspect you're right. These have been poisoned as well."

"You implied that there were more cigars than just those two," Stokes said.

Vincent nodded. "The box was more than half full."

Stokes looked at Barnaby. "We need to send word to Moran House immediately."

Penelope added, "We don't want any more inadvertent deaths."

To Southerly and Constance, Stokes explained, "My men are still there. They'll secure the rest of the cigars so no one else can be accidentally poisoned."

"You can use one of our footmen." Southerly rose and made for the bellpull.

Within minutes, a footman was dispatched to Moran House, carrying a message from Stokes directing O'Donnell to seize the box of cigars from the earl's study—carefully—and take the box and its contents to Findlay for testing.

Penelope, Barnaby, and Stokes took their leave of Constance and Southerly. On the way to the door, Penelope paused beside Vincent, who was standing back, head bowed, hands clasped before him, trying to make himself as inconspicuous as possible. She laid a hand on his sleeve, and when his head came up, she met his eyes. "Trust me. In such situations, no matter how difficult, telling the truth is always the course of wisdom."

Vincent held her gaze for an instant, then nodded and looked down.

Penelope joined Barnaby and Stokes, and they quit the drawing room and the house.

On the pavement, Stokes halted and took the packet containing the cigars from Barnaby. "I'll get these to Findlay and ensure he tests them immediately."

Penelope said, "After that, I suggest you join us in Albemarle Street."

Barnaby met her eyes, then looked at Stokes. "It's too late in the day to do much else, and we could use an hour to review what we know and decide what questions remain most urgent for us to address."

Stokes nodded his agreement and strode off to hail a hackney, while Penelope linked her arm with Barnaby's, and they headed for their carriage.

CHAPTER 9

Once again, Curtis found himself sitting alongside Mary Alder in the drawing room of the Adairs' Albemarle Street home and watching Julian, who was peering out of the window, scanning the street.

Surreptitiously, Curtis glanced sidelong at the woman beside him. Although assured that she was no longer considered a suspect in the earl's murder, Mary Alder still seemed tense, as if that reprieve could, at any time, be rescinded.

Knowing all he did of the capriciousness of the so-called justice system, Curtis reflected that he couldn't blame her.

He could, however, reassure her. Choosing his words, in a matter-of-fact tone, he ventured, "I expect Stokes and the Adairs will have made some headway by now. I'm keen to hear what they've found so we can see where the information Julian and I turned up fits into the picture."

Mary—he'd decided, circumstances being what they were, that he could think of her by her given name—turned to smile tentatively at him. "Thank you for keeping Julian busy—for making him feel he's actually contributing to the investigation." She glanced fondly at her son, then her expression sobered. "It certainly seems a complicated affair, what with the earl's involvement in business as well as politics."

"Truth to tell, he seems an odd fish all around," Curtis said.

When Mary merely nodded and went back to staring at Julian, Curtis doggedly hunted for another tack. Eventually, he fell back on asking, "How are you finding living here? In this house?"

Happiness returned to Mary's face, and he felt thoroughly vindicated.

"I don't think," she confided, "that we could have found a better, more agreeable temporary place. The house and household are comfortable in all respects, and the staff seem very accustomed to adjusting to the unexpected."

Curtis grinned. "I can imagine that the staff here have learned to take all in their stride."

"Indeed." Mary paused, then went on, "Julian and I are very grateful to the Adairs for this chance to catch our breaths, as it were. And I've actually been enjoying myself, helping with Oliver and Pip—they're such an engaging pair."

"Don't forget the hound, Roger," Curtis warned.

Mary laughed, and his heart skipped a beat.

"I would never be allowed to forget Roger," she agreed. "He's constantly around the boys, and it's lovely to see how they play with him." Her gaze went to Julian. "We've never been able to have a pet, so growing up, Julian missed that."

"He's managed, regardless," Curtis said. "He's a fine lad. You did well with him."

Her gaze on Julian, Mary's smile held a wealth of maternal affection. "I count myself lucky—he was always easy to teach. But, of course, it's now been years since I've had to deal with small boys. I'd forgotten what they're like at that age, but I've discovered that I haven't forgotten the tricks to managing them."

"I imagine, as curious as Julian is, he would have been a handful."

"He was." Pride and fondness colored Mary's tone.

After a moment, her voice quieter, her gaze still on Julian, she went on, "His father spent most of his life at sea, so having Julian with me was a blessing. Without him, I would have been entirely alone."

Her tone clearly stated that being alone wasn't a state she liked.

Curtis hesitated, then, reasoning that she'd told him something of her past, he offered, "I know all about being alone." He, too, looked across at Julian; it was easier to speak of matters like this that way. "My mother was a washerwoman in Hackney. She was alone, too, before I came, and she tried her level best to do everything she could for me. Until the day she died, she was my most stalwart supporter. Now that she's gone, even though I've gathered a good crew in the business and they're around me every day, I live alone, and yes, I feel it." He paused, then, his voice even lower, added, "As if there's something missing."

Glancing at Mary, he saw that she was regarding him with sympathy in her eyes.

"Not that I can complain," he hurried to assure her. "I've done well over the years, and now, I have a house in Red Lion Square." He paused, then confided, "Truth to tell, I bought the place, which is nice enough, because it seemed the sort of thing a man with a sound business should have. But I'm there, with Mrs. McGinnis, my cook-housekeeper, and Jilly, the maid who comes in, yet sometimes, I feel even more alone than I did when I was on my own in lodgings."

Mary nodded. "Oh, I know how that—a change in circumstances—can make one feel. It's a bit like losing your moorings, and you drift for a while before new connections form. That was one of the things I appreciated about my position with the dowager. The staff—both the smaller group when we lived in Regent's Square and the larger household at Moran House—were very settled, and they behaved more like a family of sorts." She gestured at the house around them. "And the staff here are the same. There's comfort in having others about who you know will support you, even if they're not related."

Curtis nodded understandingly. "It's odd, because you think you'll get used to it—to being alone—but the older I get, the more I find that living all alone, while making life easier in that you don't have to consider anyone else, leaves me with the definite feeling that, somehow, life lacks meaning."

Mary inclined her head. "That is so very true." After a moment, she went on, "I can't imagine how the staff at Moran House must be feeling, now that Winslow is gone. It has to have been a huge shock."

"Aye," Curtis said. "It would have been that. Especially as it seems likely that Winslow dying was pure accident, and it was the earl who was the real target. Seems he had his share of enemies."

"It does," Mary agreed.

Julian stiffened, then whirled from the window. His expression animated, he declared, "They're here!"

Mary grinned and patted the sofa on her other side. "Come and join us, and let's see if the Adairs and the inspector have any advances they're willing to share."

They heard the front door open and Mostyn's brisk steps as he crossed the front hall, followed by the sounds of Barnaby's voice and Penelope's lighter tones.

Julian came to stand impatiently beside Mary and Curtis as they got to their feet.

Penelope swept in, closely followed by a strolling Barnaby.

On seeing them waiting, Penelope's eyes gleamed. "Excellent! You're all here. We need to tell you what we've learned and see what you can add."

As she subsided onto the sofa facing Mary and Curtis, Penelope noted that the pair seemed increasingly comfortable with each other.

Fingers crossed. Unfortunately, they're both too mature and independent to be prodded.

She didn't like relying on propinquity to achieve her matchmaking aims, but in this case, she had to sit back and allow matters to progress as they would and at their own pace.

Drat.

As Barnaby joined her on the sofa, she regarded the three sitting opposite. "Just to be clear, we're all in this together. Finding out who killed the earl is a joint endeavor, so please don't hesitate to speak up if you think of anything pertinent or find anything we report strange or unexpected."

Ruefully, Mary said, "I have to admit I'm still rather reeling after hearing of Winslow's death."

Barnaby responded, "I think almost everyone is. No one imagined anyone else in the household was at risk, so we've all been jolted by the unexpectedness of the poor man's passing."

From beside his mother, Julian piped, "He was all right, was old Winslow. A bit of a stick in the mud, but everyone in the place got on with him."

His gaze on Julian and Mary, Barnaby asked, "Had there been any disagreements involving Winslow downstairs?"

Julian and Mary shook their heads. Mary elaborated, "In general, the household ran very smoothly. Winslow and Mrs. Pratchett saw to that. In our year at Moran House, there were no dramas, at least not downstairs, and even over the years we lived with the dowager in Regent's Square, we would have got wind of any wranglings when we visited, which was often enough, yet I never heard of any ructions among the staff."

She looked at Julian, and he nodded. "Never heard of any problems. Everything ran as smooth as silk."

Mostyn came in, carrying a salver which he proffered to Barnaby. "Two notes. Both arrived together just now at the back door."

Barnaby picked up the missives and studied their faces. "One's from Montague, and the other's from Thomas."

The doorbell pealed, and Mostyn hurried out into the hall. A second later, Stokes strode in, his expression rather grim.

Stokes nodded to Mary and Julian. "I'm glad you've joined us. We could use your insights into the household." He shifted his gaze to Curtis and nodded. "Curtis. I hope you have something for us, because the pressure for an early arrest is ratcheting ever higher."

"You were quick," Penelope observed.

Stokes slumped into the armchair he usually chose. "I escaped as quickly as I could. Nevertheless, the Commissioner managed to buttonhole me. I think he was lying in wait. Apparently, he's been fielding pointed questions from all levels of government and Parliament and, now, the newspaper editors. According to the Commissioner, the newspapers are currently of most concern."

Shifting his gaze to Barnaby, Stokes went on, "It seems your father and the other governors have gone in to bat for us. They're attempting to fend off the loudest voices and give us some breathing space to find the earl's killer."

Barnaby brandished the notes. "These just arrived from Montague and Thomas. I was about to see what they've found."

Stokes gestured for Barnaby to get on with it.

Smiling, Barnaby broke the seal of the first missive, spread the single sheet, and read, "Montague states that he does not have detailed knowledge of the earl's financial affairs, but he knows the earl's man of business and will speak with him tomorrow. Montague's understanding is that the earl and the earldom are in sound and solid financial health. However, he's not so sure about the minor branches of the family. He has heard that Frederick Fitzhugh is strapped for funds, and there have been rumors regarding Christopher Fitzhugh as well. And a connection—Lord Mitchelmore—is currently attempting to buy out several co-owners of a factory in Leeds and is known to be seeking funds. The younger Fitzhughs are also not free of financial woes. However, at this point, all the above is merely scuttlebutt, and Montague cannot say how serious any of the gentlemen's difficulties are. He's spoken with Thomas, and between them, they will endeavor to answer that question over the next day."

Barnaby set aside that letter and opened the second one. He spread the sheet, read, and reported, "Thomas confirms all Montague has written and adds that initial inquiries have suggested that, financially speaking, both Frederick and Christopher are sailing very close to the wind. Whether either is in danger of capsizing, Thomas cannot yet say, but he notes the possibility is there. About the earl, however, Thomas can confirm that, over the last decades, more or less since succeeding to the title, the earl has been investing in what Thomas labels 'high-risk ventures.' That said, overall, Thomas judges that the earl has been surprisingly successful, and he appears to have been deeply involved in several recent schemes concerning industrial innovations. Thomas says he will concentrate on learning more about those investments tomorrow."

Stokes blew out a breath. "Right. Well, obviously, during our interviews with the various family members, there's been rather a lot of skirting around financial difficulties."

Mildly, Barnaby pointed out, "We didn't actually ask about their financial state, but now we know more—"

"And," Penelope put in, "now we know more about the earl's parsimonious habits."

Barnaby inclined his head in acknowledgment. "Clearly, we'll need to speak with at least the male members of the family again."

In his growly rumble, Curtis said, "You might want to wait until Glendower and Montague give you more information. Then you'll know what you're dealing with. Otherwise, you're trusting these jokers to tell you the truth, and that, in my experience, is often a waste of time."

Stokes was nodding. "Best we know at least some of the answers before we ask those questions."

Penelope glanced around the circle of faces. "Let's review what we know so far."

Between them, she, Barnaby, and Stokes summarized their findings, covering the events of the day and their various interviews. They revisited their assumptions, namely, that Winslow was poisoned via the whiskey in the earl's decanter, which Stokes said Findlay had now confirmed.

"That," Stokes stated, "means that we can take it as read that the poison was, in fact, meant for the earl."

Penelope continued by describing the search for the source of the poison that had resulted in the packet of poison being found in Frederick's old room. "Mrs. Pratchett is adamant that Frederick hasn't been in that room for decades, let alone since last Thursday, which was the day on which the packet was purchased."

Mary frowned. "I'm sure Frederick hasn't been in the house since the week before last. Not until he arrived for the dinner." She met Stokes's gaze. "I can be certain because, whenever he calls, he always—invariably—comes to see the dowager. He was the most caring of her sons, and as I was always by her side during the day, I would know if he was in the house."

Pleased, Stokes scribbled in his notebook. "Every bit of corroborative detail helps." He glanced at Barnaby and Penelope. "That negates the possibility that, even if he wasn't the one who bought the stuff, Frederick handled the packet at some point and, afterward, hid it in the drawer in his old room."

Penelope nodded. "More and more, the placing of the packet of poison appears to be a bid to implicate Frederick as the poisoner."

All agreed with that conclusion.

Refocusing on Curtis, Mary, and Julian, Penelope went on, "We know Frederick wasn't the one who bought the poison because the packet carried the chemist shop's label. It was bought from Chifley's Chemist Shop."

Julian sat up. "That's in Piccadilly. Not far away."

Smiling, Barnaby nodded. "Indeed. We called on Chifley, and the assistant who served the gentleman who purchased the poison described the man, and later, the assistant confirmed for us that gentleman wasn't Frederick."

"You took the assistant to see Frederick Fitzhugh?" Curtis asked.

"The other way around," Stokes said. "And while the assistant was sure the purchaser wasn't Frederick, he was also certain that the purchaser looked very like Frederick. The assistant is adamant that he would know the man if he saw him again."

"That's useful." Curtis narrowed his eyes. "But from what Julian and I have seen of the family, Frederick's description could fit any of the adult Fitzhugh males."

"Indeed," Barnaby said. "And until we have more by way of motive or other evidence to point to the right man, we can't simply troop them all through the shop."

"Even if the assistant identified the Fitzhugh involved, it would end up being the assistant's word against that of a member of a noble family." Penelope pursed her lips. "Not an easy case to make before a judge."

Mary's expression cleared. "Ah. Yes, I see."

"But," Penelope said, "we've skipped ahead of ourselves. To return to our first interview, which was with Frederick and Imogen." In broad terms, she summarized what they'd learned. "Frederick was also happy to show me a letter he'd written, with a signature, so even before we took him to see the chemist's assistant, I was certain he wasn't the poisoner. The signature in the poison register might read F. Fitzhugh, but it was written by someone else."

She continued, describing the outcome of their visit to Charles Street and the Mitchelmore family. "Again, the earl's tightfistedness with regard to the family featured."

Penelope noticed a fleeting expression in Mary's open countenance, as if some suspicion had been confirmed. Fixing her gaze on Mary's face, Penelope asked, "Have you seen anything of that?"

Mary hesitated, then straightened and said, "Not specifically about that, but the earl demonstrating a generally parsimonious nature, certainly. For instance, he ran only one household staff—one butler, one housekeeper, four footmen, a senior and junior coachman, and one groom, one stableman, and so on. When the earl and the rest of the immediate family move to the country, to Moran Place in Gloucestershire, all the staff move, too."

Penelope let her surprise show, and Mary nodded. "I can confirm that, at present, the only staff at Moran Place are an ancient stableman and two maids-of-all-work from local families."

"So"—Penelope frowned—"Moran Place is essentially closed up."

Mary went on, "I've never worked with any other noble family, so I didn't know that was unusual, but Mrs. Pratchett and Winslow frequently grumbled over the dislocation whenever they had to move house, and after we came to live at Moran House, both explained that there should be, at the very least, a housekeeper and a small skeleton staff including a younger underbutler left at Moran Place. As matters stand, every June and November, when the household moves to the country, and every February and September, when they come back to town, there's chaos and upheaval among the staff as they rush to get the respective house opened up while shutting down the other." She paused, then glanced at Julian. "We experienced that for the first time last summer, and it was a discombobulating time for the staff."

Stokes looked up from his notebook at Penelope. "I take it that—having only the one staff—is unusual."

Her expression distinctly disapproving, Penelope stated, "Very. For a noble house of that rank, it's…well! I can't think of any comparable family who would dream of doing that."

"So," Stokes said, "that's another thing the earl stinted on. 'Tight-fisted' seems to have been his middle name."

Penelope inclined her head and went on, "The final household we called on was the Southerlys', and there we came across another, totally unexpected twist to our tale."

Barnaby explained how they'd learned that Theodore had been poisoned, and according to his doctor, it was, again, due to strychnine.

Julian looked horrified. "Is Theo all right?"

Curtis was equally stunned. "Good Lord! How did the youngster get hold of the stuff?"

"Indeed," Barnaby replied, "and yes, Julian, Theo is expected to recover fully within a few days. But from his brother, Vincent, we had it confirmed that, as their older male cousins had told us, all six of the earl's nephews were in the habit of pilfering this and that from the study and have been doing so for years. On Monday evening, while everyone else, including the earl, was in the drawing room, Vincent and Theodore slipped into the study. They didn't find any cash lying about—which was confirmed by George, who looked later—so instead, Vincent and Theodore helped themselves to a cigar each from the earl's cigar box."

With an eloquent shudder, Penelope continued, "This morning, Theodore lit his and took one puff and started choking and stopped. Stopping at that point saved him, so although he became quite ill, he is recovering."

Stokes looked up. "I took the cigars to Findlay. He'll test them and said he'd have the results by tomorrow morning. He also said that inhaling strychnine is an even more potent way for it to take effect. He said Theodore was incredibly lucky to survive. One good lungful—such as a man accustomed to trusting his own cigars would take—and he'd have been done for."

Patently appalled, Mary shook her head. "Who is doing this? Have the staff at Moran House been warned?"

"I sent word immediately," Stokes assured her, "and asked my sergeant, who's still at the house, to confiscate the box of cigars and take them to Scotland Yard. I also ordered the study closed up and guarded. No sense in taking any further risks."

"First Winslow, now Theodore." Mary looked at Barnaby and Penelope. "But surely, in both cases, the earl was the intended victim."

"So we think," Barnaby said, "but someone else put paid to the earl before he could ingest the poison." He looked at Curtis. "Have you had any luck finding sightings of a stranger lurking outside the house?"

Somewhat to Barnaby's surprise, Curtis nodded. "I put two of my best men onto it, and they checked the neighbors, and the groom of a house two doors up Park Lane says there was a man came walking up the mews from the direction of Moran House. A big, heavyset man wearing a long coat."

"Time?" Stokes asked, busily jotting.

"Apparently right on ten o'clock," Curtis replied. "The groom is sure because he heard the bells as the man went walking past."

"What chance have we of learning the man's identity?" Barnaby asked.

"It's possible we'll get lucky," Curtis said. "I'll check with the Moran stable staff first. See if they saw anything. It sounds as if this geezer had to have walked right past their stable. Meanwhile"—Curtis glanced at Julian, who looked only too eager to help—"Julian here can work his charm on the jarveys." Curtis smiled. "They like his cheery face and are often freer with information with him than with anyone else."

Julian nodded enthusiastically. "I'll start…" He broke off and blinked at Curtis.

"Aye," Curtis said, reading Julian's mind. "You'd be wise to leave the jarveys until later. Those who're about at ten o'clock of an evening won't be out driving until the afternoon. But mind, I want you to take Norton with you. Just to make sure all's well."

Julian's enthusiasm returned. "I'll come into the office in the morning, then. See if there's anything else I can help with."

Curtis nodded approvingly. "You do that." He smiled slightly and looked over Julian's head at Mary. "After all, you're still employed, and there's work to be done."

Mary returned Curtis's smile with a grateful smile of her own.

Penelope noted the interaction, but before anyone could utter another word, they all heard a dull, thudding knock on the front door.

Mostyn hurried across the hall, then they heard O'Donnell wearily ask for Stokes.

Mostyn promptly steered O'Donnell to the drawing room, and the sergeant plodded in.

He nodded respectfully to the company, then looked at Stokes. "There's no cigar box in the earl's study."

"What?" Stokes frowned.

Everyone else did as well.

O'Donnell held up his hands. "We looked and searched, but there's no box of cigars anywhere in that room."

Stokes swiveled to look at Mary. "Do you recall a box of cigars in the earl's study?"

Without hesitation, Mary replied, "Yes. It sat on the top of the sideboard behind the earl's desk. What's more, I'm sure it was there when I came upon the earl's body." She briefly shuddered. "That scene is engraved on my mind, and the box was in my line of sight. I can close my eyes, think of that moment, and see it there—on the sideboard against the wall behind the desk."

When everyone looked at him, O'Donnell shook his head. "It isn't there now." He went on, "We asked the staff if they'd moved it for some reason, but no. Seems no one's sighted it since Monday morning, when the maid last dusted in there." The grizzled sergeant dipped his head toward Mary. "The maid said it was where Mrs. Alder says—on top of the sideboard behind the desk."

As befuddled as anyone, Stokes exclaimed, "Where on earth…?"

Barnaby glanced at Penelope and saw her expression abruptly clear.

She looked at O'Donnell. "Have you searched in the room where you found the poison?"

Confused, O'Donnell asked, "Mr. Frederick's old room?"

"Yes. That one." When O'Donnell just looked at her, Penelope raised her hands and made a shooing motion. "Go and look there. And quickly. Whoever moved it might think to move it again."

O'Donnell looked at Stokes.

Stokes, who had been viewing Penelope through narrowed eyes, turned to his sergeant and nodded. "Go and check that room."

O'Donnell heaved a sigh and went.

Barnaby regarded Penelope. "Why that room?"

"Because," she said, "either the poisoner isn't very clever and lacks imagination and is still trying to convince us that Frederick is the poisoner. Or…"

When, clearly thinking, she paused, Stokes prompted, "Or?"

"Or"—raising her head, Penelope continued—"the poisoner *is* clever and knows that we searched that room earlier today and is banking on us not thinking to search there again." Still ruminating, she paused, then went on, "If they just wanted to get the cigars out of the way…and it's possible they have no idea Vincent and Theodore pilfered two cigars. But they know Winslow died unnecessarily, so perhaps they've had an attack of conscience and wanted to remove the second source of poison designed to kill the earl."

Mary shook her head. "Whoever is behind the poison, they were absolutely set on killing him, weren't they?"

"Indeed," Barnaby said. "And yet"—he glanced at Penelope—"whoever actually killed the earl, that seemed more a spur-of-the-moment act."

Stokes nodded. "I have difficulty believing that the poisoner is also the murderer. That doesn't make much sense."

"So," Curtis said, "we're looking for a spur-of-the-moment murderer and a poisoner."

"Two separate people, acting independently," Barnaby confirmed. "The first killed the earl, and the second killed Winslow and almost killed Theodore."

"Is it possible," Mary asked, "that the spur-of-the-moment murderer was a thief?" When the others looked at her, she elaborated, "For instance, if someone was sent to steal the earl's papers or learn something from them. The earl was at dinner with the whole family, and later, the company retired to the drawing room. It's likely an intruder wouldn't have expected the earl to desert his guests and return to the study when he did."

"True," Penelope conceded. "And when the earl came in unexpectedly, the intruder had no option but to hide behind those long curtains."

Stokes was following the hypothetical action. "Then the earl called Winslow in and sent him to refill the decanter, and the intruder felt he'd better escape before Winslow returned."

"He might even have taken papers from the earl's desk." Penelope looked at Barnaby. "How can we know?"

Barnaby grimaced. "Other than confirming that the papers on the desk weren't classified government documents, I didn't pay that much attention to them. There were several submissions to a parliamentary inquiry plus some private letters that seemed to be about investments." He met Stokes's gaze. "Relatively innocuous, but if some documents had been removed, I can't see how we could tell."

Stokes sighed. "We'll check what's there again and see if we can gain any insights. Whatever was on the desk should still be there."

Penelope looked around the circle of faces, then, with a degree of determination, declared, "Right, then. What do we tackle next? What's at the top of our most-urgent-to-know list?"

Stokes softly snorted and waved at her to continue.

She duly raised a hand and ticked her points off on her fingers. "Curtis and Julian will pursue the identity of the man sighted in the mews about the time of the murder. If we discover he has any links to the earl's investments—"

"Or his political enemies," Barnaby put in.

Penelope inclined her head and went on, "Or any other likely foe, then it's entirely possible that man is the earl's murderer."

She progressed to her second finger. "Meanwhile, we have the separate issue of the poisoner. Thomas and Montague are delving into the family's financial secrets, which might be the motive there. However, as of yet, we know little about any family feuds or clashes that might have spurred the poisoner." She looked at Stokes. "So I propose that, tomorrow morning, I will consult with my usual sources and see what they can tell us about the House of Moran. Even if the ladies know of no murder-worthy issue, rumor being the ton's obsession, I'm sure they'll have some pertinent information to share about the general financial state of the various branches of the family as well as their relationships, friendships, and disagreements."

Stokes glanced at Julian, Mary, and Curtis. "By 'usual sources,' she means various grandes dames and similar ladies of the Cynster family." Returning his gaze to Penelope, he nodded. "Good. We need to cover those angles, and in that regard, your usual sources are our best bet." Stokes shifted his attention to Barnaby. "First thing tomorrow, I have to report to the Commissioner." Stokes grimaced. "I may be tied up at the Yard for several hours."

Barnaby nodded. "While you're stuck there, I'll use those hours to see what my father and any of his helpful friends can tell me about the earl's politics, especially with regard to any enemies."

Stokes looked at Penelope. "I think that covers it. Or at least as much of it as we can cover by way of our next steps."

A knock fell on the front door, and Mostyn went to open it.

Everyone looked expectantly toward the hall, and seconds later, O'Donnell, appearing a great deal happier than he had earlier, walked in, carrying a polished wooden box between his large hands.

The sergeant nodded to Penelope. "You were right, ma'am. There it was, sitting on top of the chest of drawers in that room." He shifted his gaze to Stokes. "Seemed to us as if whoever left it there had just put it there for the moment, as if they weren't sure what to do with it."

"That's very likely true." Stokes eyed the box. "Did you look inside?"

"Aye. Carefully. It's more than half full of fat cigars."

Penelope looked smug. "Excellent." She glanced from Stokes to Barnaby. "Tomorrow, after our morning's endeavors, I suggest we reconvene here before returning to Moran House." Transferring her gaze to Curtis, Mary, and Julian, she added, her tone anticipatory, "Sometimes, it helps to give the guilty party a little rope to run with. In this case, by not being in the house, we've given them time to try to cover their tracks, and they've made a mistake." She nodded at the box in O'Donnell's hands. "Namely, moving that cigar box."

She glanced at O'Donnell, then at Stokes, and finally at Barnaby, taking in their not-quite-sure-what-she-was-talking-about expressions, then, with a hint of fond exasperation, she explained, "That cigar box had to have been in the earl's study when we left Moran House early this morning. Prior to that, between the time Mary saw it there and we left the house, with ourselves and various constables moving through the corridors, there was no chance for anyone to slip into the study and take the box. Even if the poisoner had thought of moving it—and I'm not convinced they did, not at that point—fetching the box would have been far too risky. And from the time we left the house until we returned midmorning, after Winslow was found dead, all the household was, by all accounts, in their beds asleep."

She tipped her head consideringly. "More, I would wager my best bonnet that what prompted the poisoner to remove and hide the box was them learning of Winslow's death, but they wouldn't have risked doing so while we were in the house. Therefore, the box was moved sometime after the search turned up the packet of poison in Frederick's old room and we left the house to go to Chifley's. That was about twelve-thirty today. So sometime *after* then and *before* the guard on the study was reinstituted after we learned about the poisoned cigars and the cigar box, someone went into the study, picked up the box, and carried it to Frederick's old room." She held up one finger. "This in a house containing only three family members and the staff—and the staff would have been rushing all around the house, catching up with their chores."

She sat back and smiled at everyone. "I believe we stand a much better chance of learning who moved the cigar box to Frederick's old room than of finding any evidence of who put the laced cigars into the box in the first place."

Barnaby returned her smile. "Excellent deduction."

His expression one of dawning appreciation, Stokes nodded. "Excellent, indeed." He looked around the group. "With the exception of Mrs. Alder—and please, do remain in this house for the nonce, as there will be reporters lurking—all the rest of us, it seems, have our tasks for tomorrow defined."

CHAPTER 10

The following morning, after noting that the newspapers had sunk their teeth into the story of the murder of the Earl of Moran and, having also learned of the unexpected and mysterious death of the earl's butler, were busy stitching the few facts they'd gleaned into a predictably sensational account, Penelope set out for Grosvenor Square and arrived at St. Ives House, on the square's north side, promptly at ten-thirty.

Although it was rather early in the day for ton events, she knew she would find at least some of her usual sources gathered over the teacups. While today's morning tea was not one of the Cynster ladies' regular at-homes, which drew a large crowd of connected ladies, given it was the height of the Season, she was nevertheless hopeful that a decent number of the family's females would be present and prove sufficient for her needs.

On opening the front door, Hamilton, the butler, smiled upon her in welcome. "Mrs. Adair. The ladies will be especially pleased to see you, ma'am."

Penelope walked into the black-and-white-tiled foyer. "Are they avidly following the latest news from Moran House?"

"Indeed, they are."

After surrendering her bonnet and coat, smiling, Penelope waved Hamilton back. "I know my way."

Hamilton half bowed, and she headed to the rear of the foyer and took the long corridor that led to the back parlor that had long been the favored haunt of the ladies of the house.

She walked through the open doorway and was pleased to find a goodly number of her favorite ladies—and her most useful sources of information—gathered in the comfortable chairs and on the sofas surrounding a central low table on which reposed a large and amply stocked tea tray.

"Penelope, dear!" Helena, the Dowager Duchess of St. Ives, was the first to notice her. "My dear girl, how fortuitous. We were just speaking of Moran's unexpected demise."

Lady Osbaldestone, seated beside Helena, asked, "Dare we hope you've been called in, along with that handsome husband of yours and that inspector chap, Stokes?"

Penelope beamed at the circle of faces. As well as Helena and Therese Osbaldestone, of the older generation, Lady Horatia Cynster, Lady Celia Cynster, and Lady Louise Cynster were present, while the next generation was represented by Honoria, Duchess of St. Ives, Patience Cynster, and Alathea Cynster.

Joining the group, Penelope sat on a love seat beside Alathea and confirmed, "Indeed, we're on the case. Along with Stokes, we've been asked to discover who killed the earl. And now, who poisoned his butler."

"Poison, was it?" Patience arched her brows. "That hasn't turned up in the papers as yet."

"And one can imagine what a furor it will cause when it does." Smiling, Honoria handed Penelope a cup of tea.

Accepting the cup and saucer, she sighed. "Yes, indeed. The whole case looks set to be a nine-days' wonder."

"So what can you tell us of the murder?" Helena inquired.

Penelope had long understood that sharing her knowledge of what had occurred was, in a way, a trade in exchange for what the ladies could and would tell her of the people involved.

She sipped, then lowered her cup and began, "Well, it started with the earl being found bludgeoned to death in his study. The murder weapon appears to have been a small marble bust that sat on a shelf behind the earl's desk." She continued relating the known facts of the case, omitting all mention of Mary, Curtis, and Julian but including all the Fitzhugh family members into whom she was seeking greater insights.

After outlining the finding of the packet of poison and stating that the description of the purchaser of the poison would fit any of the six adult

Fitzhugh males, she concluded with the tale of Theodore's poisoning via a cigar from the box in the earl's study and the subsequent finding that the box had been moved, although as yet, they hadn't established by whom.

"And that," she declared, "is where we stand at the moment." She paused to take a sip of her tea and allow the ladies to make of the tale what they would, then she set down her cup and saucer and looked hopefully around the circle. "What we most need at this point is a better understanding of the members of the Fitzhugh families—all those directly connected to the House of Moran."

"Well"—Honoria glanced around the circle—"I don't believe any of us can claim to be particularly close to any of the ladies involved." None of the others contradicted her, and she went on, "However, regarding the earl and his household, I'm equally sure we've all heard whispers and wondered ourselves about what, in fact, is going on."

Patience nodded. "At Moran House in particular."

"Indeed." Helena nodded sagely. "The oddity lies in that we are all aware the earldom has always been regarded as significantly wealthy, and we know of nothing that would indicate that has changed."

Lady Osbaldestone offered, "The Moran estate has always featured as one of the ton's most wealthy, as far back as any of us can remember."

"Some noble families," Helena said, "like the Cynsters and the Fitzhughs, have through many generations enjoyed very deep reserves stemming from the entailed landholdings and accumulated funds. Other houses are not so lucky, but usually, once an entailed estate reaches a certain worth, despite any minor hiccups generation to generation, such estates will usually remain financially solid and strong. With such wealth behind the family, there should never be any reason for pecuniary stress."

Celia nodded. "Exactly."

Lady Osbaldestone snorted. "Not to put too fine a point on it, Moran ought to be rolling in funds. Arthur, the late earl's father, and his predecessors come to that, had a knack for managing their acres and expanding their wealth in various ways."

"In a nutshell," Horatia stated, "all the Fitzhughs should be, at the very least, well-off. Instead…"

"Instead," Alathea supplied, "they all show those telltale signs that in anyone else would suggest the family is strapped for funds."

Honoria shook her head. "It's mystifying. There have been no sudden sales of properties or any of those indicators of retrenching, but the fact remains that none of the ladies—and as far as we know, none of the men of the family, either—present as being comfortable money-wise."

"Mind you," Lady Osbaldestone said, "they all hide it well, but it's the little things that are impossible to conceal—like the carriage not being refurbished and the current countess, Victoria, barely entertaining at all."

Horatia was nodding. "Certainly not on a par with what one would expect of Moran's social or political rank."

"Also of note," Celia put in, "is that the countess is not active in supporting any charity." She caught Penelope's gaze. "These days, that's rather odd."

"There are not many who have been inside Moran House in recent years," Helena said. "But those that have crossed the threshold mention outdated hangings and outmoded furniture." She arched her brows at Penelope. "You must have been inside the house. So what did you see?"

Penelope thought back. "The earl's study was…exactly as one would expect. However…" After a moment studying her memories, she inclined her head. "As usual, your information is correct. Victoria's sitting room struck me as being particularly out of fashion—as if she hadn't changed anything since first coming to the house. The dowager only moved back to Moran House last year, so her sitting room isn't so dated."

"The drawing room?" Patience asked.

Calling up her memories, Penelope surveyed what she recalled, then nodded. "In general, I focus on the people, of course, but again, you're correct. The upholstery hasn't been renewed for some time."

"See?" Helena sat back. "It's little things like that, minor details, perhaps, but taken together, they paint a picture we all interpret as penny-pinching." She raised her hands, palms up. "But in the Fitzhughs' case, why? The family coffers have to be overflowing, and yet…"

Penelope nodded. "I take your point. All of your points. Clearly, there is something strange going on financially." They needed to learn what Montague and Thomas had found in that arena. She refocused and scanned the circle of faces. "So what can you tell me of the people involved? The members of the Fitzhugh family and those directly connected?"

"Well," Lady Osbaldestone said, "you should know that the dowager countess is rather older than we are." She tipped her head toward Helena and Horatia, who nodded. "So we're not contemporaries and haven't mixed with her as much as you might think."

"That said," Horatia put in, "she's always been rather frail and, these days, appears to be fading quite quickly."

Helena said, "She keeps to her own circle of old and close friends—a shrinking number, these days—and she no longer goes widely into society."

"So you won't see her at any balls, no matter how major," Lady Osbaldestone stated.

Helena added, "What little I have heard over the years is that hers was an arranged marriage, but one that turned out very well. She was devoted to her Arthur, and he to her."

"She was an earl's daughter herself," Lady Osbaldestone said, "and while the match was made for all the usual reasons, Imelda and Arthur simply suited. They worked very well as a couple on every plane."

That, Penelope knew, was high praise, coming from the most feared of the ton's grandes dames. "What about Victoria?" Penelope asked. "The current countess?"

The ladies conferred, and the most surprising aspect of their collective insights was that while they all knew Victoria to speak with, none of them knew much about her.

"She's there," Honoria said, "swanning about the ballrooms, much as one would expect, but beyond that, I have to confess she and I have never really engaged."

The others' expressions suggested their experience was similar.

"She's half a generation younger as well," Alathea added. "And she has no children, so she doesn't cross paths with us on that front, either."

Viewing the younger matrons' faces, Lady Osbaldestone stated, "To me, the most notable comment one could make of the current countess is that, in spite of how Moran seems to ignore her along with wider society, she hasn't taken a lover, at least as far as anyone knows."

Lady Osbaldestone looked around hopefully, but no one corrected her. No one piped up to say they'd heard of any dalliance on the countess's part.

Helena mused, "Certainly, that does seem odd. Living in relative social obscurity couldn't have been what she expected when she agreed to become Moran's second countess."

Patience humphed. "Maybe she's just amazingly discreet."

With inclinations of their heads, the ladies wordlessly allowed that was a possibility.

"This second marriage of Moran's." Penelope focused on the four older ladies. "Do you know how that came about?"

"As I understood it," Celia said, "Moran wasn't all that keen, but there was pressure brought to bear from his mother and also his paternal aunts. They weren't concerned about the succession—not with Frederick there and his sons—but they felt that Moran wasn't meeting the social expectations of his rank and was unlikely to do so without a countess by his side."

Sagely, Lady Osbaldestone nodded. "And looking back over recent years, one would have to conclude that his mother and aunts were correct, but even having a countess beside him hasn't been enough to prod Moran into stepping up and fulfilling what most would see as his social obligations."

"I have heard," Honoria said, "that when it came to his own consequence, Moran wasn't one to stint, but such observations relate solely to how he presents to the world, not how his family members fare." She tilted her head. "Perhaps the deterioration in the public façade of the House of Moran has been merely a reflection of Moran's lack of interest."

"Possibly," Patience allowed, "but then there's the little things that suggest distinctly straitened circumstances affecting the Frederick Fitzhughs."

"Indeed," Alathea said. "And although Mitchelmore and Southerly—the latter especially—seem in sound financial health, I've heard rumors suggesting that the Mitchelmore sons as well as their Fitzhugh cousins are all viewed askance by the current crop of fond mamas with daughters to marry off."

"Given the Fitzhugh family's elevated social rank and that the lads themselves are agreeable, handsome, and presentable, that surely suggests some financial constraint is suspected if not outright known," Honoria concluded.

"Of course," Alathea said, "young gentlemen on the town being short of cash is nothing new. In fact, it seems almost a condition of the species—a rite of passage, if you will—and perhaps it's unfair to judge the Mitchelmores and Fitzhughs against the yardstick of our own sons."

"And our children are older," Patience pointed out. "Indeed, you are among the youngest of that generation, so in the same way you don't know much about the Fitzhugh children, we, too, are scraping the bottom of our barrel of knowledge to find what scraps we can for you."

Penelope grinned. "And I do appreciate your efforts, which you know."

Patience grinned back, and Honoria and the others all smiled.

"What about Frederick and Imogen?" Penelope asked. "How are they regarded?"

The ladies looked at each other, then Honoria offered what was, apparently, the consensus view. "Looking past the subtle signs of financial stress, Frederick and Imogen are widely viewed as solid members of the ton. They behave as the ton expects, and I—we—know of nothing, no rumor or whisper, that speaks to the contrary."

"They have children," Alathea added, "and that connects them more widely and more deeply into society as a whole. The same can be said of the Mitchelmores and Southerlys."

Lady Osbaldestone opined, "The other three of Imelda's married children and their families are viewed in a significantly more positive light than Gordon and Victoria. Whether it's the lack of children or something else, that couple were never a success within the ton."

"Primarily," Horatia added, "because of Gordon's lack of interest in being a success within the ton."

The other ladies nodded.

"In that regard, meaning the approval of the ton, or rather, the withholding of it," Lady Osbaldestone said, "Moran's attitude to not assisting his brothers, especially Frederick, while legally excusable, is widely frowned upon. Given that Frederick is—was—Moran's heir apparent, and Frederick's son, William, would follow after him, the accepted practice holds that Moran should have ensured that both Frederick and William lived in appropriate style. That Moran so openly ignored that familial obligation wasn't appreciated within the upper echelons of the ton—those circles Moran himself should have inhabited rather more."

Glancing around the gathering, Penelope saw many sober expressions and serious nods.

"We've spoken of the sons," Louise said. "Of the daughters—Imelda's granddaughters—I know Lizbet, the Mitchelmores' eldest girl, married Lord Brompton, and all seems entirely as it should be there."

Helena nodded. "A good match, and they seem to suit."

"Ah, but then we come to the next three girls, who have just made their come-outs." Her lips tight with disapproval, Lady Osbaldestone looked at Honoria, Patience, and Alathea. "You must have heard of the scheme to combine their come-out balls. Three in one! If any one incident waves a red flag as to straitened circumstances, that surely does. And even more telling, no one is imagining they'll have the use of the Moran House ballroom."

Helena was nodding. "More's the pity. It's a lovely ballroom, and no one in the ton has seen the inside of it since the old earl's day, when Imelda reigned as one of the brighter lights in the pantheon of ton hostesses."

Rapidly reviewing all she'd heard, Penelope realized there was one member of the late earl's immediate family no one had mentioned. She looked around the gathering. "What about Christopher Fitzhugh?"

Inwardly, she debated but decided not to mention that there was a good chance that Christopher was behind the poison plot. That was not yet proven, after all.

To her surprise, rather than offer any answer, the ladies exchanged uncertain glances.

Uncertain? These ladies?

"Well, dear," Lady Osbaldestone finally commenced, "I—we—have to admit that we're not quite sure what to make of our observations."

The other ladies nodded, then Honoria offered, "We—all of us—have seen signs and wondered if, perhaps, there was some sort of connection, a link of sorts, between Christopher and his sister-in-law."

"Victoria," Patience supplied. "And yes, of course, we all initially assumed that 'link' was by way of them being lovers."

"And as we noted earlier," Louise rushed to say, "that really would surprise no one, given Gordon's neglect of Victoria and that Christopher is handsome enough, and after all, he and she live under the same roof."

"Namely, her husband's roof." Helena looked ready to be censorious but also still unsure.

"The issue," Horatia stated, "is that none of us believe the connection to be a romantic one."

"It's not romantic at all," Celia said. "More as if they were each other's most stalwart supporter."

"Yet they're not exactly friends, either," Alathea put in. "It's very confusing."

Lady Osbaldestone met Penelope's gaze. "None of that should be noteworthy, really, but what makes it so is that their…whatever it might be—connection, link—is simply so intense."

"So very focused," Honoria said, "and very tightly held solely between them."

Penelope had been juggling the ladies' observations with what might —or might not—have occurred. Tentatively, she suggested, "Could they be working together toward a particular shared goal?"

Honoria's and most of the ladies' expressions cleared.

Lady Osbaldestone nodded definitively. "Yes! Clever girl! That's the impression exactly."

In other words, Victoria and Christopher might well be coconspirators.

It was a fine, midspring day, and when Penelope returned to her home, she elected to sit in the garden parlor. Through the open French doors, she watched her sons, Oliver and Pip, as they played on the rear lawn with Hettie, their nursemaid, and Roger, the ever-present spaniel pup.

Mary had been helping Hettie with the rambunctious pair, but with James, the footman, hovering nearby, there was really no need, and after spotting Penelope sitting on the sofa, Mary came to join her.

Penelope smiled and waved Mary to the cushions alongside her. "The men should be here soon, then we can see what information we've managed to gather. I've asked Mostyn to bring in sandwiches so we can eat while we talk."

Smiling in reply, Mary settled on the sofa. "You're used to this—to juggling investigations while keeping an eye on your children."

Penelope's smile widened, and she offered, "In a fundamental way, the innocent children—ours and everyone else's—are the very reason Barnaby and I work with Stokes to bring villains to justice. In the cases we consult on, were we not involved, often the guilty party would avoid all repercussions."

Mary's brows rose as she considered that. Eventually, she murmured, "I can imagine that's true."

"I strongly suspect it would definitely be true in this present case," Penelope returned.

The sounds of arrival followed by brisk approaching footsteps had both ladies swiveling to look at the open doorway.

Julian bounced in, followed more sedately by Curtis.

Julian bent to kiss Mary's cheek, while Curtis nodded to both ladies.

"Adair and Stokes are just behind us," Curtis said.

Penelope waved him to an armchair. “Sit, both of you. We’re going to eat while we confer.”

Julian’s eyes lit, and Curtis readily sank into the armchair.

Swift steps heralded Barnaby and Stokes, closely followed by Mostyn and the new footman, Henry, both bearing large platters stacked with sandwiches.

Barnaby and Stokes stood back to allow Mostyn and Henry to place the platters on the low table between the circle of sofas and chairs, then, as the majordomo and footman departed, Barnaby moved with Stokes to sit on the sofa facing Penelope and Mary.

“Is that chicken?” Stokes peered at the sandwiches on top of the pile.

“Cook said she’d send up chicken and cucumber, and egg and celery, and a few other combinations.” Penelope picked up the top sandwich from the nearest platter. “I warn you. She’s been experimenting.”

Henry rushed in with a stack of plates and napkins, and they all made their selections and sat back to munch.

After one bite, Curtis studied the sandwich he held. “Whatever’s in this, it’s delicious.”

“Hmm” came from several throats.

Barnaby had noticed that both Julian and Curtis had an eagerness about them that suggested they’d turned up something noteworthy. He set his half-eaten sandwich on his plate. “Let me report first.” He caught Curtis’s eyes. “My information on Moran’s political foes might connect with Curtis and Julian’s findings.”

The ready nods from Curtis and Julian suggested Barnaby’s guess had been right. He duly reported, “I spoke to my father, and he said that while Moran was not well-liked by his peers—my father among them—he was widely tolerated, primarily because he seemed to have interesting ideas. In general, people were willing to listen to him explain and expound. However, those interesting ideas largely revolved around the tighter regulation of labor, and through his speeches in the Lords and elsewhere, Moran had painted himself as something of a target for the various labor movements.”

Mostyn arrived, carrying a tray with mugs of ale for the men and cider for the ladies and Julian.

Barnaby paused while the drinks were handed around, then sipped his ale, lowered the mug, and went on, “According to my father, Moran’s efforts to regulate and reduce workers’ rights had reached the point that, if some of the labor movements’ more rabid adherents had learned of the proposals the earl intended to advance this parliamentary term, then to believe that he was attacked and killed by someone sent by those rabid adherents doesn't require any great stretch of the imagination.

"So," he concluded, reaching for his plate, "no sign of any clash among his peers, but him being killed by someone sent by one of the labor movements is a definite possibility."

His expression serious, Curtis nodded. "Just so." He glanced at Julian. "It took a bit of finagling, but eventually, we persuaded the earl's coachman it was better to talk to us than the police. Seems he—the coachman—was approached on Monday night by a man saying he spoke for the secretary of the dockworkers' union. The man said he wanted to know if there was any dirt the coachman knew of that might be used to persuade the earl to drop his more reactionary views. It seems it was that man who was seen by others leaving the mews that night."

Curtis nodded encouragingly at Julian.

Julian swallowed a mouthful of sandwich, then piped, "I found the jarvey that took the cove from the end of the mews to, it seemed, his home. I gave Mr. Curtis the address."

Curtis glanced at Stokes. "I'm thinking I'll drop around later this evening and have a word to see what the situation is, but on the face of it, this man—who I think must be Nate Samuel—was speaking with the earl's coachman all through the time the earl was being murdered in his study. According to the coachman, Samuel appeared at about nine-thirty and left just before the bells tolled for ten o'clock." To Stokes, who, with a sandwich in one hand, was juggling his notebook on his knee and scribbling, Curtis added, "That fits with when the others farther up the mews saw Samuel—assuming it was him—walking by."

Stokes looked at Curtis. "You know what to look for?"

Curtis faintly smiled. "Any suggestion Samuel was keeping the coachman talking while an accomplice finished off the earl in the study."

Stokes grinned. "Just so."

Barnaby looked at Julian. "The jarvey you mentioned—he only took up one man? Not two?"

"Just the one," Julian assured them. "And I asked specially. He—the jarvey—said as only one man walked out of the mews. He was waiting on the box seat of his hackney directly opposite the entrance to the mews, and he saw the man coming out of the shadows. He didn't see anyone else around."

"I'll see what I can learn," Curtis rumbled, "but for my money, and knowing how thorough young Julian here is, there was no other man lurking about Moran House at that time. Only Samuel."

Stokes grunted. "Watch yourself when you go to see him."

"Don't worry," Curtis mumbled around a mouthful of sandwich. He swallowed and added, "He and I have met before."

Stokes huffed, then reported, "Findlay sends his compliments, along with the information that the cigars were, indeed, poisoned with strychnine, and apparently, it was very craftily done."

Leaning forward, Stokes set his empty plate on the table, then sat back. "According to Findlay, who seemed quite impressed, the cap sealing the end of the cigar had been removed, a solution of concentrated poison applied to the rolled leaves, and the cap reattached. All very neat. Findlay examined the cigar Theodore started smoking, and Findlay says that not being an experienced cigar smoker, the lad had cut off the entire cap, so there was only the barest trace of the poison remaining. If Theodore hadn't, in his inexperience, overtrimmed the cap—and no connoisseur would—his first puff would unequivocally have killed him."

"So the cigars were an even more serious threat than the whiskey," Penelope observed.

Stokes nodded. "It seems so."

"Whiskey or a cigar." Barnaby met Penelope's eyes. "Whichever Moran chose that night, he was slated to die."

"Except," Penelope said, "someone else killed him first."

"At least," Stokes said, "courtesy of Penelope's quick thinking, we have all the poisoned elements contained. They're no longer a threat to anyone. Sadly, however, now that the newspapers have got the bit between their teeth, the pressure to solve the case quickly is mounting, and it'll continue to grow with every passing day. The Commissioner is being as understanding as he can be and acting as a bulwark of sorts against the press—as are the governors—but for us, the clock is definitely ticking, and we need to make some progress in identifying actual suspects and building a sound case against them."

"In respect of identifying suspects," Penelope said, "the information I gathered from my usual sources this morning might be helpful."

Stokes nodded encouragingly. "Go on."

"The conversation wandered somewhat, as such discussions do, so I'll endeavor to summarize," Penelope said. "First, among the ladies present, there was a general puzzlement regarding the family's financial state. On the one hand, all there were convinced the earldom should be significantly wealthy, and no one knows of any factual evidence that suggests otherwise, meaning there have been no sudden sales of property or whispers of similar divestments to realize funds. However, contradicting that view, over the past several years at least, the ladies of the ton have gradually become aware of the signs normally associated with straitened circumstances being increasingly displayed by members of the Fitzhugh family." She glanced at Stokes and Curtis. "For instance, the countess, Victoria, entertains at a level that is considered decidedly subpar for Moran's social rank. Also curious is that the countess is not active in supporting any known charity, which, these days, is distinctly odd, especially when judged against Moran's parliamentary rank.

"And then there are the signs like carriages not being replaced or refurbished to generally accepted ton standards, and outdated hangings and outmoded furniture, even in the reception rooms of Moran House." Looking at Stokes, Penelope said, "Those might be minor details, but taken together, they create a picture of thriftiness being doggedly and consistently pursued, but in the case of the Fitzhughs, for no apparent reason."

Penelope glanced at Mary. "Mary's dismissal is a case in point. It's a reduction in expenses for which there appears to be no rationale or reason. The dowager is known to be frail and of an age when she would be expected to have a companion, as indeed, until recently, she did." Penelope looked at Stokes and Barnaby and concluded, "All in all, there seems to be some financial situation in effect that impacts the earldom's coffers or, at least, the flow of money from those, but no one has any notion of what such a situation could be."

She paused, then went on, "The ladies also made clear that Moran's attitude in not assisting his brothers, especially Frederick, his heir apparent, while legally excusable, is not considered socially correct. Frederick, and William after him, are the heirs to the earldom, and accepted practice is that Moran should have ensured they lived in appropriate comfort and style. Further, the odd lack of funds is affecting the younger generation—both the males who are out on the town and, even more, the three girls who are about to be presented."

Meeting Barnaby's eyes, she explained, "Of all the signs suggesting that something is financially amiss within the earldom, that Imogen, Cleome, and Constance are planning a combined come-out ball for their three daughters, and they aren't planning on using the ballroom at Moran

House, which is apparently perfect for such an occasion, is unquestionably the most telling sign of all."

Mary shifted, and when the others glanced her way, she said, "I heard the…argument. Between the earl and the three ladies. They tried to persuade him to allow them to use the Moran House ballroom—and it is, indeed, a gorgeous room, albeit now thick with dust—but he said it had been shut up too long, and he was not of a mind to authorize the…" Mary closed her eyes and said, "In his words, 'the necessary expenditure to bring it up to snuff.'" She opened her eyes and shook her head. "Not even for three of his nieces at once."

Stokes, who had been jotting, glanced at Barnaby. "We definitely need those reports from Montague and Thomas."

Barnaby nodded. "Given the direction in which the information's pushing us, we should go over there and see what they've turned up so far." He met Penelope's gaze. "What you've heard might nudge them onto the right track."

"Indeed, but there's one other potentially highly pertinent fact that I learned this morning." She caught Stokes's gaze. "When I asked about Christopher Fitzhugh, I created a spot of bother in that the ladies were unsure how to explain what they've seen. It's a bit like the financial issue—a case of seeing the effects, the symptoms, but not being able to identify the cause. In short, all the ladies—and I suspect one might say, all the ton—have noticed a link of sorts between Christopher and Victoria, but no one believes it has a romantic basis. Everyone sees it as a type of friendship, and when I pressed, all agreed it was more as if Christopher and Victoria were working together toward some shared goal."

Mary leaned forward. "The staff at Moran House have seen the same thing. The countess and Christopher are definitely friends—they're forever sitting chatting together or whispering to each other. The staff put it down to them being closer in age to each other than to the earl and so having more similar interests and so on."

"Has Christopher always lived at Moran House?" Stokes asked.

Mary nodded. "As far as I know. He's certainly lived there for the past ten years I've been with the dowager." She paused, then chin firming, added, "That said, I can assure you that the staff never caught even a hint of them being lovers or anything even approaching that." She tipped her head toward Penelope. "Mrs. Adair's sources have reported exactly what the staff have seen."

"Good to know," Stokes replied.

"One last thought of my own," Penelope said. "When I was listening to the ladies struggling to explain what they'd observed with Christopher and Victoria, the word that leapt to my mind was 'coconspirators.'" She met Stokes's gaze. "That seemed the most accurate description of Christopher and Victoria's relationship."

Leaning forward, his gaze on Penelope, Stokes snagged the last sandwich left on the nearer platter. "Coconspirators, you say. To what end?"

Grimly, Penelope smiled. "That's the question, isn't it? Is it an innocent end or something more sinister?"

Stokes consumed the sandwich in two bites. He swallowed, flipped his notebook shut, then looked at the others. "While I'm sure we're all tempted to speculate, in this case, we have little leeway and no time to follow possibilities, no matter how tantalizing. With the pressure escalating, we need to focus on gathering facts."

"In that case"—Barnaby uncrossed his long legs and stood—"let's head to Montague's and Thomas's offices. Regardless of who is behind the poisonings, the financial situation afflicting the House of Moran is shaping up to be their motive."

CHAPTER 11

They had to have a clear and provable motive if they were ever going to charge any of the Fitzhughs with attempting to poison the earl. With that purpose driving them and convinced that there had to be some clue in the earldom's financial affairs, Barnaby, Penelope, and Stokes made their way without delay to Montague's office in Chapel Court, behind the looming bulk of the Bank of England.

Barnaby opened the door to the outer office, and Penelope swept past. He followed at her heels, with Stokes bringing up the rear. Montague's outer office comprised a large open area, most of which was cordoned off from the entrance by a polished wooden railing. Behind the railing, a lectern-like raised desk was placed beside a gate and faced the door, while the rest of the workspace played host to six desks at which junior clerks sat hunched over open ledgers. An air of concerted industry hovered over all.

As usual, Montague's senior clerk, Mr. Slocum, stood behind the raised desk. He looked up, saw them, and beamed. "Mr. and Mrs. Adair. And Inspector Stokes." Slocum half bowed. "If you will wait a moment, ma'am, sirs, I will confirm that Mr. Montague is free to see you." With a twinkle in his eyes, as he turned away, Slocum added, "Although I suspect he will be."

The thin clerk hurried down a corridor that led from the rear of the main office.

Barnaby stood beside a toe-tapping Penelope on the outer side of the wooden railing. Luckily for Penelope's burgeoning impatience, Slocum returned in less than a minute, his beaming countenance making his "Mr. Montague will see you immediately" entirely redundant.

Slocum opened the gate, and with a gracious nod and a "thank you," Penelope led the way through and on down the corridor. Montague's office lay at the end, and the man himself was standing at the open door.

"Welcome, my dear." Montague stooped to kiss Penelope's cheek, then held out his hand to Barnaby. "Well met, gentlemen." After shaking Stokes's hand and waving them all inside, Montague shut the door, as he did, continuing, "As you can see, Thomas is here, and I must say, we're very glad to see you."

On beholding the man seated in a chair beside the desk, Penelope's eyes widened. "Thomas! The other person we were hoping to meet."

"Indeed." Thomas rose. "And having delved somewhat into the Earl of Moran's finances, I can understand why."

He, too, kissed Penelope's cheek and shook Barnaby's and Stokes's hands.

Once the courtesies had been observed, they sorted out the seating, with Penelope, Barnaby, and Stokes pulling up three chairs before Montague's large desk. Montague returned to his admiral's chair behind the desk, his back to the windows beyond, while Thomas resumed his preferred position seated at the desk's end.

Penelope observed, "You seem to have been expecting us."

"More like hoping you would turn up and help us tease out what we're looking at." Montague waved at a collection of papers covered with neat figures that were spread over the desk.

Stokes eyed Montague's and Thomas's expressions. "The pair of you don't seem all that certain of what you've found."

"That's because we're not." Thomas nodded at Montague. "You start."

Leaning his forearms on the desk's edge, Montague reported, "I spoke with Cliffe—he's Moran's man of business. Initially, he maintained that all was above board and completely as one would expect of the accounts of a long-established landowner family such as the Fitzhughs. But when I mentioned the earl's murder and the consequent investigation and pressed him, Cliffe agreed to take another look at the accounts, just to be sure. He invited me to review them with him. I did, and he was correct in stating that nothing was amiss. But as for normal?" Lips setting, Montague shook his head. "I handle the accounts for several noble families, the Cynsters, the Chillingworths, and the Ashfords among others. I know what the allowances for various levels of family members and the amounts for the upkeep of households and so on within the haut ton should be."

When he paused, Penelope prompted, "And?"

"And what I was looking at was nothing like that." Montague met Barnaby's gaze. "The long and the short of it is that the Moran accounts are simply not in keeping with a family of that size and, especially, that social rank. Not today. Fifteen or twenty years ago, possibly. I pointed out the oddity to Cliffe, and he looked more closely and admitted I was correct. He, too, has other families of note as clients, and all would spend more than Moran. Significantly more."

Montague paused, then went on, "From all we could see, Cliffe and I concluded that, somehow, the earl had kept a very tight rein on all expenditures—personal, familial, and household. However, that only raised another question. Given we could see that the earldom's coffers were constantly being drawn down and then steadily replenished, and the inflows are, indeed, what one would expect for a landholding of that size in the here and now—indeed, the income is impressively healthy—then where are the funds going? The funds withdrawn were not deposited into any account over which Cliffe has oversight. Moreover, the earl could not possibly personally spend such amounts, and indeed, he hasn't. Eventually, Cliffe and I traced the withdrawn funds—which add up to a very significant amount—to an account at Rothschild's Bank. The account appears to be in the earl's name, but Cliffe has no records pertaining to that account."

Tipping his head Thomas's way, Montague concluded, "I immediately passed on all the information I'd gathered to Thomas."

Thomas inclined his head. "Indeed. But I should backtrack a trifle. While Montague was dealing with Cliffe, I decided to approach the Moran issue from a different direction. I'd heard the name bandied about in the context of several rather risky ventures. I thought it was odd at the time I heard it, because those ventures are not the sort even I would contemplate dabbling in, being far too uncertain for my taste."

Thomas had a long history of successfully investing in risky ventures.

"So I followed up the rumors," he went on, "and confirmed that, yes, Moran was, indeed, an investor in several of those schemes. It seems he cut his eyeteeth years ago on some of the more extreme companies floated on the promise of steam engines and railroads. Investments in such wildly speculative ventures are truly little more than bets, but to

Moran's credit, those wagers of his paid off. And, as is the nature of such ventures, those wagers paid handsomely."

Thomas linked his fingers and leaned back in the chair. "In the short time we've had, I've delved as far into the past as I could—covering about ten years—and it seems that, throughout that time, Moran had been actively seeking out and investing—very privately—in that particular type of enterprise. I dropped in on Randolph Cavanaugh, and he knew of Moran's name and, like me, had heard Moran mentioned as an investor in risky enterprises that Cavanaugh also views as too extreme to consider financing. However, he, too, knew of several Moran-backed ventures that had paid off over the years."

Thomas sat up, reached for one of the papers littering Montague's desk, waved it, then dropped it back on the desk. "I did some juggling of figures, then made my way here. If one puts together the amounts withdrawn from the estate with the probable returns from his risky investments, then by any even highly conservative estimation, Moran had to have been sitting on a massive fortune."

"That's what we were trying to work out when you arrived," Montague said. "Because from what Cliffe showed me of the earl's accounts, that massive fortune doesn't feature in any of the accounts Cliffe keeps."

Thomas put in, "It might be in the Rothschild's account or even some other account we've yet to stumble across."

Stokes was frowning. Carefully, he asked, "In terms of Moran's financial situation, what does all that mean?"

"In summary?" When Stokes nodded, Thomas replied, "It appears that over a period of more than a decade, the late earl has habitually used all available excess funds generated by the Moran estate to privately, and I would have to say rather secretively, invest in extremely risky enterprises. He's played the odds of failure versus success, and we believe that, in large part, he's won. However, where he's stashed the proceeds, we don't yet know." Thomas held up a finger. "But leave that with me. I will find out."

Barnaby regarded Thomas. "I believe you're saying that there's a very large pile of funds somewhere, and we know nothing about who else might know of it."

"Or have access to it." Thomas inclined his head. "Alternatively, and this might well be the case, he's providing finance to other risky ventures currently in development, and the money is in those companies' hands."

Thomas looked at Stokes. "It's possible that the motive for Moran's murder might lie either in access to those funds or in Moran's involvement with some as-yet-unknown risky scheme."

Stokes swore beneath his breath. "That's all this case needs—financial shenanigans."

"As of yet," Montague mildly stated, "we have no evidence of any misdeeds. Even once we learn what Moran was doing investing-wise at the time of his death, it's perfectly possible that there's no legal issue in it. Nothing illegal about anything at all."

Stokes grumbled some more.

"That said," Thomas put in, "an excessively large sum of money tends to engender covetousness, which often leads to crime."

Barnaby clarified, "So in and of itself, the money Moran had accumulated might have given rise to a motive for his murder."

"And," Penelope put in, "Moran's involvement in some specific risky scheme might also have generated a quite separate and distinct motive."

Stokes softly groaned.

They sat and contemplated the situation as they now understood it, then Penelope shook free of the mental mire and, looking across the desk at Montague, asked, "Have you had a chance to examine the financial affairs of the various family members?"

"My people have started on that," Montague replied, "and I've contacted Roscoe to see if he has anything pertinent to add. Thus far, however, the brothers—specifically the household of Mr. Frederick Fitzhugh and, separately, Mr. Christopher Fitzhugh—seem to be free of any financial wrongdoing. However, both seem distinctly strapped for cash. How deeply in difficulties each gentleman is, we're not yet sure, but if either have got into the hands of the cent-per-cents, I will shortly know."

Thomas added, "I've undertaken to look into the two brothers-in-law—Mitchelmore and Southerly. I seriously doubt Southerly is in any way underwater—he's a cautious, careful, and sensible fellow. I'm waiting to hear back about Mitchelmore. However, given that I am still waiting, there might be something relevant there."

"As for the junior members," Montague said, "the four on the town are all, to some degree, in difficulties, but from what I've seen thus far, none are sufficiently deeply in debt to provide any motive for killing the earl. Indeed, none are outside the range of incidental debt one would expect for gentlemen of their age and station."

Stokes looked questioningly at Penelope.

In response, she stated, “All your findings regarding the family—Frederick, Christopher, the nephews, and the Moran household—match the observations of my usual ton sources.” Montague and Thomas knew who her “usual ton sources” were. Penelope went on, “Collectively, the ladies reported that the Moran family, including its various branches, showed telltale signs of straitened circumstances, yet at the same time, there’s no evidence to suggest that the Moran estate, meaning the earldom as a whole, isn’t as wealthy as the ton have always taken it to be.” She held up her hands. “Viewed through a social lens, there appears to be an inexplicable contradiction.”

“I can understand that,” Montague said. “The earldom is, indeed, very wealthy, yet most of the family appear to be living on penury’s impoverished edge.”

“Exactly!” Penelope nodded. “It’s all good-quality cloth but slightly frayed at the edges.”

Stokes, busily jotting, was frowning. He paused, reread his notes, then stated, “In short, there is something odd in Moran’s finances arising from secretive investments, but as yet, we cannot say if that situation has given rise to a motive for murder, although it’s possible that’s the case.” He tapped his notebook. “In addition, we’ve established that both the late earl’s brothers and possibly one of his brothers-in-law are under some degree of financial strain but, again, cannot yet say if that is sufficient to give rise to a motive for the earl’s murder. And last but not least, we’ve confirmed that the late earl was very tightfisted regarding funds for his household and all family members.” Stokes shut his notebook and looked at the others. “As I see things, on the financial front, we need to wait for incoming information to make any further deductions.”

Montague and Thomas nodded.

Montague offered, “We might have something for you later today.” He glanced at Thomas. “Both Thomas and I have men working on learning more.”

“Good. Thank you.” Stokes tucked away his notebook and smiled. “Scotland Yard appreciates your help, as I’m sure you know.”

Thomas grinned back. “We just like solving financial riddles.”

Penelope picked up her reticule. “Come to dinner tonight and bring Griselda, Violet, and Rose, and the children, too, if you wish, along with whatever you’ve learned by that time. Shall we say six?”

Barnaby uncrossed his legs and glanced at Stokes. “We’re under pressure to solve this case rapidly, so any advance shared, however small, might get us further faster."

Stokes inclined his head. "True."

Montague and Thomas agreed.

Still regarding Stokes, Barnaby asked, "So what now for us?"

Frowning, Penelope said, "I think we should turn our minds to who moved the box of cigars." She looked at Barnaby and Stokes. "If we discount the Moran House staff, then the only ones in the house over the time the box was moved from the study to Frederick's old room were Christopher, Victoria, and the dowager."

"Well," Barnaby said, "the dowager is out, unless she instructed the staff."

"And," Penelope pointed out, "if it's true that Frederick was the dowager's favorite, why would she choose to place the incriminating evidence, from packet of poison to box of cigars, in his old room?"

Barnaby inclined his head. "Indeed. And given what your usual sources said about Christopher and Victoria being in league over something, it seems more likely it was one of them who moved the cigars."

Stokes grimaced. "What the facts seem to be indicating is that we likely have at least two different would-be murderers—the one who actually committed the deed and the one who poisoned the whiskey and cigars—and it seems possible that Christopher, Victoria, or both acting together might be responsible for the poison."

"We've always tacitly accepted," Barnaby said, "that whoever put the poison in the decanter and so carefully laced the cigars was almost certainly someone in the household."

"Someone not the staff," Penelope added.

Stokes grunted and pushed to his feet. "The pressure is on. We need results. Solid results." He nodded to Montague and Thomas as the others all got to their feet. "Let's leave these gentlemen to further pursue their financial trails—which might well reveal the motive for who actually murdered the earl—and see if we can resolve the question of who the poisoner is."

Barnaby nodded a farewell to Montague and Thomas, then waved Stokes and Penelope to the door. "Joseph, Chifley's assistant, seemed very sure he would be able to identify the man who bought the poison." He caught Stokes's gaze. "Can we arrange for Joseph to get a decent look at Christopher?"

Grimly, Stokes smiled. "Let's see what we can do."

~

More than an hour later, Barnaby stood in the shadowy nook to the right of the double doors giving onto the foyer of the main building of Scotland Yard.

Opposite, against the foyer's rear wall, Penelope stood alongside an innocuous-looking door to the left of the reception counter. She shifted impatiently, and inwardly, Barnaby grinned. He, too, was counting the minutes but, as usual, hid that rather better than his wife.

Getting everyone in position had taken time and not a little organization. It had been a bare two minutes to three o'clock before all was as they needed it to be. At that moment, the large clock on the wall behind the reception counter showed the time as one minute to three o'clock.

Given the rank of their primary suspect, Barnaby had suggested ways to make their findings watertight, and Penelope had further expounded on his notions, the upshot being that their panel of possible poison-buyers who shared a strong resemblance to Frederick Fitzhugh had expanded to five.

Consequently, summoned by a note from Stokes, countersigned by Barnaby and delivered by Sergeant O'Donnell, the first prospects to arrive had been Byron and Hugh Mitchelmore. The pair had walked breezily in at ten minutes to three o'clock and were now standing, somewhat nonplussed, by the foyer wall, a little way from and to the right of the reception counter, with O'Donnell in close attendance.

Subsequently, at five minutes to the hour, summoned by a similar note delivered by Constable Morgan, William and George Fitzhugh had strolled into the foyer. Although curious over finding their cousins also present, the Fitzhugh gentlemen had obediently followed Morgan's directive and taken up a position mirroring that of their cousins, beside the wall to the left of the counter.

Constable Walsh had been sent to fetch Christopher Fitzhugh, with orders to arrive at the Yard at precisely three o'clock.

When the city's bells tolled and the clock behind the reception counter ticked past the hour, Barnaby sensed mounting tension in all those who knew what was coming.

At two minutes past the hour, the double doors were pushed inward, and Christopher Fitzhugh strode in, his expression telegraphing that he was annoyed, impatient, and ready to be belligerent.

Coming through the doors behind Christopher, Constable Walsh encouraged him to walk toward the reception counter.

When Christopher, having noted his nephews and consequently adopted a blander expression, paced forward, Walsh took up a position before the double doors.

Barnaby shifted his gaze to Penelope; Christopher's arrival was her cue.

As Christopher approached the reception counter, she rapped gently on the door beside her.

The door opened, and Stokes walked into the foyer.

He was closely followed by Joseph Greer, Chifley's assistant.

Halting level with the counter, over his shoulder, in a low voice audible only to Penelope and the sergeant behind the counter, Stokes asked Joseph, "Is the man who bought the packet of strychnine from you on April the seventh in the foyer?"

Stokes stepped aside, giving Joseph a clear view of all the Fitzhughs in the room.

Joseph looked first at Byron and Hugh, then his gaze moved on to Christopher, and his eyes widened. "Yes!" Joseph raised a hand and pointed at Christopher. "That's the man."

For an instant, Christopher stared uncomprehendingly at Joseph, then recognition hit, swiftly followed by realization.

His jaw setting, Christopher spun on his heel and took one rapid step toward the doors—only to find himself facing the considerable bulk of Constable Walsh, with Barnaby ambling up to stand at the constable's side.

Barnaby met and held Christopher's gaze as fear seeped in and swamped all fury.

Smiling amiably, Walsh gestured toward Stokes. "I think the inspector wants a word, sir."

From the rear of the foyer, Penelope watched as, warily, Christopher Fitzhugh turned and faced the room. He took in the startled looks on his nephews' faces, then brought his gaze to Stokes, and slowly, as if he was having to force his legs to cooperate, he walked toward the counter.

Reaching it, Christopher inclined his head. "Inspector." His gaze moved on to Penelope. "Mrs. Adair."

As Barnaby strolled up to join them, Christopher cast him a look, then nodded. "Adair."

His expression bleak, Christopher returned his gaze to Stokes. "I understand you wish to speak with me."

"Indeed." In a formal voice, Stokes stated, "Christopher Fitzhugh, I'm arresting you for the murder by poisoning of Winslow, butler of Moran House, and the attempted murder by poison of your late brother, the Earl of Moran."

Penelope had expected to hear gasps from the assembled young gentlemen. When none came, she shifted and peered around Barnaby and saw that all four of Christopher's nephews were standing, staring at him with their mouths hanging open. They were literally speechless.

~

They left Christopher to stew in the interrogation room in the basement while Stokes dispatched O'Donnell, Walsh, and Morgan to Moran House, O'Donnell and Walsh to fetch the countess, and Morgan, with his appealingly youthful appearance and his engaging ways, to work his wiles with the staff and see what he could learn regarding the moving of the box of cigars on the afternoon following Winslow's death.

By the time Penelope, Barnaby, and Stokes joined Christopher in the interrogation room, he had, it seemed, realized that his spontaneous reaction to Joseph Greer's accusation had been tantamount to a confession. While they filed into the room and claimed the three chairs on the opposite side of the bare table behind which Christopher sat, he stared at his hands, clasped on the table, but as soon as they'd settled on the chairs, he raised his gaze and stated, "I put the poison into the whiskey decanter in Gordon's study." His tone was flat. "I emptied the decanter and swirled a solution of the poison inside the bottle and left it stoppered on the tantalus." He met their gazes, one by one, then went on, "But that's all I did. I didn't refill the decanter with whiskey, and I didn't force any down Winslow's throat."

When, his lips compressing, Christopher fell silent, Stokes inclined his head. "We accept that you did not intend to poison Winslow. You did, however, intend to poison and kill your brother, Gordon Fitzhugh, the Earl of Moran."

To that, Christopher gave no answer but simply lowered his gaze once more to his clasped hands.

In an almost conversational tone, Barnaby asked, "Why was that?" When Christopher glanced his way, Barnaby went on, "You're not in the direct line of succession anymore…but perhaps you imagined that if the packet of poison was found in Frederick's old room, even though he hasn't been in there for years, that would be enough to cast suspicion on him."

"You also signed the poison register at Chifley's as F. Fitzhugh," Penelope said, "presumably to provide evidence that might have seen Frederick hang."

"And," Barnaby continued, "if Frederick was convicted of the crime, the title and estate would not pass to his heirs, as they would be classed as his beneficiaries, but instead, would pass to you."

When Christopher simply stared stonily at Barnaby, Stokes prodded, "Did you think we would discover that Frederick was strapped for cash and take that as his motive to murder the earl?"

Christopher guffawed, although the sound had a hollow ring. "Strapped for cash? Frederick isn't strapped—he's desperate! Just think—he has only the same allowance as me, and he has six children, and the first of his four daughters is coming out this year. Even with Imogen's money, he's in dire straits. He's literally desperate to make ends meet. He has to find a goodly amount of money from somewhere, and soon, and his need for funds far exceeds mine."

"But you do need funds," Penelope pressed, "don't you?"

Christopher shot her an angry look and didn't reply.

Penelope regarded him for a moment, then went on, "And then there's Victoria. She wants more funds, too, doesn't she?" She tipped her head, her gaze on Christopher's face. "I can see you placing poison in the decanter, but I have difficulty imagining you having the patience to doctor the cigars. So many cigars. All so very carefully done."

Christopher lowered his gaze to his hands and remained silent, but his fingers tensed.

Gently, Penelope went on, "Was it a joint effort on your parts? You and she egging each other on? You both wanted Gordon dead, more or less for the same reason—to free yourselves from the financial constraints he had imposed on you both. Was it a wager of sorts? Which one would be responsible for his death? Other than you buying the poison, which, as it's turned out, instead of implicating Frederick has put your neck firmly in a noose—or at the very least, your feet on the deck of a transport bound for Botany Bay—your scheme was, indeed, ingenious in its way. Moran's death could have occurred at any time after you placed the twin sources of poison in his study. Each of you would almost certainly have had a sound alibi for the time of death."

Barnaby put in, "If you hadn't been so ham-fisted in your attempts to incriminate Frederick, you might even have got away with the poisoning, undetected."

"In that regard," Penelope said, "having two sources of the same poison would have muddied the investigative waters considerably. However, in this case…"

Stokes stated, "We've already sent for the countess, and we're questioning the staff at Moran House regarding the movement of the box of cigars from the study to Frederick's old room."

"From experience," Penelope told Christopher, "given that the box was moved during the day and during a period when, of the family, only you, Victoria, and the dowager were there, our chances of finding one or more of the staff who can confirm who carried the box upstairs are reasonably good." She faintly smiled. "We'll soon see."

Stokes studied Christopher's half-hidden face, then said, "You may not yet have heard, but the poisoned cigars very nearly caused another death."

That brought Christopher's head up. He stared at Stokes. "Who?"

Sternly, Barnaby replied, "Before the dinner, your youngest nephew, Theodore, stole a cigar from the box in the study. The next day, he attempted to smoke it, but the taste repelled him, and he immediately stopped. His inexperience in cutting the entire end paper from the cigar before lighting it was the only thing that saved his life. He'll live but, truly, only through pure luck."

"Vincent also took one of the cigars," Penelope informed Christopher, "but he hadn't attempted to smoke it."

Stokes went on, "We've since confirmed that all of the cigars in the box were poisoned, very carefully and craftily. Not even a connoisseur would have easily spotted the tampering. Consequently, several people might have died, not just your brother. Just as another person was, indeed, killed by the poisoned whiskey. As attempts to specifically murder the earl, both poisonings displayed complete disregard for the lives of others." He caught Christopher's gaze. "That will assuredly weigh with the judge at your trial."

Christopher's expression had turned faintly ashen.

When he remained silent, Stokes asked, "Do you have anything to say?"

Christopher refocused on Stokes, then looked at Penelope and, lastly, at Barnaby. "I poisoned the whiskey. Sadly, the plot came to naught." He shook his head. "There's nothing more I wish to say."

After leaving the attending sergeant and constable to show Christopher to his cell, with Barnaby and Stokes, Penelope emerged from the basement to learn that Lady Victoria had been brought in and awaited their pleasure in the nicer interview room on the ground floor.

Even more encouraging was the sight of Constable Morgan, waiting to one side of the foyer with one of the Moran House maids.

The girl was obviously nervous. Plastering on a reassuring smile, Penelope glided across the foyer to greet the pair, with Barnaby and Stokes on her heels.

Dredging her memory, still smiling, Penelope halted before the young woman. "Gwen, isn't it?"

The maid dropped into a curtsy. "Yes, ma'am." As she straightened, Gwen shot a look at Morgan, beside her. "I'm the upstairs maid at Moran House, and the constable here said as you'd like to know what I saw on the afternoon after poor Winslow died."

Penelope nodded. "Indeed, we would. So what did you see?"

"I was gathering the dowager's linens for washing. We were late doing that, what with all the bother of the morning, and I wouldn't normally be upstairs at that time, so I was being quiet and quick, and as I was crossing the gallery where it meets the west wing corridor, I saw the countess carrying that box that holds the earl's cigars. She was carrying it down that corridor. I thought that was odd, because the box was always kept in the earl's study, and I wondered what the countess would want with the cigars, but of course, I just hurried on."

"The west wing." Penelope raised her brows. "Does Mr. Frederick's old room lie along that corridor?"

"Yes, ma'am."

"So," Stokes rumbled, "the countess was heading for that room?"

Gwen blinked at him, then looked at Penelope and nervously said, "I'm sure I couldn't say, ma'am. She was walking toward that room, and her room isn't in that wing, but I didn't see her go in any door."

"That's quite all right," Penelope soothed. "We only need to know what you actually saw." She threw a stern glance at Stokes, then turned back to Gwen. "Thank you for helping us." She looked at Morgan. "Please escort Gwen back to Moran House."

Morgan appeared eager and glanced at Stokes.

Stokes grudgingly nodded. "Yes, take Gwen home to Park Lane, but come back as soon as she's safely indoors."

Morgan grinned, saluted, and after Gwen rose from bobbing another curtsy, steered the maid toward the front doors.

"Well!" Feeling thoroughly vindicated, Penelope turned and arched a brow at Stokes and Barnaby. "Shall we go and see what Victoria has to say?"

Wordlessly, Stokes waved her to the door behind the counter, and with a grin, she led the way.

Unlike the interrogation room in the basement with its harsh lamp-light, the interview room had a window that overlooked the rear of the building, allowing daylight to illuminate the space. When Penelope walked in, O'Donnell and Walsh were standing with their backs to the wall behind their prisoner. Victoria was seated on the opposite side of the polished wooden table, and despite the gentler light, she did not appear at her best.

Her face was pale, and her lips were pinched, and when she looked up and met Penelope's gaze, Victoria's expression held a wealth of uncertainty, combined with a large measure of apprehension.

She watched as Penelope, Stokes, and Barnaby took seats on the table's opposite side, then focused on Stokes and, in a bid for imperiousness, demanded, "Why am I here?"

Penelope sat back and watched Victoria as Stokes replied, "I should inform you that Christopher Fitzhugh has been arrested for the murder of Winslow, your late butler, and also for attempting to murder your late husband."

Victoria blinked, and her gaze turned inward. Then she looked at Barnaby. "Is that true?"

"Quite true," he replied. "We have irrefutable evidence that Christopher bought the poison that caused Winslow's death, and Christopher will be convicted on both charges."

To Penelope's eyes, Victoria had grown noticeably paler. Hoping to jolt her further, Penelope said, "And of course, now there's poor Theodore, who was also poisoned."

"What?" Victoria's eyes grew round, and her complexion lost all remaining color.

Penelope widened her own eyes. "Haven't you heard?"

Patently horrified, like an automaton, Victoria shook her head from side to side. "No," she whispered, "I hadn't heard."

Leaning forward and clasping her hands on the table, Penelope explained, "The cigars in that box in the earl's study. They'd been very carefully poisoned, and when they arrived at Moran House on Monday evening, Vincent and Theodore slipped away, waited for their moment, then raided the earl's study for what they could find. The only things they found worth taking were the cigars. They took one each."

Victoria appeared genuinely distressed. "Oh God."

"But, of course," Penelope went on, "now we've spoken with Christopher, we know that while he bought the poison and added it to the whiskey decanter, we also know he wasn't the one who poisoned the cigars."

Stokes confirmed, "He admits to the whiskey decanter but not the cigars."

With a faint, encouraging smile, Penelope continued, "So, please tell us, Victoria, why you thought to move the box containing the rest of the cigars, all of which were also poisoned, from your late husband's study to Frederick's old room?"

As if assisting, Barnaby explained, "We've heard from a witness who saw you carrying the box upstairs."

Victoria moistened her lips, then said, "I..." Her eyes darted this way, then that.

Helpfully, in an entirely reasonable tone, Penelope offered, "Because after Winslow was accidentally poisoned and died, you wanted to remove the cigars in case they tempted someone else who would then also die?"

Victoria jumped on the excuse. "Yes." She nodded. "I wanted to be sure no one else would accidentally die."

Penelope blinked, then looked confused. "But how did you know the cigars were poisoned?" She met Victoria's eyes. "You just told us—and showed us—that you didn't know Theodore had been poisoned via one of the cigars." Holding Victoria's gaze, Penelope tilted her head. "Why did you think moving the cigars would guard against further poisonings?"

Across the table, Victoria stared at Penelope. Victoria opened her mouth, then shut it. Finally, dropping all pretense, she narrowed her eyes and spat, "All right! Yes, I knew the cigars were poisoned because I'd poisoned them. But I never meant for anyone but Gordon..." She stretched out one hand as if imploring their understanding. "Truly, he so rarely invited anyone to visit, much less into his study, that the person by far most likely to die from either the whiskey or the cigars was him!"

She put her hands to her face. "I was horrified when I heard that Winslow had died. You'd already removed the decanter, so the only thing I could do was take the cigars and leave them somewhere out of sight until I could get rid of them."

From her tone, Penelope judged that was all true.

Then, with her gaze fixing on the table, Victoria uttered a disgusted sound. "What a useless pair of plotters we turned out to be."

"You and Christopher?" Barnaby clarified.

Victoria nodded. "And in the end, if we'd just waited another day, we wouldn't have needed to do anything! Gordon was dead, and Frederick would have inherited, and no matter what Christopher says, Frederick would have behaved much more reasonably. He was always a sensible soul and would have helped Christopher out of the mire and loosened the purse strings for me, and that's really all either of us wanted."

Stokes bluntly asked, "Do you have any idea who killed the earl?"

Victoria shook her head. "No. None. But if I knew who had done it, I would shake their hand and call down blessings upon them."

Puzzled, her gaze on Victoria, Penelope asked, "Why? Why did Moran have to die?"

Victoria met Penelope's gaze, then smiled tightly. "Let me give you a glimpse of what it was like being a member of the House of Moran. Gordon was the epitome of a frugal man. He was dictatorial as to expenses and turned mean and nasty if anyone questioned his views. He expected us—all the rest of the family—to live up to his mental standard of how we should, as members of the House of Moran, present to the world, but he insisted that we scrimped and saved to do it! He expected us to manage on allowances that simply weren't sufficient, and he wouldn't listen to any complaints. It was a constant battle."

They listened as Victoria outlined a host of what she termed her late husband's small meannesses, from his refusal to bestow christening gifts on his nephews and nieces, much less send gifts on their birthdays, to his stance against footing the bill for any refurbishment of the family's private rooms. "He always carried on about social standing and insisted an appropriate façade should be maintained, but simultaneously, he refused to pay for any of it."

Victoria's list was sobering; with her insights into the normal expenses of a ton family, Penelope was quietly aghast.

Finally, Victoria concluded, "The long and the short of it is that Gordon was a miser and reveled in that state."

When she fell silent, Penelope said, "Thank you for explaining." There were several aspects she didn't yet fully understand, but she knew much more than she had before.

Stokes glanced at Penelope, then said to Victoria, "Lady Fitzhugh, I'm arresting you for the attempted murder of your late husband, the Earl of Moran."

Penelope exchanged a glance with Barnaby, then rose, and Barnaby and Stokes followed suit.

Victoria looked up and met their gazes, then, her expression turning bleak, she shrugged and looked at the table again.

They quit the room, leaving O'Donnell and Walsh to escort Victoria to a cell.

On reaching the foyer, Penelope paused and thought over all Victoria had revealed.

Barnaby and Stokes halted to either side and, judging by their expressions, seemed to be similarly occupied.

Eventually, Penelope ventured, "I can understand Christopher wanting to seize the title and the associated wealth, and for Victoria, I can appreciate that the frustration and uncertainty engendered by forever being condemned to live on a frugal edge—seemingly without any necessity but solely because of one man's meanness—might have, in the end, proved too galling to be borne. Yet if the earl being miserly toward his family is, in fact, the motive behind his actual murder, and Frederick is truly as desperate for funds as Christopher believes, then Frederick is the obvious suspect—except that he remained in full view of all the rest of the family throughout the period during which the murder was committed."

Frowning, Barnaby observed, "Well, at least we've learned who the poisoner was—or rather, who the poisoners were."

Stokes grimaced and glanced at Barnaby and Penelope. "Yet despite that advance, as far as I can see, we're no closer to identifying who actually murdered the Earl of Moran."

CHAPTER 12

Pleased on one score and confounded on the other, Barnaby and Penelope left Stokes to make his report to the Commissioner and returned home.

They'd only just shed their coats into Mostyn's arms when the doorbell pealed.

Mostyn set aside their coats and opened the door, revealing Montague and Violet, standing with Thomas and Rose on the porch.

Penelope beamed and waved the four inside. "You're exceedingly prompt. Come in." She and Violet touched cheeks, then Penelope did the same with Rose. Stepping back, Penelope arched her brows. "No children?"

With a glance at Montague and Thomas, who were being welcomed by Barnaby, Violet replied, "We decided this case sounds too serious."

"And in discussing it, we'll do better without distraction," Rose concluded.

Penelope nodded. "I agree. We'll need our wits fully focused to unravel this mystery. We need to look beyond the facts, and I'm very glad you two came. The situation is quite complicated, and fresh insights will be valuable."

The knocker was plied again, and Mostyn admitted Stokes and Griselda, also unaccompanied by their children. The ladies spent a few minutes exchanging greetings, then the door at the rear of the hall swung open, and Mary Alder and Julian joined the gathering, with Curtis bringing up the rear.

"Good!" Penelope clapped her hands. "We're all here."

She waited while Barnaby introduced Mary and Julian to Montague, Thomas, Rose, Violet, and Griselda; Curtis was already known to all those there.

Then Penelope gestured with both hands toward the drawing room. "Shall we get settled and commence our deliberations?"

With expectant smiles, everyone filed into the drawing room and settled in what had become their customary places. Extra chairs had been added to the circle for Julian and Curtis, and Penelope drew Mary to sit beside her and Barnaby on one of the sofas. Violet, Rose, and Griselda settled on the sofa opposite, while Stokes, Thomas, and Montague availed themselves of the three armchairs that, with the additions for Julian and Curtis, formed an arc between the ends of the sofas, facing the fireplace.

"First," Barnaby said, "to bring everyone up to date with the latest developments, Christopher Fitzhugh and Victoria Fitzhugh have been arrested and charged—Christopher with the murder of Winslow and the attempted murder of the late earl, and Victoria with a second but connected and coincident attempt to murder the earl."

Everyone bar Barnaby, Stokes, and Penelope looked shocked. A weak "Good heavens" and similar exclamations came from various throats.

"That's a turn-up," Curtis observed, summing up the general reaction.

Into the ensuing silence, Stokes added, "The Commissioner has reviewed our evidence and approved the charges. Consequently, from the investigation's perspective, the poisoning case is dealt with and done."

"Perhaps," Thomas allowed. "But such charges, such crimes, are going to cause a significant amount of uneasiness among the ton."

Penelope inclined her head. "Indeed."

Stokes sighed and gloomily prophesized, "And that will only strengthen the voices clamoring for us to declare who actually killed Moran forthwith! If only it was that easy."

"So"—Montague surveyed Stokes, Barnaby, and Penelope—"where has the investigation got to with regard to the murderer?"

"We're still unclear as to the motive behind the attack that killed the earl," Barnaby stated.

Penelope said, "Independently, Victoria and Christopher stated that their murderous intentions were driven by the earl subjecting them to long-standing monetary pressure." She tipped her head toward Montague and Thomas. "Montague and Thomas saw evidence of that in the earldom's accounts. In essence, the earl behaved toward Victoria, Christopher, and all the rest of his family in an extremely miserly, penny-pinching fashion, despite the earldom being exceedingly flush with funds. Neither Victoria nor Christopher had any real idea of why the earl elected to behave as he did, and in lieu of any understandable reason or explanation, they both assumed his motivation arose from a vengeful form of meanness. That he did as he did because he enjoyed making their lives a constant financial and social struggle."

Barnaby nodded. "They saw his behavior as a vindictive exercise of personal power."

Thomas and Montague exchanged a glance, then Montague said, "As to that, we can confirm that three of the branches of the family—the Frederick Fitzhughs, the Mitchelmores, and Christopher Fitzhugh—are in debt. In Frederick's and Christopher's cases, significant debt. Both are in deep with creditors and increasingly desperate for respite. Mitchelmore's case is less fraught. We understand he approached the earl for a loan in order to buy out the co-owners of a factory that he and the co-owners jointly operate in Leeds."

"The other owners want to sell," Thomas stated, "but the factory is a sound business, and Mitchelmore is right in trying to hold on to it. The factory has its best days ahead of it, and for him, retaining ownership would be the better option. However, the earl refused. That meant Mitchelmore was forced to take out a sizable mortgage at business rates, which are quite high."

Thomas glanced at the others. "In short, Mitchelmore has been forced into significant debt by the earl's intransigence, but Mitchelmore is not yet at the point of sinking beneath the burden, and it's possible he'll manage well enough. However, both Frederick and Christopher are well out of their depth and floundering."

"So," Stokes said, "potentially, the earl's death benefits them all."

Thomas and Montague responded in unison, "Unquestionably."

Thomas went on, "As I expected, Viscount Southerly and his family are in rude financial health. More, it's widely known that Southerly severely disapproved of how Moran dealt financially with the other Fitzhughs. Consequently, Southerly has been almost fanatically careful over keeping his family financially separate from the earldom. Also, Southerly's sons are as yet too young to be any real drain on his coffers.

The Southerly family are the only branch connected to the Fitzhugh tree with no financial problems."

Thomas looked at Montague as if passing a baton.

Montague obligingly picked up the tale. "While the Southerlys have nothing to worry about, the same cannot be said of the young gentlemen of the family, meaning the four who are already on the town. Although none are in absolutely dire straits yet, their debts are steadily mounting and have been for some time. The more pressing issue is that, when combined with the other pending demands on their fathers' purses—Frederick with his large household and four daughters to present to the ton, and Mitchelmore with his household, a daughter to present this year, and a hefty unexpected mortgage—the younger men's debts pile yet more pressure on their fathers' ability to manage and would, of themselves, constitute a growing concern."

"Another financial straw for the camels' backs?" Penelope asked.

Montague nodded. "Indeed."

"What you're suggesting," Stokes said, "is that, setting aside Christopher Fitzhugh, Frederick Fitzhugh and Mitchelmore had the most to gain from the earl's death."

"Assuming that Frederick, when he inherits, will be freer with the earldom's funds, then yes." Montague looked at Penelope and Barnaby. "And by all accounts of Frederick's character, that he will be more receptive to assisting with family debts is a reasonable assumption."

Barnaby said, "I can see that Curtis has something to report, but before we leave the financial realm"—Barnaby looked at Thomas—"did you uncover anything more about Moran's investing?"

Thomas grinned. "I'm glad you asked, because I'm quite pleased with myself that I managed to learn what I have. While my assistants pursued the paperwork, I tracked down two investors who, in the past, had joined Moran in separate investments. Neither have any current association with him, and both were happy to share their views of him as an investor."

"And?" Stokes prompted.

"Essentially, both told the same story. Namely, that Moran was a careful and rather possessive investor, always wanting to know every last little detail and insisting on being kept informed of every financial and also operational decision." Thomas glanced around the circle of faces. "That level of involvement by an investor is unusual. My sources said that Moran always drove a hard bargain and, in their view, was himself driven to ensure his chosen project—the one in which he'd invested capital—succeeded. Indeed, they maintained he was obsessed with success to an extraordinary degree. While the two projects my sources had helped fund were wildly successful, both men had heard of other projects that Moran had backed that had failed, in some cases spectacularly, and they suggested that his current behavior was in reaction to those past failures."

Stokes narrowed his eyes. "Any hint of anyone likely to bear a grudge because of one of those past failures?"

"Or Moran's obsessiveness with regard to his current projects?" Barnaby added.

Thomas shook his head. "No. And I would say that, in general, with company failures, the shoe would be on the other foot. Meaning as an investor who'd lost money, Moran might bear significant ill will toward those involved in the failed project."

Montague was nodding. "That's usually the way risky ventures play out—it's buyer beware, quite literally."

"That," Thomas went on, "brings me to Moran's current projects—or rather his interlocking web of projects, which is really one gigantic project. It involves constructing shorter railway branches radiating from the stations at Edinburgh, Glasgow, and York." Thomas grimaced. "My contacts don't reach that far north, so I can't report from anyone on the ground, as it were, but I understand this project—in all its various pieces—is in the very early stages of planning, and they haven't even got to the point of approaching farmers to put lines across their fields."

"Historically," Montague said, "it's at that point—the actual laying of line—where difficulties arise."

Thomas tipped his head. "The interesting thing is, when one looks at this project, the scope and intent of it, if one looks beyond the concomitant risks, it makes a great deal of commercial sense."

"So," Barnaby said, "likely another winner for Moran?"

Thomas waggled his head. "Possibly. But the one fly in the ointment is that, in being the principal backer, Moran was risking an extremely large amount on the project. He's already put in an eye-watering sum, and if for any reason the project fails—or even just hits hurdles and progress slows significantly, as often occurs with such ventures…" Thomas shrugged. "Suffice it to say that any other man would be staring at ruin."

"Could Moran have weathered such a failure?" Penelope asked.

"Yes," Thomas replied, "but the damage would be significant, and I don't just mean to his wealth."

Thomas met Barnaby's gaze. "I dropped in on Randolph Cavanaugh and ran the project and Moran's involvement with it past him, and he was as viscerally horrified as I. Moran has risked an awful lot of his wealth on what amounts to a single throw of the dice—a single project that could hit major problems in so many different, unpredictable, and unknowable ways." Thomas shook his head. "To anyone who invests prudently, this is the very opposite of that. I've built an investment business based on taking risks, but I would never take a risk like that."

"What I'm hearing," Penelope said, "is that on the one hand, the Earl of Moran forces his family to exist on the cusp of penury, while on the other hand, he's been taking enormous risks with funds he presumably amassed from the earldom's coffers, augmented with capital gained from previous successful risky investments."

She paused, then concluded, "In a nutshell, he's been expanding his investing capital and actively pursuing risky ventures while simultaneously stinting his family at every possible turn." She looked at Thomas and Montague, then at Barnaby. "Do I have that right?"

Montague and Thomas inclined their heads, and soberly, Barnaby said, "I believe you are entirely correct."

"Essentially," Thomas said, "he was robbing Peter to pay Paul, with Peter being his family and Paul his latest risky investment project."

"That is, indeed, a reasonable summation," Montague said.

Frowning, Stokes asked, "But does that get us any closer to identifying who killed him?"

When no one answered, Stokes looked at Curtis. "What have you learned?"

Curtis squared his shoulders and reported, "I managed to catch Nate Samuel last night. We had a good jaw about the earl." Curtis dipped his head toward Barnaby. "It seems the workers' unions are well aware of that bill Moran was aiming to push, and Samuel had been delegated to find something—anything—they could use as leverage to persuade Moran to back off."

Almost eagerly, Stokes asked, "Did Samuel find anything?"

Curtis shot Stokes a commiserating look. "No. And he's tried. He's turned over all the usual stones and asked all the usual coves who can tell you whispers of the nobility doing things they shouldn't—things they wouldn't want other people to know about. However, there's not a single rumor like that about Moran. Samuel and his governors were quite disgusted, you might say, that the man seemed to have no exploitable secrets at all."

Barnaby humphed. "Not of the illegal sort, at least."

Stokes sighed. "Investing in risky ventures is no crime."

Curtis went on, "I asked Samuel if he'd heard of anyone else having a beef with Moran, and he said he hadn't. As he assured me, if he had heard of anyone, he would've been around to speak with them right away, to see if there was anything in it his governors could use."

Stokes frowned. "Is it likely that anyone from one of the workers' organizations—not necessarily Samuel—took it upon themselves to murder Moran?"

Curtis shook his head. "You're clutching at straws. As far as I've heard, the union bosses have kept their push against Moran and his ideas to themselves." He shrugged. "Makes sense. Learning someone's secrets in order to essentially blackmail them isn't the sort of enterprise you tell the newspapers about. And now, they're just happy that he's gone and grateful to whoever did the deed."

Julian shifted, and when everyone glanced his way and smiled encouragingly, he raised his chin and reported, "I spent today working through the jarveys who cover that area of Mayfair. I spoke to all of them I could find, and all said that last Monday night was pretty quiet, as Mondays often are, and they didn't see anyone suspicious about Park Lane or any of the streets around Moran House." He paused, then confided, "I know lots of the locals, of course, the servants and grooms and such of all the houses 'round about, and I checked with them, too. There were enough of them out and about—at back gates or going in and out of stables—to be sure, and other than the Samuel bloke Mr. Curtis spoke with, no one spotted anyone they didn't recognize on the streets or in the lanes that night. Samuel was the only person, stranger or not, wandering about in that area at that time on Monday night."

Stokes grimaced and looked at Penelope. "Am I right in thinking that, in Mayfair, between nine and ten-thirty is generally a quieter time of the evening?"

Penelope nodded. "The ton will have driven off to their evening's engagements and not yet returned." She met Stokes's gaze. "So yes, if the murderer had come to Moran House, clambered over the courtyard wall, killed the earl, then walked away, they should have stood out." She tipped her head to Julian. "One if not more of Julian's sources should have seen them."

Stokes sighed. After a moment of cogitation, he said, "So with regard to the murder, we're still left with the conundrum of the terrace door, which was open but should have been shut, and no evidence whatsoever that anyone came in from outside the house by clambering over the lane wall and, after murdering the earl, left via the same route. In fact, all the evidence we do have insists that no one did."

"More," Barnaby went on, "over the same period, all the family, including all the most likely suspects, were in the drawing room, in full view of each other."

They were pondering those perplexing facts when Mostyn walked in with the news that dinner awaited their pleasure.

Penelope rose and waved everyone to their feet and toward the door. To Mary, Curtis, and Julian, she said, "Don't think of slipping away. You're as much a part of this investigation as anyone, and our habit when we reach impasses such as this is to put aside the investigation for the duration of the meal and fill our heads with conversation about our families and anything else that interests us. Then, when we come back to the drawing room afterward, we return to the case with fresh eyes and open minds."

"Or so we hope," Stokes muttered as he fell in with the other men, and they followed the ladies from the room.

~

As matters transpired, there was no shortage of topics to be discussed over the dining table, given that the children of the couples present were at the stage of growing up fast.

"You turn around," Griselda said, "and they've somehow grown another inch! I swear Megan is going to be as tall as her father."

Violet countered, "Martin's reached the stage of running Gilda off her feet. And now he's learned to throw a ball, I've had to move all the breakables into cupboards."

"Hettie mentioned that there was to be a balloon ascension in Green Park in two weeks' time." Penelope looked around the table. "Shall we make up a party and take the children? I'm sure they'd enjoy seeing a balloon go up."

Everyone readily agreed, and the date, time, and place to assemble was settled, with Julian invited to help with the younger boys and Mary encouraged to come along and stroll with the ladies.

"We'll bring William and Alice, too." Rose looked down the table at Julian. "They're nearer your age and will help keep the little ones in line."

Smiling, Griselda said to Mary, "With the children absorbed, we might get some time to actually catch our breaths."

Eventually, with the dessert of chocolate-and-raspberry charlotte consumed and the plates cleared, the company rose and repaired to the drawing room.

Penelope sat in her accustomed place. She waited until the others had resumed their seats, then firmly stated, "We're missing something—the piece of information that, if we knew it, would make sense of all else we've learned. I suggest we begin again, but from a different perspective." She looked around and raised her brows. "Who gains most from the earl's death? Who was most desperate for any ease his demise would bring about?" She held up a hand as a point they'd made a day earlier struck her. "And what was the event that triggered our spur-of-the-moment, plainly not a planned killing?" She met the others' gazes. "No one picks up a bust sitting on a shelf and smashes in someone's skull because they planned it that way."

"No, indeed," Rose replied. "But as for who gains the most, surely that has to be Frederick Fitzhugh. However"—she tipped her head—"was he the most desperate?"

"Desperation," Thomas stated, "depends very much on the individual's state of mind."

Knowing Thomas's history and that it made him something of an expert on that subject, Penelope had to acknowledge that was true. "I agree with both observations. However, Frederick was in the drawing room when the earl was killed, so he isn't the murderer." She looked around the circle of faces; everyone appeared as puzzled as she. "That's what I meant by saying we're missing something. There has to be someone else who, for whatever reason—money, politics, or something else entirely—was desperate enough to do the deed and wasn't in that drawing room."

Barnaby stated, "We've found no evidence of an intruder approaching the house, let alone gaining entry to it, whether to steal documents or with the intention of killing the earl."

Penelope replied, "No intent, remember? The killing of Moran was a spur-of-the-moment act."

Barnaby paused, then inclined his head. "All right. Let's pursue the issue from that angle. 'Spur-of-the-moment' implies that some event in the immediately preceding period incited someone to murder the earl. So"—he looked around the gathering—"what was that event? Given all our evidence indicates that the murderer was someone who was inside Moran House at the time, what occurrence compelled that person to act?"

They all glanced at each other, then Griselda looked at Barnaby and Penelope. "The dinner occurred." Griselda turned to Mary. "Was the dinner that night in any way unusual?"

Mary frowned. "Not especially. Over the years that I was with her, the dowager occasionally arranged family dinners..." She paused, then inclined her head. "But, yes, this one was a little different. She called it with only a few days' notice and specifically insisted that everyone attend, including all the children, meaning her grandchildren."

Mary looked at Griselda, then met Penelope's gaze. "I wrote the invitations. The dowager's hands are crabbed with age, and she can't grip pens anymore. And judged against previous occasions, the short notice was unusual, and although, in general, the children attend, the directive that they were to be there wasn't customary, either."

Penelope narrowed her eyes. "We need to learn what was said at that dinner."

"And," Violet added, "if anything out of the ordinary happened."

Mary said, "I wasn't present, of course, so I'm afraid I can't answer either question."

"Hmm." Penelope tapped a finger on her knee. "Which of the attendees is most likely to give us a straightforward and honest account without seeking to fudge to protect the family?"

"Imogen." Barnaby met Penelope's gaze. "None of the men would be reliable witnesses, and Cleome and Constance will try to preserve the family's façade. Admittedly, Imogen is unlikely to volunteer anything, either, but if we ask the right questions, even if she's reluctant to reveal whatever it was that happened, she will answer truthfully."

Penelope nodded decisively. "That would be my assessment, too." She looked at the others. "To learn the truth of what occurred at Moran House on Monday evening, asking Imogen is our best bet."

CHAPTER 13

The following morning, as early as possible—that being the relatively early-by-ton-standards hour of ten o'clock—Barnaby, Penelope, and Stokes were admitted to the Fitzhugh residence in Hertford Street by the kindly but faintly disapproving butler.

He showed them into the drawing room. "If you will wait here, sirs, ma'am, I will ascertain if the mistress is available." His tone suggested he was making no promises.

They sat and waited.

As the minutes ticked by, Stokes stirred, then grumbled, "The Commissioner was almost pleading this morning for me to make an arrest for the murder. Apparently, the arrest of the poisoners—sensational as those were—has only whetted the rabble's appetite for learning who killed the earl."

Barnaby humphed, and Penelope looked toward the closed drawing room door.

A minute later, they heard footsteps crossing the hall tiles, and Imogen came in.

They rose to greet her.

"I'm sorry to have kept you waiting—a minor kitchen crisis, I'm afraid." Her gaze searched their faces; she was plainly surprised to see them. She waved them back to their seats and moved to claim the armchair facing the sofa on which Barnaby and Penelope sat. Tentatively, Imogen said, "I must admit I feel a trifle stunned. We've only just heard

—over breakfast—that Victoria and Christopher have been arrested for attempting to poison Gordon. Is that correct?"

Barnaby inclined his head. "It is. They confessed, Christopher to placing strychnine in the earl's whiskey decanter and Victoria to lacing his cigars with the same poison."

Looking pained, Imogen shook her head. "What is the world coming to?" After a second of pondering that, she refocused on Barnaby and Penelope. "But that's not why you're here." She folded her hands in her lap and asked, "How can I help you?"

Barnaby and Stokes had agreed that, in this interview, Penelope should take the lead.

She began, "With the poisoners identified, our attention now is concentrated on identifying who actually killed the earl."

Imogen nodded. "Of course."

Clearly choosing her words, Penelope went on, "Christopher and Victoria cited the earl's peculiar insistence on household frugality and his severe limiting of their personal allowances as their primary motive for wanting to do away with him." When Imogen merely nodded again—transparently unsurprised by that revelation—Penelope continued, "Given the timing of the murder, we realized that we have not yet learned what the purpose of the dinner that immediately preceded the murder was. We understand that it wasn't one of the family's regularly scheduled gatherings."

Imogen waggled her head from side to side. "Well, it wasn't one of the regularly scheduled events, that's true. Although the dowager does organize occasional family dinners, this wasn't one of those."

"What was the dowager's purpose in calling you all together?" Penelope asked.

Imogen hesitated. Her expression stated she knew the answer but was unsure if she should share what she knew.

After a second of silence, Penelope gently said, "We could, of course, ask the dowager herself, but within mere days, she's lost one son to murder, another to his own ill-advised actions, and lost a daughter-in-law, as well. If you would share what you know, we might avoid intruding on her at this fraught time."

Imogen's eyes narrowed fractionally, and her lips thinned, but then she sighed and surrendered. "Yes, of course. Poor Imelda. I can't imagine how she must be feeling. I was planning on going to see her later today. I'll take the girls—they always cheer her up."

Penelope nodded encouragingly, then prompted, "The dinner?"

Imogen thought, then stated, "I don't think any of us realized what she had in mind, but once we were all seated about the table and the main course had been served, she sent the staff from the room."

Penelope's brows rose. "The dowager did?"

"That might seem odd," Imogen allowed, "seeing Victoria was there, after all, but in all the ways that matter, Imelda still rules that house. She was the dominant mistress, and it was she who sat at the foot of the table, opposite Gordon at the head. Victoria sat beside Gordon at that end."

Penelope's brows remained high. "I see. That must have added to Victoria's frustration."

"Very likely." Imogen sighed and shook her head. "I still can't believe she thought to poison Gordon." After a moment, she continued, "Anyway, what happened next, about the dining table, was thoroughly unsettling." She paused, and it was plain that what she was about to reveal wasn't by choice. "Imelda invited each of the men around the table to describe to the group what their current financial situation was. Only Vincent and Theodore were exempt." Imogen drew in a tight breath, and her hands, clasped in her lap, tightened. "It was…hideously awkward. Christopher was seated on Imelda's right and was the first she commanded to share that information. Of course, he tried to avoid doing so—any man would—but Imelda was relentless. I've never seen her so… *ruthless* in imposing her will. When Christopher balked and demurred, she started giving the answer she'd asked him to provide."

Imogen drew another, deeper breath, then let it out with "I don't know how she managed it, but she knew everything about all of us. How she gathered the information, I can't even begin to imagine, but she had it all, chapter and verse. We all learned how much Christopher owed his creditors, and that he was behind in paying his clubs' dues, and that he'd recently approached a moneylender and taken out a sizeable loan.

"Christopher was horrified, but while he was, on the one hand, sunk in embarrassment and mortification, he also seemed somehow defiant over it. But Imelda refused to countenance any hint of challenge. She looked straight down the table at Gordon and said, 'This is what comes of your neglect.'"

"His neglect?" Penelope asked.

Imogen nodded. "That's what she said—what she accused Gordon of. And of course, many would say she was correct. Gordon was deliberately ignoring any familial claims on his purse. He's been doing that since he succeeded to the title." Imogen paused, then focused on Penelope. "Do you need to hear the rest of it?"

Penelope glanced at Stokes, who silently nodded.

Looking back at Imogen, Penelope said, "Please. If we're to identify the murderer and dispel all suspicion from other family members, we do need to know."

Imogen grimaced, then nodded and went on, "After Christopher, Imelda moved around the table to Byron, then George. I was shocked to learn that both were sinking into debt, and I rather thought Damien—Mitchelmore—was taken aback as well. I know Cleome was shocked. After that, Imelda excused Southerly—she stated she knew he wasn't in any debt—and passed over Gordon and Victoria and moved on to William, then Hugh, and then Damien. I knew about William's and Hugh's debts, of course, but I was surprised to hear that even Damien was in need of money. I hadn't imagined that was likely, but the amount was such that, as we all knew, Gordon could have easily loaned him the funds."

Imogen swallowed and shook her head. "It was becoming quite excruciating for, of course, every man tried to hide or play down his situation, but Imelda dragged their dirty linen into the open for all the rest of the family to see."

Penelope tilted her head. "And then she got to Frederick?"

Imogen nodded. She grew paler, then she closed her eyes, drew in a breath, opened her eyes, and with her gaze fixed over Penelope's head, stated, "We are in dire straits. We're only just managing day to day." She waved one hand in a helpless gesture. "Again, Imelda knew it all. She had every last detail, and I know for a fact that Frederick hadn't told her anything at all."

Imogen paused, then said, "I suspect she got some of the information from the children. They all love her, and whenever they go to Moran House, they always go and natter to her. She must have kept close track of all they let fall, and while I daresay the younger ones and the girls wouldn't have understood the implications of what they shared with her, Imelda certainly did. She's lived a long time in the ton and knows how to draw sound conclusions from observations of all those little things one rarely thinks to hide, at least not from one's children."

Imogen fell silent, then she glanced at Penelope. "You asked for the dowager's purpose in arranging the dinner. Imelda's purpose in subjecting the entire family to that ordeal was to bring home to Gordon the damage he was doing to the family as a whole with his…as you put it, frugality. Imelda had another term for it: his miserliness.

"She blamed him for each of our woes, specifically and explicitly, and truth to tell, in doing so, she wasn't wrong. Anyone can get a bit hard-pressed at any point in life, and according to generally held precepts of how an earldom is managed, Gordon should have stepped in to lighten the burden until whoever had faltered could find their feet again. That's all it would have taken. He could easily have helped everyone out. Yet he refused to. Always, he refused, even to just advance a small amount on an allowance. And the allowances he paid to the family members—to Frederick, Christopher, Victoria, and the dowager, and the smaller annuities to Cleome and Constance—have not been increased since his father set them, and that was years before the old earl died, which was nearly twenty years ago!"

Barnaby asked, "So Gordon forced his family to live on straitened means and kept all the earldom's income for himself?"

"Yes!" Imogen drew in a calming breath. "Or at least, so it seemed to everyone. And given Imelda's performance at the dinner table, she believed that, too."

Frowning, Penelope asked, "Would it be accurate to say that the dowager organized the dinner in order to reveal the financial difficulties all of the family are facing in the hope of forcing the earl—shaming him, even—into changing his ways?"

Imogen took a moment to consider, then nodded. "That would be my reading of her intent. She was determined to push him into acting to ease the financial pressure on the rest of the family."

"What was the state of the dowager's relationship with the earl—Gordon?" Barnaby asked.

Imogen hesitated, then said, "Years ago, when I married into the family, I would have said the dowager viewed Gordon with no small amount of pride, but as the years rolled on, that pride faded and was replaced by…frustration, exasperation. Emotions of that sort." She paused, then added, "Over the past few years, her attitude to him soured even more, and over the past months, since he moved her back into Moran House, the exchanges between them that I've witnessed have held more than a touch of bitterness."

When Imogen said nothing more, Penelope asked, "What happened at the conclusion of…what you've termed the dowager's performance? How did it end?"

Imogen sighed. "After the last of the men—Frederick—had confessed all under her direction, Imelda looked straight down the table at Gordon and said, 'Well? This is your family. What are you going to do about this sorry state of affairs?'"

"And?" Barnaby prompted.

Imogen's features hardened. "Gordon's expression had grown only stonier as the revelations progressed. He responded to Imelda's challenge by dismissing it. Literally waving it aside, along with the dowager and all her efforts, too. He said it wasn't his concern what we all got up to. That he wasn't our keeper. Then he rose from the table, crossed to the wall, tugged the bellpull, and when Winslow and the footmen came in, ordered them to clear away the plates."

Imogen met Barnaby's gaze. "That was Gordon all over. He cared nothing for the family or what we thought of him." She paused, then continued, "It was all dreadfully awkward, of course—we'd all been forced to air our financial difficulties before everyone at the table—and there we were, trying to carry on as if the previous half hour hadn't happened."

"The dowager?" Penelope asked.

"She was furious, of course. White with fury and also so very disappointed." Imogen hesitated, then added, "I also sensed she was cast down in a way. She'd tried her damnedest to get Gordon to save the family—or at least, help us all—and she'd failed."

Meeting Penelope's eyes, Imogen said, "Imelda's not in the best of health, and the effort of her performance that evening had to have cost her dearly."

Penelope nodded. "Is that how the dinner concluded?"

"More or less. Certainly, the fireworks part of it. Nothing more was said of financial matters. The children saved us, filling the silence by asking silly questions of each other, then the meal was at an end, and we rose, and the company progressed to the drawing room, as we usually did."

"Did all of the company retire to the drawing room?" Barnaby asked.

"Yes." Then Imogen amended, "Well, except for George, who I've mentioned to you before, but he rejoined the gathering shortly after we'd settled in the drawing room."

"What happened next?" Penelope asked.

"Gordon told Winslow to bring in the tea trolley. Gordon looked at the dowager and made a snide comment that he was sure no one was keen to prolong the evening."

"So the tea trolley was brought in almost immediately?"

"Within five minutes. As usual, the dowager poured. Gordon took the first cup, drained it, set it back on the trolley, and announced he was going to his study, as he had business to attend to." Imogen shrugged. "He left, and the repressive atmosphere lightened somewhat. The rest of us sipped our tea, then Cleome, Constance, and I realized we might as well make use of being there together to discuss the details of the girls' come-out ball."

Frowning, Penelope asked, "When did the dowager leave?"

Imogen replied, "She chatted to the girls for a time, then she said she was tired and had Hugh call for her footmen. They arrived, and she left us. That was just on nine-thirty, which is the time she usually retires upstairs."

Penelope glanced at Stokes, who had been taking notes throughout.

Acknowledging Penelope's look with a small nod, he said to Imogen, "To confirm—no one else left the drawing room until after the earl was found dead and the alarm was raised?"

"That's correct," Imogen said. "I can definitely state that none of us left." She paused, then went on, "Truth to tell, we were still rather shell-shocked. Most had a second cup of tea. We were all still trying to find our feet…and forget that we'd told everyone of our difficulties and been forced to listen to theirs. You might imagine that we'd all scuttle apart as fast as we could, but in reality, we all seemed to feel…a sort of kinship, now we all knew each other's darkest financial secrets, as it were."

Penelope nodded in understanding, then looked at Barnaby and Stokes. When neither indicated they had further questions, she returned her gaze to Imogen. "Thank you for being frank with us. We appreciate your honesty."

Imogen colored but looked relieved. She glanced at Stokes.

He inclined his head to her. "I believe we have all the information we require. I doubt we'll need to take up any more of your time."

They rose, and Imogen showed them out of the room and accompanied them to the front door.

On the pavement, Penelope halted, and Barnaby and Stokes joined her. After the door had closed behind them, she sighed. "I believe I'm starting to see the light motive-wise, but I still have no idea who, exactly, killed the earl."

His hands in his greatcoat pockets, Barnaby said, "We need to return to Moran House and question the staff more closely regarding the period immediately preceding the earl's death."

"The answer to all our questions has to lie in that house." Stokes looked at Barnaby, then at Penelope. "There are pieces of this puzzle we're still missing."

~

They made their way directly to Moran House.

Stokes tugged the bell chain, and the door was opened by Jeffrey, the lanky footman-cum-acting-butler.

Round-eyed, Jeffrey stared at them, then stammered, "Er…only the dowager's at home…" He blinked and, focusing on Stokes, hopefully asked, "Will the countess and Mr. Christopher be returning soon?" Then Jeffrey blushed and hurried to explain, "We're all wondering, you see."

Stokes took pity on the fellow. "No, son. They won't be coming back."

Shock infused Jeffrey's expression, and he froze.

Penelope stepped past Stokes and took charge. "You don't need to bother the dowager. We're here to ask the staff a few last questions."

Responding to her tone, Jeffrey straightened. "Yes, ma'am." He stepped back and allowed them to enter, then closed the door and led them to the servants' hall.

With Stokes on his heels, Barnaby followed Penelope into the large chamber. Despite being abustle with numerous staff busy with their chores, everyone seemed subdued, and a sense of waiting for some axe to fall blanketed the room.

Seated at one end of the long deal table, Mrs. Pratchett looked up, saw them, and quickly rose to her feet. She looked at Penelope. "Lady Victoria and Mr. Christopher?"

Penelope glanced at Stokes, who replied, "Both the countess and Mr. Christopher Fitzhugh are in Newgate, awaiting trial."

Mrs. Pratchett paled. "Lord have mercy!"

The rest of the staff, all also shocked and stunned, drifted toward the housekeeper as if seeking reassurance from her and each other.

Stoically, Stokes stated, "One of the prison wardens will, no doubt, arrive shortly to fetch some clothes and personal items." Reading the question in many faces, Stokes added, "We seriously doubt you will see either again."

For a moment, Mrs. Pratchett looked lost, then her features hardened, and she focused on Stokes. "Were they the ones who did for Winslow?"

Penelope replied, "Christopher Fitzhugh confessed to placing the poison in the earl's whiskey decanter. His intention was to poison the earl. At the same time, Lady Victoria laced the earl's cigars with the same poison, again hoping to kill the earl but, instead, nearly killing Theodore Fitzhugh. She's confessed to her actions as well."

Mrs. Pratchett and the staff exchanged speaking glances, then Mrs. Pratchett, lips set, faced Barnaby, Penelope, and Stokes and nodded. "Good, then. They're where they deserve to be and will receive their just deserts."

Penelope said, "We have a few last questions we would like to put to the staff as a whole." She glanced at the group gathered about the housekeeper. "Are all the members of the staff here?"

Mrs. Pratchett turned and surveyed those assembled, then dispatched the maid, Gwen, upstairs to fetch the dowager's maid. Mrs. Pratchett turned back to Penelope and declared, "Other than Hilda, we're all here."

"If you don't mind, we'll wait for Hilda and Gwen to join us." Penelope waved Mrs. Pratchett back to her chair. "There's no need to stand."

Penelope sat, and Barnaby and Stokes settled on the bench beside her. Mrs. Pratchett consented to return to her chair, and the older cook and another maid claimed places opposite the investigators, but most of the younger staff, including Jeffrey, remained standing in a loose group behind Mrs. Pratchett and the seated women.

A clatter of footsteps on the servants' stairs heralded Gwen and Hilda's arrival.

Mrs. Pratchett waved both women to seats along the board. "The inspector and his friends have a few more questions for us."

As soon as Hilda and Gwen had settled, Penelope said, "We need to clarify the dowager's movements so that we can be sure we know where she was and at what time on the evening the earl was killed. We know where she was to the point of the family returning to the drawing room. We know she dispensed tea from the trolley, then we've been told that, at about nine-thirty, she summoned her footmen, Edward and Thomas."

Penelope raised her gaze to the pair of burly footmen, who were ranged behind the cook and Hilda. "Please tell us where the dowager went next."

Edward and Thomas looked at each other, then Edward returned his gaze to Penelope and said, "We carried her, in her chair, up the main stairs, through the gallery, to her room."

Thomas nodded. "Like we do every night."

Penelope inclined her head. "And that night, when you got to her room?"

"We set down the chair, and I opened the door, and Mrs. Alder—" Edward broke off, then explained, "When we were called, as she usually did, Mrs. Alder followed us from the servants' hall and came up the stairs with us and the dowager. So when I opened the door, Mrs. Alder wheeled the dowager into her room, just as she always did."

Thomas added, "And Hilda was there, waiting to help with the dowager."

Penelope shifted her attention to Hilda. The dowager's maid-cum-dresser was a stoutish, solid woman with rosy cheeks and soft-brown hair. She projected the air of a countrywoman rather than one town bred. Penelope smiled reassuringly. "So you were there, waiting, when Mrs. Alder wheeled the dowager into her room that evening."

Hilda nodded. "Yes, ma'am."

"And what happened next?"

"The dowager waved Mary away. She said she wouldn't need Mary anymore that night, and Mary went off."

Penelope frowned slightly. "Was that usual—the dowager dismissing her companion as soon as she reached the room?"

Hilda waggled her head. "It didn't happen every night. Sometimes, the dowager liked Mary to read to her for an hour or so. But on other nights, like on Monday night, the dowager was in one of her crotchety moods and didn't want to be read to."

"I see." Penelope nodded encouragingly. "So Mrs. Alder left, and then?"

Hilda's expression remained open, and her answers flowed without restraint. "I was waiting to help the dowager get ready for bed, but after fretting for a moment, she declared she wasn't yet sleepy, what with her mind being too full of things."

"Things?" Penelope asked.

Hilda shrugged. "Just 'things'—she didn't say what."

When Hilda didn't go on, Penelope gently prompted, "So then…?"

"She—the dowager—sat and stared at the fire for maybe five minutes, then she had me call the footmen back. She wanted to go down to the music room."

Penelope blinked and sat straighter. "The music room?"

Together with several of the staff, including Mrs. Pratchett, Hilda nodded. "Aye. Oftentimes, she found it hard to settle, so she'd go down there and…well, just sit in the dark and peace for a while."

Mrs. Pratchett cleared her throat and, when Penelope, Barnaby, and Stokes glanced her way, explained, "The dowager used to play the pianoforte and the harp, both quite beautifully, when her hands were still good. She used to play to soothe herself, and these days, she just likes to sit in that room and, I suppose, remember."

"I see." After digesting that, Penelope raised her gaze to Edward and Thomas. "I take it you returned to the dowager's room and carried her down to the music room."

Both nodded. "Yes, ma'am," Thomas said. "We left her there, just as we always did when she wanted to be alone."

Envisioning the dowager sitting in her chair, all alone in a room full of memories, Penelope frowned. "But if she's alone, how can she summon you when she wishes to leave?"

Mrs. Pratchett leaned forward. "Oh, the dowager can walk, ma'am. Just not very easily or for long. She always has a folding cane with her, tucked under her chair's seat, so she can stand and reach for the bellpulls whenever she wants to call us."

Penelope stared at the housekeeper, then rapidly rearranged her assumptions. After several moments dwelling on the newly emerging picture, she looked at Edward and Thomas. "When did the dowager summon you back?"

Edward shared a glance with Thomas. "Must've been about ten after the hour?"

Thomas nodded. "It was in the middle of all the ructions, what with the earl being found dead."

Edward returned his gaze to Penelope. "We carried the dowager from the music room to the bottom of the main stairs, but then she heard all the commotion and asked what was going on. We told her that Mrs. Alder had been found standing over the earl's dead body, and Winslow was saying as she—Mrs. Alder—had killed the master."

"How did she react?" Penelope asked.

"Shocked," Thomas stated. "She was thoroughly shocked and stunned, just as you'd suppose."

Edward nodded. "She was right taken aback. Hardly surprising."

"She went deathly pale," Thomas said, "but then she rallied and ordered us to take her to the drawing room." He shrugged. "I suppose she could hear that the others—the rest of the family—were still there."

"We carried her to the drawing room door," Edward said, "and I opened the door, and she rolled herself in."

"She didn't call for us again until much later," Thomas said. "When the police were leaving."

Edward confirmed, "We carried her upstairs to her room then." He paused, then added, "You saw us, I think."

Penelope nodded. "We did."

Hilda offered, "I was in her room—I'd stayed there, waiting—and that time, she was ready to get into her bed."

"I see." Penelope suppressed her incipient frown and looked first at Stokes, then at Barnaby. Both simply met her eyes and volunteered nothing. Returning her gaze to Mrs. Pratchett and the assembled staff, Penelope inclined her head. "Thank you all. I believe that's all we needed to know."

Everyone rose, and Mrs. Pratchett and the maids bobbed curtsies, and Jeffrey hovered, ready to conduct them to the front door. Penelope waved Jeffrey on, and with Barnaby and Stokes behind, she followed the acting butler toward the mansion's entrance.

On reaching the foyer, she halted on the tiles, and Barnaby and Stokes flanked her. Facing Jeffrey, she stated, "We should take a look at the music room. If you could show us there?"

"Yes, ma'am." Jeffrey bobbed a bow and turned toward the corridor that led past the study.

They followed him down that corridor, past the study door, then he turned in to another corridor, running at right angles to the first.

Halfway along that second corridor, Jeffrey halted before a door and set it swinging wide. "The music room, ma'am. Sirs."

Penelope walked into the room. Her gaze fell on a grand piano that squatted in one corner, angled toward the room. The opposite corner hosted a large standing harp. In front of the harp, a love seat stood to one side of the space in the room's center, while a small chaise sat on the other side, in front of the piano. A quick scan of the surfaces of the piano and the side tables set beside the love seat and chaise confirmed that the room was kept dusted and ready for use.

Penelope halted in the middle of the room and looked out through the windows that took up most of the wall opposite the door, their curtains drawn wide.

She waited while Barnaby firmly dismissed Jeffrey. "We'll call when we're ready to leave."

When she heard the door shut, and Barnaby's and Stokes's footsteps drew near, she gestured to the view beyond the wide windows and the French door between them. "And there we have it. The explanation of everything, and the one thing we didn't know."

Stokes grunted, and Barnaby shook his head as, along with her, they looked out into the courtyard—the same courtyard the French door in the earl's study opened onto.

"That's why the French door in the study was open," Stokes said.

"And if you recall," Penelope said, "earlier, Jeffrey told us that, about a year ago, the earl ordered Winslow to unlock that door every morning and relock it when doing his rounds at night. It was about a year ago that the earl moved the dowager from Regent's Square to live, once more, under this roof."

"You think it was at her insistence that the earl had the French door unlocked?" Stokes asked.

Penelope pulled a face. "Given what we've learned of the earl, I imagine it was more a case of him growing irritated over having to get up from his desk and his papers and unlock the door whenever she thought to approach via that route."

"She visited him in private, trying to influence his behavior," Barnaby hypothesized.

Penelope nodded. "I suspect so. That fits both their characters—his resistant and recalcitrant and hers doggedly determined to advance the overall good of the family."

Staring at the French door, presently shut, Stokes exhaled heavily. "I'm having a hard time believing where the facts are leading us."

Penelope didn't reply, but went forward, opened the French door, and stepped out, onto the gravel. She looked down. "No step. That would have made coming out here easier."

Barnaby joined her, along with Stokes.

While Stokes wandered toward the study, looking in the same direction, Barnaby said, "You have to admit, it's hard to accept."

Frowning, Penelope nodded. "It all fits, yet I find myself asking, 'Is that what really happened?'"

With a soft grunt, Stokes hunkered down, his gaze on the graveled ground.

After exchanging a glance, Barnaby and Penelope went to join him.

With one blunt fingertip, Stokes pointed at a deep depression, round and about the size of a sixpence. "She needed her cane to go back and forth. She has to lean heavily on it, and as it's been less than three days since she last came this way, we can still see the marks left by the end of the cane." He raised his hand and directed their attention to the line of similar indentations, spaced out along a route leading to the music-room door. "Most likely, she holds her cane in her left hand, so these marks were made when she returned to the music room." He swiveled on his heels and pointed to another set of similar indentations on the other side of the graveled path. "And that's the trail she left when she went to the study."

Penelope and Barnaby studied the imprints, then both straightened.

Stokes rose.

He looked at Barnaby and Penelope, who both looked steadily back.

Stokes arched a black brow. "So what do we do now?"

For a moment, none of them spoke, then Penelope heaved a sigh and said, "Now, we go and speak with the dowager and ask her why she killed her eldest son."

CHAPTER 14

They found Jeffrey hovering in the front hall and sent him to request an audience with the dowager.

He returned almost instantly. "The dowager says she'll see you now."

The immediate reply put Penelope on her guard, and after they'd climbed the stairs and she entered the dowager's sitting room, she knew her instincts were sound. The second she laid eyes on the old lady, sitting upright in her Bath chair beside the fireplace, the shawl over her knees militarily straight, and her chin raised in a challenging manner, Penelope felt sure that the dowager had been expecting them.

Unlike the previous occasion when they'd been in that room, today, the curtains over only one window had been drawn back, leaving much of the room wreathed in soft shadows, yet plainly by design, the dowager sat in a shaft of early-afternoon light as if signaling that she had nothing to hide. Indeed, a sense of serenity cloaked the old lady; she seemed at peace with herself, confidently so, yet her assurance was mellowed by a tinge of…was it rueful regret?

Feeling the gravity of the situation settle on her shoulders, Penelope halted and waited just inside the door until Barnaby and Stokes joined her, and Jeffrey drew the door shut. Then, with an innocuous smile on her lips, she walked forward.

On reaching the armchair angled toward the dowager's chair, Penelope curtsied. "Ma'am. Thank you for obliging us."

With a smile of gentle yet apparently sincere pleasure, the dowager inclined her head. "Mrs. Adair." The dowager waved her to the armchair.

Barnaby had followed Penelope, and the dowager inclined her head to him, acknowledging his bow, then she smiled at Stokes, as having halted deeper in the room, he straightened from his obeisance. "Well met, Mr. Adair. Inspector."

Barnaby didn't sit but took up a stance behind Penelope's chair, while Stokes elected to remain at a distance, almost swallowed by the shadows nearer the door.

After settling in the chair, with increasing wariness, Penelope met the dowager's faded-blue eyes. The awareness she detected there had her dispensing with caution. "You know why we're here."

A statement, not a question; the dowager took it as such, and graciously, she inclined her head. "I knew this moment would come the instant I learned that you and your husband were assisting with this case. You"—her gaze shifted to include Stokes—"and the inspector have made quite a name for yourselves." The curve of the dowager's lips deepened. "I was confident you would figure it out."

Penelope allowed, "We believe we have, yet…it would help to hear your reasons for why you picked up that marble bust and smashed in your son Gordon's skull."

The dowager's lips faintly twitched. "It was rather dramatic, wasn't it? But ladies are a great deal less squeamish than society likes to paint us. My only regret was that I hadn't known that Mary was scheduled to deliver the list of my engagements to the study at ten o'clock. If I had, I would have delayed my action until such time as she was no longer in contention as the murderer." The dowager met Penelope's gaze. "It was never my intention to have dear Mary caught up in the killing. Please do assure her of that and of my continuing regard for her and Julian."

Penelope nodded. "I'll tell them."

She waited, but from the dowager's expression, the old lady was in no hurry to reveal her reasons. Not unless they asked the right questions; she was waiting to see them perform. Accepting that, Penelope ventured, "Why, exactly, did you arrange the dinner on Monday evening?"

Her gaze on Penelope's face, the dowager tipped her head. After a moment, still steadily regarding Penelope, the dowager stated, "That's not where or when this story starts."

Penelope widened her eyes. "When does it start, then?"

"Many years ago," the dowager replied. "Beside my husband's deathbed."

"The previous earl?"

The dowager nodded. "Yes. My Arthur. He passed in 1824, when Gordon was thirty-seven years old. Gordon's first wife, Ursula, had died seven years before that. Sadly, their marriage lasted only three years before a fever took her, and as a way of recovering from the loss, Gordon grew increasingly absorbed with investing."

Her gaze growing distant, the dowager paused as if surveying the events of the past. "Initially, Arthur and I viewed Gordon's early successes with some pride, but by the time Arthur was fading, he had already detected symptoms of what he—Arthur—referred to as 'that damned trait.' He meant a family trait, one he'd seen in one of his uncles and also one of his brothers. The trait was, in essence, an obsessive nature, where the pursuit of one endeavor overrides all other considerations. Those affected feel perfectly justified in focusing on only that one thing and neglecting all else."

The dowager's chin rose, and she went on, "Arthur knew, of course, that Gordon would inherit the title and become the earl and that, therefore, the responsibility for the well-being of all those dependent on the earldom would fall to him. However, in his final days, Arthur began to fear that Gordon was afflicted by the trait and would grow obsessed with his single endeavor, that being, for Gordon, investing, and progressively and increasingly, Gordon would neglect all his other responsibilities."

She paused for a moment, then looked at Penelope. "I was the daughter of an earl, and, like Arthur, I was brought up to understand and accept—indeed, revere—the concept of a nobleman's familial responsibility. Because of his experiences with his uncle and brother, Arthur honored that calling above all else. He knew in his bones how important supporting and nurturing one's family was."

When the dowager fell silent, Penelope guessed, "You made a promise."

The dowager nodded. "I did. Just before he passed, in his very last hour, Arthur asked me to promise that I would ensure that the Fitzhugh family—the family he and I had built—did not fall victim to 'that damned trait.'" Steadily, the dowager held Penelope's gaze. "I gave Arthur my word that I would ensure that the Fitzhugh family thrived."

Penelope held her tongue and waited.

After several seconds, the dowager lowered her gaze, then she sighed and eased back in her chair. "The crux of the problem was that I didn't appreciate that Victoria was no Ursula. Ursula understood about family, and although she and Gordon didn't have any children, she was devoted to the next generation of Fitzhughs, and she was able to influence Gordon to a significant degree. While Ursula was alive, I had reason to believe that all was well and Gordon had been drawn back from succumbing to the trait. Then Ursula died, and in the aftermath, Gordon deteriorated, leading to Arthur's fear and my promise to him. My first act—mine and that of Gordon's paternal aunts, who were also aware of the trait—was to press him to remarry, and when he married Victoria, I hoped she would be able to deal with Gordon as Ursula had. That she would draw him away from the seductive lure of the trait."

The dowager paused and seemed to gather her strength before continuing, "Unfortunately, after their marriage, thinking I was doing the right thing by Victoria, I moved to the house in Regent's Square, and because I wasn't here, in this house, I was unaware of how badly Gordon was behaving—how deeply the trait was affecting him. My other children never liked to complain about Gordon to me, and of course, in their younger years, I hadn't encouraged them to carry tales. I had my own circle, and it only rarely overlapped with Gordon's."

She sighed, and it seemed to come from the depths of her soul. "After returning to this house—and the irony of it is, that move was driven by Gordon's adherence to the dictates of the trait—I realized that Victoria had never stood any chance of rescuing Gordon from the trait's clutches. It's likely that by the time she married him, he was past the age of being influenced by anyone, let alone a pretty lady ten years his junior. He was too deeply ensnared. I saw that when I returned, and gradually, I realized just how far beyond bearing matters had progressed. Over the past months, I sought and gathered as much information about the family as I could, and viewed through the prism of my promise to Arthur, the full picture was horrifying.

"Gordon had gone unchecked for too long. I pleaded with him to change his ways, but of course, he wouldn't listen." She paused for several long heartbeats, then in a quieter tone, said, "Then the doctors told me I had only weeks, perhaps a month, to live. My strength has been fading for some time, and I am, indeed, ready to go, but the news meant that I had only a short time in which to keep my promise to Arthur."

The dowager shifted her gaze and fixed it on Penelope. "So I arranged the dinner on Monday evening as a way to confront Gordon with the full gamut of the results of his familial neglect. All at once, in a forum in which I hoped he would be forced to pay attention. My aim was to jar him sufficiently so that he opened his eyes and saw the reality of the damage he was causing. Or more correctly, was allowing to happen."

She shook her head. "He refused to pay the slightest attention. As if the problems of the family were of no account to him. And I knew he had the funds. I have my trusted sources, and I know how much money flows into the earldom's coffers month to month, year to year. I know that income is more than enough—by a very long chalk—to allow Gordon to increase the allowances to reasonable levels, and just that alone would have enabled the others to climb out of the holes into which they've tumbled." She recaptured Penelope's gaze. "It would have meant nothing to him financially, yet he wouldn't do it. He preferred to risk that money in his many ventures."

Penelope blinked; she'd wondered if the dowager had known much of Gordon's investing.

Seeing her reaction, the dowager smiled. "Oh, I know all about those as well. His latest scheme is quite fantastical, and I daresay, given his record of success with such investments, he might well make a mint." She shook her head. "But that was never my point. I didn't begrudge him playing investor. But I abhorred him ignoring the family's financial health in order to plow more and more capital into his investments."

Regarding Penelope, the dowager tilted her head. "It had become an illness of sorts with him. He was addicted to...the sense of power and euphoria he felt when an investment paid off. I could see it made him feel invincible and that his business acumen was beyond compare. That spike of euphoria and the rush of power and pride were drugs he grew to crave above all else." Her features grew stern, and she nodded. "Yes, it was an addiction—no more and no less—and so he wouldn't listen to reason."

The dowager exhaled. "So the dinner on Monday was my last and final attempt to make him see and change his ways. When he refused..."

Penelope waited, but when the dowager remained staring into space, gently, Penelope supplied, "That night, you walked from the music room to the study."

The dowager nodded. "He'd dismissed me—me and all that I'd tried to show him. He'd effectively disowned the family. He'd refused point-blank to care about the family at all. He'd reached the point of only caring about his obsession."

"His investments," Penelope clarified. She hoped Stokes was jotting everything down.

"Yes." The dowager's chin sank toward her chest. "I went into the study, and he glanced up, then ignored me. When I neared the desk, he still refused to look at me, but instead, he said, 'No matter what you say, I'm not going to change my mind.'" She drew a slow, slightly shuddering breath and raised her head. "So I walked to the shelves behind the desk. I think he thought it was merely a ploy to make him look away from his papers and turn to me and engage, so, of course, he continued to ignore me." She paused, then went on, "So I picked up the bust, and using every bit of my remaining strength, I smashed it down on his head."

The dowager drew another slow, shuddery breath. There was not a shred of guilt to be seen in her face or heard in her voice as she went on, "I waited only to make sure he was dead, then made my way back to the music room."

She looked at Penelope, then raised her gaze to Barnaby, then shifted her head to look down the room at Stokes. "I suspect you already know the rest, but that is how the Earl of Moran was killed."

Returning her gaze to Penelope, the dowager went on, her voice raspy and tending reedy as she hurried to say, "I kept my promise to Arthur. It was he and I who gave Gordon life. It was within our purview to take back what we'd given. He was our firstborn, and it was his duty to keep this family, the Fitzhughs and all its branches, healthy and secure. In that respect, Gordon didn't fail so much as refuse to act. So I removed him. Frederick will make a much better head of the family."

Stokes walked nearer, and the dowager looked at him and smiled—serenely, confidently. "Don't worry, Inspector. You won't need to prepare a cell for an elderly countess. You have one countess on your hands already, I gather, and I'm sure that must be putting the amenities of Scotland Yard under significant strain."

The dowager shook her head and, with her voice lowering and fading, said, "A feckless, reckless pair, Christopher and Victoria. If only they'd had the sense to speak to me, I would have saved them from their now-inevitable fates."

Stokes shot a puzzled and concerned glance at Penelope.

Penelope caught it, then looked again at the dowager, who was struggling to keep her head raised.

In sudden comprehension, Penelope half rose and peered around the dowager at the small table beyond the dowager's chair, until then hidden from their sight. On the table stood a small dark-brown bottle. Sinking back onto the chair, Penelope stared at the elderly lady. "You've taken laudanum."

A faint smile curved the dowager's lips. "Clever child. Yes. My family is now safe, and my work on this mortal coil is done. I'll be with Arthur soon, and he'll absolve me. He'll understand."

Her features eased, and her lids lowered. "It won't be long now. I can feel it drawing me under. It's quite gentle, you know." She paused, and her next words came in a whisper. "I'll be gone soon, and I have few regrets, and those I have, my last testament will put right."

With an obvious effort, the dowager raised her head slightly and smiled, still serenely, at the three of them now gathered before her, then her lids drooped, and she whispered, "Farewell, Mrs. Adair. Mr. Adair. And Inspector Stokes."

"Indeed." Violet directed a sharply interrogatory look at those named. "What, exactly, happened?"

From the head of the table, Barnaby met Penelope's eyes and arched his brows.

Beside her, as he started on his lemon blancmange, Stokes muttered, "You're the storyteller here, which definitely makes you the best one to answer."

"Very well." Accepting the role with a dip of her head, Penelope ate a spoonful of the delicious dessert while she gathered her thoughts, then commenced, "We told you—and swore you all to secrecy on the subject—that the Fitzhugh case was one of filicide. However, given the dowager countess had taken her own life—a life that, regardless, was slated to end within days—there seemed no point in bruiting abroad the facts and putting her family, the innocent people she'd killed to protect, through the diabolical wringer of the consequent sensational publicity. Moreover, the Fitzhughs and the connected branches live within the ton, so the rumors and their likely impact would have been considerable and wide-ranging."

She paused to assemble the facts she had to impart into some semblance of logical order. "The closing of this case was complex, convoluted, and extended over several weeks. On realizing what the dowager had done, we debated, then removed the bottle of laudanum and summoned the housekeeper and the dowager's maid-cum-dresser, Hilda. Both were devoted to the dowager and, we judged, would wish to witness the old lady's passing. As they did. We also remained until the dowager breathed her last. It was all very peaceful and serene, as I'm sure she would have wanted."

Penelope paused, then added, "In many ways, given what she'd done and, more importantly, the reason why she'd summoned the courage and the determination to kill her own son, we, too, felt she deserved to be accorded all due respect."

From the head of the table, Barnaby said, "For the Fitzhugh family to survive, Gordon, the late Earl of Moran, had to be stopped, and in all truth, the only way he could have been stopped was by being killed."

Penelope nodded. "Indeed. And the dowager not only had the understanding to grasp that, she also had the iron will—bolstered by her promise to her late husband—to do what needed to be done."

"It was clear," Stokes said, "that she hadn't made the decision to murder her son lightly. Far from it. She'd done her best to make him see the light and change his ways, but he'd refused. Repeatedly. We didn't feel that she deserved to be vilified for taking the ultimate step to protect her family."

"I suppose," Violet said, "if one considers that we send soldiers onto battlefields to protect this country by killing our enemies, then the dowager killing the man who was threatening to harm the rest of her family is difficult to condemn."

"Just so," Penelope said. "After we'd witnessed her death, we returned to Scotland Yard with Stokes. All three of us spoke with the Commissioner, and it was immediately and abundantly clear that this case was going to require careful handling."

"In the end," Barnaby said, "a meeting was convened at which the Commissioner and the three of us presented the case to the assembled governors of Scotland Yard, along with members of the government as well as several Law Lords." His lips twitched as he looked down the table at Penelope. "The ton was further represented by Lady Osbaldestone, the Dowager Duchess of St. Ives, and the current Duchess of St. Ives."

"And her husband, and Chillingworth, Calverton, and Raventhorne as well," Stokes added. "It was quite a gathering."

"We presented the case as one of justifiable homicide," Penelope said.

"Not an action to be recommended," Barnaby said, "but one that could be understood."

"Ultimately," Stokes said, "all those attending agreed that no good would come from allowing the case to become public knowledge and, indeed, that innocents would be harmed if the facts of the matter ever became widely known."

"So," Penelope said, "we concocted a tale of some unknown person gaining access to the earl's study via the lane, the wall, and the courtyard. The courtyard door was unexpectedly open, and there were signs in the gravel that someone had approached and retreated that way. That was all true."

"What our unknown person's motive was, we couldn't determine," Barnaby said. "It was impossible to prove whether it was a simple theft gone wrong or an attempt to remove political documents—for example, the parliamentary submissions Moran had on his desk—or if the intruder had intended to murder the earl all along. As for possible culprits, a theft from a Park Lane mansion could have been perpetrated by anyone, and the earl's political enemies were drawn from a sufficiently wide spectrum of people that there was no shortage of potential suspects."

"In the end, that was the story that was released to the newspapers and the avidly curious public," Stokes said. "And thus, the mystery of who actually killed the Earl of Moran will, officially, remain unresolved."

Penelope sighed. "It took more than a week to sort all that out, but I'm pleased we were able to preserve the dowager's secret and protect her name and that the genuine outpouring of grief over her death, so close to that of her son, was unmarred by any further sensational revelations."

Those about the table took a moment to assimilate the tale, then Griselda said, "So thanks to the dowager, the Fitzhugh family as a whole are now able to get on with their lives." She looked at Penelope. "How are they doing in that regard?"

"Quite well," Penelope replied. "Imogen is proving an exemplary countess. She's a caring soul, just the right sort of person to take charge of the staff at Moran House. As for Frederick, the dowager was correct in predicting that he would make a much better earl, at least from the family's perspective. Courtesy of the dowager's final family dinner, he'd learned of his relatives' financial difficulties, and as soon as the reins were firmly in his hands, he set about assisting the others out of the holes they'd fallen into."

"On a broader stage," Barnaby said, "I have to say that I, together with many of Frederick's peers, such as my father, are quite impressed by what we've seen of the new Earl of Moran thus far. Frederick's taken up the reins without any sense of ill will toward Gordon, and when I spoke with Frederick after the formal reading of the wills—both Gordon's and the dowager's—he seemed resolute in righting the Fitzhugh ship." Barnaby smiled. "I crossed paths with him more recently, and he actually had a spring in his step. He was confident that all had been resolved and that none of the family were any longer under stress in any way, and more, he'd just come from the legal firm who managed Gordon's investments, and they'd informed him that all the current investments were performing well and looked set to continue to rise in value."

Thomas raised a hand. "I can verify that. The late earl might have been an impossible-to-live-with miser, but in choosing investments, he had a golden thumb."

Curtis arched his brows. "So despite all, the late earl was the investing genius he thought he was."

Montague pulled a disapproving face. "Up to a point."

"That point," Thomas clarified, "being when he eventually risked too much on some chancy endeavor and his house of cards came crashing down. Trust me, with men like him, at some point, it would definitely have come to that."

"Indeed." Montague nodded sagely. "Such a reckoning always comes."

"It seems the one thing the late earl didn't understand," Griselda observed, "was that being an earl and managing an earldom wasn't all about him."

Spooning up the last of her blancmange, Penelope nodded. "Exactly." Spoon poised, she went on, "He didn't understand that, in this life, no man is an island, existing solely by and for himself, with the outcome of his actions confined only to himself. Family is the most fundamental aspect of human existence. Gordon Fitzhugh chose to ignore that and reaped his just rewards."

"The dowager must have felt pushed to her limits to act as she did," Violet said.

After swallowing her last mouthful, Penelope explained, "Given her illness and her encroaching death, she felt she had no choice. Her time was nearly gone, and she had to make a stand, and when Gordon refused all her entreaties, from her point of view, with her promise to her husband to keep, she had no option but to act decisively. She didn't have much time or any other way to put right what was so amiss."

Glancing around the table at the others finishing their desserts, Penelope reflected that, in many ways, for her, it had been a privilege to have known the dowager, even for so brief a time. To have heard her reasoning and witnessed the unwavering commitment to family that had guided and driven her.

Mary laid down her napkin and, looking up the table, said, "In a letter to me that accompanied her will, the dowager explained that she didn't continue to protest my dismissal because she knew she would soon die, and to her mind, it was better not to have me and Julian involved in the escalating situation between her and the late earl." Mary's smile was fond as she went on, "She bequeathed us—me and Julian—a very tidy sum. She also left generous gifts and personal messages for all the staff. She was truly a gracious lady."

Barnaby grinned. "This case was a lesson in never discounting a gracious old lady. Given her age and infirmity, no one would have expected her to seize control of the earldom's reins in the way she did, and by acting so decisively, she definitely achieved her aim."

"That aim," Penelope said, "being to put the Fitzhugh family, including all connected branches, back on an even financial keel, as they always should have been, there being no reason they shouldn't have been."

She looked around the table at the familiar faces of her and Barnaby's closest friends and smiled. "I suggest that the moral of the story of the killing of the Earl of Moran is to never underestimate the power of a grande dame, no matter how frail she appears."

Some chuckled, and everyone grinned. All clearly agreed.

At the other end of the table, Barnaby reached for and raised his glass. "To the late Countess of Moran, who succeeded in saving her family."

"Hear! Hear!" rolled around the room, and everyone raised their glasses and drank.

~

Several hours later, Curtis followed Mary and Julian onto the porch of the Adairs' house. Mostyn closed the door behind them, and they descended the steps to the pavement.

All the others were still inside, chatting in the drawing room, but Julian and Curtis would be working from first light tomorrow, hunting through Islington for an old lady who had wandered off from her home. They were determined to find her and would need their wits about them to do so and had opted to go to their homes and get a decent night's sleep.

Julian glanced up and down the street—presently devoid of hackneys—then turned to Mary and Curtis. "I'll go down to Piccadilly and hail a carriage and bring it back."

Mary said, "All right," and Curtis nodded, and Julian hared off, loping down the pavement toward the bustling thoroughfare at the street's end.

Curtis stood beside Mary, and they waited.

After a moment, Curtis glanced sidelong at Mary. In his eyes, she was a beautiful, mature lady who personified comfortable practicality with a touch of gentrified elegance.

After all she'd been through and with what he saw as her steady courage in the face of disruption and near-disaster, he thought her quite perfect.

He'd been dithering and dallying over speaking to her for weeks. Now, after spending the evening with their friends, he screwed up his courage and, thinking furiously, ventured, "All that talk of family and how the dowager valued family so highly she killed to protect it."

Mary turned and fixed her fine eyes on his face. When he hesitated—not certain anymore about where he was headed—she nodded. "Yes. I thought she was very brave."

He hauled in a breath and said, "I've seen"—he gestured vaguely at the house behind them—"that family is central and important. It's a critical element for living a good, satisfying life." He paused, cleared his throat, then holding her gaze, managed to say, "I was wondering…"

After a second, she tilted her head. "Wondering what?"

Resisting the urge to close his eyes, he blurted out, "If you might possibly see us—you, me, and young Julian—forming a family of our own."

Her eyes widened, and he rushed on, "I just thought, what with you both being alone now, and me being alone as well, rattling around in my big house just across the square, and it just seemed…"

When she blinked, he swallowed and croaked, "I don't know how these things ought to be done. Perhaps I shouldn't've asked. I don't want you to feel awkward or anything if that's not what you want. Heaven forbid! The last thing I'd want is for you to feel in any way obliged, but—"

She stepped closer, came up on her toes, and pressed her lips to his.

For an instant, he froze, then his senses reeled. But before he could decide if he dared kiss her back, she drew away, leaving him stunned.

She looked into his eyes, then smiled and patted his arm. "You're an admirable man, Ronald, and if you're trying to suggest that you're amenable to making me Mrs. Curtis, then I would like you to know that if you made such an offer, I would accept."

He felt his eyes grow round. "You would?"

She nodded decisively. "I would." Holding his gaze, she said, "You're not the only one who values the comfort—and the strength—of family. Oh!"

Her exclamation came as he swept her into a tight embrace and kissed her as he'd dreamed of doing, soundly and thoroughly.

The sound of hooves clopping on the cobbles finally penetrated, and they broke apart, Mary holding on to her hat, and Curtis holding on to her.

A hackney drew up at the curb beside them.

On the box beside the jarvey, Julian was beaming fit to burst. He cheered, leapt down to the pavement, rushed to them, and flung his arms about them. "Yes! *Yes!*" He looked up into their bemused faces. "I'm so glad! So very glad!"

Curtis smiled and hugged him back. "So are we, lad. So are we."

From the corner of his eye, he glimpsed movement in the window of the house behind them. He turned his head and saw Penelope, Barnaby, Stokes, Griselda, and all the rest, beaming down at them.

He looked at Mary and Julian, tipped his head to the window, and shifted so that they, too, could see.

Huge smiles broke over Mary's and Julian's faces, delight there for all to see. With his new family-to-be, Curtis beamed and waved at their joyful friends, then they turned, climbed into the hackney, the three of them squeezing onto the seat, and with a final wave to their well-wishers, they set off on their next adventure, on the next stage in the journey of their lives.

~

~

Dear Reader,

Curtis, owner of the Curtis Inquiry Agency, first appeared in one of the early volumes in *The Casebook of Barnaby Adair* series, *Loving Rose*, and he subsequently played a part in several of the more recent installments. Although not one of those to be found gracing the ballrooms of the ton, I couldn't resist wondering through what circumstances the dogged Curtis would meet his match. In light of his frequent involvement in investigations assisting Barnaby, Penelope, and Stokes, it certainly seemed feasible that, one day, Curtis would stumble across a lady—the right sort of lady—who needed his help in extricating herself from a bad, possibly criminal situation.

And so it proved when Curtis's professional mentoring of young Julian Alder leads to Curtis meeting Julian's widowed mother, who is under the threat of an unwarranted charge of murder. Naturally, Curtis turns to Barnaby, Penelope, and Stokes, and the group plunges into the challenge of unraveling the many tangled threads of the Earl of Moran's life in order to determine not simply who wanted the man dead, but who actually accomplished the deed.

I hope you've enjoyed returning to London and the heart of the haut ton in this latest installment in the adventures of Barnaby, Penelope, Stokes, and friends. Information about earlier volumes in THE CASEBOOK OF BARNABY ADAIR series—*Where the Heart Leads*, *The Peculiar Case of Lord Finsbury's Diamonds*, *The Masterful Mr. Montague*, *The Curious Case of Lady Latimer's Shoes*, *Loving Rose: The Redemption of Malcolm Sinclair, The Confounding Case of the Carisbrook Emeralds*, *The Murder at Mandeville Hall, The Meriwell Legacy, Dead Beside the Thames, Marriage and Murder, The Murder of Thomas Cardwell, and The Curse of Ill-gotten Gains*—can be found following.

Barnaby, Penelope, Stokes, Griselda, and their friends and supporters will, no doubt, continue to tackle the solving of crimes with their customary enthusiasm. I hope they and their adventures unraveling mysteries and exposing villains will continue to entertain you as much as they do me.

Enjoy!

Stephanie.

For alerts as new books are released, plus information on upcoming books, exclusive sweepstakes and sneak peeks into upcoming novels, sign up for Stephanie's Private Email Newsletter http://www.stephanielaurens.com/newsletter-signup/

Or if you don't have time to chat and want a quick email alert, sign up and follow me at BookBub https://www.bookbub.com/authors/stephanie-laurens

The ultimate source for detailed information on all Stephanie's published books, including covers, descriptions, and excerpts, is Stephanie's Website www.stephanielaurens.com

You can also follow Stephanie via her Amazon Author Page at http://tinyurl.com/zc3e9mp

Goodreads members can follow Stephanie via her author page https://www.goodreads.com/author/show/9241.Stephanie_Laurens

You can email Stephanie at stephanie@stephanielaurens.com

Or find her on Facebook
https://www.facebook.com/AuthorStephanieLaurens/

RECENTLY RELEASED:
The twelfth volume in
The Casebook of Barnaby Adair mystery-romances
THE CURSE OF ILL-GOTTEN GAINS

#1 NYT-*bestselling author Stephanie Laurens is back with a complex case in which her favorite sleuths must wade through the attendees of a ton house party to discover which one was moved to murder their host.*

When the genial and highly regarded Sir Montague Underhill is found murdered in his own orchard, Inspector Stokes is dispatched, together with Barnaby and Penelope Adair, to Patchcote Grange to uncover the culprit. But a fashionable house party provides a large cast of potential suspects, and when the investigators learn what business Sir Montague had been dabbling in, the challenge before them grows even larger.

Richard Percival has bowed to familial pressure and agreed to attend a tonnish house party at Patchcote Grange, where the gathering's unabashed aim is to introduce eligible gentlemen to suitable young ladies. Two of Richard's elderly aunts have assured him that Miss Rosalind Hemmings will make him the perfect wife, and after meeting Miss Hemmings over dinner on the first evening of the party, Richard is sufficiently intrigued to be willing to learn—indeed, he's even looking forward to learning—more of the unusually direct young lady.

But on coming downstairs the following morning, he hears an anguished scream for help. On racing outside to the orchard from whence the scream came, he finds his possibly-intended standing over the very dead body of their universally well-regarded host, Sir Montague Underhill. This is clearly a matter for Scotland Yard, and Richard wastes no time in summoning Barnaby and Penelope Adair and Inspector Stokes to the company's aid. For, indeed, very soon, it becomes blatantly clear that the murderer is one of those presently residing in the house.

On arriving at the Grange, Penelope, Barnaby, and Stokes are confronted with a dauntingly large cast of potential suspects. Wedding through the throng takes time, but on uncovering Sir Montague's private means of earning a little extra cash, it becomes ever more likely that his murderer is, indeed, one of the guests at the house. All too soon, the questions facing the investigators become whether Sir Montague learned a secret someone was desperate to conceal, and if so, what secret was powerful enough to compel an otherwise reasonable man to murder?

A historical novel of 85,000 words interweaving mystery, crime, and a touch of romance.

The eleventh volume in
The Casebook of Barnaby Adair mystery-romances
THE MURDER OF THOMAS CARDWELL

#1 NYT-*bestselling author Stephanie Laurens returns with a perplexing case in which her favorite sleuths must untangle a web of interconnected motives to identify the man who killed Thomas Cardwell.*

When Thomas Cardwell, an upstanding man-of-business, is murdered, Roscoe enlists the aid of the best investigators in London – namely Barnaby and Penelope Adair and Inspector Stokes of Scotland Yard – to solve the puzzle of why anyone would want to kill a man as honest as Cardwell.

Dispatched by Roscoe, London's gambling king, to learn what "nefarious activity" an upstanding man-of-business has stumbled upon, Jordan Draper—Roscoe's own man-of-business—arrives at Thomas Cardwell's office to discover Cardwell very recently murdered.

Soon, Jordan finds himself working alongside the Adairs and Inspector Stokes as they search for clues as to why anyone would kill a man as unthreatening as Cardwell. Unexpectedly, Jordan finds himself drawn to Cardwell's family, especially Thomas's sister, Ruth, and as the investigation progresses, the greater Jordan's compulsion to find the murderer and bring the family resolution and respite grows.

Clue by clue, motive by surprising motive, the investigators seek to identify Cardwell's murderer and, along the way, uncover the "nefarious activity" he'd sought to bring to the authorities' attention. But in a case cluttered with intertwined motives and a web of potential suspects related to each other as well as the victim, finding the kernel of truth amid the chaff is no easy matter. Only through enlisting the help of the investigators' wider circle of supporters do they make any headway, and on the heels of uncovering a cascade of crimes, they finally—*finally*—close in on the man who murdered Thomas Cardwell.

A historical novel of 77,000 words interweaving mystery, crime, and a touch of romance.

The tenth volume in
The Casebook of Barnaby Adair mystery-romances
MARRIAGE AND MURDER

#1 NYT-*bestselling author Stephanie Laurens returns with a puzzling case in which her favorite sleuths must untangle a slew of secrets to expose a coldblooded murderer.*

When a middle-aged spinster is found strangled in her country cottage and scurrilous gossip implicates Henry, Lord Glossup, he appeals to Barnaby and Penelope Adair along with Inspector Stokes to unravel the mystery of who killed Viola Huntingdon.

Henry, Lord Glossup, arrives on Barnaby and Penelope Adairs' doorstep and begs their aid—and that of Stokes—in identifying the murderer of Viola Huntingdon, a middle-aged spinster who lived a largely blameless life in a country cottage in a tiny village close to Henry's home. As Stokes has already been tapped to take the case, the investigators travel to Salisbury and thence to Ashmore village and throw themselves into the case.

While initially Henry was touted as a suspect, he is quickly eliminated, and with the help of the victim's sister, Madeline, the investigators set out to discover all they can about the victim and who might have wished her ill. In such a small village, with a commensurately small population, the list of possible suspects is short, but the existence of Viola's 'secret admirer, H' has everyone stumped. First, how could Viola, living in such a small community, have had a secret visitor, a man no one saw except at a distance? And who on earth is he, this H?

As the investigators piece together the clues of missing jewelry and sightings of H and follow the leads generated by opportunistic thieves, dodgy jewelers, and local moneylenders, a picture emerges that points to only one conclusion. But in small villages, things are rarely as they seem. Have the investigators got the right man in their sights, or have they been led astray?

A historical novel of 82,000 words weaving mystery and murder with a touch of romance.

The ninth volume in
The Casebook of Barnaby Adair mystery-romances
DEAD BESIDE THE THAMES

#1 NYT-bestselling author Stephanie Laurens returns with a confounding case that sees her favorite sleuths acting to save a friend wrongly accused of murder.
When a detested viscount is found murdered by the banks of the Thames and Charlie Hastings becomes the prime suspect, Barnaby and Penelope Adair join forces with Stokes to discover the real story behind the unexpected killing.

Charlie Hastings is astonished to find himself accused of murdering Viscount Sedbury. Admittedly, Charlie had two heated altercations with Sedbury in the hours preceding the man's death, but as Charlie is quick to point out to Stokes – and to Barnaby and Penelope – there are a multitude of others in the ton who will be delighted to learn of Sedbury's demise.

As Penelope, Barnaby, and Stokes start assembling a suspect list, Charlie's prediction proves only too accurate. Yet the most puzzling aspect is who on earth managed to kill Sedbury. The man was a hulking brute, large, very strong, and known as a vicious brawler. Who managed to subdue him enough to strangle him?

As the number of suspects steadily increases, the investigators are forced to ask if, perhaps, one of their suspects hired a killer capable of taking Sedbury down. With that possibility thrown into the calculations, narrowing their suspect list becomes a futile exercise.

Their pursuit of the truth leads them to investigate the many shady avenues of Sedbury's life, much to the consternation of Sedbury's father, the Marquess of Rattenby. Rattenby does not want Sedbury's distasteful proclivities exposed for all the world to see, further harming the other family members who Sedbury has taken great delight in tormenting for most of his life.

In the end, the resolution of the crime lies in old-fashioned policing coupled with the fresh twists Barnaby and Penelope bring to Scotland Yard's efforts.

And when the truth is finally revealed, it raises questions that strike to the very heart of justice and what, with such a victim and such a murderer, true justice actually means.

A historical novel of 62,500 words interweaving mystery and murder with a touch of romance.

The eighth volume in
The Casebook of Barnaby Adair mystery-romances
THE MERIWELL LEGACY

#1 NYT-bestselling author Stephanie Laurens returns with her favorite sleuths to unravel a tangled web of family secrets and expose a murderer.

When Lord Meriwell collapses and dies at his dining table, Barnaby and Penelope Adair are summoned, along with Inspector Basil Stokes, to discover who, how, and most importantly why someone very close to his lordship saw fit to poison him.

When Lord Meriwell dies at his dining table, Nurse Veronica Haskell suspects foul play and notifies his lordship's doctor, eminent Harley Street specialist Dr. David Sanderson. In turn, compelled by a need to protect Veronica who is at Meriwell Hall as David's behest, David calls on his friends Barnaby and Penelope Adair for assistance.

However, as the fateful dinner was the first of a house party being attended by the local MP and his family, the Metropolitan Police commissioners also consider the Adairs' presence desirable, and consequently, Barnaby and Penelope accompany Stokes to Meriwell Hall.

There, they discover a gathering of the Meriwell family intended to impress the visiting Busseltons so that George Busselton, local MP, will agree to a marriage between his daughter and Lord Meriwell's eldest nephew, Stephen. But instead of any pleasant sojourn, the company find themselves confined to the hall and grounds while Stokes, Barnaby, and Penelope set about interviewing everyone and establishing facts, alibis, and the movements of those in the house.

To our investigators' frustration, while determining the means proves straightforward, and opportunity reduces their suspect list, motive remains elusive, and their list of suspects stays stubbornly long.

Then the killer strikes again, but even then, the investigators are left with the same suspects and too many potential reasons for the second death.

What did the killer hope to gain?

More importantly, will he kill again?

At last, the investigators stumble on a promising clue, yet following it requires sending to London for information, and their frustration builds. As the clock ticks and they doggedly forge on, they uncover more and more facts, yet none allows them to identify which of their prime suspects is the murderer.

Will they get the breakthrough they need, one sufficient to exonerate the innocent?

When the answer arrives, they discover that the Meriwell family legacies are more far-reaching than anyone realized, and that the crimes involved and the motivation for the murders is far more heinous than anyone imagined.

A historical novel of 78,000 words interweaving mystery and murder with a touch of romance.

PREVIOUSLY RELEASED IN THE CASEBOOK OF BARNABY ADAIR NOVELS:

Read about Penelope's and Barnaby's romance, plus that of Stokes and Griselda, in

The first volume in
The Casebook of Barnaby Adair mystery-romances
WHERE THE HEART LEADS

Penelope Ashford, Portia Cynster's younger sister, has grown up with every advantage - wealth, position, and beauty. Yet Penelope is anything but a typical ton miss - forceful, willful and blunt to a fault, she has for years devoted her considerable energy and intelligence to directing an institution caring for the forgotten orphans of London's streets.

But now her charges are mysteriously disappearing. Desperate, Penelope turns to the one man she knows who might help her - Barnaby Adair.

Handsome scion of a noble house, Adair has made a name for himself in political and judicial circles. His powers of deduction and observation combined with his pedigree has seen him solve several serious crimes within the ton. Although he makes her irritatingly uncomfortable, Penelope throws caution to the wind and appears on his bachelor doorstep late one night, determined to recruit him to her cause.

Barnaby is intrigued—by her story, and her. Her bold beauty and undeniable brains make a striking contrast to the usual insipid ton misses. And as he's in dire need of an excuse to avoid said insipid misses, he accepts her challenge, never dreaming she and it will consume his every waking hour.

Enlisting the aid of Inspector Basil Stokes of the fledgling Scotland Yard, they infiltrate the streets of London's notorious East End. But as they unravel the mystery of the missing boys, they cross the trail of a criminal embedded in the very organization recently created to protect all Londoners. And that criminal knows of them and their efforts, and is only too ready to threaten all they hold dear, including their new-found knowledge of the intrigues of the human heart.

FURTHER CASES AND THE EVOLUTION OF RELATIONSHIPS CONTINUE IN:

The second volume in
The Casebook of Barnaby Adair mystery-romances
THE PECULIAR CASE OF LORD FINSBURY'S DIAMONDS

#1 New York Times *bestselling author Stephanie Laurens brings you a tale of murder, mystery, passion, and intrigue – and diamonds!*

Penelope Adair, wife and partner of amateur sleuth Barnaby Adair, is so hugely pregnant she cannot even waddle. When Barnaby is summoned to assist Inspector Stokes of Scotland Yard in investigating the violent murder of a gentleman at a house party, Penelope, frustrated that she cannot participate, insists that she and Griselda, Stokes's wife, be duly informed of their husbands' discoveries.

Yet what Barnaby and Stokes uncover only leads to more questions. The murdered gentleman had been thrown out of the house party days before, so why had he come back? And how and why did he come to have the fabulous Finsbury diamond necklace in his pocket, much to Lord Finsbury's consternation. Most peculiar of all, why had the murderer left the necklace, worth a stupendous fortune, on the body?

The conundrums compound as our intrepid investigators attempt to make sense of this baffling case. Meanwhile, the threat of scandal grows ever more tangible for all those attending the house party – and the stakes are highest for Lord Finsbury's daughter and the gentleman who has spent the last decade resurrecting his family fortune so he can aspire to her hand. Working parallel to Barnaby and Stokes, the would-be lovers hunt for a path through the maze of contradictory facts to expose the murderer, disperse the pall of scandal, and claim the love and the shared life they crave.

A pre-Victorian mystery with strong elements of romance. A short novel of 39,000 words.

The third volume in
The Casebook of Barnaby Adair mystery-romances
THE MASTERFUL MR. MONTAGUE

Montague has devoted his life to managing the wealth of London's elite, but at a huge cost: a family of his own. Then the enticing Miss Violet Matcham seeks his help, and in the puzzle she presents him, he finds an intriguing new challenge professionally…and personally.

Violet, devoted lady-companion to the aging Lady Halstead, turns to Montague to reassure her ladyship that her affairs are in order. But the famous Montague is not at all what she'd expected—this man is compelling, decisive, supportive, and strong—everything Violet needs in a champion, a position to which Montague rapidly lays claim.

But then Lady Halstead is murdered and Violet and Montague, aided by Barnaby Adair, Inspector Stokes, Penelope, and Griselda, race to expose a cunning and cold-blooded killer...who stalks closer and closer. Will Montague and Violet learn the shocking truth too late to seize their chance at enduring love?

A pre-Victorian tale of romance and mystery in the classic historical romance style. A novel of 120,000 words.

The fourth volume in
The Casebook of Barnaby Adair mystery-romances
THE CURIOUS CASE OF LADY LATIMER'S SHOES

#1 New York Times *bestselling author Stephanie Laurens brings you a tale of mysterious death, feuding families, star-crossed lovers—and shoes to die for.*

With her husband, amateur-sleuth the Honorable Barnaby Adair, decidedly eccentric fashionable matron Penelope Adair is attending the premier event opening the haut ton's Season when a body is discovered in the gardens. A lady has been struck down with a finial from the terrace balustrade. Her family is present, as are the cream of the haut ton—the shocked hosts turn to Barnaby and Penelope for help.

Barnaby calls in Inspector Basil Stokes and they begin their investigation. Penelope assists by learning all she can about the victim's family, and uncovers a feud between them and the Latimers over the fabulous shoes known as Lady Latimer's shoes, currently exclusive to the Latimers.

The deeper Penelope delves, the more convinced she becomes that the murder is somehow connected to the shoes. She conscripts Griselda, Stokes's wife, and Violet Montague, now Penelope's secretary, and the trio set out to learn all they can about the people involved and most importantly the shoes, a direction vindicated when unexpected witnesses report seeing a lady fleeing the scene—wearing Lady Latimer's shoes.

But nothing is as it seems, and the more Penelope and her friends learn about the shoes, conundrums abound, compounded by a Romeo-and-Juliet romance and escalating social pressure…until at last, the pieces fall into place, and finally understanding what has occurred, the six intrepid investigators race to prevent an even worse tragedy.

A pre-Victorian mystery with strong elements of romance. A novel of 76,000 words.

The fifth volume in
The Casebook of Barnaby Adair mystery-romances

LOVING ROSE: THE REDEMPTION OF MALCOLM SINCLAIR

#1 New York Times bestselling author Stephanie Laurens returns with another thrilling story from the Casebook of Barnaby Adair…

Miraculously spared from death, Malcolm Sinclair erases the notorious man he once was. Reinventing himself as Thomas Glendower, he strives to make amends for his past, yet he never imagines penance might come via a secretive lady he discovers living in his secluded manor.

Rose has a plausible explanation for why she and her children are residing in Thomas's house, but she quickly realizes he's far too intelligent to fool. Revealing the truth is impossibly dangerous, yet day by day, he wins her trust, and then her heart.

But then her enemy closes in, and Rose turns to Thomas as the only man who can protect her and the children. And when she asks for his help, Thomas finally understands his true purpose, and with unwavering commitment, he seeks his redemption in the only way he can—through living the reality of loving Rose.

A pre-Victorian tale of romance and mystery in the classic historical romance style. A novel of 105,000 words.

The sixth volume in
The Casebook of Barnaby Adair mystery-romances
THE CONFOUNDING CASE OF THE CARISBROOK EMERALDS

#1 New York Times *bestselling author Stephanie Laurens brings you a tale of emerging and also established loves and the many facets of family, interwoven with mystery and murder.*
A young lady accused of theft and the gentleman who elects himself her champion enlist the aid of Stokes, Barnaby, Penelope, and friends in pursuing justice, only to find themselves tangled in a web of inter-family tensions and secrets.

When Miss Cara Di Abaccio is accused of stealing the Carisbrook emeralds by the infamously arrogant Lady Carisbrook and marched out of her guardian's house by Scotland Yard's finest, Hugo Adair, Barnaby

Adair's cousin, takes umbrage and descends on Scotland Yard, breathing fire in Cara's defense.

Hugo discovers Inspector Stokes has been assigned to the case, and after surveying the evidence thus far, Stokes calls in his big guns when it comes to dealing with investigations in the ton—namely, the Honorable Barnaby Adair and his wife, Penelope.

Soon convinced of Cara's innocence and—given Hugo's apparent tendre for Cara—the need to clear her name, Penelope and Barnaby join Stokes and his team in pursuing the emeralds and, most importantly, who stole them.

But the deeper our intrepid investigators delve into the Carisbrook household, the more certain they become that all is not as it seems. Lady Carisbrook is a harpy, Franklin Carisbrook is secretive, Julia Carisbrook is overly timid, and Lord Carisbrook, otherwise a genial and honorable gentleman, holds himself distant from his family. More, his lordship attempts to shut down the investigation. And Stokes, Barnaby, and Penelope are convinced the Carisbrooks' staff are not sharing all they know.

Meanwhile, having been appointed Cara's watchdog until the mystery is resolved, Hugo, fascinated by Cara as he's been with no other young lady, seeks to entertain and amuse her...and, increasingly intently, to discover the way to her heart. Consequently, Penelope finds herself juggling the attractions of the investigation against the demands of the Adair family for her to actively encourage the budding romance.

What would her mentors advise? On that, Penelope is crystal clear.

Regardless, aided by Griselda, Violet, and Montague and calling on contacts in business, the underworld, and ton society, Penelope, Barnaby, and Stokes battle to peel back each layer of subterfuge and, step by step, eliminate the innocent and follow the emeralds' trail...

Yet instead of becoming clearer, the veils and shadows shrouding the Carisbrooks only grow murkier...until, abruptly, our investigators find themselves facing an inexplicable death, with a potential murderer whose conviction would shake society to its back teeth.

A historical novel of 78,000 words interweaving mystery, romance, and social intrigue.

The seventh volume in
The Casebook of Barnaby Adair mystery-romances
THE MURDER AT MANDEVILLE HALL

#1 NYT-bestselling author Stephanie Laurens brings you a tale of unexpected romance that blossoms against the backdrop of dastardly murder.

On discovering the lifeless body of an innocent ingénue, a peer attending a country house party joins forces with the lady-amazon sent to fetch the victim safely home in a race to expose the murderer before Stokes, assisted by Barnaby and Penelope, is forced to allow the guests, murderer included, to decamp.

Well-born rakehell and head of an ancient family, Alaric, Lord Carradale, has finally acknowledged reality and is preparing to find a bride. But loyalty to his childhood friend, Percy Mandeville, necessitates attending Percy's annual house party, held at neighboring Mandeville Hall. Yet despite deploying his legendary languid charm, by the second evening of the week-long event, Alaric is bored and restless.

Escaping from the soirée and the Hall, Alaric decides that as soon as he's free, he'll hie to London and find the mild-mannered, biddable lady he believes will ensure a peaceful life. But the following morning, on walking through the Mandeville Hall shrubbery on his way to join the other guests, he comes upon the corpse of a young lady-guest.

Constance Whittaker accepts that no gentleman will ever offer for her—she's too old, too tall, too buxom, too headstrong…too much in myriad ways. Now acting as her grandfather's agent, she arrives at Mandeville Hall to extricate her young cousin, Glynis, who unwisely accepted an invitation to the reputedly licentious house party.

But Glynis cannot be found.

A search is instituted. Venturing into the shrubbery, Constance discovers an outrageously handsome aristocrat crouched beside Glynis's lifeless form. Unsurprisingly, Constance leaps to the obvious conclusion.

Luckily, once the gentleman explains that he'd only just arrived, commonsense reasserts itself. More, as matters unfold and she and Carradale have to battle to get Glynis's death properly investigated, Constance discovers Alaric to be a worthy ally.

Yet even after Inspector Stokes of Scotland Yard arrives and takes charge of the case, along with his consultants, the Honorable Barnaby Adair and his wife, Penelope, the murderer's identity remains shrouded in mystery, and learning why Glynis was killed—all in the few days before the house party's guests will insist on leaving—tests the resolve of all concerned. Flung into each other's company, fiercely independent though

Constance is, unsusceptible though Alaric is, neither can deny the connection that grows between them.

Then Constance vanishes.

Can Alaric unearth the one fact that will point to the murderer before the villain rips from the world the lady Alaric now craves for his own?

A historical novel of 75,000 words interweaving romance, mystery, and murder.

ABOUT THE AUTHOR

#1 *New York Times* bestselling author Stephanie Laurens began writing romances as an escape from the dry world of professional science. Her hobby quickly became a career when her first novel was accepted for publication, and with entirely becoming alacrity, she gave up writing about facts in favor of writing fiction.

All Laurens's works to date are historical romances, ranging from medieval times to the mid-1800s, and her settings range from Scotland to India. The majority of her works are set in the period of the British Regency. Laurens has published over 80 works of historical romance, including 40 *New York Times* bestsellers. Laurens has sold more than 20 million print, audio, and e-books globally. All her works are continuously available in print and e-book formats in English worldwide, and have been translated into many other languages. An international bestseller, among other accolades, Laurens has received the Romance Writers of America® prestigious RITA® Award for Best Romance Novella 2008 for *The Fall of Rogue Gerrard.*

Laurens's continuing novels featuring the Cynster family are widely regarded as classics of the historical romance genre. Other series include the *Bastion Club Novels*, the *Black Cobra Quartet*, the *Adventurers Quartet,* and the *Casebook of Barnaby Adair Novels*.

For information on all published novels and on upcoming releases and updates on novels yet to come, visit Stephanie's website: www.stephanielaurens.com

To sign up for Stephanie's Email Newsletter (a private list) for heads-up alerts as new books are released, exclusive sneak peeks into upcoming books, and exclusive sweepstakes contests, follow the prompts at http://www.stephanielaurens.com/newsletter-signup/

To follow Stephanie on BookBub, head to her BookBub Author Page: https://www.bookbub.com/authors/stephanie-laurens

Stephanie lives with her husband and a goofy black labradoodle in the hills outside Melbourne, Australia. When she isn't writing, she's reading, and if she isn't reading, she'll be tending her garden.

www.stephanielaurens.com
stephanie@stephanielaurens.com